THE DRACONNADE

MILES HAWKE

Cromwell Publishers

First published in 2002 by Cromwell Publishers,
405, King's Road, London SW10 0BB.

Internet: www.cromwellpublishers.co.uk

E-mail: editorial@cromwellpublishers.co.uk

Paperback ISBN 1 901679 34 9

DEDICATION

To **Louis Chavasse**, late descendant of the French Huguenots

My son, **Stephen Michael**

And my daughter, **Claire Louise**, on whom the tale was partly based when she was a mischievous twelve year-old – which she still is!

ACNOWLEDGEMENTS

I wish to acknowledge assistance from several persons and places. These include:

The Curator, Bridport Museum, Bridport, Dorset.

Flagship Commander King's Navy Fleet, Flagship *HMS Victory*, Portsmouth

Sarah Harbridge, curator
Bridgwater Museum Bridgwater Somerset.

Curator, Taunton Museum, Taunton, Somerset.

Lyme Regis experience Museum
The Promenade
Lyme Regis (Very helpful in their brief existence.)

Lyme Regis Philpot Museum, The Buddle, Dorset

The search of a 12 year old maid for
her natural mother and step-father
complicated further when she finds her
mother was a known woman buccaneer
Anne o' the Indies and her marriage of
convenience to Bristol born Ned Teach,
better known as Blackbeard the pirate

The 17th century was a turbulent
time and the maid Clarissa and her
guardian Miss Wilks realise as they ride
the Exeter *Post Chaise* that the proposed
landing in Lyme of the Duke of Monmouth
and his intent restoring the Protestant
crown would complicate matters, heralding
the beginning of the infamous rebellion.

Miss Martha Wilks' mission is to
safely transport a royal *whispered pardon*
document clandestinely afforded to the
pirate king, Captain Henry Morgan, which
originated from his monarch Charles II

The *DRAGONNADE* is defined in English dictionaries as *"The persecution of Protestants in France during the reign of Louis X1V by means of an army of dragoons who were quartered upon them: a persecution by means of troops"*

The French monarch Louis X1V welcomed the news that a Catholic king was about to ascend the English throne. He offered huge sums of money in the guise of loans if the new English king would prevent English privateers from attacking French or Spanish galleons bearing gold and silver ingots from the Potosi mine in the New World.

On February 6th 1685 Charles II was declared dead: Unfortunately he left no legitimate heir or bloodline successor. Charles II was popularly thought by the public to have been poisoned by his brother, James, Duke of York. Constitutionally, only James could lay serious claim to ascend the throne of England. James had an impressive reputation as a fighting Admiral during the 1st & 2nd Dutch Wars; he had also proved a worthy naval administrator. Professing publicly to being a Roman Catholic, James II when crowned king and firmly ensconced, made it known he would punish co-religions and more conventional traditions of England's Sunday church services. This was a direct threat to the hard-won Civil War rulings earlier that century, also subsequently the restoration of the English monarchy by way of the exiled Charles II in 1660 some three years after the death of Oliver Cromwell and his English Republic. Legal edicts against foreign intervention or influence, although ancient, were enforceable back to the times of Elizabeth I and Henry VIII. Some thought that this would encourage Louis XIV of France to intervene in the running of the country from across the English Channel. Louis XIV was also to enforce later that same year in October, revocation of the Edict of Nantes and driving out of France of the Protestant Huguenots, many ending up in London, King James II now found he might have bitten off more than he could chew by declaring the country to be wholly Roman Catholic. James counted on a distinct lack of interest due to the wearying of a war torn land under Cromwell and the Civil War of the 1640s. The country recovered well under Charles II, to find a short time later the upheaval was starting again. King Charles II turned England's fortunes under the auspices of the Jamaica-based pirate, Captain Henry Morgan.

A dark liaison was agreed under the letters-of-marque and letters patent documents and soon newly built shuttling three-tiered treasure ships ferried gold and silver to England. But the plundering of foreign merchantmen and the more heavily armed fighting man-o'-war galleons of the marauding French and Spanish had to stop under the new Catholic king, who did not wish to incur the wrath of the French and Spanish. James also had to consider the wishes of his Catholic wife, Mary of Modena.

Strip away the romance from pirates and their ilk to show them for what they are, and remove the fancy titles they afford themselves - Barbary corsairs, buccaneers, freebooters and an even more respectable affectation of "privateer", and underneath you will find thieves and murderers. Dispel visions of moonlit seas and a galleon under full sail held back in forward speed by drag barrels in fishing nets and with dark souls with murder in their hearts hiding in her gunwales. Destroy also thoughts of their ship bearing silently down on a gaff-rigged sloop or a Dutch flute - for this was the wicked ways of bloodthirsty pirates on the high seas. Pirates were the first employers to take out insurance policies for their crews: captains, surgeons and deck officers, right down to lowly powder monkeys who refurbished ordnance below on the gun decks. There was recompense for injuries sustained in battle.

> *loss of a right arm 600 pieces of eight or six slaves;*
> *loss of a left arm was 500 pieces of eight or five slaves;*
> *a left leg 400 pieces of eight or four slave alternative.*
> *For an eye 100 pieces of eight or one slave - loss of a finger*
> *was classed as the same as for an eye.*

The only thing asked of a pirate crew was total loyalty. Neither should they individually nor collectively conceal booty, or try to abscond from the ship. Either act would result in the perpetrator being evicted from the pirate community or worse still - death by garrotte.

The pirate king Captain Henry Morgan was sent to England to stand trial for piracy, yet when news of his successful sacking of the world's most prestigious gold and silver mart, Panama City, was made known, Morgan became more popular than Drake. All thoughts of his going to trial and the Tower were forgotten, and in due course he returned to Jamaica, sent on his way by a most grateful king. When the 3rd Dutch war broke out, Morgan was made deputy Governor of Jamaica and knighted. King Charles II presented him with a silver snuffbox with his image portrayed, its perimeter encrusted with diamonds.

Morgan once again began his privateering for the king and in the name of England and her colonies his fleet continued to roam the seas around such places as, Maracaibo, Puerto Principe, Portobello, Panama, Cartagena, Tortuga, Isle la Vache and nearby Hispaniola.

Edward Teach, more commonly known as "Blackbeard the pirate" hailed from the port of Bristol and purportedly was an acquaintance of Henry Morgan's. Their paths rarely crossed, but when they did,

Morgan begs a favour from his comrade in arms, Black Ned, that when next he reaches England he is to locate and transport back a documented pardon afforded him by the late king, Charles II. The reward will be a velvet purse containing 2,000 silver pieces of eight, Black Ned acknowledges rumours abounding where Morgan is reputed to have taken 400,000 pieces of eight from the sacked Panama so saw no reason to doubt the generous amount on offer.

Infamous scoundrels such as Stede Bonnet, Calico Jack Rackham and Bellamy and likewise Edward Teach, did privateering along the American coastline from Boston to far away Vera Cruz in the south. It was on one of these piratical cruises that Black Ned Teach spied and admired the woman pirate known as Anne Bonny, real name Anne Bone: Anne renouncing her penniless sailor husband James Bone, for the more handsome dashing infamous pirate called "Calico' Jack Rackham. A liaison ensued and resulted in Anne sailing off to sea with Rackham to become the world's first woman pirate. Soon her reputation preceded her and she became known as Anne o' the Indies. Jack Rackham persuading her to dress as a man whilst cruising throughout the Indies, and the trip turned out to be one of hell fire piracy and debauchery.

All went well, despite the pickings being scarce; they had fared reasonably on the high seas. However, within months Anne found she was with child and Rackham coldly placed her ashore in Cuba. Anne decided to go to England for safe haven, and this was where her baby girl was born in the name of Clarissa Lovelace. Later that same year Anne met and fell in love with Ned Teach and in a small church in the port of Dartmouth, she tied the knot. Allegedly after the ceremony before any honeymoon could take place, Ned was shanghaied by a naval press gang as he left the church, dragged off to be forcibly pressed into service with the King's Navy and a fighting Man o' War leaving port that night. Anne Teach, née Bonny diligently looks after her little maid, Clarissa, but eventually, tiring of the long wait for Ned's return arranged for a guardian and friend of the family to look after the maid. Financial provision was made for the child's welfare and a Miss Martha Wilks the one chosen to look after her. When Clarissa Lovelace is eight years old, Anne leaves to find either Black Ned Teach, her erring husband of just a few hours all those years ago, or even 'Calico' Jack as an alternative.

The woman pirate slipped away to sea and reverts to her former name of Anne Bonny, better known to naval authorities as Anne o' the Indies. At 12 years old, some four years later, Clarissa Lovelace Peach (abbreviation thought not to link the child with her piratical parents) is becoming curious about her missing mother and stepfather, Ned. Martha Wilks, on the other hand, was approached by King's man and agent of the Crown on behalf of a loyal servant to the late king. D'Arcy Ingrams knew the link with the child Clarissa and her roguish parents persuading Miss Martha Wilks to deliver the document known as The Whispered Pardon. The sealed parchment was from the late Charles II to be delivered to Sir Henry Morgan transported via Black Ned Teach - his go-between. Deciding the time was ripe for the maid to meet up with her step-father, Ned and maybe discovering more recent whereabouts of her mother, Miss Wilks agrees to deliver the document by way of the Exeter stage to Bristol, then to Dorset and an old inn in the coastal town of Lyme Regis. In so doing, Martha Wilks decides to take the child on the Royal Mail stage journey with her, and thus began the adventure of a lifetime.

The spinster Martha Wilks and the young maid Clarissa Lovelace Peach's stage journey corresponded in June 1685 with rumoured news of a possible landing in Lyme Regis of an army of rebel soldiers. James, Duke of Monmouth, coerced by England's disgruntled aristocracy and prised out of a comfortable exile in the Dutch Free States with his uncle who was the Stadtholder, King William of Orange.

The Duke of Monmouth was to attempt a rebellion and was promised finances and ordnance backing from the select number of Protestant Royalists, providing he attempted to regain the English crown on behalf of the loyal and the free. William of Orange, Stadtholder of the United Provinces, encouraged the intrigues, contributing by revealing the plot to James. The wily William offered to land an army on the West Coast of England to quell and crush any revolt or rebellion against him. But this possibly was a ploy to join forces with Monmouth's army in Dorset, assisting also the Earl of Argyle's attempt at a pincer movement by landing up country on the coastline of Scotland.

Henry Morgan was in the Dutch Free States having his portrait painted by the artist Rembrandt. He also awaits news of Monmouth and the outcome of his rebel invasion of England. Henry Morgan muses whether to commit his fleet of pirate vessels to the Protestant cause. It was another facet of reasoning behind sending Black Ned Teach over to England; apart from the pardon document which would clear his name, for this would restore Morgan's reputation as a fervently loyal patriot should the war be seen to be won on the land.

This is where we pick up the story.

Chapter One   LETTERS OF MARQUE

ANNIVERSAIRE DU BOUCANIERS

Huddled 'round the log-fire's smoke, tales of old 'bout Ships of Oak
Clay pipes lit, an ale or two, dancing flames in smoke so blue
Air flung with adventure tales, of crashing seas and Force Nine gales
Flagstones smooth, cold to thy feet, countered by the log fire's heat

Tankards clash with an ale or two, clay jar swings from me to you
Odours of 'baccy, rum and snuff, bright twinkling eyes so proven
tough
A hook, a stump and there a patch, brass buckles shine as I lift the
latch
Laughter and songs all known so well, fair near drowned the old
ship's bell

It drifted in upon a breeze calling us shipmates to Seven Seas
t'was over now and time to go, our voices died as we made to row
Aboard the longboat swinging 'fro, oars a-creaking keeping low
'Heads down lads and no redress; remember always the Exciseman's
Bess?'

Jolly Roger flying clear, as we approach shipping oars for fear
Of fouling gunwales, gun-ports t' boot – piped aboard to drum and
flute
Longboat stowed, anchors aweigh, dawn caressing a bright new day
Lusty shouts from a distant headland, sails a-cracking as they fall and
stand

Musket fire rips a sheet, our returning cannons deny defeat
Men in the rigging, our sails unfurl, bows a-whipping surf to a curl
This be the life, ye keep thy quill, thinking them lines fair makes one
ill
Feel o' Doubloons, Ducats or Eight caring little for the morrow's fate

Mors Vincet (Death Wins –pirate's motto)

The effervescent hiss of raindrops drummed continuously on the smooth shiny flagstones of the courtyard of the hostelry known as the Blind Beggar Inn. Above its recently thatched roof barbed veins of forked lightning tore from charcoal grey clouds and these moving veils chased away the reverberating claps of springtime thunder. A stiffening wind began to moan a lament, laying emphasis to England's unseasonable cool April climate, and it was this inclement combination of weather that hastened an early nightfall.

The rain-drenched driver of a nearby racing post chaise yanked at the collar of his brown great coat upright against the worsening squall, galloping horses were nudge-bumping into each other with exhaustion as their drumming hooves pounded a dirt road in the distance. Wiping rainwater droplets from his eyes, the coachman decided it might be prudent to take an early stopover and allow the worst of the gathering storm to pass. Deciding on the nearby hostelry at the edge of Kings Wood, knowing that which by seventeenth century precepts was a spacious detached and fairly modern building. It lay under a steeply pitched roof; its beamed exterior panelling looked fresh painted with a creamy distemper. It contained five Spartan furnished bed chambers, a galleried walkway overlooked the dining area below, but the mine host did not object to bona fide" travellers slumping where they sat over the well-scrubbed tables, that was providing they paid for a meal and copious amounts of brackish red wine and watered down ale.

A broad tunnel under the tiered frontage allowed access to a flag-stoned courtyard at the rear, inside this inner sanctum the Exeter mail stagecoach and team eventually cantered in. Almost unnoticed a gangling rider on a black stallion trotted in soon afterwards and dismounted in a shadowy corner, the restless animal appearing irritated at being abandoned by its master though ignoring the skittish mood of the Arab bloodline beast he attached its leather halter to an iron ring of an outbuilding and there the horse would remain for the stable boy to attend it concluding his other duties. At that moment, a young boy stood alongside the ostler to see to the snorting coach and team which clattered into the cobblestone yard. The man in black leaned casually against an outbuilding door and snorted cheap snuff from a silver snuffbox, he was there intending to make the acquaintance of one of the passengers whose name was Wilks.

Dressed in a black silk tricorn and riding cloak, thigh-length boots, and a broad leather belt which secured a claret coloured three-quarter length tunic coat and where a white ruff spilled out of its high collar. His informant advised the contact was a middle-aged school-teacher travelling with a companion aged twelve years, this affiliation made them easy to locate as the rider had spied them from a low hillock earlier that day. Wearily the five passengers alighted with difficulty due to stiffness from a bone-shaking journey part way up from Exeter in Devon. This stopover would be their final stay before ongoing up to the broad capital of London town. Furtive and shifty-eyed the lone rider was obviously a road agent, a highwayman who made it his business to check on the outward appearance of the coach passengers prior to robbery. There was no point in holding up a post chaise filled with prisoners heading for Bedlam or better known as Newgate prison in the city. Several years earlier when he ended up shooting it out with two well-armed guards, he had been lucky to escape with life and liberty. Now disguised he allowed himself relaxation and to stay at the Blind Beggar Inn the night before any robbery took place. Mainly because it was a known stopover for the regular stage and occupants. A black patch down over one eye was enough to disguise his sallow features, for this would be the only thing the terrified occupants would recall whilst being robbed of their valuables. Only this time the robber held prior knowledge that one passenger was carrying something of great import. It was a parchment document for the pirate king himself, Captain Henry Morgan. Signed, sealed by Parliament and Charles II, not the new Catholic monarch. James II ascended to the English throne in February that year. Allegedly, the secreted document was to be a pardon for misdemeanours of the pirate, his cronies and probably worth a small fortune to any third party. Disparaging cries had come a day earlier from the motley bunch of sea-devils gathered at the coastal Ship Inn near Lyme in Dorset, they were there to accept delivery from a known female courier go-between. Only he, Jess Mandrake would be allowed to intercept this document for safe delivery, their premise the royal document might be bait in a trap.

An enormous rosy-cheeked woman, whose bonnet part-hid her fleeting glances toward him, clutched at the hand of a slender young girl as together they gingerly stepped down to mud and straw covered ground from the stark interior of the coach. Rubbing darkened stubble on his chin. Mandrake thought this must be the contact and trusted go-between for the pardon document. He watched fairly nonchalantly as the couple scurried to stand in the entranceway of the rear scullery door, there they paused to turn and look directly at him. As a returning smile was offered, the highwayman bowed low and doffed the flouncy feathered black silk hat. Haughtily twirling her red cape over her broad and well-rounded shoulders, the woman now smirked coyly from under fluttering eyelashes, she dallied momentarily before entering. Suspecting the task might be easier than first thought, the highwayman made his way forward and paused on nearing the woman and her ward. Cautiously allowing them to enter first, then following on to await the lady's pleasure after booking in to the hostelry.

"Where is thy daughter." Jess Mandrake said gulping mouthfuls of coarse bread dipped in the greasy stew platter lying in front of him on the table. The discarded bonnet exposed the dark-eyed woman attentively watching her new acquaintance relish and thus consume his meal. She was attractive yet overweight. Her rosy cheeks tinged further as she anticipated his advances.

"We'll not be disturbed for the maid is exhausted and is now to her bed. Although she be my entrusted ward, and not my daughter, a more jovial little maid ye could not wish for and I would be proud if she were so and that's a true fact so it is."

Concluding his meal sometime after the woman due to his in-depth questioning, the robber pushed away his greasy wooden trencher platter to lean comfortably back in the bench settle. Looking around him to gather his thoughts he then slid quietly toward her. The others had left, presumably gone to their bedchambers for the night.

The inn had a lived-in feel about it, decorated in expensive flock wallpaper and hung with country prints. Ornate beamed ceilings and white alabaster panelling seemed strange after so many nights hiding away under the stars. Twenty minutes later and having supped copious amounts of ale, they entered the woman's bedchamber to settle down for the night.

She held out a hand and smiled a comely welcome.

"Here Mr. Mandrake you come and sit over here by me."

Patting rough-stitched fabric covered upholstery with her long graceful fingers; the gesture and dark eyes invited him, as did the writhing of the seductive body movements. Dimly lit, the tavern's chamber was scantily illuminated by smoky wax tallows affixed inside sooty metal-framed lanterns that were scattered about the room. Plumping a scatter cushion allowed the well-fed grinning man down into the comfort of the wooden framed upholstery. His thoughts seemed to dispel completely as the laughing woman gracefully slid up toward him on a pert rump. "I've rum for thy entertainment." She smiled and poured golden liquid from a pewter flask, the highwayman nodded and after taking the tiny goblet allowed his free hand to be taken up and clutched seductively into her lap. Mysteriously her raven-coloured hair lay unpinned and gracing her bared shoulders of an emerald-velvet travelling gown. Her hair lay in a kind of symmetry, dark curls flicked up enhancing her wispy see-through lace top gracing a fulsome bosom. Her heaving breasts drew the man's eyes eagerly down to enticing glimpses of a paled skin. They kissed. The woman opened her wide mouth as if to consume him whilst sucking eagerly into the wide red abyss and sparkling white teeth, her wide-eyed innocent sensuousness now abandoned for the sake of lust. The moist kiss bolstered his waning spirits and even affected her own mood. Relaxing the women became philosophically languid, curiously with a soft emotive tone she inquired, "D'ye think not, my dear Jess Mandrake, that love be an off-shoot of lust." Sighing deeply with the foreplay taking place and having the desired effect, she further reasoned,

"Or be it merely a companion to a much deeper love within thy breast."

His needs becoming urgent the half-naked man whose tongue flicked eagerly around the heaving cleavage of the woman's plunging neckline, finally paused and found enough time to murmur with a very masculine sincerity, "I think it be everything that be handsome in the union of man and a woman about to make thundering love." Darkly and with malice aforethought he truly reckoned that verbal or any other type of foreplay was an unnecessary delay to the real business in hand, that was to propagate the species of humankind. Twinkling dark eyes met and danced on his as impishly she finally murmured,

"Why my dear Jesse ye hath the lips of a liar."

"You my dear Miss Martha Wilks, spinster of thy parish." Sliding

18

his hand gently along the length of her stockinged thigh he concluded with, "ye have the thighs of an angel."

They exchanged a quiet smile, as further excursions into her loosened clothing were no longer resisted. A bouquet of spring flowers lay upon the skin and he warmed and responded to their closeness. Holding hands they swayed gently back and forth in the preamble to love making. Perhaps clasping of hands was the way our ancestors chose a sexually compatible mate. As he moved too close too quickly his inquiring fingers were restrained in hers - for lovers needed time and she chastised him by saying as much. Eagerly he'd undone another button of her flowing dress revealing an abundant cleavage, the firm swell of her bosoms heaved moist with anticipated passion. Black-lace edging of her under garments tantalised and encouraged his instincts further. Slipping an arm round her waist he began to cosset her ample waistline. An annoyed wriggling made him realise she was uncomfortable with so much attention to this part of her torso. Instead his hand finally settled for the curvature of her full rounded hips. "Now then Mr. Jesse Mandrake you leave my love handles alone." She giggled playfully and butterfly kissed his cheek with her fluttering eyelashes. When his other hand fondled her firming breast slowly and with much desire she began to respond. Eagerly he sought and found the firm peak of her nipple by slipping his free hand down into the black lace void. Suddenly feeling vulnerable the woman said urgently, "will ye slow down sire, for goodness sake."

Not caring or listening, the road agent stroked the foothills of her bosom for he knew it was an erogenous zone on most women, his fingers titillated and raced almost without touching over the palest skin he'd ever seen. Her nipples distended pink and erect as he paid lustful attention to them, showering them with kisses and as her clothes slipped one by one away to the floor. Martha Wilks was not a young woman yet the gentle act of coupling made her appear more and more beautiful by the minute for the lusty highwayman. Preventing his eager hands from removing any more of what was left of her wispy lace under-garments, she indicated with her eyes the door should be bolted and the curtains around the enormous four-poster bed should be closed. Jess Mandrake returned from placing a wood beam across the metal hasps on the only entrance to the chamber, fully darkening the bed to find the job had been completed in his brief absence. Revealed by scant items being cast aside, her body highlighted by solitary soft candlelight telling secrets of her supple torso. Relaxed on the pillows now, Martha Wilks' nipples had grown to the size of saucers. Jess Mandrake paid particular attention to them as the lithe bodies began to sway to invisible music the way lovers do. Recalling how pleasurable it was to be helped from one's clothes when the helper is a tantalising woman full of urgent desire with long slender fingers. Each performing individual deftness of touch. Soon the bared individuals faced each other fervently determined to become one. Hearts pounding in unison they moved closer and closer, soon to gaze directly into the other's eyes. The former preamble of courtship now over, they felt impatiently for the other's desires. Soon the highwayman followed her down to the bumpy surface of the straw-filled mattress as she slid from his arms. Smiling up at him she spread her legs and revealed herself by way of invitation and to further his delight. Incandescent licking flame lit their shadowy draped surroundings. Pupils enlarged, heightening the moment for both, flicking his tongue and roving his hand whilst reclining on his elbow soon made the woman writhe in ecstasy. Eventually moved she directed his attention by showing a preference to the region of her clitoris. Kissing everywhere his lips roving relentlessly over her torso for an eternity. Eventually ardour swept over them as they felt and yearned for each other's needs and wants - soon they were one. Writhing, moving slowly at first, then quickening according to the other's mood. Tenderly clutching eagerly at every horizon of their moist bodies as they glistened in the soft warming candlelight. Rising and falling only to finally shudder after many inexorable moments to a sublime feeling of mutual ecstasy - they came together in a crescendo of spasms of delight. A gentle cry escaped her lips as digging her fingers into his buttocks, mercilessly, she held onto the writhing body on top of her. Relaxing the once sensuous fingers, allowed time to gently extricate himself, prevented momentarily by an insistent hand behind his neck for she needed to feel him a little longer, her wants for this more personal sensation was much to allow his instincts to relax and recover. Moments later the amorous forms and by way of mutual agreement, allowed the other to separate alongside to a spent silence for they had thought and loved as one. Several minutes passed while their hearts returned to normal with a fluttering wave of sadness. Their only link now was entwined arms lying side-by-side on the deep recesses of the mattress, and sleeping for an hour or two until they became chill, cold but refreshed becoming aware also that the bedside candle was also spent. Suddenly the man sat up and shook his head with vigour, adjusting his eyepatch she noted his one good eye that rolled alarmingly.

"What's wrong." The woman cried, alarmed at the disturbance and dropping a self-conscious hand between her legs to hide her real nakedness, relaxing when the man smiled.

"Thy bewitching body is making me feel faint with renewed passion." Her expression took on a wicked glint as exquisitely she replayed the mating game, adding,

"If thou be feeling giddy then mayhap ye should put thy head between thy knees. It always seems to work for me."
The robber grinned and lowering his head between eagerly parting legs in front of him and he took great pleasure in the squeals of renewed delight emitting between gasps of completely rejuvenated pleasure.

The following night

"Stand - hold hard or I shoot." A dark cloaked figure atop a rearing black stallion appeared suddenly in front of the post chaise and its team racing at full pelt. Snorting nostrils, the slither of horses hooves on mud strewn tracks, stretched water-logged reins slipping through the driver's fingers all hindered an immediate reaction to the barked command. A long-barrelled flintlock pistol exploded simultaneously with a lightning flash - illuminated the storm-lashed night with an eerily blue flicker - accompanied with an echoing thunderous "crack" from above. Howling calamitous winds and a rain storm which snapped swaying tall forest boughs as if arid twigs crushed underfoot, gusting squalls funnelled through dark avenues of trees on that ancient toll route known as Exeter Way. Screams of terror were cut short, drowned-out by a resounding fracturing of wood and metal as unable to recover momentum on the bend, the hurtling conveyance overturned on the single track road, crashing over onto its side in bordering roadside thickets. Fallen writhing horses tried in vain to free themselves of twisted, splintered shafts and traces. Stretched thongs of

21

leather rein continued to securely bind together the quadrupled team of skittish horses. To halt the team at any kind of speed in those narrow lanes near Axbridge was impossible. Exhilarated by an English springtime's inclement weather, the hysterically whip-cracking driver had encouraged his fresh team of four up to their bit-between-the-teeth galloping speed limit. The lone horseman wearing a long black cape and felt tricorn slowly climbed down from the still nervously stepping stallion, to stand amongst bloodshed in the coach and the fallen squirming beasts of the broken mail conveyance. A slim bladed knife flashed into view and he cut them free murmuring, "There my beauties you're free of your ribbons - be off with you."

So saying the wet gleaming muscular torsos of the downed beasts flung themselves free of the wreckage, struggling upright made off to the night snorting with a frenzy that comes only with downfall. One horse skipped sideways into a mud sinkhole and stumbled. To prevent himself being stepped upon the road agent threw himself arms-akimbo, rearwards, accidentally flinging the dagger over his head to nearby undergrowth, the beast righted its footing to tear after the others into night rains whinnying furiously. Recovering, the highwayman straightened up and flicked spattered mud from his clothing with a thinning leather glove. Only then did the lone rider survey the horrendous damage to the fallen post chaise. A flicker of annoyance came from under the black wild silk neckerchief pulled up and hiding most of his face, bulbous, the black eye patch left one eye free to scan this unexpected turn of events. Drawing and gripping a second loaded flintlock pistol across his chest, thus preventing ingress of rainwater, slowly the wiry figure climbed up onto the upended conveyance. Cautiously inquisitive he peered down over an opened horizontal window. Accumulated rain water tipped from the felt gulley of his tricorn hat, it cascaded downwards deluging the upturned face of a young girl crouched and now whimpering inside.

"Please don't you kill me sir." She lowered her gaze to stove a baggy sleeve across her moisture-soaked forehead. A silent deliberating took place and he withdrew to other business. When she looked up again the black shape of the road agent had gone.

"Where are you sir?" Watching and waiting the girl suddenly panicked and screamed out, petrified at being left alone that raging night, changing her plea to a throat catching sob, the slim, dark-haired

22

child added a convincing reason for her plight. "The others are all dead - please don't you leave me here, sir."

"So they are." The hunched black figure reappeared in the splintered opening above her and stood where it used to support the locked mail trunk, this he turned his attention to and opened with the butt of his heavy weapon.

The highwayman's mind was in turmoil. No one would believe his tale about the accidental upending of the mail conveyance, so maybe it was best he took the surviving maid to commandeer her voiced truth of the incident. Giving this further thought as he rummaged, glancing away from the desperate gaze of the girl. Eventually appearing to find what he was looking for by exclaiming a satisfying grunt. "At last 'tis the bundle of letters for Morgan." He flung the wooden strong box to one side the highwayman strode to a still spinning coach wheel, seconds later the still spinning iron rim severed the red ribbon which bound seal and parchment together. Time-hardened wax seals and their bindings split to fall scattering about his feet as he went through document after document,

"Damnation and God's hellfire the main document b'aint here!"

Further whimpers came up out of the wreckage,

"If you please sir." The shocked and crash weakened girl was heard trying to free herself from her heavy travelling companion, the dead weight bound her slender legs to the up-turned door frame, her guardian school mistress knew nothing of her struggles. Even the stilted conversation with the highwayman for her neck had been broken on impact; at twenty stones body-weight the woman's corpse made a formidable anchorage on the trapped girl's leg.

The man's voice percolated the damp night air as he reached down to her.

"Here lass, give me thy hand." The formidable looking gothic figure in black stood aloft of her and lowered a gloved hand down through the upturned window, bracing his thigh boots took up a firm astride of the frame, then attempted to pass a length of leather strip which was the reins down. "Your hand." He commanded impatiently as he would be gone from that place. Only to fall silent as she appeared to hesitate and complain mysteriously.

"I daren't sir for I'll surely snap!" Looking down at the girl in her red velvet dress noting how darkening rain spots stained it like blood.

The Highwayman threw back his head and cackled coldly. Ceasing he soberly informed the trapped girl folk did not `snap".

Fervently the maid insisted of her plight.

"I surely will sir for I'm only little - d'you see."

"So you are girl so you are. But if ye take the line and thread it under the fat one I shall endeavour to lift her bulk away from thee."

Successfully concluded moments later his high boots and buckled knees took up a creaking strain, for this was the only view she had of the stranger hovering darkly above. The man already calculated it was to be a snatch and grab at the body, assessing her bulk to be some 280 lbs. A bone wrenching jerk and hold later dourly he inquired if he had been successful.

"Aye 'tis done, sir - I can move my legs freely." She scrambled clear as the woman's lifeless corpse was lowered back down into her splintered coffin.

Throwing the stretched leather reign to one side allowed the late Miss Wilks to settle atop three other bodies in the post chaise coffin. A hand released a sheaf of dried parchment documents bearing similar wax seal crests to those detected by earlier searching. The lost package cracked open and the contents fell from her opened up fingers into the darkness of the post chaise interior.

* * *

It was exceptionally cold for April. The fine English spring having failed again that year, more rain than the heavens could hold were released to fall upon the heads of the lone horseman and his terrified young captive clinging on behind him on the galloping black stallion. Wind squalls finally died with the waning of night. All about the shadowy fleeting figures on the speeding beast was now subjected to a deathly calm. Apart from the repetitive drumming hooves as they rhythmically pounded the rutted mud-strewn track, there was silence which preceded the song birds dawn chorus.

The Eastern hemisphere showed belligerency in clinging onto darkness. Silvery streaks reached lazily from faraway foothills, as clear indication a moody dawn was not far off. Unused to being hauled unceremoniously up and out of a carriage window, the girl thought how a footman usually placed a velvet-covered stool for her shoe; on the other hand, when you are twelve years old anything can be an adventure. Occasional whimpering came from the terrified girl as sinewy thighs slipped from the muscular back of the racing stallion, the night-black beast thundered in soundly whipped hysteria. Suddenly a notable change of hoof-tone diverting across a freshly furrowed field made the girl feel they neared their secret destination. Which was just as well because she could feel her cold-cramped fingers slipping from dark folds round the road agent's waist. Desperately bouncing about on the hurtling animal's buttocks, flung up and down rhythmically made it difficult for her to cling for dear life. Feverish galloping to goodness-knows-where gave her a feeling of her very life slipping away, praying aloud above the noise of the thundering hooves `please keep thy servant alive oh lord" the youngster burying her face into the horse-man's shoulder blades.

"Best make it a plain prayer," she thought for the Good Lord would not hear above all this commotion. Then suddenly it was over! The snorting and perspiring horse and its riders at last halted outside an obscure hostelry thatched with fresh golden straw.

The crumbling country inn looked for all the world that it had fallen from the heavens above, so had a brief benediction been answered. They must be near the sea for a pounding and swish of receding waves on pebbles broke the crisp dawn air somewhere far beyond a rising copse. She thought too she spied a distant sand dune in the dawn's half-light. Dawn. They must have ridden hard all night, for it was barely nine-of-the-clock when her dead guardian checked her brass carriage clock, poor woman, her on an errand of mercy too.

The Highwayman reached behind and firmly gripped the slender girl's waist. Roughly he lowered his weather-beaten passenger to the ground alongside the sweating and panting horse. Falling to lie prostrate on the straw-strewn earth, the girl lay there looking up at the panting beast that'd galloped through the night in the raging storm. Sweat taking the place of dampening rains, the hotly steaming beast mashed the ground with a stomping front hoof. She began to wonder if its action suggested after all it was not the place to halt their journey, as the girl rose to her feet to flex her aching limbs she took time to look about her in somewhat confused bewilderment. Suddenly the rickety door of the old inn opened wide and an ochre filtering light spilled to the ground in front of her, followed by a diminutive woman dressed in long flowing skirts, mob-cap and fluttering shawl draping rounded shoulders now burst into view. The girl glanced away and down in fear of her life as a back-lit figure stood motionless, silhouetted in the doorframe only looking up when her shrill voice and black shadow moved to appear at her stockinged feet.

"A maid!"

Now looming in front of her with her hands on her hips, there swayed a larger-than-life, middle-aged woman shaking her head in a totally exaggerated display. Her round moon-face was smudged with soot and smut her twinkling eyes burned out of a raging face. She came closer and it was only then that the girl spied her wild spiky orange hair, florid as a basketful of fresh drawn carrots.

"What in God's name did ye bring a maid here of all places, Jess Mandrake." Side lit now by faint lantern light from the opened doorway, it fell across a kindly face. Sniffing disdainfully, the woman swiped at her nose with the back of a dampened hand. The squawking voice rang out in staccatos sounding like the irritated crack of a whip. Yet the woman called her abductor by his full title of `Jess Mandrake" - there was a name to remember. "A place full of vagabonds and ne'er-do-wells, hell's teeth man, whatever possessed ye." Her bulk was that of the late Miss Martha Wilks, again this was the first thing that sprang to mind as her hand was scooped up and dragged off towards the inn door.

"And what are we about to be calling ye child."

"Clarissa ma'am - ''tis Clarissa Lovelace."

The kindly woman mellowed and leant over to softly inquire if she was a bastard child or fortunate enough to hold a gentleman's surname.

"That'll be Peach, ma'am, for my full identity be Clarissa Lovelace Peach."

Nearby the swirling of a black cloak heralded the dismounting of the horseman, his black silk tricorn torn from his head and he fanned himself irritatedly. Under the black hat a heavy black velvet cord and bow secured the lank dark hair tied at the nape of his neck. A sickly pallor and bony-sharp features now distinguished themselves to the girl - revealed clearly by the faint yellow light from an opened doorway. She felt a reassuring shake from the woman's massive work-callused hand.

"Don't thee worry none child, for old Pernickety be here to protect thee."

The highwayman growled, "Inside woman, I'm thinking we'd best be discussing this worrisome affair inside. The skinny maid and my bones be fair froze from unseasonable chill winds and driving rains." The gloating sneer and sharpening one-eyed glance offered to the shivering maid, now appeared more of a silent warning to keep her tongue still over the previous night's occurrence. Unhitching the reins of his mount he looked about him angrily,

"Where's thy blasted ostler - that dolt of a stable lad."

The unkindly interpretation of her slender frame was felt to be unnecessary and most embarrassing, yet the inquiries about the missing stable boy heightened her consciousness of a stable nearby. And with it came a rancid stench of rotting straw and horse dung which hung thickly in the air. Looking up from comforting the girl the woman commanded patience from the highwayman.

"Tom will tend thy steed, just leave him bide there to cool its heels."

Clarissa still felt the sting of embarrassment rising to her cheeks at the disparaging reference, yet felt a comforting squeeze of encouragement from the perpetually smiling woman. She confided warmly, "Pernickety be my name and be my nature too. I don't stand nonsense from those who do so frequent my ale house." Giggling she added, "Fuss and fear naught, Pernickety be here." Then led the way towards warmth of the doorway, side-slapping herself in merriment with a free hand as she went. Guiding her she combed long fingers through the tangle of her wild hair and tossing her head defiantly at the glowering observation of the highwayman.

Miss Pernickety and the girl stooped to pass through the low beamed doorway, part-turning to watch the rickety oak door close on a new found freedom, Clarissa felt her heart skip a beat. Then as the door closed she thought she glimpsed a half-naked youth with sprigs of straw in his hair hurrying to tend to the highwayman's horse. Scantily clothed his appearance conveyed that he had been disturbed from his slumbering on a bed of straw in the nearby stable. Once established inside, her innermost thoughts suggested she should keep her own counsel. Relaxing she sniffed ale-laden air of the ale bar which fell thickly to her flaring nostrils, and yet the long room itself was welcoming and hung with a pleasing warmth and atmosphere. Blue smoke wafted around, probably irritated by the draught from the opened doorway, it swirled upwards toward the age-gnarled beams of the low ceiling. This was originally cream in colour but now it was stained a molten copper with many years of stale tobacco smoke and their accompanying fumes. Here and there slumped bodies of men lay crumpled awkwardly across the well-scrubbed tables, stiffening, Clarissa recalled the horror of the coach crash, for these too were likened to the broken corpses of her memory. Sprawled casually in an austere somewhat claustrophobic clutter of the wooden bench settles and sensing her fear the woman whispered reassuringly.

"Oh don't ye pay no never mind to them bodies lying over there for them's not dead - just dead-drunk, aye that they be - and all from the evening afore's ale supping."

Smilingly companionably they passed by flagstones lightly dusted with sawdust. Clarissa was gently pushed down into the corner of an enormous inglenook fireplace. Placing a log onto greying embers, she gave a smart kick from a brass-buckled shoe to give rise to a thousand sparks. They glittered, and moments later a lick of flame gave way to a roar and a renewing heat warmed her.

"Before the flames get too hot for thee why Don't ye place thyself on the black-lead hob to be just like one o' my copper pans." The woman then noticed the girl sniffing. "Here now what are you snorting at young `un. Not got the night fevers have 'ee." Pernickety watched firm denial by a shake of her head and grunted relief then hurried off to tend to the coming days business. Pressing duties included provisioning for the road robber and due to the unpredictability of the man was to the fore and uppermost in her mind. Clarissa sniffed the air and quite cautiously she looked about her, then recalling words from her evil saviour who had mentioned earlier at her growing apprehension when faced with abduction or death, "Thou needn't afear for thy safety child for "tis much fatter fish I've to fry this night."

* * *

A scuffed brown leather thigh boot stirred the girl from her exhausted slumbering, partially opening one eye she peered through

28

her long lashes to spy a man shrewdly staring hard with one part closed and one glinting eye. Moving in closer the dark stranger doffed a silver-braided black tricorn with one hand to hang it to swing on the vicious curved hook affixed to his other limb. Bending lower he offered up a lantern whose light side-lit his face causing a twinkling of a gold earring, she felt his warm ale laden breath and his braided black beard tickled her fully awake as it touched her face. All the girl ever read and had been taught about pirates and privateers was there. A white ruff and cuffs of his flaxen-coloured blouson shirt. Blue breeches, thigh-length boots of a well-worn nature, and one of which surely must have disturbed her respite. Distantly a voice called the bearded one to task.

"Ned! Come thee back here and leave the maid be in her slumber." Regaining full use of her senses to recognise the command as that of Miss Felicity Pernickety - what a strange name to be sure. Careful to spy the bearded one straighten and withdraw to do as he was bade, she allowed herself a gentle stretch to restore her limbs, all set against the broad back of the retreating pirate. Revived once more, wondered if she should cross the well-worn flagstones to join the woman sitting amongst the men. Though now they were apparently discussing something quite important. By yellowy light of the many spluttering tallow fat candles, a deal was struck the far side of the room. Palms were spat upon and snatched-grips sealed some silent bond. Later voices would rise then subside; a drinking table would shudder as a fist pounded its scrubbed wooden surface laying emphasis to some salient point.

Babbling of urgent conversation would occasionally die away as the door was flung wide and a stranger entered to demand ale and stabling for the night, fearful of the king's eavesdroppers and spies abounded. Low denomination silver coins, spot cash for many rejuvenated tankards of foaming ale was collected and flung to a nearby barrel head.

The ale room hung with a velvety warmth and darkness, only pools of light from the many candles and lanterns offered some sort of sparse illumination, this dulled luminescence highlighted the austerity of well scrubbed tables and settles. Although hunger pangs swept over her, the girl decided it was prudent to remain in her corner of the great inglenook fireplace. Or at least until the kindly women glanced her way again, then the girl might carefully acknowledge or wave back without the other rogues noticing. Her eyes drifted to the nicotine-stained ceiling where knurled beams held an assortment of dusty bric-a-brac. Expanding candleholders made of air-blackened brass also tarnished with sooty smut, several bunches of faded purple heather and dusty dried hops, teazles, sun dried grasses or straws hung from each corner. Clarissa remembered how Miss Wilks explained how old houses and hostelries used dried grasses and flowers to soak up the profusion of pipe smoke and cooking smells. Then each summer they were exchanged for armfuls of fresh gatherings. Turning her attention to the rest of the room she spied oaken doors leading to other parts of the inn, and nearby in the fireplace, black iron pots, pans and skillets hung sentry over her head. A battered scuttle of split logs completed the arrangement, also broken clay pipe stems and bowls lay scattered carelessly in the hearth grill. A moulding on one broken pipe bowl resembled a wheat-sheaf now where had she seen that design before, it was a thieves' market-place as wares were sprawled randomly over nearby tables for she presumed what were prospective purchasers, supped their ale at bench settles across the room. Her thoughts were abruptly interrupted by a raised voice, that of the night robber.

"Hast thou seen my Bess?" The voice rose above the hubbub of the crowded room and filling fast with boisterously arguing men. Mandrake's favoured acquisition purloined recently from the Somerset and Devon militia ordnance tent, and deftly removed as they'd boisterously consumed their field rations nearby. Left unattended in that den of iniquity though loaded with black powder, the all important flash pan lay empty, and therefore the lengthy weapon would offer sparse comfort for attempted theft or misuse of the musket.

""'Tis over by the lass," another answered in somewhat bored tones as he threw down a pasteboard jack of diamonds. Very soon a dark shape loomed closer than was comfortable, and then pausing only to take up the propped musket from the corner and once again it was prudent for the girl to pretend to be asleep. Moments later the black shape turned away and crossed the room again to join the others in the game of primero.

The girl squinted, opened her eyes and watched him as she recalled that the roaming naval press gangs and dockyard units in

Dartmouth carried the tall weapons. She noted cautiously how the highwayman furtively manhandled the lock mechanism whilst glancing about him.

A chill wind sighed down the broad shafted chimney causing a brief glow to rise in the iron dog basket, greying ash crowned the red-tipped embers of apple faggots and lay like a scattering of snow. Occasionally a flurry or sputtering would take place and then a spark or two would rise on a grey spiral of billowing smoke.

"Oh there you be at last little maid." Miss Pernickety appeared and was bending over her offering a clay bowl of thick steaming gruel. "My goodness but ye've slept all day and best part o' a raucous evening - God's teeth ye must be starved, lass."

"I am ma'am and I thank you most kindly for thy goodly offer of sustenance."

"Well now, them's manners them is." Pernickety beamed her pleasure at the young girl's company; it was pleasant indeed to have another lass with which to converse and pass the time of day - even if she was a mere pubescent maid. "Art afraid, lass?"

"Aye, ma'am, I be afraid for my lack of permanence in this frightening place and dreading naught more than being sold into a tavern-girl's existence."

"Fear not little one for I'm thinking thou art a goodly lass and I'll do my best to look after thee." A continuing wide-awake nightmare of doubt and fear waned in the comforting exchange with the kindly woman, the girl's shivering ceased and she forced a smile into the glinting somehow mournful woman's look. "Now eat up and look lively afore the dullards doth spy a square meal and take it off thee for their own sustenance." She placed a torn chunk of unleavened bread on the wooden trencher of steaming food. Taking the offered bowl and nestled it to her lap, then to her surprise the fat woman slid down the wall alongside her and started to chuckle. Offering more chunks of the dried out darkened bread adding cheerily she'd baked it herself.

"Odds bodkins little girl tuck in heartily or you'll never grow big like old Pernickety. Not that ye'd have a preference, eh." Cackling brightly, Clarissa felt herself relaxing and enjoyed mopping the bread to a thinning greasy_liquid, even though it smelt strongly of coarse flour. Eating her meal Clarissa disguised as much relish as was humanely possible, yet able to take note as the woman took pains to

31

point out varying wares on nearby tables,

"Look what the nice but wicked gentlemen have brought to trade from o'er the waters, rolls o' fine silks and coloured yarns. Gentleman's snuff boxes o' silver and pewter along with great kegs of "baccy and rumbullion." Half-dozen petticoats under multi-coloured full length skirts rustled with excitement. She went on and on in excited tones, her voice growing more stentorian. "Booty Cognac, red and white wines smuggled from Normandy - all thus keeping me and my friends to a manner we'd all like to get accustomed to." She laughed so loudly that this time her mob-cap fell over her eyes until she snatched it away - pursing her fulsome lips in a comic mock-embarrassment. Clarissa felt herself laughing and finishing her meal placed the bowl to the stones alongside, suddenly voices were raised again and both pairs of eyes followed the noise to the far shadowy corner, heated questioning came from a group of men occupying a table near the broad entrance door.

"T'was near the old king's hunting lodge in Axbridge I tell you." A fist crashed on to the tabletop, pewter tankards flipped into the air and crashed to spill their amber coloured liquid contents everywhere. A flattened palm swept the amber liquid to the sawdust-covered floor.

Pernickety lowered her voice and spoke to the girl from behind the palm of her raised hand. She bent closer to the girl's ear, "Whist little maid we'd best be hushed for a while." Squeezing her hand gently to make a point, noting that in the distance another man rose menacingly to his feet and swung a vicious looking metal hook. Pounding down upon the bench table it seemed to be attached to what was left of his left arm. Then he threatened the first with a scathing statement.

"Ye'll be a telling of us next that it were an act o' God, Jess, so avast ye dirty bilge scum try telling us the truths of all this evil matter."

A huge bulk of a man with the black beard interfered at this moment, rising to fix his grip to the hook then forced it again to the first man's side. "I think I'll be a hearing o' the tale from the highwayman for t'was he that did the dirty deed that brooding night."

They all slumped to sitting positions as the bearded one went on, "dandy's and fops they might have been yet blood were spilled unnecessary like - so the lads and I reckon ye best tell us why ye felt why thy chosen attack was decided upon."

Black Ned Teach also knew his over-cynical men were long

corroded by the indiscipline of boredom, especially after this latest escapade which would intensify defeat on land. They too had relied upon this paper pardon and forgiveness of Morgan's and their own past wickedness in the far off Indies. The room fell mortal silent as the drunken highwayman rose unsteadily to his feet, Clarissa putting this down to the ale quaffed over the past hour or so.

She found herself gripping the woman's hand tighter and tighter as the man with the curly black beard drew a cutlass from its scabbard. Watching as he placed it atop the table surface and where they all now sat patiently awaiting an explanation. Mandrake hovered, pewter tankard in hand and propped up by stiffening the backs of his legs against the bench seat, his thighs jammed hard against the over crowded table. It seemed to be the only way he could stand securely, then eventually he spoke in a softening mock sincerity,

"It didn't stop," pausing to scan the frowning expressions of the sea of upturned faces to note their eyes were sullenly lowered in obvious doubt. Protesting Jess went on with his side of the story. "The post chaise conveyance and its team o' four didn't pull up when so ordered - it tried to out-run a flintlock he did . . . Only he didn't, if ye can see my thinking?

Coachman sprang from his perch like a wild man possessed and fell under his own wheels. The dolt of a coachman kept going and the conveyance upended itself, all that were inside died o' broken necks, only the maid squatting o'er there in the inglenook survived." Lowering his head whilst choosing his next words, "the mail coach was fresh from a second relay and the buffoon were still blasting on his damnable post horn, normally this signalled arrival at his destination only he were jubilant in a fast turn around of fresh horses or some such like. This eerie noise forewarned of his approach and I could choose my moment and point of ambuscade - but imagine my horror." Jess threw up his arms in mock horror, "when he rode a rock on the side o' the road after ignoring to heed my strict command to stop."

Jess nodded menacingly towards the girl. Cruelly his words brought back the fresh memory and innocence of her fellow travellers, the lying road agent beheld a most hateful stare from the girl, deadly unforgiving Clarissa's expression afforded a warning of eventual retaliation. A blank stare looked at he who abducted her as she recalled that terrifying dash on horseback to the safety of the old inn, spying too that he'd discarded his black high boots.

Now he sported brass-buckled shoes and white hose noticeable under half-length velvet breeches. Topped off with a three-quarter length red velvet frock coat, thin neckerchief of dark silk which clung lightly to his throat like a black shadow and on their initial encounter the self-same neckerchief covered his face up to his patched eye. The black silk tricorn tilted at a rakish angle, and the embroidered silver braid around its brim stood him apart from the rest of the seated men in the hostelry. Although he was now being browbeaten and badgered sorely by the rest. Clarissa inquired why he of all folk looked to be the more affluent than the rest of the roguish looking band of vagabonds.

"That's because he be a gentleman o' the road, child." Lowering her voice she added with deadly sincerity, "Old Jess Mandrake be the devil incarnate. T'was a goodly surprise to thy servant when he told of rescuing thee from a coach spill."

"Aye ma'am a spill that he himself caused - so he did."

Clarissa displayed her displeasure with narrowing eyes. Miss Pernickety chided the girl for her pessimism about the one known as Jess the Pearly. Eighteen hours earlier the frail appearance of the maid on arrival convinced her she was either too ill or frail to do anything more than but sleep. But now she was on fire with hatred for the regular drinker of her inn.

"Aye, little maid thieves and vagabonds all of 'em, and there be some more roguish than others - I be afraid that old Jess be one of 'em."

"And the others be they sailors, ma'am. I heard one talking of the sea and its mortal perils whilst voyaging in warmer climes abroad."

"Privateers with creditable letters-of-marque or dastardly pirates on the high seas. They bring their ill-gotten booty to the old Ship inn to trade 'em against quaffing ale and such like." Squeezing her hand to assure safety of sorts her jowls puffed as she went on, "irritation was that they'd all hoped to change their wicked ways for a king's pardon." Sucking and picking at her teeth she added, "corsairs be mustering their wooden ships up the coastline of Lyme Regis, though half their vessels be only fit for mast-less hulks of prison ships to sit upon the Thames Estuary in the city of London."

"Yes ma'am, but why bother with such men when we have the

king's navy." She then feared her frankness had been her undoing as the grip slackened.

"No silly goose for they be just the folk to know far off lands like Tortuga, Maracaibo, or manifold inlets of Port Royal in Old Jamaica. Such places you and the likes o' Pernickety barely heard tell of. Why "tis rumoured Black Ned be acquainted with Henry Morgan his own self." Pressing a forefinger to her lips she whispered,

"Methinks little maids like ye best be seen and not heard, eh." Nodding across the room she snapped, "You make no never mind o' that heller, Jess," sucking her breath in she released it through her blackened teeth with a sigh, "I doubts somehow if the dolt will breathe the morrow's air."

"Why, because he killed my companion, Miss Wilks?" The girl responded a strange excitement at potential revenge.

"Oh, who be she then?"

"My guardian, ma'am. Her on an errand of utmost mercy, too." The girl whispered. Pandemonium broke out from the other side of the room, the woman and the girl exchanged nervous glances then back toward rising anger of men as they shouted threats and obscure reasoning.

"Paper pardons b'aint worth no mind, pardons be spoken and not scribed."

Jess looked furious and held the one-eyed challenging gaze of the black bearded man rising to face him. Rising to a full height of over six feet to stand in confrontational opposition to the highwayman, Ned Teach spat,

"Then where be thy proof, Jess Mandrake." Holding his gaze he leant forward onto a fearsome hook attached to what presumably was a left hand. His spread-eagle fingers of his right hand heavily bedecked with jewel-encrusted gold and silver rings.

"Proof." Came the stuttered reply.

"Aye man, proof, some say folk do sometimes go back on their word now Don't they just. But if the house o' royals puts it to the scribe then "tis binding - see!"

Jess took up the challenge. "Who so says such grand words."

"I Black Ned do so say." He sniffed uncertainty but continued, "For it be common knowledge amongst the brethren." He nodded to the shouts of approval around him.

35

Clarissa found herself rising to her feet, yet the voice which rang from her dry throat was unrecognisable, sounding more like a canary trill she cried out in a lull of conversation,

"Are ye the one they call black Ned Teach, sire."

His voice unquestionably the authority of her stepfather, vaguely familiar to her from early childhood whilst growing up in the naval town of Dartmouth. Challenged by a slip of a maid, the huge man turned slowly around to look across the smoke-filled room and toward the maid Clarissa. Staring hard and with his back turned on the highwayman, and with a room falling as silent as the grave he inquired, "Who be you to bear witness to my identity little maid." A dangerous liaison to nurture if the pirate failed to recognise her.

Delicately-boned the girl in her innocence likened to porcelain standing in that den of lions.

"I be thy step-daughter, Clarissa Lovelace Peach, sir."

Jess slowly picked up the musket and pausing only to prime his flintlock mechanism, then withdrew a powder horn from his belt. Silently uncorking the cap he levelled off the weapon to pour a tad of black powder into the flash pan, then closing the guard he checked on the leather pad gripping the razor edged flint. Only after he'd snapped the flash guard shut did Black Ned realise what he was up to with the weapon, to lay emphasis to his actions Jess then placed the weapon on full-cock with an audible double `click". But at the same instant a broad-bladed cutlass flashed its way into the firm grip of the pirate. Poised now they steeled themselves for the oncoming fray - a scurrying mass exit from the old inn took place in moments. Drunken seamen sobering quickly at the thought of injury or death becoming a reality, they upturned tables and settles rushing for the wide-flung inn door. Tallow stumps and the strategically placed lanterns were tossed aside and extinguished in the evacuation and darkness grew in pools around the room. Jess jerked his head from side to side as he watched with a darting eye, standing solemnly with a raised gun his other hand rested atop the quillon hilt of the slim rapier blade at his side. When the commotion subsided, only the females and warring adversaries were left. The grudge fight was on at last. Cheering from outside the grimy windowpanes came from gaunt faced men, anxious with the gambling fever as they debated the outcome. Money quickly changed hands on the outcome of the forthcoming onslaught. Nut-brown faces pressed hard against the thick panes of glass once final bets were laid and paid. A gold earring twinkled on one pirate, broken teeth offered a knowing grin on another's face, yet another grimaced and tore off a red striped bandanna to wipe a fevered brow. All smiled anticipation on their wagered outcome and the babbling, though muted, filtered inside the smoke filled ale smelling room to add to an already charged atmosphere. Silence and stillness inside was broken as Jess excused his actions with a necessary justification.

"The maid over there witnessed a gaggle o' murders I'm thinking "tis best that she be put down with a musket ball here and now."

The desperate girl blurted out another plea, as inexorably she felt so alone.

`Please sire - "tis thy stepdaughter, Clarissa. "

"What was that child, what dids't say." Ned's flashing dark eyes darted from distraction to distraction as he gripped the hilt of the curved blade, the sharply-honed cutlass would split a hair on a man's head. Now scythe-like, it whistled through the air in a wildly exaggerated figure-of-eight, the fight-hardened pirate knew he could only threaten retribution and not reach across the clutter of upturned furniture for his pair of pistols - useless and a deal of distance away on a far-flung table. The girl's voice stated once more quite lucidly,

"My school teacher guardian held a paper-pardon to her purse. She said she was to be a `go-betwixt' for thyself and the pirate king, Captain Henry Morgan of Jamaica."

Moving forward to whom she felt might be her long-lost step-father as she tried desperately to recognise the wild-eyed rogue with a vicious-looking hook affixed to his left hand, though recalling the habit of platting red-tassels into his jet black beard from early childhood - yet why did he only have one arm.

"Wilks, D'ye say. Martha Wilks the schoolmistress - well I never, blast my hide. Thy name child - dost say it were Clarissa Lovelace?" Smiling broadly from behind the tousled matt of black facial hair, Ned Teach picked his way across the room toward the wide-eyed and terrified girl.

""'Tis thy maid sir and "tis mortal glad I be to have found thee in this place."

Mandrake hovered before the girl his musket aimed from the hip at her slender torso, noticing the weapon she cried out to the only one in the room who might save her. Responding to her plea Ned turned and offered a final ultimatum to the highwayman.

"Jess put up thy weapon or I'll put you to the skewer."

The overhead whirling of the cutlass flashed further warning in the remainder of dimming lights in the ale room as the two faced each other all the while circling slowly. Each man looking for the edge, a stumble over fallen furniture, a distraction from the jeering drunken oafs at the window or merely a dropping of one's guard. For one to survive a fight to the death one has to evaluate one's opponent's mental and physical strength capabilities with any chosen weapon. Casting aside doubts of by-gone lack-lustre performance with blade or bare-knuckle, stomach-knotting and blood-tasting battle in waterfront beer taverns or below decks after a drunken cheat's game of Primero. Brawls or more friendly rough and tumbles amongst the crew, for hand-to-hand combat was any pirate's stock and trade, especially haranguing or spurring others to blood-thirsty killing and fighting. It was too late for Jess to back down or change his mind over despatching this witness to his potentially ending up on the gallows at Tyburn. The combatants stared across the divide between them of ten short feet. Then the highwayman seemed to make up his mind and turned back to the girl. A resounding boom along with a hurtling ball of yellow flame sent the maid hurtling backwards to slam into the white distempered wall. Slithering down the uneven wall left red stains to smear the off-white distemper behind her, consciously staring a disbelief in her watery-blue eyes and with her paralysed frame slipping down alongside the fireplace, she found it difficult to speak as a sickly taste sprang to her throat as she swallowed.

"I be thy step-daughter, sir."

Miss Pernickety screamed and fainted dead away. Instinctively Jess tossed the now useless weapon to one side with a clatter of metal and wood, at the same instant he withdrew the rapier from its belted scabbard. Black Ned gave a terrifying scream of anger all the while whirling the razor-sharp cutlass wildly above his head as he picked his way purposefully across the floor clutter towards Jess the Pearly. Once within range he found the prodding and jabbing of the rapier kept him at bay.

Slowly he gathered his wits over the needless death of what he took to be his long lost stepdaughter, a white-knuckle rage overtook his senses and distorted stratagem of preplanned attack on his adversary. Waving the left arm with the hook affixed distracted the road robber momentarily as he focused his almost hypnotic gaze on it, Ned swiped back with the broad thrash of the half-moon shaped cutlass, hacking and parrying with the more cumbersome weapon. Distracted with thoughts of how he should have despatched this treacherous villain whence hearing of the bungled mail robbery attempt, now he and others would fail to reap the full pardons for their wanton misdeeds in the name of the crown.

Jess cursed the oversight and a flicker of fury came to his singular gaze as he realised too late the girl was no real threat to him. He should have despatched the man alongside him first then concerned himself with the slip of a girl. Also he was too far away from the only door to freedom and could no longer think about escape, the only thing was to fight his way clear. Knowing his slim-pointed rapier could do naught against a heavier blade if allowed forward into any given close quarter foray. His left-handed jabs were alien to the pirate as they now stood at right angles to each other. Sensing the fearful reach of the prodding rapier, Ned seized up a fallen footstool by thrusting his hook into the timber squab. Holding it ahead by way of a shield until he could move within slashing range. Jess grinned at what he considered to be a futile gesture and thrust forward into the wooden seat - burying the tip that arched its resistance. Feeling abruptly the sudden over-balancing weight of the floor furniture, Jess's expression dropped as only now did he realise the futility of his reaction. As with ancient adversaries coming up against the pilum - he too was left with an unwanted encumbrance on the slender rapier. The Roman army's invention of long spears with soft-metal heads encircled with retaining groove, pierced defending shields of their enemies. Only to find the Roman soldier's javelin was left secured in their shield then to bend under the extended weight. This is what now happened to Jess's rapier - stuck on the tip was a heavy foot stool, with no way of withdrawing to further his planned onslaught. Struggling led to it snapping off altogether and right up to the hilt. Confusion and growing panic gave Ned the chance to glance briefly at the girl. A growing pool of dark red blood grew around her upper body as she lay on her back. Turning back towards the road robber he noted his pleas for mercy and blurted excuses for this unwarranted attack upon both him and the girl.

Distracted momentarily as a faint cheer rose from outside and flurrying hands spied through the hostelry window grabbed at their wagered winnings. Black Ned's eyes turned to focus on the lamentable coward his hands clasped together with the hilt of the rapier, sagging at the knees cringing in front of the wavering cutlass. Yet what mercy had he afforded his adopted ward lying at his feet and in her own life's blood. Spinning on his heel and in a thrice it was over, the highwayman screaming out in horror as the curved blade pinioned him, thrusting the blade so ferociously it went through his left side and into the lining of the wall. Jess" eyes bulged like chapel hat pegs. Strangely the spectre of death in the making remained upright, when suddenly a blackening tongue lolled from a corner of his cruel mouth.

The cross-quillon hilt of the rapier tilted from relaxing fingers and it fell along with spurting blood in a resounding clatter to the stone floor, gasping incredulously until his senses finally left him and his head fell forward onto his chest. Gruesomely, the pirate chief bent forward to cock an ear for his opponent's death rattle - only it never came, so leaving the cutlass protruding from the corpse he did what all victors did at the scene of battle - that of wiping the blade of his opponents" blood then wiped it across his forehead. Without a backward glance he moved swiftly to the fallen girl's side and there to kneel and scoop up her tiny hand in his, and at his touch the fallen girl's eyes flickered open and her painful gaze searched his face straining for recognition in his eyes as he moved into her field of vision.

Catching her breath she said,

"I be thy Clarissa, sir, dost thou not recognise thy own step-daughter, sir?"

"Aye girl thou be my little daughter alright, though too many years have passed by without contact and I fair nearly failed to recognise thee."

The girl took hold of the half-moon spike and drawing attention she registered more confusion in her pained expression. Ned smiled and unfastened the hook, revealing a flexing left hand complete and healthy. "It were my guise so's no one would recognise a wanted felon from the wanted posters hung up in Lyme town." Confused he looked at the tiny creature sprawled on her back, blood leached from an upper chest wound.

Black Ned Teach stared in motionless stupefaction at the doll-like creature on the flags in front of him, as she coughed one more time and then lay quietly still as she felt a red veil draw itself slowly down over her eyes to lose consciousness...

* * *

*Primero - forerunner of the modern game of Poker

Chapter Two   SMUGGLER'S MOON

In thee thy morning's light
I spy ye shining silver bright
I spy ye standing shivering
in golden dew a quivering

Mystical light that follows ye
transformed now for all to see
Majestically into Venus flight
revealed by gentle waning night

Have a care of this my plight
spying ye in thy morning's light
forsaking others my spirit cling
Peace tranquillity ever bring
Poem: Morning light of Venus

The full moon shone like a piece of freshly minted silver. Billowing storm clouds on the horizon and the crisp night air held a deal of mystery about it and the brilliant moonshine backlit a handful of stars in the heavens. Stella Maris and the great Dog Star Sirius, Orion's belt and little Pleiades outshone by much larger sisters. Distantly and like an elderly woman gathering her skirts, gunmetal clouds began to skate hither and thither across a great void to portend of worsening weather. Out of the all-enveloping darkness the man and woman became aware of distant footfalls as they clattered on the shiny cobble-stoned slope. This hill was Silver Street; it led precariously steep down to Lyme Regis harbour side and manifold moored ships contained within its ancient Cobb quayside. Men's lowered voices came in their direction and prompted the woman Pernickety and her manservant Jake into reacting. They drew back to crouch down into an alleyway and hid themselves smartly into a scudding moon shadow.

"Mayhap preventives, Pernick." Jake whispered from behind his cupped hand.

"Preventive water guards Don't shine their appearance that way,

Jake." The woman reasoned in equally hushed tones. "Hush up and watch out for the maid. She just might call in her delirium." Nudging him she urged, "I did advise ye to stop the blood's flow." The woman tried to rearrange the wound pad as the man held the precious bundle under his armpit.

Walking two miles from the old Ship Inn had taken its toll, now the gentle pressure on the wound caused the girl's eyes to flicker and open. Softly she began to moan with a renewed pain, the woman pressed a gentle finger to the child's blueing lips and bade her be quiet on pain of death. Especially if they should be caught abroad on that moonlit night.

Clarissa's conscious eyes bore more than just a tad of confusion and anguish looking out from the cloth shroud hiding her from head to toe. Her brow furrowed under the shock of tousled dark hair, already paled as her complexion took on an eerie white glow from the moonlight. Jake nodded towards nearing voices,

"Revenuers - maybe Pernick." Jake rasped through his gritted teeth, for he hated revenuers. The woman Pernickety dragged her manservant and his precious bundle of gathered rags up into an alleyway between a row of tiny terraced cottages. The outskirts of Lyme Regis the Dorset village was normally quiet at this hour of the night, though she felt it might be a different story when they approached the harbours edge, and decent folks were to their beds at this hour. The only sound now echoing across the night air was the approach of the gang's footfall above a distant hiss of a rising sea washed beach. Pernickety crept to the corner of the end house and flicked her head round and back in a flash. There she spied bowed backs of tub men with shoulder-born double liquor kegs slung between braces of jute. A known safe way of transporting contraband in their handy-sized 4 gallon barrels. A flash of her copper-coloured hair in bright moonlight was all it took. The brief movement recorded and exposed by one of the batmen. Their hushed voices died and the nearest, cudgel in hand, dived after her and dragged her back into view from the narrow alleyway. Gripping her shoulder he shook her roughly with one hand growling at her, his face barely an inch from hers, "Don't ye be a knowing better than that, missus. Especially at this God-forsaken hour o' the night." A voice devoid of emotion held cold-bloodied logic for her stupidity in identifying the trawling column of smugglers. Realising who they must be the woman spun away from eyeball contact to face the brick wall. Calling urgently she advised her night companion,

"'Tis the gentlemen o' the night, Jake, best be facing the wall with the maid until they do so pass by and go about their business this evening."

Releasing his painful grip on her, the ruffian then nodded and grunted his approval of her reaction. Then he turned to watch her companion do likewise. Bending forward he whispered a final caution. "Tub men allus use this route so best be more alert next time, missus."

Sliding away into a moonlit shadow, Pernickety saw him run to catch up the weaving column of trudging tub-carrying men. This final caution left behind racing hearts and sweaty palms. She moved to her burly manservant, noticing he too had paled and looked quite green in the soft moonlight, "hardly revenuers, Jake, thou couldn't have been more wrong." Scolding him gently he joined in her nervous cackle of relief. Clarissa regained full consciousness and inquired from her cradled position as she wiped her eyes who the men were.

"Bless ye child for you're back with us, eh. Well there be a rhyme in these parts o' Dorset." Pernickety held Jake's arm insisting the child be comforted before they continue. "Goes like this." The middle-aged woman burst into a trilling which jarred her companion's nerves and impatience. "Them's that ask no questions b'aint told no lie, so watch the wall whilst the Gentlemen go by, so watch the wall m'dears when the Gentlemen go by." She indicated they could walk on as she persisted in enlightening her further.

"'Tis tub men, Clarissa, rum smugglers from the harbour ships. Them's that carries casks o' rum and brandy and their damnable batmen. Twas one o' them devils that grabbed old Pernickety here, they dark rogues and their damnable cudgels. D'ye know weren't be nothing for one o' them to pound thy servant to the cobbles."

Releasing Jake's arm so the journey might continue they moved cautiously off their shoes picking their way over the polished moonlit cobblestones. Eventually it became difficult to keep their balance on the steepening slope of the winding hill known as Silver Street, wending its way to the harbour. Clarissa murmured the song somewhat deliriously.

"When the gentlemen go by, m'dears. So face the wall when the gentlemen go by. So face the wall when the gentlemen go by."

In her delirium, and watching as the full moon was chased away allowing storm clouds to gather in front of them. Half-hour passed before a cloudburst finally sent the huddled group scurrying into a porched doorway. They were now in the midst of the town of Lyme Regis itself and awaited respite from the torrential downpour.

"Who's there?" a voice called out from an opened window above, muted only by the hiss of the sudden torrential spring rain storm, "state your business or be off." His voice demanded somewhat irritatedly. Pernickety stepped out from the stone clad porchway and craned her neck,

"Whist to your irritation sir, "tis only travellers abroad and sheltering for a moment under thy porch canopy on this wretched night - and one an injured maid, too."

Silence from the voice above reinforced noise of lashing rain on her upturned face. Withdrawing to a drier spot enabled Pernickety to think the resident had retired once again back to his bedchamber. Moments later and as they made to leave, a bolt was shot from the door behind them, and welcoming candlelight spilled outwards to the wet street.

A man wielding a sooty lantern opened the narrowed oak door with its loud creak.

Renewed rain spats blew inwards onto smooth dusty-dry flag stones within the doorway and this offered encouragement to a sense of urgency.

"Best be coming inside. Please bring the injured girl out of the night air." Standing to one side the middle-aged man dressed in nightshirt and raggedly tasselled cap allowed them to pass into what turned out to be an apothecary's surgery. As luck would have it the Samaritan turned out to be a retired ship's doctor with a wealth of experience in bullet wounds. A dark shadow silhouette on the far side of the main room flitted around busying itself lighting lantern wicks around and about the room. Increased illumination revealed a woman with wild black hair, deftly prancing around betwixt lanterns wielding a lighted tallow taper. On seeing her, Pernickety drew back into the doorway making a grab for Jake's arm. Gently but firmly she was pushed forward once more into the room.

An explanation came from their saviour.

"It's only my housekeeper Meg - she'll not afford you any harm." The doctor smiled a reassurance and waved them to a bench.

"Please be seated so's I might tend the maid's injury." His tied bun of dark hair was loosely secured with a black velvet ribbon. The others watched as he dragged off his white night attire revealing dark breeches and brass buckled adorned leather shoes. Donning a white calico surgeon's gown he crossed the room to wash his hands in a porcelain bowl of cold water, then moved towards Clarissa. Pulling back the raggedly cloak that had been draped around her, binding the girl to the crook of the manservant's arm. "God's teeth woman. How on earth did this wound come about? How long has the girl been devoid of consciousness."

"It comes and goes, if you please, sir," Pernickety said.

"To you madam I am the local sawbones. An apothecary. A ship's doctor if you prefer and my name is Temple. Now I repeat - how did the maid come by this shoulder wound. A musket ball is the only explanation, especially the way it has torn the flesh on entry." He drew the child away from Jake's arms and spoke over his shoulder as he walked to a well-scrubbed table in a parlour surgery. Placing the child gently down he made to cleanse the wound. His floor length gown became darkened with blood as he busied himself to save the girl's life. Time passed like an eternity to the young girls" saviours. Jake had lit a fire in the grate with the previous evenings dying embers, fresh dried logs encouraging combustion, recovered from a nearby iron scuttle. Flame soon popped angrily in a soot-darkened grate adding greater illumination to the shadowy room, giving light and warmth to the occupants of the damp parlour in the small terraced cottage.

A sudden loud banging at the front door brought a hush to their voices and movement within. Doctor Temple did not cease with his surgical treatment of the injured maid; instead he raised his voice enough to be heard by the others in the room.

"One of you see who is at the front door before they awaken the whole village this night." Recovered metal chunks of ball thrown into a pewter tray gave up a tinkling noise. Somehow giving credence to the importance of his work with the injured maid. Pernickety licked her forefinger and thumb running to each pewter candle holder in turn squelching its light, leaving a bare remainder illuminating the operating table. Turning her attention to the pounding on the front door, Pernickety finally shot the bolts, on opening it she peered into the darkness. Tallow candles in a wavering black lantern outside the door temporarily distracted her until gradually a youth's face appeared. Suddenly the face rose as if by magic and flew past her like some ghostly transition. The boy in rags crumpled to the stone floor in front of the flickering fireside, whose light enabled the woman to recognise her stable lad. Thrown bodily into the room, he now cowered on the flagstones where he landed.

"Tom," the woman cried in anguish, "what be ye a doing out on such a night." It was all she had time to say before being bundled sideways to be squashed behind the heavy oak door to the wall. Eventually relaxing to swing and release her into a crumpled heap. Pernickety and the lad looked at each other then back up to the doorway, whereby a man dressed in black stood framed.

"This un yorn?" He stooped and held the gaze of the woman then looked to the boy. When there was no response he glanced over his shoulder and closing the door strode forward toward them. Reaching down he swung the woman to her feet and then crossed to the lad and did the same with much less effort.

"Clumsy great oaf," Pernickety began until the man clamped a huge hand over her mouth. Pressing his face to hers he threatened menacingly, "'tis the second time of this night I have taken it upon myself to warn ye woman. Once again I be asking ye - is this brat yorn?"

Feeling her head nod up and down in his grip he relaxed the hold, then hearing a noise spun on his heel, a long flintlock pistol grew in his other hand.

"Thee in the corner there? State thy business here sir."

The newcomer had spied the doctor working by a faint glow of candlelight.

"Now you wouldn't want a surgeon to leave his patient and identify a tub-man's batman would thee, stranger." The doctor grumbled head-down, breath coming in pants through a white mask as he feverishly worked on the wound. Segments of heavy shot were flung with bright metal grips into a bloodstained kidney-shaped dish as the surgery continued unabated.

The man in black relaxed and sheathed his pistol into a broad belt around his waist, and then strode over to check on the torrent of shot in the dish, grunted acknowledgement then resumed his place back by the fireside. Blackened lanterns and candleholders dripped and gave off an annoying stench of tallow as once more they began to illuminate the broad interior of the room. Meg, the doctor's silent helper went unperturbed about her business lighting them all again. Filtering light revealing the identity of a tall man dressed in black, contrasted drastically with a red spotted necker-chief tying back a full covering of dark hair. A deep scar traversed the smile line on his left cheek; this countered devilishly by a pair of bright twinkling blue eyes deep set in a rugged sunburnt face. Rubbing his cold hands together he threw his bulk to a bench settle alongside the fire. He looked this time to Jake for further questioning,

"And where might ye figure in all these goings on, eh, big man?"

Jake was not of a small frame by any yardstick, yet the voice that answered him fair trembled with fear. Advising the stranger how he worked for the woman Pernickety. That the maid Clarissa Peach had been fired upon in their coastal hostelry situated up the road a spell. How he'd bore the unconscious child for several miles with hope of finding a ship's surgeon in Lyme harbour. Faltering only when Jake reminded him how the batman had spied them earlier on the brow of the lengthy long hill that was the far end of silver street. Appearing satisfied the man called for rum to keep out chills of the night. Pernickety nodded and said she would do her best, then inquired if the big man might be thus excused. The stranger gave his silent permission for him so to do and the man crept cap in hand from the surgery through the front door. Patting the wooden settle alongside him when his flitting gaze fell upon the open-mouthed youth shrinking back into the shadows, he moved cautiously away.

"Don't ye harm the boy," Pernickety began, "for he be my stable lad and hasn't seen a mortal thing this night - have you Tom."

"Nay ma'am." The youth wiped a raggedly sleeve across his face perhaps to hide fearful beads of perspiration breaking on his brow. "Nary a thing." Then rising from all fours he did as he was bade and slid alongside the stranger. The high-backed settle held barely enough room for three adults, having outward sitting space of some ten inches - it was mortal uncomfortable for any length of time. Yet cosy enough in front of the fire on such an inclement night. Once seated the man stared hard into his very soul. This inadvertently rude practice prompted a strange retaliation from the youth, unseen by the boy, or so he thought, he held erect fore and little fingers downwards. The devil's horn gesticulating curse-avoidance was spotted by the man, he laughed and threw a friendly arm around the lad's bony shoulders. Plucking a straw sprig from the sad rags draped over him, guffawed more belly laughter before saying sincerely,

"Don't thee be a'feared lad, no harm will befall thee this night. Not from my hands any-road-up - I shall merely bide a while by this cheery fire for a warming noggin o' thy mistresses rum then be gone into the night about my business."

Pernickety, noting Jake was well down the road, now plucked up courage to advise him the building was a doctor's private dwelling and not a smuggler's haunt - as were many such domiciles in the town centre of old Lyme. The woman took audience with the doctor to inquire if porter, ale or rumbullion was to be made available for the stranger's thirst. Dismissing Meg with a wave of his hand to fetch a ship's decanter. When she returned she held two flattened based and pear-shaped crystal vessels. While this activity took place in the background, Tom, strangely warmed to the stranger alongside and on impulse said behind cupped hand,

"Take me with thee, sir. I don't want to go back to cleaning stables. Take thy servant to sea for an apprenticeship in piracy and smuggling.

"Why should I be a doing that lad. What possible use can a son of a gun like thee afford thy servant here." Accepting the pewter tankard that came along-with a glower from Pernickety, he winked a knowing secrecy to the lad as he took a deep draught of the vessel's contents.

"Son of a gun, sir?" the lad queried, avoiding the woman Pernickety's glare, as she grimaced and turned away half-suspecting some intrigue soon lay between man and boy. Making further nuisance endeavouring to assist in the operation on the apparently lifeless form. The man leaned over the boy's ear and whispered with a grin, "bastard child o' freebooters and old salts of the seven seas."

He emptied the vessel and banged it down alongside, swiping ale moisture from the corner of his mouth with the back of his hand. Or maybe this was merely to warn the women not interrupt their manly yarns. Tom could only speculate in silence.

"Ye see lad the only place privy to a bit o' quiet was betwixt the cannons should a sailor's lass give birth. Saves blocking a busy gangway below decks on board a ship-of-the-line. Especially if a sea-action was due. It was entered in the ship's log as a man child to be a son of a gun." Grinning he took another deep draught from the battered pewter tankard. "Why even the naval term `show-a-leg" or a "purser's stocking" comes from ladies of the night venturing on board and staying over. Anybody still swinging in a hammock after first light had to identify itself to the boson's call."

The stranger produced a silver snuffbox and watching the lad's reaction a forefinger and thumb forced a pinch to each nostril in turn. The atmosphere became thick with the aromatic smell of fine tobacco dust. Yarns of life on the high seas continued for the best part of an hour as more ale was enjoyed and quaffed in a quite deliberating manner.

"Well I remember I were present at a necessary careening o' the good ship Reverence. At a place called Bucklers Hard on the Beaulieu River, Hampshire. Men pulled lines of a part finished hull onto her side at low tide whilst moored on the shallow riverside. Exposing her hull below the water line. Summer heat had sprung its hull and deck boards, seams were caulked by hammering jute line then tarred by a team standing on a floating raft. They set about filling in the oakum and black pitch, fired so's it sticks firmly onto wood and protecting it from the Teredo worm and other mollusc. Also it made for a sure-fired watertight seam."

Having little to do but keep clear from under the doctor's feet, Pernickety snorted disapproval and called for the man to stop filling this impressionable lad with adventure tales of the sea, such knowledge of sea-faring best kept away from someone so young as her stable boy. Tom apparently did not agree with her impatient fury.

"Please be telling me more good sir." He encouraged, desperately avoiding his mistresses scolding stare. Then for reasons best known to him, the batman took note of the woman's presence and then tried to shrug off the glamour of the sea.

"Sailors away from home and the safety of land eventually fall foul of the dreaded scurvy, lad. Men's teeth fall out. Their mouths ulcerate. Huge wheals of black and blue showed up on thighs and lower legs." His words began to percolate as the lad registered horror in his gaze. "And them's that suffered so were plied with celery seed tea. Or maybe Stag Horn plantain and other coast land-gathered weeds for their aching bones or hot tempers which accompanied." Rising to his feet with a knowing smile towards the placated female he crossed the floor to push a draped hop sack curtain clear of the window. The small manifold iron-glass panes were tinctured with beady chains of humidity and condensation from reverse side chills of the night. Rubbing a space in the mistiness he looked out and said thoughtfully aloud. "The storm squalls be abating and we've a second rum walk awaiting my presence in the jolly boat. Soon I'd best be wending my way." Dropping the curtain into place he turned to offer gratitude to the doctor, "I be thanking ye for your kindness in sheltering my weary bones, apothecary." Ignored, he shrugged his broad shoulders then noticing a window settle slumped momentarily as he searched his pockets for a clay pipe. Lighting the well-worn pipe he waited patiently for any reaction from the doctor. Moments later, after clearing-up clattering noises of surgical instruments had been completed, the surgeon joined him at the window seat, although he continued to wipe his hands free of blood. The doctor indicated he should move and make room alongside him as he now wished to converse.

"How be the maid, apothecary - thy other visitors tell of a fractured musket ball wound suffered at the inn not far from this place."

"How did you know it was a partial ball which hit the maid."

"A solid ounce of lead would have put paid to her tiny form otherwise."

"Aye, you're right of course. The musket load must have split in two when fired from the breech. Too high a black powder charge can cause poorly cast lead to fragment. Air trapped in the casting expands on violent explosion." Doctor Temple indicated the girl would live yet she lay unconscious at the moment. Nodding towards the man's silver-hobbed lanyard ring fixed to the butt of a protruding pistol, he said in a whisper, "Thy servant suspects ye b'aint no tub-man sire. Thy pistol be naval militia issue, so if ye are a King's man and so just what is thy business here this night?"

Chapter Three SILVER STREET

When hair be red there be plenty to dread
when her hair be blond ne'er be the bond
when hair be grey thus seen many a day
yet if hair be black thy bond be exact

When her eyes be red they miss their bed
when her eyes be grey they're going away
when her eyes be green - jealousy's been
when eyes be blue then doubtless I'm with you
Poem: Maids

"My job was to locate the maid Clarissa Peach and her close companion, Miss Martha Wilks. Although I must confess it does my heart good to hear the girl will survive the shoulder wound."

The King's man had failed to introduce himself. However, he whispered a confidence of his mission into the ear of the surgeon apothecary doctor James Temple. Journey-worn and exhausted the agent of the crown requested and had been denied sustenance or liquor until he revealed his true reason for being there that night. Ignoring necessity to advise anyone he had been commanded by Louis Duras to eliminate Ned Teach on his excursion to England seeking Morgan's paper pardon. A rare opportunity not to be missed and not affording as normally Ned Teach rode the high seas off the Spanish Maine, or hid himself amongst one of many islands off the Indies. Still enraptured with the late king's image, Morgan was at that moment in the Dutch Free States seeking out and commissioning the painter Rembrandt. Reputed to be a fine artist known in Holland specialising in chiaroscuro. This purportedly to be a delicate technique balancing light and shade. Rembrandt was to reproduce Morgan's piratical image yet graced in gentleman's lace and silk finery.

The scabrous spy stood unrepentant in front of the doctor and held his gaze for a mite longer than was polite. Suspecting affiliation to the Protestant cause, yet the moment for him was cautiously salubrious. Almost memorable as the other's true intentions were summed up. Temple eventually relaxed and offered a grim smile and knowing nod.

"The maid has lost a deal of blood and yet if she does expire it certainly won't be from lead poisoning." James Temple grimaced and added in a lowered tone, "Sea spy, eh? King's man from one o' the ships moored off the Cobb, no doubt. Pray tell me what is an injured innocent to your intrigue this dark night." Following the lead allowed himself to be taken by the arm and guided to a wooden settle by a glowing fireside, waving the dozing lad away for his own good, indicating to his new found and like-minded compatriot they should sit close that the others might not overhear.

"Your name, sawbones, be somewhat familiar to me, for 'tis said ye have a direct sympathy for any invasion by this Pretender to the English throne." The chaise-silver snuff box set with diamonds appeared and glinted opulent in the candlelight. Offering up the dusty snuff which was declined by the other, instead he watched as a line of fine brown tobacco dust was placed to the back of the man's hand. Snorting the mixture he took a head-back gratification and awaited the burning reaction to his senses.

"Ship's surgeon retired, sir. Dr. James Temple thy humble servant, sire." The stranger politely mimicked Head falling in brief salute and this courtesy, Ingrams placed a huge hand on the shoulder of his seated companion as he squeezed sincerity into his words.

"Look squire Temple, I may look unto thee to be a bilge rat up to thy gentlemanly kind." No response came to his self-humility so the sea spy snorted a sneeze from his irritated nostrils instead as he thought up a suffix to his words. Eventually he wiped his nose saying,

"I should inform thee I be here in thy locale on a mission of some import." Relaxing his grip a harsh stare affixed to the other's eye. Ingrams warned solemnly. "If I were to tell thee my name it is not to be banded abroad loosely - wouldst do me the honour of taking this on board." Watching the doctor agree he proudly puffed himself up with self-importance confessing one of two identities. "D'Arcy Chavasse Penhalligon formerly of the Huguenot Protestants o' the Francs." Slapping the doctor on the back as he confided, "But ye can refer to me as `D'Arcy Ingrams, some say King's man and I too am thy humble servant." The terse nod was acknowledged as Temple fell silent with his thoughts. A white clay pipe was produced by Ingrams stuffed with coarse shag, lit with a spill from a still glowing ember. Clearing his throat Ingrams said, "As far as thy patient be concerned, she be witness to a mail robbery and illegal killings of its passengers. It happened night afore last." Puffing fiercely on the stem garlanded his head in smoke and misted a dour expression.

"How did ye come by this knowledge." Temple rose to recover a silver flask of rum and two small pewter cups, pulling the stopper he made to pour generous measures of the golden liquid. Ingrams grumbled inaudibly personal discontent. "Thy servant has long sorely convinced himself, no good would come of traversing the country-side in one of them new fangled conveyances."

Temple confided the woman Pernickety told of the maid surviving the incident in the Ship Inn. Yet confessed not a word had passed between them about a robbery. Tilting his head he quaffed a measure of rum. The fiery liquid burnt a warming passage down his throat, sore relief after the iron smell and inevitable taste of the maid's blood. He found himself starting to relax in the company of another professional that night. Caring little for the trade and intrigue or accompanying hazards. "How come ye on this coach accident."

"T'was a deliberate ambuscade and resulting wreck would be more the like." Ingrams too swigged at the pewter cup then said, "I was despatched from Parliament to keep spy on documents meant for a gathering o' Corsairs up the coast a spell from Lyme." Producing a rolled parchment from inside his clothing, he passed it over pointing out the official red wax seal and securing ribbon. Temple recognised them as being little acknowledged or publicised letters-of-marque or patent.

"Guardian o' the maid Clarissa be one Miss Wilks, past-tense, God rest her soul, she in turn was supposed to be a giving these documents to her gentleman friend, him being one o' the pirates and all. Only she was killed dead and cut off in her prime along with other innocents on the coach." Shrugging his powerful shoulders helplessly, he recalled the situation. "I was riding behind the careering coach in fearful winds and lashing rains." He took a swig of rum to conceal a personal embarrassment, "I spent a mere thrice relieving myself when the stage were robbed, wrecked under my damnable nose."

Doctor Temple lowered his head to hide his growing smile at a scene pictured and building in the recesses of his fatigued mind. Yet allowed him to conclude his gruesome tale.

"I barely had time to pull up my breeches when for I were in the saddle again. Yet when I arrived on the desolate scene of carnage and murther - the maid had disappeared. I knew she was alive but must have been abducted. The highwayman had not located the papers, I had occasion to retrieve them from the corpse of the designated courier, the school mistress guardian of the maid Clarissa." Sighing in exasperation at the futility of the waste of life, and also the greater task as a result now lying in front of him. "I've now to find a way o' getting these documents to the ne'er-do-wells without revealing my presence in Lyme."

D'Arcy Ingrams reached into the folds of his clothing and produced a small brass carriage clock with traditional single marking hand and minute calibrations. "I found this on the body o' the dead school mistress. Ye best be giving it to the maid when she be fit to be told of its whereabouts." Ingrams grimaced at the thought.

Temple didn't understand but half of the conversation yet held out his hand for the timepiece,

"Mayhap she'll see it should she survive this night." Rising from the settle with the object he placed it to a wall cupboard, locked the door and withdrew the cast iron key from the brass escutcheon. Drawn down alongside again by D'Arcy Ingrams to add a suffix to his words before the subject cooled and was forgotten forever.

"The maid be a witness to whosoever did the dastardly deed. So it be best she survive for I need to question her opinions at length." The man alongside rubbed his chin stubble. He muttered something about `devils and demons spiking his guns every which way he had turned for the past few nights. Feeling it was the rum talking on an empty stomach rather than the man, Temple left the room briefly to check on his fragile patient. In an upstairs room Meg looked up from mopping the girl's brow and shook her head, indicating there was little or no change in the maid's condition. Back downstairs crossing over by way of a hand-held candle holder to where the sea spy sat, Temple barely had time to refill his and his unwelcome guests" cup with rum when the woman Pernickety joined them. Slinging her bulk between them on the wooden settle spilled both their drinks. Appearing oblivious to this fact and the doctor's prior movements she advised both men of the girl's progress.

"The maid's to your bed just as ye suggested, doctor. Sleeping like a babe she be. And ye were true accurate about thy tot of brandy - she be out like the fluttering flame of a wind blown candle."

"Is my maidservant with her?" Temple could not be bothered to explain and thought of a way to encourage her absence in favour of listening to the rest of the spy's tale. He watched her nod and suggested," Meg will need to be diligent over the need to staunch the flow of blood. Alcohol can thin it out quite drastically." Then noted how the woman resisted any effort to leave. Temple thought of an alternative way to be rid of the woman, turning once more to Ingrams he said deliberately,

"Mayhap this good woman will be able to cast light on your highwayman's identity."

D'Arcy Ingrams eyes lit with a realisation. Rounding quickly on Pernickety he grabbed her arm and barked a question close into her ear. "Identify thyself woman and that of the road agent." He squinted directly into her gaze before adding threateningly,

"Now be giving us the truth for this man be of some import to thy humble servant." She made to rise but was roughly jerked back down to squat on the hard surface of the oaken settle.

"Miss Pernickety to ye sire, and I am thy servant." A square of linen was produced and wiped over a fervently perspiring brow as she calmed herself. Taking deep breaths and with heaving bosom the woman stated matter-of-factly,

"I be mine host of the old Ship Inn up the coast a spell nearby Uppe Lyme in the county of Dorsetshire."

Ingrams nodded and confided with a broad grin into the churlish expression of the woman.

"Aye, I've heard o' ye and thy ale house. ''tis nought more than a haven for vagabond youth, smugglers and pirates." Shaking his grip free from her arm Pernickety grimaced and glowered into the tub man's eyes.

"As for anything else, ye'll get nothing from my lips." She blood cursed him lively and gave a firm toss of her head. So much so as to loosen the red rag that held wild red hair back from flashing eyes brimming with hate.

The man's voice tried to relax her,

"It b'aint be ye I be after, missus, just the bounder which did for some innocent travellers abroad a while back. The maid will tell me should she survive, apparently that be debatable according to the good doctor here." He leaned forward filling the woman's face with his own dour expression, "the name o' the villain will suffice. I'll be saying nought more o' my predicament and thy own illicit trade with Devon smugglers."

Pernickety pushed a lank of hair back and nodded, "Well not that it'll do thee a bit a good as "tis said the knave be stone dead - skewered by." Lowering her voice obscured a blurted identity. Then her eyes popped white with fear as suddenly she felt the muzzle of a pistol to her ribcage, shoved up under an ample bosom. "Damn yer eyes tubman t'was the one they call Jess the Pearly." Slowly the pistol was withdrawn from under the rising swell of her breasts then as she breathed freely a smile flickered relief. Quick as a flash, resumed her terrified look as it was thrust back into the cleavage of her low cut dress. Adding to the terror was the audible double click as the wheel lock weapon was placed on to full cock.

"Now why not be a clearing of thy conscience with the rank of the man who put down the highwayman. He must surely be a titled gentleman due to thy protecting him." He deadlamped her by closing one eye and tilting his head to one side, glowering piercingly with the other. Eventually the woman screwed up her eyes and shook her head in fear.

"Don't ye curse me none for I b'aint done folk any harm this night." Seeing him relax his peculiar lopsided pose she shrugged her mighty shoulders and admitted reluctantly. "It were Ned Teach. Him and others like him were lying low at my hostelry awaiting official government documentation. These documents were to be passed on to old Harry himself." She looked undone.

"Old Harry?" the doctor queried. "And who is Jess the Pearly?"

"Henry Morgan, Assistant Lieutenant Governor to John, Earl of Carberry Lord Vaughan of Port Royal in old Jamaica." D'Arcy Ingrams explained and seemingly satisfied rose swiftly to his feet. "Though "tis said the assistant governor having aspired to his diplomatic rank gave up bountiful debaucheries and that he was now contentedly married running plantation on the island." He rubbed his chin nervously, more of a habit than anything before continuing, "He was always a heavy drinker - especially with close comrades in arms. Swilled ale and rumbullion with reputed zest and quite unmatched by the best of them." Stuffing the pistol into a low slung broad leather

57

belt around his waist, he began pacing in front of the fire as if totally alone analysing dark thoughts, so much so that the sea spy failed to hear the good doctor repeat his query.

"Why Pearly - presumably this is a nomme de guerre?"

Sinking into his innermost thoughts, Ingrams kept his own counsel only the way a spy could, yet sometimes polite conversation was the only way forward in times of stalemate and dead end to a mission. Though on pain of death there was many a slip betwixt cup and lip - and well he knew it. He took a deepening draught from the drinking vessel. Finally Ingrams came back to the moment and interrupting his own thinking to voice scant knowledge of the robber rogue.

"Rumour has it the left eye be false, replaced many years since with a large white sea pearl to his blind socket - be that not so woman." He watched her head nod in a reluctant though confirming silence. Again the doctor interrupted turning pent-up frustration onto the shivering woman by his side. Maybe fired by the injured maid lying nearby. Poking at her with a deliberating forefinger he asked:

"The other villain who came to rescue and thus defended the maid's honour - was he so titled as was thought? In other words a dastardly knave of the same ilk."

Pernickety shook her head in frightened defiance yet again, offering naught more than tight-lipped dumb insolence to the bullies encircling her person. The night was giving way to daylight and D'Arcy Ingrams would be gone from that place. Then he watched from a distance as the woman rose up from the settle and turned to look down upon the doctor.

"Ye've been kind to me and my chosen ward, doctor, and for which I shall always be in thy debt. If the other brute of a tub man doth overhear our conversation - so be it. I hereby advise ye that I be addressing your goodself and thy goodself alone." She drew a breath," Clarissa, the maid stated in front o' witnesses that Black Ned be her step-father, "tis thought child's mother be better known as Anne o' the Indies. She be her true mother and reputed to be a dastardly pirate herself, though Black Ned be her step-father, and "tis rumoured the maid were sired by another - one known as "Calico Jack Rackham". Anne Bone was born near Cork in Ireland, a daughter of a lawyer who emigrated to the Carolinas where he became a wealthy planter. Yet because a girl child had been born to him from an illicit love affair by

58

his employed maid, the lawyer dressed her up as a boy child until his legal wife died. Anne Bone grew up a tomboy showing to be a maid of spirit. Eventually she ran away to marry a local sailor called James Bonny. Disowned by her father, Anne was spirited away by her youthful spouse to the port of New Providence." Pernickety snorted her disapproval then her voice lowered as she confided,

"Whereby he promptly lost his new wife to the advances of dashing Calico Jack. And who persuaded Anne to join him on his next cruise of piracy throughout the Indies." Ignoring glances of slighted disbelief at her detailed revelations she concluded, "pillaging pickings were poor, all went well until Anne discovered she was with-child." Then hissed disapproval. "Calico Jack placed Anne Bonny ashore in Cuba and little is known what became of her or her child - baby girl. Though it's suggested they came to England where she met and married Ned Teach in the naval town of Dartmouth. Ned was press-ganged and forced to take the king's shilling ending far away on a ship o' the line." She cocked a snook at the fates.

"Anne Bonny left the girl child to be brought up by a guardian friend, a woman called Wilks. Anne Bonny, for she retained her married title, mayhap be back with that sea-devil Jack Rackham unless he's already dangling from a navy yard arm somewhere. The girl Clarissa knew nothing of her true blood kin, only Ned who took her as his own kindly - before having to make good his escape back out to sea last evening." The woman caught the eye of Ingrams from across the room and feeling afraid of the brooding stranger, she continued in lowered tones with her story. "Ned must have figured highly in the maid's memory. Anne brought the babe to England for edification o' sorts or mayhap she were actually born here. Any road up the girl Clara be intelligent and she doth sport beautiful manners." Nodding over her shoulder she added in a lowered tone, "Unlike some rogues I could mention and poke at with a damp stick." Scowling and turning her back to make a point. "Ned Teach be a strange kettle of fish under fire. T'was not always generally known that he be ruthless. Yet were it he that fathered such a delightful babe as the girl then t'were gentle and loving father he'd surely be." A tear welled in her eye as she concluded matronly, "And it be only natural Ned would want to clap eyes on the maid again if only to spy how she be faring by growing into a goodly lass and young lady."

D'Arcy Ingrams returned to the settle pushing the floor snoozing stable boy to one-side, lifting his boot side-swiped the dying embers with a kick. Sparks burst forth and rose whirling on the curl of smoke around the darkened lip of the open chimney. The woman watched him cross the room for a rum refill and then turning confided to the doctor.

"That heller b'aint interested in anything of import," snorting contemptuously nodding after the retreating figure, "he be more interested in where his next tot o' rum's coming from."

Dr. Temple shook his head in disagreement and spoke of his reaction to their earlier conversation together, "I don't know woman somehow I sense him to be an honourable man."

Making sure Ingrams was still out of earshot she confided her closest secret.

"Ye see doctor - Jess the Pearly weren't so despatched as first thought."

"Not killed dead you say." Temple dallied with her colourful phraseology.

Sucking her breath she released it slowly,

"He were only mortally wounded."

Temple smiled at the woman's mistaken interpretation of the man's wound but let her continue without interruption. "Black Ned's lightning blade pinned him to the wall and it was thought that he were dead. His mates were summoned and arrived to find him barely clinging to his life force. A cutlass thrust severed his arm taking most of the force. Pinning him to the wall only released when his confederates secreted him to a safe haven. Lord only knows where for thy humble servant fainted dead away." She sat again and looked him straight in the eye. "Trouble is doctor, if Jess the Pearly were to survive his wounds, I be feared a terrible vengeance will be reaped upon the poor little maid. Though Ned can look after himself."

The Doctor rose to the mantelpiece, he removed a long clay pipe from the wrack he stuffed it with tobacco and taper-lit the mixture from a glowing coal ember, then raising his head he blew a veil of smoke over his shoulder before speaking softly so's not to arouse Ingrams and the sleeping stable boy Tom. Knowing also that if he used silence as a thought-provoking weapon he might glean more information. It worked, irritated at his seeming detachment and inner tranquillity the woman whispered further insistence.

"Don't ye agree that if the maid be a witness to robbery and coach murder Jess the Pearly will find us unless we be on our way as soon as possible." The woman's pained expression was unnecessary, as Temple had already made up his mind to offer care to his hapless patient. Rising from the high-backed settle he tapped irritatedly the pipe which had gone out on him. Watching its dried tobacco remnants fall into the fire, then he replaced the clay pipe for later use.

"The maid Clarissa will remain safe here until well enough to rejoin your goodself and thy giant manservant. Leave me contact thee rather than risk discovery o' thy adopted ward. Let me know where ye'll be a month hence. Worry not about mine own silence, woman, though I insist knowing the identity of the child's step-father in case he should arrive on my stoop seeking her."

"If anything should happen to the maid doctor, ye better hope and pray he don't for he be the piratical heller be known locally hereabouts as `Blackbeard the pirate."

Chapter Four   MONMOUTH BEACH

Do not come within my space
or encroach too near upon my face
for it's forbidden to enter close
my eyes look inward become morose
Stare you out or fill with tears
blurring your image over the years

They will hold you off or in esteem
or finally shut to end a dream
Opening afresh to blink new light
putting worries and cares to flight
Poem: Inner Circle

11 June 1685

"Nineteen days at sea, gentlemen and it would appear we are here unannounced."

The voice with the authority of a king suited the man with flowing wavy brown hair and blue eyes. His white-lace neckerchief gathered treasonably with a blue ribbon of State. By way of contrast his dark green velvet frock coat pleated at the waist, trimmed with burnished gold thread, wrapped with cross-over shoulder leather straps supporting a slim bladed sword to his side, a short bayonet to the other. The ensemble of weaponry complete with a large pistol, Damascus twist silver wire bound its lengthy barrel, noticeably protruding from a dark blue cummerbund. Red breeches and leather calf length boots, all these accoutrements adding to a splendid image of the man standing before distinguished gatherings at the Olde George Inn in Lyme Regis.

"As you may know the Stadtholder in the Hague gave me good advice to take commission from the Emperor against the Turks." A murmur circulated the room, "however," pausing for silence, "My companions, so called fugitives from the `Rye House plot" persuaded thy servant to do otherwise." A rousing cheer went up from the thirty or so men crushed into the tavern's main room, shouts rose as individuals called, "Claim your rights, m'lord," and `Now or never" raising a hand for a cessation to the friendly outbursts he said, "My heartfelt thanks gentlemen. To be practical I had little choice in the matter. My esteemed uncle, the William of Orange was embarrassed at the presence of Charles II's Protestant son and rightful heir to the English throne on his door stoop."

Smiling through another cheer from the mixture of noblemen and knaves now so obviously at his feet.

"We are deeply honoured sire ye should choose Lyme Regis to take up your army and recover the crown of England." Gregory Alford thought it best to find out as much as he could and milk the moment and atmosphere of the gathering, intending to ride to nearby Honiton to warn of the danger and raise the alarm. Yet as Mayor of Lyme his presence was required above others in the motley crowd. James, Duke of Monmouth glanced at the man hard perhaps trying to look into his very soul, for maybe he was the predicted Judas warned of by his Dutch relative in the Hague and a local soothsayer. Beginning the duke went on,

"My original destination was Torbay, suggested by my advisors in the Dutch lowlands, yet warships abound the English channel and so we mariners made for safe haven in your fair township of Lyme." Monmouth lied knowing full well their town was a prime destination. In the Great Civil War Lyme was noted for its Puritanism in defying Charles I's nephew Prince Maurice. In formal siege the defence inspired by two colonels, Robert Blake, later Admiral Blake of Bridgwater, and John Weare both who were relieved by the Earl of Essex. A symbol of Parliamentary support in the predominantly Royalist West Country.

"Therefore with goodly grace and fair favour of all present here this night I thus proclaim myself rightful heir to the true throne of England."

The packed gathering fell as one to a bended knee and called the words, `The King". Then rising to their feet they cheered rousingly.

James Scott, the Duke of Monmouth, allowed himself a broad grin as he was lofted to the shoulders of two of the large musketeers. Ducking his head was carried from the room to a separate chamber where drinks were poured liberally for his immediate aides. In a moment of brief respite between raucous conversation and planning,

Monmouth tried to push to the back of his mind more relaxed days in the Hague of the Amsterdam Free States. Whereby ice-skating, dancing and socialising with his beloved mistress the Lady Wentworth was preferable. Indeed, just as his father Charles had with his mother the mistress Lucy Walters or `madam" as he'd preferred. A fine woman of distinction, good taste and breeding despite unknown emissaries of the Pope spiriting away a black box containing their marriage lines. Purportedly authenticated and witnessed by unknown notaries of the day. Despite all this, he must, for posterity sake, oppose his wicked uncle's rise to the throne of England. For it was a weary war torn England reeling from oppression of Oliver Cromwell's Republic, then transition to his eldest son Richard as Head of State, albeit for a brief eight months henceforth to be known as `Tumbledown Dick". He too now in lordly obscurity and exiled across the water in France. Lucky in fact to escape arrest by the `Rump" Parliamentary guards on trumped charges of State Treason. Then Monmouth brought to bear his thoughts of his own treasonable act of landing a warlike army to retrieve the throne for the cause. How Argyll, the son of the covenanting Earl, along with `Hannibal" Rumbold had set out prepared for war in Scotland. By carrying the rebellion to the highlands in a carefully planned and strategic pincer movement down from the north. Back to the moment, arriving at Monmouth's side, Joseph Tyler began to read out a formal declaration. The work of a man later known as the plotter, the right Reverend Robert Ferguson, whose words denounced King James II's right to wear the crown,

> "We therefore do declare James, Duke of York to be a
> Traitor to the Nation. Tyrant, and usurper to the Pope,
> and a murtherer* an Enemy to things goodly and noble."

D'Arcy Ingrams pushed his way through milling bodies in the Lyme tavern, desperately looking round for the man who would be king; a musketeer volunteered information that the Pretender had retired. It would be best he be left undisturbed, for the morrow was to be a great day for a gathering army outside in the streets. Relenting the soldier suggested that he might best be served by William the lord Crofts, and who was at the gathering that night. In a trice Ingrams was formally introduced to him.

"Your business, sire?"

64

The greying sallow-faced man, thought to be in his late sixties had inquired of him. Surly in manner only, as his face held the serenity and knowing calm as that of a Monk. His eyes questioning the King's man being there suggested,

"Hast thou extended thyself, or dost thou bear useful information for the Protestant cause this night."

Ingrams pulled from his person a small sheaf of bound parchment with the cumbersome House of Commons seal in crumbling wax. A finger spun the tube of parchment tightly to release its bondage, the missive passed from knavish fingers to nobleman's hand, and the hand that snatched the document was adorned with jewel encrusted gold and silver rings. The man held the paper away from his eyes in traditional manner of the short sightedness of gently advancing years, as quietly he read aloud.

`The Bearer of this document be allowed without hindrance,
demand or occasion, free passage on the furtherance of his duty
to the Parliament of the Day. Dated this day of 17th April 1685"
signed Lord High Privy Seal

Throwing the document aside as if it were an assailant's cudgel, he stared hard at the bearer of the missive, finally coming to a silent decision a sentry was summoned. Moments later D'Arcy Ingrams was ushered into an ante room as precursor to the main bed chamber of the man who was now known to be the Pretender. Standing for several minutes in the darkened room whilst tapers ignited candles, one of two sentries lightly bent over and awakened Monmouth lying atop the bed linen of an enormous four-poster. The Duke, fully dressed, rose on his elbows to glean the face of the man interrupting his repose, then to fall back ascertaining that there was no immediate recognition of the intruder's shadowy features.

Ingrams, not to be outdone, seeing his chance of an interview waning confided a need for dire urgency. "A word my Lord Duke I beg of thee."

"Majesty - dolt." The pike-wielding sentry alongside the spy leaned menacingly toward him having bellowed the command into his ear.

"We are not set in stateliness yet, Guthrin, be patient with this fellow."

Propped up in the bed, James, leant back against the carved ebony headboard, yawned a silent request for a brief interlude. This gave Ingrams time to note the relief dominated by a centralised roaring Lion's head, it was circled by a hazelnut and wild berry cluster. Heads of twinned horses leapt outwards from portrayed artichokes, pear, plum and profusion of summer fruits. Gargoyles and Gorgon supporters with front legs of a horse in lower corners were part concealed by the wild silk pillows. D'Arcy Ingrams' attention reverted back when the man cleared his throat to speak. Looking tired and humbled, his full dress commanded a daunting yet fraught reclining figure. He fluffed at the white throat ruff then nonchalantly tugged at lace spilling from his tunic sleeve ends as he bade the visitor pray continue. Awakened rudely he was prepared to listen to the interruption yet not wanting to prolong conclusion with needless protocol.

"Sire, I bring a document from the Rump Parliament, mayhap if ye were to spy the missive with thy own perusal it would convince thee of my sincerity."

"We have been informed of your qualifications, D'Arcy Ingrams, and we think they are in order - prithee proceed." Monmouth desperately needed to rest. Although by remaining fully clothed the flight to a safe haven was at least prepared.

"My lord, certain parties in the capital have but your very best interests at heart. Mindful of thy enthusiastic spirit and loyalty to thy cause, yet fear the English nation is weary and tired of past civil wars. So dost thou think this be a goodly time for thy venture?"

With one blow of his pikestaff the boisterous Guthrin took a side step and knocked Ingrams to the ground, where he fell on all fours to the foot of the huge bed. Alarmed at the interruption to their conversation, Monmouth rose clear of his pillows to chastise the impetuous and over-zealous guard. Eventually he bade both sentries leave them to their debate, to await his bidding outside the bedchamber and thus stand guard in the adjoining anteroom. D'Arcy Ingrams, from a sitting position, watched the routed sentry do his master's bidding then begged permission to rise and approach closer. This courtesy was declined suspecting mischief now the guards had left and they were alone. Instead Monmouth inquired, "How come ye doth know of my account here in Lyme," Monmouth began.

"I am here in the county of Dorset by default, milord, randomly chasing paper documents issued by your father the King before his untimely demise. They concern the pirate king, Henry Morgan residing in and around Port Royal on the island of Jamaica."

"Ah, pirates - bless their evil black hearts and wicked ways."

It was a strange reaction for one so obviously in authority of his task.

Monmouth reverted to his original questioning and concluded from Ingrams' presence, "Surmised by the death of my father such a venture would be undertaken, eh." Watching Ingrams' head incline continued with solemnity.

"Keeping spy on the Rye House conspirators of 2 years past, eh."

Monmouth rubbed his chin thoughtfully; a rueful smile took the place of vulnerability. He waved the visitor forward to within striking distance.

"Thy audience is so granted Mr. Ingrams and thy reputation precedes thee."

Ingrams was abashed by the information he was not incognito and felt more persona non grata instead as he rose to confide urgently.

"The Mayor of Lyme Regis has ridden to nearby Honiton warning of thy presence here, milord Duke." He lowered his eyes, as a contrived humility conveying this was nothing to do with his presence there that night.

"The Mayor of Lyme has betrayed me?" Monmouth rose and moved from the bedclothes like an animal clearing undergrowth. "Well the good Lord had his Judas and so I apparently have my Gregory Alford." The moment of piousness passed as the two faced each other much closer in the semi-darkness.

"May I speak about something weighing heavily on my mind, milord."

"We think thy loyalty does not require permission." The Duke shrugged off the vague misnomer yet felt he needed to prolong original reasoning. "You see D'Arcy Ingrams - good sir - We have thought long and arduously over coming to England from the Free States of Holland. Whereby leaving the comforting love of good women, rich victuals and merriment of court. However becoming a slight embarrassment to the Prince of Orange, and on the death of my father, deciding if one was to die for a cause it should for the goodly and noble one. That to rid England of my Uncle James." The Duke

67

turned away to pace. "Either that or to undertake some inauspicious foreign adventure and fly into obscurity." He turned and looked hard at Ingrams. "I was encouraged by my uncle to invade."

Adding thoughtfully if somewhat recklessly a treason aloud, "Mayhap York be the rightful claimant if he were not so unpopular with the common people."

A look of momentary disdain passed over the gaze of the man in front and yet however brief, it was recognised by the Duke.

"Mayhap ye think otherwise, sir, so then why pray am I discussing affairs of state to a complete stranger."

Ignoring the challenge, Ingrams strode up and down the floor as if to search for the correct approach to such poignant questioning. The Duke obviously sought help from him. Ingrams thought he must have made an impression, albeit a vague obscure impression. Yet an impression all the same. Before the King's man could muster courage to react to something that might make his life worthless as a traitor to the cause, Monmouth's shadow grew alongside with an imposing presence some command without effort.

"Ye appear to have lack of faith for the task in hand, D'Arcy Ingrams. Though your thoughts would not go amiss at this juncture." Pausing for an answer that never came, the shuffling equerry appeared reluctant to put voice to inner thoughts. Monmouth's tone darkened with dignity as he continued, "mayhap ye are thinking about the fleeting muster of men outside the inn. A distinct lack of cannonade, and muskets, pike, cavalry and capable English swordsmen." He sighed a harmony of thought, adding quickly, "I too have these noted problems to my heart, yet other factors bewitch me in my hour of need."

"Such as, milord."

Monmouth seemed relieved at response. Despairing at earlier non-cooperation from the one alongside, and Monmouth began a slow rambling monologue more for the sake of communication with a like mind.

"Only a fool or buffoon would undertake such an impossible task with such a lightly equipped land army. Be this credence to thy thoughts, Ingrams." Not waiting for an answer his mouth took a downturn as snarling a monosyllable normally best kept to that of a whisper. "Barbary corsairs."

"Sire?"

"Pirates, buccaneers, the dried meat-eaters of Tortuga, the island some ways off Santiago and Hispaniola. The buccaneers would land on Ile a' Vache, there they slaughtered and dried the carcasses of beef cattle, thus provisioning for many men on their lengthy voyages. Thus sustained this diet enabled few in number to attack and overwhelm huge landed armies. Even carracks and lateen-rigged galleys or Spanish galleons larger and of better equipages than themselves, all were taken as spoils. Beef and rum put fire in their bellies. If this did not work, as they approached a larger vessel than themselves, a misdirected ball into the main deck of their vessel would give encouragement."

The Duke fired with historical imaginings rolled his eyes wildly with excitement. "Dost know their motto, Ingrams. Apart from a displayed skull and cross bones pennant whilst bearing down and engaging enemy shipping."

Ingrams indicated he'd had dealings with such rapscallions and murmured,

"Mors vincet - death wins."

"Aye, sir for they would cry out `Come all ye brave boys whose courage is bold will ye venture with me and I'll glut thee with gold - have ye zest for a fight - then "tis dire dealings this night" Ignoring the accuracy of his earlier reply, Monmouth carried on, "The Spanish are a cruel race. They have prompted tortures of such barbarity if their enemy were caught napping.

One technique, perfected by a man known to Corsairs as "the exterminator", Louis Montbars, was French and a native of Languedoc. Reading of attributable cruelty of the Spanish in the Indies, decided to join the men of Tortuga."

The Duke grimaced at recollections of earlier research, "like attracts like."

"What pray has this to do with the task in hand, milord Duke."

"Patience my dear fellow. You interrupt the flow of thoughts that I voice with reason and dedication to the honour of one's fellow warrior. Ah yes, Montbars. Well on sailing to the Indies, Montbars on joining others soon became a leader of note. Many of his dire tricks with prisoners cast his wicked reputation far and wide. In one instance he would nail one end of a man's intestines to a post, unrolling them by stinging the poor devil into a dance of death with a piece of burning wood to his hind quarters."

Monmouth folded his arms and stole a glance at Ingrams to gauge reaction.

"Surely these monsters were not typical of buccaneers, though such community would attract depravity and those drawing from pain." Ingrams offered breaking his controlled silence.

It was as if Monmouth failed to hear him as he continued in a mesmeric daze, merely to shock his visitor or perhaps to summon up his own waning courage.

"Then there was Francis L'Olonaise, a buccaneer chief. Who on returning from Maracaibo, so great was the blown fame, volunteers to serve him outnumbered requirements."

"Would my lord confuse one issue with another?" Ingrams began, "mayhap information has reached thee denied to others." Choosing his words carefully. But again the man who would be King failed to react to provocation.

Unfortunately the Duke's attention once more fell on the evil L'Olonaise. The monologue began as if the Duke had first hand experience of the pirates.

"Sailing off on his next expedition he was armed with an army who were well disciplined and officered equal to that of any in the World." He took a deep breath and straightened himself physically as well as mentally. Stretching to his full height, he began to pace the room like a caged lion. "His barbarities were notorious even amongst the most hardened of ruffians. Plundering, ravishing, burning and torturing, this he delighted doing in his most dastardly of deeds." The Duke now seemed to hold a glazed over look about his eyes. "On one occasion L'Olonaise drew his cutlass and cut open the breast of a Spaniard. An enemy sailor who refused to say if an island ambuscade lay ahead of the main landing party." Monmouth's voice fell to a rasping whisper. "Extracting the man's still beating heart with sacrilegious hands, L'Olonaise began to bite and gnaw at the organ like a ravenous wolf saying "I will serve you all alike if you shew me not another way." The significance became apparent as his face fell to his hands and mumbling he repeated the phrase through his fingertips.

"If ye shew me not another way."

D'Arcy Ingrams no longer recognised him as a gentleman.

Laboriously he'd plumbed the depths of his memory of terrifying pirates and whose desperate adventures had impressed so vehemently.

Monmouth returned to the bedside, throwing himself exhausted to the brocade coverlet that now lay dishevelled on top of the straw filled mattress. The four-poster canopy cast a shadow from the cluster of candles scattered about the tiny room. Shoulders hunched Monmouth sat sideways to the bed, looking like Atlas supporting the trials troubles and tribulations of the world. Perhaps Monmouth had - perhaps also it was time for Ingrams to leave. He could then allow him to thus escape into the welcoming arms of Morpheus.

"I think it best if I take my leave, milord."

"Methinks ye are right, D'Arcy Ingrams, King's man and sea spy, however my point was that one appears to have a rabble rather than rebel army. Yet the determination of the masses will thus achieve anything if they so wish it." Monmouth swung booted feet onto the bed allowing his head and shoulders to fall back to the wild silk pillows, and the sigh which expired was not one of despair but one of sheer frustration of what was to come. Surreptitiously glancing toward the man about to leave the room without so much as a by-your-leave, Monmouth thoughtful with fatigue remonstrated somewhat loudly, "And how about thee, D'Arcy Ingrams, wouldst thou nail my guns too." Before an answer was forthcoming, a terrible grinding and muffled mechanical noise somewhere in the folds of the canopy material above made its presence disturbingly felt. Ingrams found himself sprinting across the room from the doorway, and as he ran towards the four poster heard a ripping which pierced canopy material above. Glancing up he spied it was now stretched beyond recognition betwixt enforced draping and the sharpened points. Rows of spikes split the cloth and then shuddered to a halt. The primary gear having concluded its 1st stage. Suddenly rumbling began again and it appeared the spikes were hovering and about to fling themselves downwards at full pelt on whosoever was below. Without a care for his personal safety, Ingrams dived full-length forward in flight - bowling Monmouth to one side from atop the brocade covers. Momentarily, Ingrams replaced the reclining figure of the man who earlier lay spreadeagled across that part of the huge mattress, that split second was long enough for the overhead spikes to release themselves, hurtling downwards to pin a thigh-length leather boot

71

firmly to the mattress. A far-away deep rumbling began once more as the machinery went into renewed life, and as the pinned man struggled to free himself - slowly the bed base began to rotate on its own axis. Monmouth rose swiftly from the floor to grab at Ingrams free booted ankle - but it was too late. Swivelling noisily, the booby-trapped contraption took the struggling man out of sight to his fate on the underside of four poster mattress; apart from the thunderous rumbling noise, the last Ingrams heard was Monmouth screaming for the guards outside to lend a hand. Assistance which would come too late to be of any help to the hapless hanging-man swinging upside down in total darkness supported only by a lengthy iron nail through a left boot. Instead of life flashing before him in a myriad wave of thoughts, the spy could only think of the lengthy conversation with the Pretender to the English Throne. Moreover the man's preoccupation with pirates, their code and their motto lived by with the blood and fire of glorious battle - mors vincet - death wins!

(*belief that James II poisoned his brother Charles II Feb 1685)

Chapter Five THE BLACK DOG INN

I miss your touch I miss your smile
I miss the passing of the while
with skin so sweet and eyes so blue
I miss the meaning of me to you

Poem: Missing You

"It'll be summer skies with winter eyes, ye mark my words our Jake. Or this b'aint the Black Dog tavern in old Lyme's broad humpty-backed hill Silver Street."

Miss Felicity Pernickety grumbled profusely at her pantryman as, back turned to him she glanced out of the iron-glass windows. It was her way of warning her manservant to guard his tongue whilst conducting social intercourse with an evil visitor. The old building, liveried in black and white and of a half-timbered and stepped design, its broad portals opened onto the busying street and thrown wide to passing trade, for anyone wishing to enter the prominent ale-house to slake their thirst on that hot sunny morning in June. Pernickety scrubbed a window settle clear of porter stains, occasionally glancing through thick image-distorting window panes to warn D'Arcy Ingrams or Dr. Temple should they happen along the boarded side walk. Lyme Regis town was full of strangers going about military training for the cause. Few having occasion to sup ale until the sun was well over the yardarm. Ale-quaffing, as any red blooded male would confirm, was deemed a sovereign cure for any such soul's darker despair.

Felicity Pernickety unscrambled her thoughts, concluding her task took a peek over her shoulder at Jake's reaction to an earlier snub. She had taken him to task for daring take dalliance with her goodly nature, by requesting midday vittles out of time. Jake had looked confused. He was a giant of a man and cravenly nursed a giant fellow's appetite, now angrily denied he tugged at the faded leather pouch bursting with dried and rasping tobacco leaves. Rising from the oaken settle stalked across the sun-shadowed room to the mantelpiece, whereby he snatched a bowed clay with the longest stem he could select. Feeling they were always the coolest smoke, filling it impatiently, crossed back to silently regain his corner seat in the bowed window. Anticipated chastising came as soon as he reseated himself alongside their dark visitor.

"I hope ye'll be a purchasing that our Jake and not just a borrowing the like." The woman scolded, irritated more at the company Jake was keeping rather than anything else. Fearing divided loyalties as she paused briefly having turned her attention to scrubbing tables from the previous evening's revelry. If her simple-minded manservant accepted the gold Louis on the table top for information about the maid, or even if he were recruited for the Protestant cause - she would be at a loss without his broad back and company. Yet fearing more that the kindly slow-witted giant would mistakenly allow a slip of his tongue be their undoing by offering convalescence for the child.

Inwardly, she'd been pleased at the change of venue from the Olde Ship inn on the coast, for it seemed fitting she should be tending the girl now her injuries were on the mend. Old Gregory, the ensconced landlord of the Black Dog Inn reluctantly agreed a two month change of venue, the tavern keepers were a close-knit gaggle and it took moments and a yard of ale to persuade the temporary swapping of their thriving hostelry. Each mine-host agreeing to look after the other vintner's interest, mayhap encouraging a little gentle smuggling, and this Gregory's spirits and his trade a world of good. Watching him go, feeling him to be a piously good-natured soul. Yet one who'd fare better with a bit of life tucked under his belt. He'd taken himself off to Pernickety's place of work some six weeks past, leaving the girl Clarissa to grow well mended from her ferocious ordeal. The stilted conversation between her manservant and his visitor had become strained, it was the reasoning behind him choosing that moment to help himself to a smoke whilst in the main ale-room. A thinning quarter-part of a cartwheel penny rang onto the flagstones beside her, recovered with a grunt by the doubled woman. As she peeled it from the flags, head turned her eyes flashed a silent warning, straightening to bite hard at the silver coin to test its validity. Satisfied she then placed it with deliberation deep into the pocket of her discoloured apron. "Ye be a dullard and certainly no genl'man our Jake." She sniffed her contempt, tossing her head angrily, "least wise ye paid for the churchwarden clay and that makes for a pretty change."

74

Jake glowered the woman into a silence. Turning away feeling it was time to conclude business, not be distracted by a well-meaning woman's small talk. Darkly scowling the man alongside dressed from head to toe in dusky black cloak gathered closely about him that hid his disablement. If one could see under his cloak a pinned-up sleeve of his frock coat would tell a tale.

Furtively his battered black silk-edged tricorn was tilted down over an eye patch, the predominantly bony and hooked nose was sweat-moistened for he was well over-dressed for that warm morning. He swigged at his ale whilst enlarging on past experiences. As the pitcher of ale passed backwards and forwards, the greater the embellishments. Tipping the hooped leather tankard up he drained bitter flat dregs, whilst smacking his lips with a suggestion for more. The earthenware pitcher slid his way across the tight planking of the well-scrubbed wooden table once more.

"Many days I've wasted since recovering my mobility enough to locate the dead girl's father." His food and drink stained clothing hid wound-swabs, blood-soaked bindings part-identifying the felonious road agent now depicted on fly-blown Wanted posters about town. The hat pulled down over his face accompanied by a raised elbow hovering about his face when not supping ale.

"I've advised ye, it's vital he be found for conveyance of my privileged information, thus having dire pecuniary interest for thy servant."

Glowering with his good eye rolling it round and round heightening the whites.

"Aye to put him to the sword no doubt." Jake puffed blue smoke to his face by way of silent contempt, raising his eyebrows he stared a defiant challenge. Part-turning with a mischievous grin he spoke between puffs of blue smoke.

"And it's no good ye do thy self trying to dead lamp me back with thy good eye, Mandrake," pointing the smoking stem of the clay, he reasoned, "'tis only part-way good ye'll do thyself, bearing in mind a black patch rides thy other vision." Then watched in horror as the highwayman dry washed his face exposing the creamy white sea pearl filling the left socket.

"If it's dead lamping ye'll be a doing of then I have a natural expertise."

The dead eye socket was like a red hole burnt into his face. Pernickety turned her head and began scrubbing vigorously, she'd seen that look and heard Jess's tone afore, also there was the maid to protect and think about as this man knew naught of her clinging nearby to life, for if he knew then he would dearly love to dispatch her to kingdom come. Pernickety knew Jess the Pearly was harrying for confirmation of the girl's death and not Ned as he'd purported earlier. Her fleeting thoughts raced but were interrupted by her manservant's sudden raucous laughter.

Jess, in anger, a hand falling atop a flintlocks hilt protruding from his thigh boot holster. "Be ye certain sure thou needs to find the Corsair afore he finds ye." Jake rose his huge bulk to face Jess eyeball to eye patch now back in place. "Only ye can little afford to lose any more of thy limbs."

A devil's spark came into his eye and quick as a flash, a long-bladed knife grew in his fist, substituting noise of a pistol report for a silent weapon. Etching at his throat the bright blade leached a line of blood, held against a growing lump in the tall manservant's throat. Not seeing the knife only now he felt the keenest blade when he tried to effect a nervous swallow. Jess leaned on him confidently wielding the knife deftly in the grip of his right hand. The man's halitosis-laden breath snatched at Jake's thoughts as he tried desperately to hold his breath. Partly to avoid having his throat slit, partly due to the foul emission of ale fumes.

It wasn't a Sunday morning yet a solitary, soulful bell rang out from the nearby church. Another such chime struck. It was only when the wiry form originally leaning forcefully against him went limp. Suddenly he slid down-wards to the floor and Jake realised what had happened. Confirmed when the knife relaxed and disappeared, also the copper warming pan in Pernickety's hands was lowered from the attack position. Jess the Pearly went out like a candle in the wind. He would offer precious little mischief for a short while at least. A further cut to Jake's throat was a reaction from the struck road agent, thankfully as superficial as that of his first attack. Full of praise for his bravery, apologising for her foolhardiness, the woman threw down the copper and quickly made to stem blood from the wound.

"I didn't know the bastard held a knife to thy throat, our Jake. 'tis mortal sorry I be for putting ye to any further hurt this day." Her hand withdrawn as Jake stooped to pick up his broken clay pipe. Pernickety hurried off for a fresh-dampened rag returning to twist water from the cloth. Urged him return to the settle to give the blood a chance to congeal. Fetching a pitcher of ale and goblet, knowing this would keep him from moving too far from his seated position. The tending done, Pernickety returned to the prone figure, with great strength she dragged his body by his high boots into a ground floor anteroom. Locking the door with an iron key and this she placed in view on the mantelpiece. Scooping another clay whilst there, the first broken in the furore, she stuffed chain strands of tobacco into it and lit the contents with a spill from a smoker's candle. Sparks showered downwards and bluing smoke wreathed her wild red hair. Puffing merrily at the foot-long receptacle the woman crossed the room endeavouring feverishly to keep its combustion alight. Alongside she cooed as she passed the smoking Churchwarden, "Quaff thy ale, our Jake, for t'other were spilt in the squabble with that heller, Jess, and kindly be a taking this token smoke for thy courage."

Miss Pernickety made a forlorn sight as her features were not built for simpering over a male, least of all her lowly paid, slow-witted cellar man. Thankfully the fawning ceased and Jake found himself nodding a contented gratitude, puffing the dying embers of the pipe to re-ignite its combustion. Murmuring thoughtfully he confided a worry, "Aye, Pernick, and I thank ye for thy trouble and concern." Billows of smoke shrouded his face as he withdrew the clay from between his lips and glanced toward the open doorway. Rebuking her with a mournful questioning statement, "Mayhap that's what we be having ourselves now, Pernick - trouble. Ye realise the Pearly was probing about the continuing existence of the maid. If he found she were still alive he would be joyously looking forward to killing her." Noting a concurrence he added, "The highwayman has a villainous tongue but he b'aint sure the girl be still with us, yet quoted rumours about Lyme that apothecary Temple entreated a young niece for gunshot wounds."

Shaking his head in growing despair billowed much smoke about him. Pernickety patted his shoulder advising him not to worry too soon, the whispering lightly to his ear in case overheard, she said,

"Jess the Pearly will not find her in the roof attic, and young Tom checks her betwixt his kitchen chores and stabling responsibilities." Smiling her reassurance, "Tom be a good lad; he'll report any change in her condition by the hour." Flopping alongside the gentle giant was the only time the enormous woman felt comfortable with her own obesity, only when briefly residing next to someone as large as her manservant did she feel of a normal size and weight. She confided concern no warning had been given about the highwayman's presence in the harbour town back streets, despite an assignment of watchful eyes and informants of Inn regulars. Palms were greased and heads cautioned about a need for discretion if indeed they spotted the evil road agent. Most wanted posters had been torn down up the length of the main Silver Street, probably destroyed by the scoundrel himself.

"Normally we'd have warning of Jess's whereabouts and when he was recovered enough to come after the maid and Black Ned - any road up, Lyme Regis town be full o' Redlegs joining the Protestant cause."

"The Pretender here you say - ah, so Monmouth must be the reason for all the fly-blown activity around the beachhead and harbour entrance to the old harbour Cobb. When did ye come by this information."

Pernickety told of men clamouring to sign enrolment papers knowing full well her manservant to be a strong contender, endeavoured to deny such knowledge.

"T'were yesterday evening and word flew about like a wind-fanned wild fire. ''tis a wonder ye did not hear the powerful whisper abroad on the street."

She wondered if she should voice her misgivings knowing already where the man's loyalties lay.

"King Monmouth issued a royal warrant laying claim to the English throne, asking for volunteers for the rebel army - as was thought on the death o' old Charlie II, the Pretender be raising Protestant armies o' labourers and crofters to fight against his wayward uncle, King James II."

Distracted only from her monologue when the tiniest tinkle of a silver bell charm made its urgency felt in the room. Jake looked over towards the carillon dangling from a silken thread through a finely drilled hole in the plastered ceiling. Hurriedly the woman rose and made off toward the stairwell door, placing her hand on the doorknob she turned and tutted loudly, "Whatever pray could the child be wanting - for sure she's had her vittles earlier this morning and I'm certain sure she enjoyed the same."

Jake choked on his ale and spat an unheard protest as the woman part- vanished inside the stairwell to hearken closer to her adopted ward's shrieking.

"Ye deny me a morsel o' my vittles woman, yet not a maid who thus consumes barely crumbs from thy kitchen table and that which I would find necessary to leave on my finished trencher."

Pernickety's torso-less face reappeared briefly as she tried to reason with him.

"Maybe the maid be fitful with fever and therefore ye allus feed a fever. Now I must away to tend her restlessness."

Jake relented and nodding agreement said, "Aye. Mayhap she heard the commotion with the highwayman and is part-feared for thee. Aye, she be a goodly maid." He rolled his eyes upwards to the floor above. "How be the bairn faring for I never think to inquire of her health. She be a goodly soul never a once I heard her complaining of her wounds."

"I told 'ee Jake she be better from the wound but be fretful and fitful with fever."

"Yellow Jack?" The retired ageing seafarer was shocked at the possibility.

Shaking her head she grinned at his concern as she made to climb the kite-winders to the tiny attic somewhere above them.

"No, "course not - just a reaction to the good doctor's herbal potions and the shoulder wound's almost healed. It were great luck the ball broke in bits when Pearly fired his Brown Bess at her - the maid took a fragment o' lead in her left shoulder but it didn't do for the bone." Reaching for the stout wood banister rail in the stairwell, turned for the last time and stated matter-of-factly. "Watch out for that heller in the store room. He'll be a sore head when he comes round from his unconsciousness and that might not be too long now." Making to ascend the narrow steps she called,

"He be a goodly surgeon that doctor Temple, we were in lady luck's pocket to stumble upon his tiny seaman's shore surgery that fearsome night."

"If he's so wonderful where be he then for the past twenty-four hours?" Jake snorted. "Why b'aint he up there in the attic"

She erected a forefinger to her lips insisting on silence about the maid's whereabouts. Then informed in hushed tones, "Cause Temple be aware o' the rumours abounding this week about the doctor's niece staying at his surgery."

"The maid's still his patient, Pernick. We paid fair his dues."

The staircase door closed and fearing retaliation from what she was about to say, called from behind a closed door as she ascended the rickety treads.

"Because our good practitioner has absconded his practice for the time being and he be off to submit his services for the cause as field surgeon in the duke of Monmouth's army."

Jake's mouth fell open and another clay pipe split asunder after crashing from a toothy grip spiralling downwards to the stone flags. His bright eyes dulled.

Pernickety had other things on her mind to concern her as she made her way up to the attic - had she put the fear of God into the maid with earlier tales. Trying to put the maid's mind at rest and dismissing bustling activity beneath her high window. Clarissa had noted with fear crowded streets abounding with rebel troops and their assortment of cavalry and strutting scythemen. `A cruel and murderous weapon, the scythe" - she had been told. Some Devon militia had deserted their regiment in favour of the Pretender bringing a more disciplined armed presence with muskets and their Civil War Cromwellian helmets. Polished headgear had been immediately recognisable to the woman, with their cross-foil guard frontispiece, and their cruciform leather belts held either bloodletting cutlass, rapier or broadsword alike. Secreting other dire weapons in tall thigh boots and their leather tunics.

Now mayhap this blurted knowledge be giving her nightmares; oh, at the time she'd smiled at her cock-a-doodle-doo words probably understanding little and caring even less of what was said - merely excited at the attention received from a caring mother figure. Pernickety had responded, and cuddling her to her breast, said,

"Though thou hast the spirit of a fighting tomtit, missy, thy nature be that o' the cuckoo and ending in another's nest."

Jake was left alone to guard their dishonoured guest and for his part, melted into deep thought. Staring at the blank white wall intently as he absentmindedly listened at every stay creaking and groaning its protest. Whilst his mistress traversed her way upwards he followed her blind progress by staring at the dusty wall opposite, perhaps slightly enjoying the muted pandemonium of timber under stress. The manservant imagined her matronly form, head-lowered and heavy breasts almost touching the treads in front as laboriously she climbed a precariously steepening wooden slope. It was probably why she'd chosen to live on a ground floor level, traversing narrow stairwells after a noggin of rum or a cup or two of liquor was beyond any sensible reckoning. Why even the flaskers had much bother temperancing her mortal testing of their bursting casks on each clandestine night delivery. Years had passed before he'd been able to work out that wherever he and his mistress resided, albeit rented hostelry or part-time labouring in hostelries, gentlemen of the night, tub men and their thuggish batmen would miraculously appear with contraband wares, that was until Jake finally caught her out. Pernickety was spied atop a rickety ladder using a mixture of clay and mortar adhesive, affixing broken green wine bottles bases under the roof eaves, this turned out to be the `traders of the night" secret sign, a portent advertising unto which an "open for business sign" was there for all to see. Yet to passing innocents abroad, translucent emerald-green roundels were but embellishment to the gable ends and eaves of the half-timbered buildings. Jake's thoughts were rudely interrupted as quite unanticipated, a piercing scream from the roof garret prompted the big man to forget his wound and dash to the fireplace. Taking up the iron key from the beamed mantelpiece, turned to open up the door that held the highwayman, only now the storeroom was completely empty.

Chapter Six　　THE WHISPERED PARDON

Yellow eyes o' fire its head jet black
red mouth a gaping fangs all drawn back
white teeth bleeding scaring all Man Jack
toss a coin for vittles and Rum to cheer
then leaping Black Dog will disappear
Poem: The Black Dog
* **

Earlier in the attic

The effect of daylight through the four narrow iron-glass panes of the attic window was heightened being struck by the growing strength of a noonday sun. It having risen well clear of the black and white frontages of the tiered buildings opposite, as the bright beams pierced the tiny cramped room. Silver Street was a steep hill down through Lyme Regis town and was also the main thoroughfare down to the waterfront harbour side. Street traders set up their stalls and sold their wares alongside and opposite the broad opened up front door of the Black Dog Inn. The sunshine afforded immediate rises of temperature to the room through the tiny patchwork of bulbous salt-stained crystal panels. Mystical, the effect was that of a myriad hue in ever-moving shafts of brilliant blued sunlight. Trapped within the beacons of light were minuscule backlit flecks of suspended dust that revolved and undulated within its wafting grip. Entertainment indeed for the girl as she lay propped up on chicken-feather-filled pillows. Looking out from her grimy bed, a straw-filled pallet with harsh blankets and a coarse bed sheet of yellowing calico. Staring in an hypnotic daydream, she watched the pin-prick movements of arrested particles as diverse as the very universe itself. It was certainly enough respite and entertainment for a recovering girl in a foul garret tucked up under shabby eaves of the old inn. The sunbeam's nucleus directed rays past her face to land on a bricked-up fireplace, devoid of the location in her temporary sickbed berth. Earlier fearful thoughts wrested her out of a fitful and restless slumber. Since the sun came up she'd tossed and turned in the crude but safe haven of the crib. Her restlessness perhaps accountable to her now feeling much better from the wound in the upper chest area of her right shoulder. Complaints about remaining bed bound were ignored by her kindly mine host, Pernickety. Looking round the attic that stank acridly of damp and mould, stained walls erupted accompanying humidity. Mysterious shapes formed on the white lime-washed walls about her in the evenings. Mornings were completely different. She lay there gazing at her enjoyable sunlit surroundings feeling irritatedly helpless as any child could of twelve short years. Many thoughts raced as she lay some weeks recovering from the near-death experience. Yet on the other-hand inside every young girl was an equally young woman waiting to come out. A transformation had come over Clarissa Lovelace-Peach rebounding the way she had from death's door. Visions and deep insight into the folk about her and their lives - for good or evil. She took satisfaction in regaining her strength. Feeling well enough to rise from the sick bed and face the world and her enemies again.

Tom, her friend and stable-boy of the inn, and when trade slackened, would refresh her bedside water jug, for him this was excuse enough to tarry a while from his many duties with the Black Dog's overnight boarders and their horses. Business was brisk - he'd said, especially with many strangers in Lyme town and all. Informing the girl the inn was full to bursting with men deciding whether to throw in their hand with the Pretender. Though not in daylight hours. Ongoing, the intensive training of three rebel army units went on in nearby sunlit fields, urgently prioritised to the maximum duration and length of the sultry midsummer day. An hour earlier Pernickety had sat with her and took due note of the child mentioning a `scratching" noise coming from the fireplace. The woman discounted this phenomena, placating her by saying.

"Well this be the Black Dog Inn so if ye see an apparition of a black dog thou must toss it one of these silver farthings." Delving into her medical bills shrunken purse, willing offered for essential medication and herbal cures, but these had taken their course on their dwindling finances.

Finally she came up with a scattering of a few silver farthings and thus placing a handful to her bedside table she had added with a ring of warning,

"Poor beast be a troubled land-locked spirit ever seeking to escape cruel bondage of when it were alive." Glancing furtively about her confided, "the mutt were a robber's dog and beaten cruelly to death by a highwayman. Legend has it the dog's owner were a footpad who happened upon a stage hold-up here in Silver Street, intervening, hoped for a share of the spoils. A fight broke out and the dog were kicked to death its distraught master shot dead on the spot." Then the woman told of the road robbery that took place several years ago outside of this very inn which was promptly renamed. "The black spectre doth portend `a violent death to its beholder" and then mentioning that for spiritual protection she had to toss a coin at the beast if it materialised, reiterating a dire need to chant a rhyme which must accompany the coin.

Then before leaving to tend to her business, Miss Pernickety had insisted the maid learn it by heart, adding as she slammed the tiny attic entrance door and to take away the fear of God from her gaze - chortled the `black beggar" will leave thy precious sight forever. A withdrawing finger pointed to the scattering of low denomination coins placed by her bedside and within easy reach. Her cackling traversed the stairwell as she went down the stairs.

A bedside tabletop contained one pewter candlestick with a stump of tallow inserted. A tinderbox for lighting the candle and a terra-cotta vessel with thick drinking tumblers alongside. Cast aside and forgotten by the woman retiring downstairs, lay a wooden trencher with remainders of a greasy meal. A fine square of linen weighted on four corners with china beads, kept flies off a few sweetmeat treats left for her delectation in a silver pot.

Apart from this item of battered furniture and the crudely-built though warm comfortable bed, the attic bedroom contained little else, though a chamber pot had been slid under the bed for relief - should she require it. Translucent wax lighting flickered in the evenings, ever moving shadows formed disturbing silhouettes of mystical beasts of flesh, fish and foul. These danced menacingly on the four whitewashed walls. Earlier, Pernickety whilst feeding and comforting the girl, allayed voiced fears of moving shadows and things which go `bump" in the night.

Cell-like her little attic for the past few weeks, now began to feel quite oppressive, and nightmares were waking her in a bath of perspiration in the small hours - visions repeated to her host told of a dark stranger, a man on horseback who visited the scene of the post chaise wreck. How she'd envisaged this darkened shadow remove the secreted paper pardon from the body of her Miss Wilks; four corpses lying incarcerated in the splintered coffin undiscovered for many weeks after she'd been abducted. This she was then told by the scoffing woman to be a nonsense. Discounted with a casual wave of her hand as the subject was speedily changed, yet when her visions revealed a sinister black dog the woman took her very seriously.

To the extent a little known rhyme affording protection from any ghostly canine apparitions considered unwelcome to little or large strangers visiting the old haunted hostelry, unless of course, her kindly patron was trying to allay fears about the missing government document.

A sudden groaning and creaking noise from across the room began again and the cringing girl now thought she spied a panel across the fire hearth move. The whirling shafts of clear sunlight kept up its transparent barrier that lay between darting eyes and a shadowy corner the opposite side of the room. There it was again only this time it was coupled with a loud `crack" and this noise made her sit bolt upright in the rickety bed. Shivering with fright, now wringing her hands in fear, Clarissa clasped at her discoloured calico nightshirt. Gathering it closer to her chest, hardly recognising her own rasping voice, the girl began chanting loudly as she fumbled for a silver farthing lying on the bedside table...

`Yellow eyes o' fire head coal black
red mouth a gaping fangs drawn back
white teeth bleeding scaring all man jack
so toss a coin for vittles Rum to cheer
leaping black dog please disappear"

Suddenly a faded thinly stretched brocade fire screen flew outwards and down to the floor and a very sooty highwayman materialised and emerged from the sooty chimney.

On hand and knees the pain tortured expression of a soot-blackened face was offered sideways on to the terrified girl, his face with the bulbous black patch displaced precariously to one side it showed the creamy ball in a blind socket. Slowly and with great laborious effort, Jess Mandrake moved up out of the black chimney hole. His tricorn hat knocked on a beam and tilted over his good eye, grimacing yellow teeth steeled themselves against another shower of falling soot as he clambered from the mound of loosened firebricks. Looking like the phantom image of the black dog, purporting to roam the inner sanctum, the incarcerated robber burst to freedom out of the wall and into the horrified girl's bedchamber and her life again. Breathless with fear the girl's wavering voice began murmuring the rhyme louder and louder, her eyes screwed up tight against the enlarging apparition. Failing to see his bony frame emerging, having escaped entombment up internal chimney rungs from the storeroom directly below, taking an age to break the back of the fired clay bricks - bursting out of his confinement in a cloud of brick dust and loosened soot into the attic grate. The highwayman had not realised the girl was in the building, yet alone survived the inflicted musket ball wound weeks earlier in the Ship Inn. Yet now as the fresh dust and soot settled on his shoulders, he could partially spy her by clearing the dust from his good eye. Pausing on all threes, Jess silently decided his next move. Yet the spectre conveyed to the bed-bound young girl was for all the world - that of the legendary black dog. It was then that a flashing silver coin came down the sunbeam to hit him directly in his good eye. The excruciating agony added to Jess" pain-racked and wound-punished body, head spinning, and rocking back on his haunches and knocking his head - clasping his bloodshot eye. Blinded temporarily as he desperately tried to protect the amputation wound. The bloodied pad affixed to his short arm socket, also nursing a ringing headache from the woman's blow to the back of his neck. Now this demented maiden's voice fair screaming a chant about a black dog was flinging her damnable pocket money at him. Had the whole world gone mad. His head now clearing, Jess gathered his thoughts and realised this was the opportunity he needed to despatch the maid, thus disposing of the only living witness to a gaggle o' murthers. Temporarily blinded, Jess stumbled clear of the rubble and struggled to his feet, clutching the painful left stump and reeled toward her. Clarissa, still cringing she clasp-gathered the grimy bed sheet to her chest, realising at last that it was not the apparition she'd thought and flew from under the bed linen to bound out onto her feet. Marvelling aloud she wondered about the apparition in front of her paralysed figure.

"Gracious - the spectre of the ghostly animal be rising to his feet like a man."

Reaching out without looking for another silver farthing as suddenly the attic door opened so fast it hit the wall with a bang - distracting the sooty highwayman for a moment. Tom the stable boy ran into the attic and immediately summed up the situation. Running forward towards the girl, glancing desperately around for what had scared her and wondering why she stood rooted to the spot in dusty shafts of midday sunlight. Bewitched she continued to mumble the ode to the ghost of the black dog. Tom dashed up and grabbed at her hand, spinning on his heel to drag the stupefied maid from the room. Jess fell grinning backwards against the narrow door of the attic tossing his tattered cloak about him as he did so. Closing with impetus and thrown weight of his sooty body. Desperately Tom looked for an escape to the solitary window of the room. Calculating immediately that the orifice was too small for clambering through in a hurry. Also not appreciating the stepped design of the building meant an overhang would throw them three storeys to a cobbled street beneath them. The newly opened up fireplace with its bricks strewn across the floor appeared to be their only choice. Quickly drawing the girl close up under his armpit that made them move as one, now he could move swiftly without resistance as they dived into the sooty void. Jess's vision clearing meant he anticipated this darting action by the children and throwing his arm out - made to grab them as one. Forgetting the piled obstruction of scattered bricks on floorboards to shoot past the cowering figures as if he was rolling about on marbles. As the highwayman careered past the open mouthed children now on their knees, as they made to dive into the inky blackness, missing them and flailing the air as he inadvertently circumnavigated the room - his shins hitting the side of the bed to dive head-first through the attic window with a resounding crash. Glass fragments showered the crowded gathering below, as the farm labourers and serfs massed in queuing groups for the signing into Monmouth's army. Guffaws of laughter from the street greeted the blustery anger of the highwayman's soot-blackened expression as he struggled to free himself from his enforced bondage. Slowly with controlled temper he sought to free himself from the jagged shards encircling his throat. A careful manoeuvre which would take enough time for Tom to move the stunned girl into the opening, guiding her fragile frame still dressed in the calico nightdress rearwards down the sooty metal fire rungs. Deciding not to repeat the road agent's route, Tom hauled her gently down into the wishbone join of the main chimney breast. There they would change direction to emerge in the main room of the inn. Downstairs Jake stared at the empty storeroom and the soot-piled hearth, then hearing the commotion from the attic above him, he leapt for the stairwell door and jerked it open. He was just in time to see Pernickety's bulk sliding backwards through the opening, crashing into his shoulder she bowled them rearwards to land the far side of the room against the inglenook fireplace. Lying for a full minute, Pernickety, fair winded she eventually spoke of what she'd found in the girl's bedchamber. "Devastation and destruction be everywhere up there, our Jake. The maid be gone - vanished in terror no doubt from the phantom trying to squeeze into the street out of a broken window."

Jake lifted the woman clear and they began to brush themselves down as they decided their next move.

"I tell ee', our Jake, it be a living nightmare up in the maid's room. The spectre of the dog be jammed tight in the attic window still wearing its black tricorn." Pernickety failed to realise the significance of what she said until her manservant observed.

"Dogs, phantom or not don't wear no tricorn hat, Pernick. It must be our missing highwayman thou spied in the room." Placing her bulky frame from him to one side, he made to investigate further. Before he could take his leave he was distracted by a nearby scraping noise, accompanied by a dull thud and falling soot down into the fireplace alongside them. Falling upside down into the hearth came muddled black images of the children, unrecognisably black as the ace of spades as they clambered to their feet. They made off towards the kitchen of the old Black Dog Inn without a sound.

"Argh, two black devils now Jake, they be multiplying by the minute." She sucked her breath and squealed, "largest beast ye ever did spy in the attic window now two of its offspring be in my fire grate. Pity t'wern't a'fire with burning faggots, for they'd surely gone back to hell where they belong."

Jake helped her back up to her feet chuckling gently at the innocent naivety.

"Pernick ye slow-witted witch, those b'aint black devils they be humankind."

He glanced at the movement past the opened kitchen doorway

adding he knew who they were; "'tis thy adopted ward and Tom and they've just made off with thy fresh baked homity pie from the bread oven." He brushed soot from his shoulder and helped her straighten her crumpled raggedly clothing. "Those soot blackened faces looked very much like Tom and the maid, if I not be mistaken. And I've a fair idea who the black devil be in thy attic, too." He slid past the woman crossed the flags and began ascending the staircase.

Pernickety ran to the kitchen and closed the door of the bread oven, then dived back into the main room she spied the anteroom ajar and peeked inside. Realising what her faithful manservant meant, a whimper burst forth and came from her lips and gathered momentum as she dashed to the stairwell and expounded,

"That bastard Mandrake has escaped our Jake, now ye be careful up there."

The woman fair ran up the narrow staircase to enter the attic close behind, then rounded on him as he pulled back from staring down the open fireplace.

"He was there I do so swear to you our Jake." Climbing up from his knees he brushed soot from his grubby breeches and placed a cautioning finger to his lips as together they listened at the opening. A cursing and swearing came from within the black hole, something had made it down the internal rungs and appeared to be clambering out of one of the ground floor fireplaces. The woman spied something and retrieved the dusty eye patch from red brick rubble. Glancing quickly at each other before rushing back to the stairwell. It was too late. With a clatter the door slammed shut at the base of the stairs, they knew securement was permanent until an iron bolt on the outside of the door was shifted. The highwayman, for it was he that had extricated himself from the window, knew bulk of the woman and her manservant was too great, this prevented them following his escape down the chimney. Dancing a seaman's jig whilst yelling triumphantly, fled off down scullery cellar following sooty footprints now clearly visible on the flagstone steps. Though inwardly he was red-faced with shame as he raced after the runaways. His six-foot tall aching frame shocked beyond measure. It had been a fraught day yet had yielded fruit, now he sought to even the score by despatching the only living witness and thus save his neck from the Tyburn gallows. Recalling a foolish night several weeks hence when he allowed the strip of a girl's continued existence, for now she could inform the world of his shortcomings as a road agent. Then Jess spied smutty stains sweeping downwards into the bowels of the earth. Wine cellars of the old building, obviously linking it to a catacomb of caves adjoining the sea wall at the overhanging undercliff. Well known locally to be frequented by smugglers who found it convenient to arrive by boat, then transferring wares and casks along the sea-washed link. Rubbing the stubble of his chin the highwayman stood angrily pondering his next move.

* * *

•

Soot-blackened ragamuffins ran pell-mell with their feet barely touching the worn steps downwards to the subterranean cellars and cave system beneath the kitchens. Tom, exploring the way only curious young boys did, discovered the escape route to the open sea several weeks earlier. Halting their headlong flight into dank darkness, the children paused to tinder strike a part-used brazier Tom pulled down from an iron holder on the wall. Jerking Clarissa to a standstill, releasing her hand to fire-raise a flickering flame that now licked at the cave walls eagerly. When radiance grew in strength, pocketed the pewter tinder box then they dashed, torch held high, deeper and deeper into the tunnel system toward seagull noises of the distant water front.

"Tom," the girl cried slithering to a halt, hand flung up to her ear.

Resisting his trawling grip, she slowed to eventually lean exhausted against the watery walls of the rock tunnel. "I must rest a spell - I beg of thee."

Moisture leached quickly damp-staining her sooty calico nightshirt, she shivered and glanced about her. Wrenching her hand free she placed a forefinger to her lips the cupped hand continuing to listen intently. The stable boy's rasping breath caught in his throat momentarily as he eventually insisted,

"It's the sea, Clarice beau, for we be but a few short yards to the beach. This smuggler's tunnel comes out at the water's edge of the North shore. There be a discarded row boat - we can escape across to Gold Cap."

"Shh..."

Cold-looking the lad into silence by the shimmering orange-red light of the spluttering brazier, endeavouring to concentrate on more than just an echoing swish of receding waves on rocks she cried out in a hushed whisper.

"There dost thou hear that groaning noise somewhere ahead of thee." Pointing urgently to where a crossroads of tunnel systems met a few short yards ahead. "I be certain sure it be a man moaning in dire pain."

Tom afforded her a sidelong glance inquiring also why the girl thought it could be a man and not a woman in purported difficulty.

"Cos in inky-darkness a female would cry out in fright or fear - that's for why I be telling thee to hush up - hearken a while." They moved to investigate.

Slowly they crept forward with bated breath intent on catching any inflection of extraneous sound above faraway crashing waves. Arriving at a cavernous bell mouth join in the tunnelling whereby caves met. They craned their necks blinking upwards against dripping water droplets. Holding high the searing torch, Tom made the girl start with sudden fright as he yelled, "Hoy." And waving it above his head to illuminate a moist darkness.

"Whist," Clarissa warned, "take care mayhap it be Mandrake taking shortened routes to thwart our escape."

"No. He be a looking for us in the Black Dog, he'd never find the secret passage down this far with half vision." Gripping his wrist she forced the burning brazier to ground level having suddenly noticed their undoing. The lowered orange glow revealed splodges of smudged soot, this had left a telltale trail leading directly up to where they now stood shivering.

Tom gasped a realisation that they were more vulnerable than at first thought. A quick glance into the eyes of the girl told him she too decided they should move on at once. They made to run onwards when a commanding male voice from above bade them do otherwise and bade them remain where they were.

"No please don't go - tarry a while for I be in dire straits above thy heads."

Far-flung echoing words caused them to look about them and eventually up to where a voice rang around the smooth walls of cavernous void. The flickering torch was but a thinning glimmer when

91

held up against the vast dark space above them and that which revealed nothing. The cliff ceiling drew together in folds formed by the sea in times gone past, then it parted into a gaping bell-mouth cleft on high. Then to their horror yet more echoing words from unseeing ghostly tones repeated over and over its plight. Aghast, Tom fell to his knees dragging the girl with him, crossing his heart then the girl's several times, praying fervently in mumbling penance.

Clarissa's enforced kneeling hurt her knees on rubble of loosened flints and sea-washed pebble stones, seaweed chains indicated the caves were washed clean by the regularity of incoming tides. She rolled her eyes in fear for was it the almighty come to claim them for their past adolescent sins.

"Help my plight young uns. Help me for I be a dangling like a fish on a line above thy tousled heads." The voice sounded weak and despairing from fatigue.

Looking at each other in wonderment, Clarissa gripping Tom's waist as they rose as one to their feet, holding the torch higher to illuminate the raggedly-hung folds of a sea-water-formed rock ceiling. In fear-gripped terror they clung together like a statue of lost souls in torment pondering their next move. It was decided for them.

"Coins - silver and gold coinage which ye are most welcome to for thy trouble. A pocket sundial also fell from my person as is there by thy feet."

The voice complained of cramp forming in his legs then quickly went on to say,

"When ye locate my fallen property on the cave floor, look heavenwards for ye'll find me suspended above. I spy thy torchlight and find it a great comfort - help me I beg ye both."

Tom led Clarissa on bended knee, she was in a weakened state still clawing and affixed nervously to his waistband, moments later they found the articles strewn across the well-trodden cave floor. Rising to their feet in amazement, the ragamuffins still fraught from chase and attempts on their own lives now looked to help another in danger. There in gloom of a rock ceiling fold, barely visible and suspended by one boot, a man hung upside down from of all things - what appeared to be a spacious bed base.

"We spy thee sir. How may we help thy plight from so sheer a rock face."

Clarissa took the lead in comforting the poor dangling wretch.

"A rope. 'tis only possible with a rope." Confirming their willingness not to abandon him, and after confused deliberation they slowly made their way toward the exit and a welcoming sight of the sky and sunlight once more.

Clarissa saw their position past the bell mouth offered a clearer view of the catacomb's egress to an unsettled sea. Eventually standing on the waved-formed cave ledge, they now found themselves barefoot in several inches of spume. The restless ocean heaved and swirled strands of seaweed up onto the broad entrance. Distantly a heat-inspired sea mist rose speedily silent to girdle white crested wave tops, this partially hid the landmark of Gold Cap across a horseshoe shaped bay. Stamping their feet in a rising tide brought blood-coursing stinging relief to the bitterness of standing on a wave-washed floor. All about them heaved with swirling chains of dense weed clumps, as a rising tide ran without check and continued to batter the smuggler's grotto with a freshening breeze. At once the bobbing ten foot row boat became apparent to them as it writhed against its whipping rope painter. It lay alongside the water bathed ledge resisting a snatching riptide as best it could. Above the undercliff protected them from prying eyes, their activities remained private on the north shore of Lyme. Observance came only from a scattering of herring gulls whirling as they dived for fish in the rising swell. Tom pointed to something in the row boat amongst its lobster pots and remains of black webbing fish nets. There was a coil of rope, but would it be long enough for their needs.

"Tide's coming in - We'll have to be quick. It fills the caves at high water to a depth of several feet." He went back into the cave and forced the still burning torch into a crag on the rock face. So saying he sprang into the boat as it rose from a dip to a swell. Fully stretched, the tender of sound bottom took the boy's weight, barely altering its course upwards as he did so. Once aboard Tom threw the crab and lobster pots ashore exposing a smell of rotting fish in the gunwales of the boat - someone had a fishing trip not too many days hence. Twirling the thin rope over and over his forearm he soon gathered it into a coil and threw it for all he was worth on shore. Warning the girl away to one side due to inaccuracy of flight on a heaving and moving wooden sea platform. Clarissa took up the painter's slack and tugged the boat level with her good arm, this independent action allowed Tom to leap ashore and retrieve the broad coil of jute and then to make their way back into the cave. Pausing only to retrieve the brazier they soon found themselves beneath the hanging man where they threw down the rope coil. Pondering and cogitating upon renewed analysis of the situation. The waning torch placed carefully up out of the gathering waters rising under their chilled feet, Tom looked up as a voice inquired.

"Has lady luck favoured the brave?"

The disparaging utterance from on high held a ring of despair, even the inherent echo now began to sound weary.

"Aye sir, fortune did not desert us in our hour of need." Tom retorted placing the burning torch to a metal clasp on the side of the cave wall. "We nurse an insoluble problem though - how will we fetch the rope to thee."

"Can ye climb like a monkey lad." The voice inquired, "for `''tis like such an animal ye'd have to be thus reaching up to my hapless self."

Tom scanned the ragged wall of the cave sides and cupping his hands called, "Aye, that I can." Spying the walls further said, "though it be fair steep and with scant hand holds."

"There are a few objects which might help thee in thy ascent."

With a loud clatter three varying sized daggers fell from the suspended man to a spot alongside. Tom thrust them into the rear of his leather belt.

"The sea." Tom had an idea and rounded on Clarissa, "Are you strong enough to go back to the cave entrance." Watching her nod he explained his reasoning.

"When the tide is right the cave will begin to flood to several inches. When this takes place thou must gently tug the rowing boat, by first untying the painter, deep into the cave to a place beneath the bell mouth."

So saying he began to climb towards a ledge, using one of the daggers he dug deep into a fissure as hand hold. Thrusting others as he went further and further up the rock face. She watched momentarily as the hand holds now held one by one, his bared feet. Slowly he moved ever upwards.

"What if the tides overcome me?" Clarissa exclaimed, realising she was left to her fate and a swell of the rising waters.

"Pass up an end of the coil afore ye leave us." Tom reached to grasp the end of the offered jute. Adding, "Fetch the boat girl or the fellow and thy servant will surely be done for."

"But the highwayman?"

"If he has knowledge of these caves then he'll also hold knowledge of flooding. No, Jess Mandrake will bide his time till after high water."

Tom's voice began to become patience-strained, the girl placated him by saying she would go at once. So doing she left them to their fate and crept away.

As she reached the daylight again Clarissa realised the flooding of the caves had more than begun. A furore came from the row boat as a plummeting flock of seagulls scavenged the silver darts of dead fish in the gunwales. Paddling in bared feet as waters lapped well above her ankles she realised the soot would be washed away. Kneeling in several inches of warm seawater, briefly she rinsed her legs and calico nightgown. Now feeling refreshed, rose to begin her task of dragging the craft back again. The boat was full of seabirds scavenging for dead fish in the bottom of the row boat, they had been revealed by the earlier task of tossing lobster pots to the shore. Tucking the calico nightshirt into her bloomers bared her knees as she swished further into unknown deeper water, she reached into the boat and grabbed an oar. Waving the heavy spar dissuaded all but one seagull. A hungrily persistent and large black and white creature with fearsome yellow beak - an irritated yet wisely mature herring gull. It resisted her efforts and stood his ground firmly in the middle of the seat looking downwards into the bilges between swipes from her wavering weapon. Clarissa snorted and placed the oar back alongside the obstinate sea-gull. He for his part was interested only in dead fish trapped underneath the wooden grill, with the danger passed it proceeded to delve his long yellow beak between the wooden struts to satiate his hunger. Falling backwards with a squawk against a leather bucket as Clarissa took the strain of the painter.

The tide was such she could freely attempt to float the boat inwards to the cave entrance. Disconnecting the landed end of the painter from an iron ring, proceeded to tug the skiff deep into the undercliff along with her yellow-eyed, deeply resentful and somewhat preoccupied passenger. Following a distant light of the burning torch, Clarissa eventually reached the cross way of the tunnel. Resounding bumps against the cave wall heralded her presence back with the boat, arguing voices stopped and one called out.

"Clarissa. I be trapped too." Tom's voice, shrill with fear came from about fifteen feet or so above the ground. Then the stranger's voice chuckled.

"We mortal males have found ourselves in sore predicament, Miss, now we must rely on thy good offices to rescue us from our joint predicament." Despairingly it added in quieter tones to the trapped boy several feet below.

"Mayhap it be best if we resign ourselves to our fate young Tom."

Clarissa looked around her and spied the continuing endeavours of the huge sea bird. It was a monster and determinedly hungry. A glimmer of an idea came to her. Creeping up on the grubby creature from behind, she tipped the empty upturned leather bucket over its head and pressed downwards. Trapping all but one of the yellow legs and part span of a flapping wing. Grabbing the other end of the thin rope she hurriedly tied it around the freed leg. Relaxing her weight momentarily, swiftly seized the other, with a flick of her wrist affixed the line to both.

"Tide be rising behind ye - be quick I beg of thee."

Tom called from a ledge up close to the inverted D`Arcy Ingrams. Then he added despairingly, "If you stay in the boat you must reach the entrance before it reaches the roof, apart from the bell-mouth it will not fit under this part of the caves."

"Quiet Tom or I'll leave ye both to thy fate - I'm doing my best and do not thank ye for thy interruptions." The infuriated sea bird threw off the bucket and took flight up to the restricted air space under the bell mouth roof. Once at altitude it flapped around gaining little height where it could, especially up toward the suspended man and boy. Finally fluttering exhausted downward into the rising murky tide and splashing muddy sea water into the girl's face and arms. Above the captives realised what was happening their voices rang with fresh encouragement.

"Aye "tis a goodly maid thou art - try to send the angel of mercy this way." Ingrams cooed encouragingly to the girl.

"The hungry creature must be after the dead fish in the bottom of

96

the boat so see if any remain hidden underneath the central barge boards."

Clarissa desperately clinging to the raging bird with her good arm, delved around underneath the wood grill finding handfuls of pilchards with the other.

Gathering strength and resolve tossed them skywards up to the dark recesses of the rocky bell mouth ceiling, she became elated as the bird took off again weaving upwards after the pitched flying fish. Again the girl recovered the pilchards and threw ever them upwards, eventually satiating its desire for fish the bird became used to flying the chasm, which held the man and the boy. The bird whirling like a deranged kite in a gale, now tiring of the fishy enticement, sought to free itself in any way possible. Diving again and not wanting to drown due to securement of its feet, brushed the swollen water surface and rose upwards with a flurry of feathers. Its efforts to rise out of sight towards the suspended man, made the girl realise she was fast running out of rope. As the glowing torch began to splutter and dim, Clarissa could hardly spy the whirling white bird as it ascended higher into the gloom above.

She balanced herself inboard clinging to the rope, feeding it out then gathering in slack when the bird dived to settle alongside her in the boat.

She then thought of something to bring the situation to an end and screamed out in sheer frustration like a dying shriek of a banshee. Deranged cries from the gull rang in echoing terror as it shot upwards like a returning shooting star to the heavens. Tom nearly fell from his perch as he made a grab for the passing creature. Ingrams almost passed out due to horrendous funnelling of sound into the bell mouth. Then it happened and with a loud snort the hanging man swung himself like a pendulum and desperately seized at the passing sea bird. Suddenly it was all over. Grasping the bird by the whipping line, clinging frantically with one hand to the handle of the dagger he sought to free the flailing feet of the now upside down flapping gull. Before being sent hurling downward to a watery grave, he called to Clarissa to tie her loosened end of the dangling rope to the boat seat spar.

One-handedly shaking the bird clear and tying the end of the rope around his waist he cried triumphantly, "I have ye my angel - for bringing haven to a mortal man in such dire straits ye must surely be an angel from God." In his haste to undo the rope affixed to the bird, Ingrams dusted the air with feathers and downward flying objects befitting to a frightened creature, who, earlier had dined on a banquet of stinking fish. One such object befell the maid as kneeling down she clung to the inside of the boat as it spattered her and the sides of the cave walls.

"Don't ye hurt the creature - it was he that saved ye both - not I."

Endeavouring to cleanse the mess from her tousled hair - rebounding backwards into the bilges as the sea gull hurtled past making off toward the cave mouth. Clarissa completed her task of personal hygiene and now craned her neck to see what was happening on the cave roof, the dangling stranger managed somehow to tie the rope line to a pinnacle rock point where he'd been suspended. Now he began to swing precariously back and forth like a bell hammer. Sliding downwards he headed for the boy swinging past many times before grabbing at him. When low enough down the jute Ingrams coiled the rope around his wrist and reached over for Tom seen to be perched on a shelving ledge. Grasping him then lowering him to suspend between his knees enabled him to cling to the swinging rope between them. They clung suspended briefly whilst the lad released himself from the strangle hold and slither downwards to the boat. Ingrams then uncoiled his wrist and slid speedily after him, leaping the last couple of feet with sheer relief and joy for the long hours spent suspended. Lifting the slender maid into his arms he thankfully kissed her on both cheeks until they bloomed with a rose-red tincture. Turning to the lad who also saved his hide, cowered back at thought of receiving the very same and very traditionally French treatment. Instead graciously took the offered hand of a more English and reserved friendship token, this shaking took place so violently the lad rose and fell on his toes many times on the bobbing row boat deck head. Composure regained, and with a deep sigh of relief, all Ingrams could do for several moments was but grin stupidly at the two mortal souls who gave him back his very existence. Eventually he sighed deeply and composed himself ready for the next move, that was to vacate the cave system before they became trapped inside with the growing tides.

"Release the rope lad whilst I recover the daggers which helped save us." He reached upwards yet prevented from going further by the lad who said, "They're here sir." Slashing jute away from the seat spar, straightening he offered the blades in the palm of his hand. These along with the silver coins and pocket sundial. Gratefully Ingrams retrieved the coins and made to secure the sundial in his clothing. Only when the lad looked interested did Ingrams explain. "You take a reading by the shadow thrown by the gnomon, there are tables on the reverse for corrections to latitude." He explained then eagerly thrust the articles away with a grateful grunt, shouting urgently that they should be gone from that place. Clarissa looked past the balancing man struggling to stay upright in the rowing boat, his cramped legs likened to that of a sailor long-voyaged and regaining his sea legs. What became reality was the tunnel entrance toward the waterfront, apart from where they were moored temporarily in the bell mouth, all escape routes including that one was now flooded to within a few inches of the roof. Pointing this out she sucked in her breath with a growing fear.

"We can always climb aloft again," the stranger chuckled loudly at the look of horror on their faces so quickly added, "Yet I feel the need of a breath of fresh sea air so into the water with ye both and grab the stern of this trusty craft." Peeling off his white blouson shirt he bade Tom do the same, "It may snag and restrict ye as thy torso passes under the rock ceilings." The girl's modesty was left intact, though cautioned further about trying to avoid becoming trapped by keeping low in the water when behind the towed row boat. Somehow it was finality of loud hissing as the torch extinguished itself in the rising waters, urging on the dishevelled group in the overcrowded craft. A discussion regarding merits of remaining in the bell mouth and ride incoming tides, or to escape to fresh sea air and new found freedom concluded. There was no real choice. Part-sinking the craft by filling it with swirling seawater from the leather bucket took only a couple of minutes and now it rode the rippling flow only an inch from being swamped altogether. Tom and Clarissa splashed into the water behind the stern and gripped the bobbing tiller then watched as Ingrams did the same, only this time gently over the bow. Calling cautionary advice to breathe only when they were able betwixt hollows and clefts in the tunnel ceiling they cast off.

The restless ocean heaved and swirled dark waters into the cave system. Single and double stranded chains of seaweed, divided by fierce currents clung to their faces and were peeled away irritatedly. Crashing surf was heard pounding the north shore outside the nearing cave entrance. A rip tide made its presence felt with the sheer force, twisting currents sweeping under their trailing bodies made them realise the power of nature. Chill winds sighed past their faces barely clear of the choppy surface as they were blindly towed behind the part-sunken craft. D'Arcy Ingrams swimming fervently ahead and towing the boat as best he could, one stroke forwards and two back, seemed to be the order of the day. Yet the King's man knew it was better to die fighting for his and the children's lives, rather than dangling under the bell mouth hollowed out cave for an eternity of death. As the darkening waters flooded in unabated, threatening to drown these children barely out of their infancy, D'Arcy Ingrams began to swim and tow the heavy boat toward the cave entrance slit, all the while with the hole reducing in size as it ensnared dazzling orange rays of an evening sunset.

Chapter Seven DOUBLOONS DUCATS & PIECES OF EIGHT

Mayhap thou see thyself as others do
thy looking glass image always untrue
thou shalt spy never the real me
I see ye as thou wilt never see

Reflecting kindness perceived
hiding flaws having once deceived
beauty beholden granted skin deep
friendship forever mayhap to keep

Image in the lake be one we accept
time be the thief unto everyone crept
yea time be the thief of every thing
it steals in the night to even a king

Poem: Thy Image

`Thus was consumed that Famous and Ancient City of Panama, which is the world's greatest mart for silver and gold in the whole world, for it receives the goods into it that comes from Olde Spain, in the king's great Fleet and likewise delivers to the Fleet all the Silver and Gold that comes from the Mines of Peru and Potosi"

Henry Morgan circa 1671

James II of England and Catholic Majesty to the land, brother of Charles II deceased that year on 6th of February 1685: lowered the neatly rolled document after reading aloud the exploits of the pirate king. The ancient missive was from the government of the island of Jamaica many years since passed, sent by way of a reminding persuasion of just how useful the buccaneer has been to the Crown. Recently arrested, Morgan had been tried for treason and attacking Old Spain, jailed, released and pardoned - then remarkably knighted, and returned to Jamaica as assistant governor. Now the pirate enjoyed life and of a more secure status and position, a somewhat restless albeit frustrated Morgan, chose to emphasise dire need for pardoning misdeeds perpetrated raising revenue for England. Huge triple-decked treasure ships had been constructed, shuttling backwards and forwards to and from the Indies, clandestinely orchestrated by the shrewdness and dexterity of the reinstated Charles II. All in the name of the crown and which swelled the coffers ready for war, if needs be and if fate dictated.

"Mayhap the writings of the man doth capture my liege's imagination." Louis Duras, Earl of Feversham, anticipated incorrectly concurring reaction from his king. A fleeting smile crossing lips did little for his audience's composure.

James snorted indignantly. "Morgan is an egotistical butcher who minds himself nothing yet gold silver and or bloodlust, and methinks the latter certainly not taking the hindmost."

James strode past the Earl awaiting response, mindful of his position he did not suffer fools gladly. Large plans filled his resolute if egotistical mind. Protestant opinion from the masses never doubted or underestimated for one moment. If despotic power was gained, he would use it to further his religion in the same manner as did Louis XIV of France.

In this brief time of the year of James' accession to the throne, Louis, king of France revoked the edict of Nantes by persecution known as "the Dragonnade" - quelling without compunction the last resistance of the Huguenots. James already in letters had approved the persecution practised by the French monarch, and was much befriended and grateful of him. For the last two years of his brother Charles' reign, James, had played a part in running of the English realm. Probably arranging the 250,000-pound sterling for not forming and delaying beyond reasonable duration a duly elected Parliament. This suggested and paid for by the Sun King Louis himself. Exploiting the victory which Charles, by compliance, and using time by an ignominious foreign policy he had gained much for the House of Stuart.

His accession to the throne, for James, seemed to him to be the vindication of all the conceptions for which he felt he had always stood. All he thought he needed to make him a real king, on the role model established in Europe by way of Louis XIV, was a loyal Fleet and a fine standing Army. Well trained, equally well equipped. Warlike command appealed strongly to his nature.

He, James, had fought under Turenne, and had fought in the forefront of many bloody actions at sea. Now to form sea and land forces devoted to his Royal authority. To his noble personage was to be the foremost object of his mind. Here too was the key with which all doors might be opened. Rump Parliament proud and politically minded nobility restored triumphant Episcopacy, the blatant Whigs along with sullenly brooding Puritans. All would take their place once the king of England possessed a heavy tempered, sharpened sword.

Everyone was awe-struck, spell-bound by the splendour of France under absolute control of the wealth and power of absolute monarchy.

The power of the French nation, now its quarrels were stilled and its force united under the great king, a main factor of this their magnificent age.

Why should the English not rise to equal grandeur by adoption and duplication of such similar methods? Behind this there swelled in the breast of the King, great hope he might reconcile all his peoples to the old faith of Catholicism and heal Christendom. Considering it to be devoid of direction for past generations. He was therefore resolved that there should be toleration amongst all English speaking Christians.

James was a convert to Rome, he knew secretly he too, might be considered a bigot, and there was no sacrifice he would not make for the faith. These grand plans filled James's resolute and obstinate mind as he strode the long room of the palace. Suddenly he spoke his thoughts out loud, forgetting his wandering mind had not advised his companion of tangential thought. "Toleration will be the first step to the revival of Catholicism."

"My Liege," Duras inquired after suffering silence with stout dignity which becomes an Earl, yet felt this outburst, totally devoid of conversation-continuity failed him. Now the man in the grand robes bedecked to lay others insignificant, appeared to be rambling incoherently.

Spying carefully his king from the corner of his eye, he summed up the man to be cold, haughty and strutting, yet with none of the attributes or political ability of his demised brother Charles. He, though created Earl of Feversham, had not the loyalty of an Englishman, and as a dyed-in-the-wool Frenchman, needed close contact for his other most proper liege. Also happy to command the

English standing Army periodically then to make his reports back to France accordingly.

The long flowing wig of James brushed him aside as head bent forward he paced the room, tapping the rolled parchment to his lower lip. Finally placing it to his spacious desk he rounded once more on Louis Lord Feversham. Raising the original questioning which commanded the audience in the first instance.

"You say letters of marque for Morgan were signed by my brother quite sometime before his death."

"Obviously my Liege." Duras regretted his quick tongued response and almost equally nimble command of the English language. Unusual indeed for him.

France might have the guillotine, yet England had the scaffold at Tyburn and with it went the awesome might of the headsman's axe. Many a lapse of thought to roguish tongue had cost a man his head in this backward country.

James however must have been deep in thought as he allowed the remark to go unchallenged, continuing unabated on a differing tack.

"The hearth tax, window tax, all these a soul could appreciate and be mindful of value to the government's coffers. Yet letters of marque to some piratical rapscallion, sailing for sport outside the jurisdiction of lands and laws is much too much." He swept grandly with flourish into a chair on the far side of his broad desk, continuing his speech with a note of bored solemnity in his tone. "Then what pray has happened to these aforementioned letters-of-marque, reprisal or patent. Most of all, the missing pardon.."

"Apparently my liege they did lay underwritten on the late king's desk in his quarters. Someone, a loyal cleric mayhap. Decided and took it upon himself to forward them along with agreed, and authenticated paper-pardons for those piratical scoundrels named and placed thus so." Duras moved to a commanding position before the King's desk. Leaning forward on his fingertips to lay emphasis to his words, he eagerly reflected the gleam in the King's eye.

"A damnable Pardon." King James, not really surprised at confirmation that the document had gone missing, bemoaned and repeated the news. "An official pardon for Henry Morgan." Bushy eyebrows raised demanding the full story. "Morgan's knighthood came after the spell in the Tower, my liege. The pirate granted a verbally whispered pardon, though it was originally thought possibly nothing scribed in writing. Your late brother decided upon this latter move, mayhap after granting the man his assistant governorship in Jamaica island."

Hesitating, mentally treading the need for deft transposition of thought into word. Most carefully he added, "It was deemed appropriate and to authenticate validation of his position in the Caribbean against."

"Pray continue.." James leant forward and swept his advisor's poised hands from the marquetry inlay of his ornate desk. Menacingly he suffixed his words, "Against old Spain, eh. Mayhap thy tongue escapes thy more elusive thoughts by way of a convenience or conscience, sir." He watched as the Earl straightened himself, his brow puckering and eyelashes fluttered nervously.

"I'm afraid my Liege, pirates tend not to differentiate betwixt flags of Nations or their convenience. Only what may be aboard, having been charged upon and then scuttling their galleons be consumed as contraband victuals, or indeed, casks of wine."

"Oh, and what about your own country - France."

"Oui, my Liege. I too am thy humble admirer, I along with my country, sire be thy greatest ally. France too might also be subjected to Captain Morgan's whims. If England were to receive its share of spoils from our galleons, well sire, it could be a smite embarrassing for thee and thy English command." Stiffening, Duras pondered whether the chosen phraseology could be misconstrued as delicately veiled threats.

"So these letters should be recovered the ones of Pardon and marque," James concluded ignoring any thoughts of recrimination at that point, "dost know where said documents lie, Feversham," the king said ignorantly the latest fear registering in the eyes of the man standing erect in front of him.

"I have despatched one D'Arcy Ingrams, my lord. To chase and trace their secreted passage from thy palace kingdom to ends of the earth, if necessary."

"This Ingrams fellow. A scoundrel no doubt. One mayhap supposes, purports to hail from the `devil's acre"." His reference to Old Pye street of London town was nonetheless accurate. Yet Duras conveniently failed to assert this den of iniquity and thieves was his man's cover - for Ingrams and also for his own security reasons. Instead he reckoned, "Aye - possibly my liege. It is surmised Morgan lies anchored in the Indies or conceivably wandering the Netherlands, even England itself. Purportedly waiting forgiveness from the Crowne." Then unnecessarily elaborated on the great treasure ships invoked in King Charles II's shuttling of great voluminous hoards of Spanish gold to the English coffers in years and months gone past.

"You obviously thought we did not know of this bounty, my Lord Feversham. Mayhap such information comes from envy-tainted-lips." The cock-a-doodle doo words were emphasised by a fluffing of the throat ruff with jauntily flung fingers.

Ignoring his king's provocation, Duras tried to continue, "I am reliably informed, Morgan, dared not legally set foot in England after hearing of the death of his friend. Your brother and the late king. Compromised somewhat he paid an old adversary into doing his dirty work of spying on thy Realm and verily to test the waters of discontent. Mayhap for goodly enough reason. He might reside once more in the cramped cells of thy fearsome Tower."

"Adversary eh." James" face broke into a rye smile. "Teach - it can only be Ned Teach." Rising to his feet he clapped his hands in delight at the incline of his informer's head. Duras drew back from the desk edge as a corona of curls flashed his face one more time. Happy to compose himself as the Martinet pranced from behind the desk into a cross-armed sailor's jig. Pausing to affirm his assumption so he looked at him again for confirmation.

"Aye my liege. ''tis the infamous rogue - Blackbeard the pirate."

"A bird in the hand be worthy of two in a privet, eh my Lord Feversham."

A cough drawing attention to his need for explanation was allowed with another toss of the King's head, as he pranced merrily around the eight foot wide desk.

"Henry Morgan did thus save the island colony for the Crown. That is after Admiral Penn initially wrested it from Old Spain many years afore him, sire." Duras relaxed and folded his arms expecting chastisement that never came.

"It is spoken of throughout the land as the pirate king's greatest momentous achievement. This apart from the sacking of Panama along with many ransoms, weaponry, cannonade and several hundreds of thousands of pieces of eight silver and gold coinage." A pursed lip sealed with his forefinger tapped thoughtfully brief. Removing the digit concluded a loud statement of fact. "Sire the man is a ferocious demon yet a living legend of his own time."

James's mood for dance passed quickly now the cards were down. He strolled back to his desk and twisting the seat sideways-on sat down. Crossing his legs then shuffling his shoes, caused silver buckles to glint gold in light of many wavering candles. A full minute elapsed before he deemed it necessary to break his own enforced silence. Stalking him mentally after recalling many slips of the knave's tongue - baiting him verbally again asked.

"Dost thou dally with our intellect my Lord Feversham?"

"No my Liege. Nary a once." The soldier came wearily to attention.

James rose to stride up and down, glancing up occasionally from the head down position preferred whilst pondering great matters of State. Pausing to turn and face Duras face to face. "What to do my lord, eh, what to do. Henry Morgan, renegade pirate chief of old Port Royal Tortuga and Maracaibo, eh." Turning away he picked at a hang nail. The quite human gesture was appreciated by Duras, perhaps lulled into a false state of security by the sort of thing a commoner might do, absentmindedly he spat with jocularity.

"Aye. Harry to his friends." Duras instantly regretting the confidentiality,

Yet the levity fell onto deaf ears. However, he surmised sensibly, it might be prudent to be careful with his patron and benefactor. Hurriedly he added,

"Captain Morgan delivered the `Coup de Grace" to Spanish hegemony in the past sacking of Panama. Thus saving Jamaica and especially a planned attack on Port Royal itself. Yet in this the year of our Lord 1685, Francais is the most powerful of all countries and not `Old or New Spain"." The Earl of Feversham made one last desperate plea on behalf of the assistant governor of Jamaica. Belying too, lay the problem of treasure ships invoked by the old king's edicts of the realm. Knowing full well the English coffers would feel the draught should this source of booty revenue dry up overnight. Morgan had his uses alright for one-third of all captured enemy gold came here.

The king failed to appreciate the gravity of the situation and the need to placate Morgan's piratical knaves.

"Every last man-Jack deems it awestruck dallying with the Barbary Corsairs." Duras stated knowing it would spark reaction and enchant pictures in his sovereign's mind.

The king took up a legendary coloration by saying, "Yet what a terrifying sight it must be for a crew of a merchantman sailing peacefully along, with a pirate brig bearing down and overhauling her. Eh, Duras. Then if the ship were captured, its crew given one chance to join Morgan or be keel-hauled." James looked to the Earl for reaction to his surmising, yet only a blank expression whilst deep in thought came forth.

"Black flag of the skull and cross bones hoisted. Billowing sails snatching at Southerlies and other winds known as the Songs of the Trades. And so with fire in their bellies, mayhap a cables length from victory, they would hoist their motte of skull and bones to bear down on a Brigantine with mad Morgan screaming, `Avast ye bilge scum. No prisoners. Look lively lads for ''tis grog for them's that cut the most throats." James reiterated solemnly, "Did'st know my lord Feversham, sometimes whole bodies were hoisted aloft in iron gemmaceous," he shuddered visibly. "Hung from the masthead to rot. Victim swayed with the roll of the ship clad in a coiled armour. It boded well as a warning to their prey and to strike terror into the hearts of their enemies." He raised an eyebrow when his colleague became mindful and showed a spark of interest. "Before an attack and poised for the kill, they would thrust guns into body sashes or belts after testing barrels without ball - thus to see if either was rusted - man or armament." Leaning forward to eyeball Duras and holding his gaze said, "Attacking and disposing of their enemies - blood of the kill would remain on their clothing and bodies. For all true buccaneers refuse to wash bodies from the last kill. Considering it a symbol of good fortune. The last time they had such was on entering the world shackled to their mother's cord."

The Earl of Feversham shuddered at the picture conjured up in his mind by the cold leering tones of his king. It put his own yarns into the rear of his mind forever. Pulling himself together and holding his employer's challenging grin decidedly became inclined to change the subject of buccaneer's and their wicked ways. Yet before Duras had a chance to appease further, resounding commotion outside the long

108

room caused both to glance toward the portals. The act echoed force as the doors swung to walls with a fearful crashing noise. Unexpected in that late middle-of-the night hour.

A third swept past the sentries and fell head-bowed to one knee, his breeches slewing on a loose Persian rug, thankfully to run out of impetus just in front of his monarch. "Majesty, sire." He cried anxiously.

"Rise and give thy message." James, having little time for theatricals of his minions, they detracted from his own occasional more privileged cavorting.

"News of a document of some import from Lyme in the county of Dorset, sire."

"Yes, yes, we know where our harbour towns lie within the kingdom. One also knows of the legendary rip tides of Lyme bay - thy message sir." James became irritated for it had put paid to his ribald yarns of the Barbary corsairs.

Rising to his feet the guard tore off his black beret-style cap adorned with lengthy feather, he twisted at the headband nervously. Head still bowed he continued to avoid the king's dark glower and appeased nervousness by glancing at the king's colleague. "A rider from a staging post speaks of a letter from the mayor of Lyme." He glanced down again to humble himself once more.

"Speaks of a letter. Well sir, where is this letter."

"It rides with the Exeter post chaise, sire." His eyes avoiding the burning challenge of James. "The rider was advised to ride on ahead thus warning of its presence to your majesty and of its great import."

James strode past the guard and confronted Feversham with a dulled look in his eye, "We are surrounded by numbskulls and dimwits no less." Raising his tone he added, "Pray tell - why is the letter remaining with the mail coach." Without raising his eyes the man spoke softly, perhaps anticipating his wrath,

"Thy Majesty's missive would be privy to thee and thee alone sire."

Throwing his hands out amidships then aloft in total despair, James caught the eye of Duras, who decided it was in his own interest not to give credence to the mystery. James could not be bothered to reply to the messenger, instead offered dourly, "The hour grows late, I feel it is time for one to retire. my Lord Feversham. We bid thee good night and in our weariness would beg of thee to advise this dolt of a messenger to thus inform one of the document's arrival - whatever the hour." So saying, James swept away without a backward glance, patience tried beyond reason. The humbled servant dismissed Duras did as he was bade, and rising from a deep bow on hearing the far door slam shut he tugged at a bell tassel. This was a summoning, a prearranged signal for some hidden minion manservant to lower the central candelabra. The smooth action trundled earthwards and swiftly allowed careful snuffing as the conical pewter hood on a pole did its job. As the spacious windowless room flooded with darkness, the Earl took a last look around and closed the huge door on the private quarters of the king. Striding away from the chambers accompanied by deep thoughts, pausing in the brightly lit corridor to glance about him to see if he remained alone. Dry washing his face with trembling hands seemed to clear his senses as he whispered aloud, yet to himself perhaps by way of reassurance.

`Where art thou D'Arcy Ingrams - damn and blast your eyes."

Louis Duras strolled slowly, he endeavoured to clear his head of the king's dalliance with his spirit, offered bespoke apologies met reaction and had been a dangerous indifference to the rank and majesty of his English monarch. Duras recalled how the conversation had gone off at a tangent and about of all things - pirates. Yet little did James know or realise that latest rumours had it, Henry Morgan had chanced upon a likeness in oils of the late king Charles II. Since then, nothing would satisfy Henry Morgan lest he portray his own likeness reflecting that of the late king, a curled black wig accompanied much adorned finery in lace and silk. Love knots strangely adorning the ensemble tied from head to foot. A single peacock feather shimmered with every movement of a curved black hat. Bright coloured breeches and fine hose which glistened in dullest light, whilst his shoes had silver buckles of such enormity in hot sunshine plain folk were duly dazzled. Other ornaments included a pair of Damascus-twist silver wired long-barrelled pistols, thrust deep into his broad waist band of ruby coloured satin. A bejewelled dagger tucked into either a high thigh-length boot or lowly hose garter, if so bedecked for flaunting a finery in social revelry and dance.

Morgan the Terrible as he'd become known, was a well earned notoriousness that would live in the heart of Englishmen forever.

Certainly any soul who'd suffered at some Spanish mis-treatment, including Morgan himself, would recall how he matched seamanship with seamanship, and eventually their worst cruelty.

It was beyond reasonably measurable doubt that as a cabin boy from Bristol, Morgan was probably sold to a merchant venturer, or mayhap kidnapping a maid with child closely followed by an irate parent with a fearful loaded weapon.

Whose hatred of the Spanish equalling and fervent as that of Francis Drake's legendary lust for Spanish blood, matched only with his ferocious blade and fine seamanship. There was another side to Morgan which few and only those who served with him became privy. To signify a great victory over the Spaniards Morgan would hoist a decapitated corpse to the yard-arm, there to swing in such silk and satin finery for all to see and become mesmerised, especially with the severed head lashed to its own feet. The gory practice became known on Jamaica island as "Morgan's mummery". A cruel rogue cherished by his own men due the system of insurance for each and every high or lowly rank at sea. Wounded or maimed, each seafarer under his direct command would receive, 600 pieces of eight for loss of a right arm, or six slaves. Slightly less for a left arm and for leg or legs. 100 pieces of eight for an eye and for a finger and should an unfortunate be so relieved of his manhood, Morgan would jest they of all would deserve and receive 6 handmaiden slaves.

Duras knew Morgan commanded ten ships and a thousand men to command at whim or whit, to do battle or merely luxuriate between and guard the most heavily defended lair in the world. Vast caches of wealth accrued from his and his men's one-third share of the order of letters of marque. A booty balance sent monthly to England on lumbering treasure ships of the line. Louis Duras thought of the terrible circumstances in which this naval giant could descend upon England's shipping and channels, silently at night to reap a terrible harvest of slaughter and death upon the king's fleet. Therefore he would advise his sovereign monarch to enlarge quickly and guard against such unimaginable horror.

Failing to secure enough cannon gun powder to fire a warning shot to the town of Lyme with quayside cannon on the wind-blown Cobb, knowing Monmouth's arrival would now go relatively unnoticed, Samuel Dassel, a customs outrider, slipped quietly away at night with his colleague, Anthony Thorold. First they rode to nearby Crewkerne and after some provisioning for several days ride sped off towards London. Once there, after two days and nights hard riding, presented themselves to the Member of Parliament for Lyme, the right honourable Sir Winston Churchill. Hearing and realising the urgency of such dire tidings he at once took them, accompanied by his son, John, to the royal apartments of the king of England. At four a. m. James II was awakened to hear the grim news of Monmouth's arrival at the port, immediately rewarding the exhausted riders with the princely sum of twenty pounds apiece - the king wasted little time in issuing his battle orders. Gregory Alford's missive sent by coach arrived later that day of the 13th of June 1685 and was read out to a hastily convened House of Commons, less than thirty-six hours after the Duke of Monmouth's landing at the pebble north beach at Lyme Regis.

Honiton 11th June 1685

"May it please your sacred Majesty this evening betwixt seven and eight of the Clock House clock came a Naval Ship into the bay of Lyme Regis Dorset not showing any colours."

This message read out to a hastily convened House of Commons, the king's standing army was on full alert assigned to the east and to the west coastlines to cover the rising West Country rebellion. Almost immediately the following proclamation was issued by the assigns of the bill makers John Bill (deceased) and a man called Henry Hills.

Thomas Newcombe printers to the king's most Excellent Majesty circa June 1685.

A Proclamation

JAMES R

Whereas we have received certain information

112

that James Duke of Monmouth, Ford, late Lord Grey
- outlawed for High Treason, with diverse other
Traytors and Outlaws are lately landed in an
hostile manner at Lyme, in this the county of
Dorset and have possessed themselves of our said
Towne of Lyme and have sent and dispersed some
of their traytorous complices into neighbouring
Countreys to incite them to joyne them in
open rebellion against us.
We do hereby, with the advice of our Privy Council
declare and publish the said James, Duke of Monmouth
and all his complices, adherents, abettors and
adviters, traytors and rebels, and do command
and require all our Lieutenants, Sheriffs,
Justices of the People, Mayors, Bayliffs and
all other of our Officers, Civil and Military,
to use their utmost endeavour to seize and
apprehend the said Duke of Monmouth, Ford, late
Lord Grey and all other persons that shall
be aiding and abetting the aforesaid persons
and every of them to secure until our further
pleasure be known as they will answer the
contrary at their utmost peril.
Given at our Court at Whitehall this 13th day
of June 1685 and in the First Year of our Reign
God save the King

Eyes will meet and a fuse is lit
fingers touch hearts flutter a bit
the two now beating gently as one
when the gentle act of love is done

When you leave I die a while
return again to find my smile
candle - its flame brighter for two
shadows flitting and eyes so true

Gentle words mindful gentle fare
smiling kindness to show we care
sipping wine is tasting love
worn as easily as a glove

Poem: Friendship

* * *

"I be savaged by a raging thirst and a famishing hunger."

The rowing man complained bitterly to the children as he rowed out to the open seas, having navigated the broad-beamed jolly boat out of the Cobb harbour into the rising swell and also a spreading gold-tinged indigo blue summer dusk... The waning of day now resplendent in a golden sunset dived after glittering droplets of blood on silver-topped wavelets.

An after glow of faint waning light, silhouetted the distant ship tilting nervously at her anchors.

D'Arcy Ingrams inhaled deeply the raw sting of salt winds as robustly he cherished his and the boy's new-found freedom from being inverted unceremoniously in the dark of a bell mouth cavern. His thoughts then turned to darker ones - those of revenge. Impossible against a four-poster bed and yet if he found the perpetrator who'd contrived to kill the Pretender, inadvertently placing himself in danger, the fellow would die a thousand deaths. Though somehow the King's man felt his secret mission might fare better now he was well and truly bloodied. Or so the smirking man consoled himself. A midsummer sun's fiery cauldron slid gracefully beneath the choppy swell in front of the shivering children's gaze. The girl half-expected to spy a transference of the sun's scarlet trails to appear under a vast blued dusk. In its wake the stark afterglow afforded indigo highlights of a crystal clear horizon, stars appearing faintly in the growing night sky. Earlier several hours were spent outside the cave entrance, recovering and then drying their saturated clothing. A welcoming respite in consuming a deliciously baked full-sized, fresh-baked homity pie. A hundred nautical yards or so from the ship, the sea spy Ingrams had requested the binding of their row boat's oars, and a heated discussion debated chances of their otherwise being discovered. The sea around them would soon be peppered with ball and grape if they were found prowling the well armed ship at fall of night. Tom trembled as he watched his bound blouson shirt securing the end of an oar fleetingly appear then dip down into velvety waters of the Bay. Muffled oars was excuse enough for shuddering in the growing light of the faint round moon hung low with mist, growing out of the horizon of an eastern sky as the craft pulled from swell to swell. The girl too, felt rising chills despite for the sakes of modesty being allowed to keep the calico shirt on. The original jubilant smile froze on her face when they left harbour, for a cool breeze and fine misty sea spray made the garment damp and uncomfortable in next to no time at all. Partway between the overall distance of ship to shore, small darkened shapes rose and fell in their line of sight as they stared past the doubled-up rowing man.

"There's something in the water ahead of ye." The girl urgently pointed over his shoulder, part-rising to her feet and unbalancing the headway. Stooping as in the stance of an old crone, gesticulated fervently across the port bow.

"Driftwood ahoy - port thy helm sir," Tom screamed at him also now spying the danger, letting go of the tiller he dived for'ard arm raised to pinpoint the direction. Then bent and clasped the sides of the rowing boat making ready to lend a hand or allow for some change in their nautical direction. Brackish water slopped the bilges about their bared feet - yet this was unfit to consume on a naturally anticipated bout o' the squitters. Shipping oars for fear of being swamped by standing children or striking a heavy part-submerged lump of saturated wood, Ingrams looked about him. Row boat rocking perilously, the reluctant skipper bade his excitable crew take heed of the real jeopardy of a mid-ocean capsize. Calming Tom's frenzy he spied the reason for his fervour, flotsam broke surface a yard in front of the bow. Silence befell them as an assessment was made of what came slowly up to and alongside the tiny craft. Age-blackened, a writhing necklace of trencher sized buoyancy corks broke surface creaming the nearby swells into a curl.

"Booty cognac." Ingrams spat, relieved, and reaching out with an oar, made to retrieve it for their parched thirst. Hove-to the occupants of the boat hung larboard whilst Ingrams stretched out opposite and reached for the part submerged corks supporting the light-gauged water-logged rope. Gathering hand-over-hand found it held huge sunken casks. One by one appearing briefly at the surface. A knife was produced and one anchorage weight was cut by an impatient Ingrams, the rest allowed to slide once again beneath the sea.

Taking precious minutes to transfer his agreed cargo of one of the half-ankar casks slung one fathom beneath the surface. Releasing the other end of the line which held sinker stones, this prevented the illicit contraband breaking surface until collected on selected tides by boathook and lantern.

Moving off again the large cask lay wedged in the bilges, it contained four and a half imperial gallons and filled most available space in the small boat. Though Ingrams held little hope for the toxicity of its contents as marks of the teredo worm could be spied to his trained eye, and yet he said nothing.

A breeze freshened and the distance between both vessels diminished to less than a quarter nautical mile. Persevering strokes with plodding oars having taken their toll over the sheer expanse of sea. Though the tiller steering coped adequately betwixt the girl and her attentive young male companion. D'Arcy Ingrams answered the lad's questions regarding smugglers and their contraband wares dumped at sea in dead of night.

"Most casks these parts contain white brandy, all spirits conveyed are supplied uncoloured, most purveyors adding burnt raw sugar cane for coloration on point of delivery. Breton in the form of Roscoff or

Cherbourg be the merchant venturers' choice for closeness and convenience. A sealed wax tub of colour tint sent along with each cask to be added after the spirit had been run. Trouble is the average strength of the liquor varies - most are 70 above proof, and many a reckless imbiber has met a sticky if merry end quaffing a contraband spirit of 180" above proof. Avoided if possible by the supplier or merchant venturer, because expenditure to his reputation was damaging beyond belief and any extra mention of out-of-pocket cost."

Ingrams knew this to be true as he too was a reformed smuggler, transferring allegiance to thus become an errant king's messenger, charged this night by fates and auspices with looking after the young lives crewing his vessel.

The amber moon turned to silver as it rose clear of the warmth of land and came over the darkened waters, this too enhanced the translucent aquamarine of night. It gave a mystical ambience to their plight in the heaving tender. An eerie luminosity took the children by surprise, as they both stared at the sky to take their minds off the journey. A few distant pinnaces were spied by Ingrams racing the horizon, though none came within but a few cable lengths of their own headway. Tenebrous, the wavering silhouette of the three-decked galleon beckoned as rhythmical circles of the oars made an almost foundering headway as they dipped on gathering swells of a slipping rip tide. Their quiet efforts overlooked by the distant purple haze of a horse-shoe shaped coastline and the ever dominating peak of Gold Cap. Another pathway of yellow light on the water took the form of a golden riviere, undulating from twin lanterns overhanging a ginger-bread stern as they rowed closer and closer. Majestically proud, the bulk of the man o'war became apparent as they swept underneath an enormous anchor rope to sloping sides of the hull. Reaching up to an opened-up lower decked gun port, Ingrams steadied the small craft as it fell and rose on a leeward swell. Looking up towards the bulwarks he checked for movement on the upper deck. The Portoise, housing a vast ordnance of cannonade pointed land-ward. A natural foreboding swept over them as the ship heaved and groaned on its stretched moorings. Wooden creaking flexed and combined with the slap of seawater on the thickened hull would hopefully hide their tenuous presence. In the middle distance a sea-shanty was loudly voiced by a rowdy crew obviously very drunk somewhere amidships. Ingrams

117

mused as he turned his attention once more to the children.

"Pass the maid Tom, help her over the clutter" Only to snort impatiently when the girl coward to draw away from him. "Slither thyself over the barrel to get yourself to my side." Ingrams demanded curtly.

"Why do you require her services, sir?" Tom inquired sliding a comforting arm around her shoulders adding proudly. "She be in my jurisdiction until I be able to return her to the safe auspices of the Mistress Pernickety."

Ingrams relented to advise of his plan. Gesticulating up through the gun port he said quietly,

"I be thinking mayhap she'd squeeze her little self into the gun port. Some-thing you and I good sir, would find mortal difficult in so doing. Then she was to make her way according to my orders I have yet to suggest." He stretched a hand out to assist her passage over the spirit barrel. "Either that or you can shin up the anchor rope - for that be the only other way we can board." Reasoning abounded. Tom checked agreement with the girl to then help her slide over the barrel and make towards the bow end. Eventually she stood waveringly upright alongside Ingrams as he flashed a short dagger under her nostrils.

"Take this knife child and only use it for thy defence if ye have to."

"Bless you, sir, I wouldn't know how even if opportunity afforded." She cast her eyes down in a perpetually girlish embarrassment.

"Then hide it on thy person for it might be just the job to open a clasp or cabin door lock in some haste." Ingrams watched her secrete the slender handled stiletto into the folds of her clothing.

"Tell me again why we need to go aboard ship, sir."

The rowing boat tilted violently and threw them into a huddle at the bow head. Sideways on - the tiny craft was endeavouring to resist inrushing shore-born tides. Reaching down he corrected the slippage with an oar and recovered a modicum of leeway. Ingrams then said with a hint of irritation in his tone.

"We need to find thy father girl. He be the one befitting to get documents from my person to the private notice of Old Harry Morgan himself."

"Captain Henry Morgan." Tom said from the stern of the row boat.

"Aye, Harry to his friends." Ingrams' look anticipated her co-operation then added, "And thou advised thy servant that thou wants to see thy parent again."

"Aye sir, ''tis the nature I began my long journey from Dartmouth. I will do as ye ask of me." She smiled prettily and he felt drawn to her innocence.

Ingrams circled strong hands around her waist ready to lift her towards the black gaping hole and part-protruding cannon muzzle. Resisting because she needed confirming directions once aboard the ship. It bothered her getting to her estranged piratical father, who, it appeared, did not believe her when she had advised him of her mission. Hesitancy and a firm grip prevented and delayed access to the spacious gun port. Confused and worried, voicing concern of how she would make it safely before a loose member of the crew might murder her as a spy. She was to be offered up as the smallest being aboard a vessel full of pirates and cut throats. But Ingrams and Tom himself were both men, she voiced feeling that her most worldly companions in the small boat were more befitting to this task. Why pray then could they not climb anchor ropes or scale the steep sides of the swaying ship to do the bidding.

"I know your thoughts little one, but a man even young Tom's size - seen to be clambering aboard a darkened boat this late in the evening would be shot on sight. Now a maid. Why they be curious and a superstitious crowd, these old salts, and think `''tis ill luck to have a women aboard ship without invite. Especially appearing at dead of night in bare feet, pantalettes and a grubby old calico nightshirt." Smilingly he reached out stretching his arms to transport Clarissa up to the lower gun port on the rise of a growing swell. Briefly she clung to the very end of the cannon barrel, then swinging her legs pendulum-fashion into the portico itself, was suddenly gone from their sight.

"Safest place for us now me lad be moored off the gingerbread stern." Ingrams said as he watched Tom gather the oars and made to guide the little row boat along the length of the huge ship.

"Thy maid will be alright so don't fear for her safety - fear for ours." He released his stretched up grip on the edge of the gun port and regained his seat. Taking the oars over he made to row. Tom squatted part astride of the liquor cask so's he might whisper-soft to the rowing man as slowly they edged along the over-hung hull.

"'tis of great mortal import that I see the maid Clarissa again, sir." Tom blurted to him in a hushed whisper.

"Aye, lad so ye shall. If it be love in thy heart thou be confessing then I D'Arcy Ingrams shall do all in my power to help thee. Ye be my hero o' the caves, thy very presence here in this craft humbles me. Aye, ye certainly were my saviour in climbing those craggy walls to offer thy help." The lad went to talk but was prevented by Ingrams shipping an oar to quickly place a hand over his mouth. They neared the watch quarter. Gently rowing with one hand and once past the danger, he released his grip allowing conversation.

"But it was the maid Clarissa and the giant sea bird that brought the rope to ye sir. She be lovely and I be fair smitten with her purity and loveliness."

Ingrams lowered his head to smile for a man never forgets his first love and no matter how young she be, that man will remember her until his dying day. Heaving-to he shipped both oars to look upwards at the gingerbread stern of the vessel, the fleeting moon light clearly showed a vessel name that was unrecognisable to the sea spy "THE MARACAIBO'. D'Arcy Ingrams found and held a loose whipping stern line and this checked their landward drift. Stowing the oars to the shallow gunwales, Ingrams slid into his frock coat and pulled it closer around his shoulders against an exposed breeze. The normal reaction set against growing coolness because they were now out of the lee of the ship. This chill reminded both occupants that their shirts were still muffling the oar tips. Moodily he watched the boy carefully releasing his own garment, ringing it dry, then with some difficulty pulled the damp linen about him. Proceeding to rub his sleeved arms furiously as if the friction would dry the fabric. Tom shivered as he looked to Ingrams for a modicum of sympathy. The spy's reaction was to offer a low grumble at the lad because he'd only untied one shirt - forgetting that he wore his frock coat now. Tom untied the other with little consideration, ringing it out briefly he passed it to the bow for yet further disapproval. None came. The garment was snatched impatiently away from him and slung casually over the half-ankar cask for the breeze to do its work. Ingrams then slid off the planked seat to reside lower in the craft and make himself as comfortable as was possible. Tom kept glancing first at the huge oval of sodden barrel wood amidships then at the dark-haired man trying to ignore his obviousness huddled in the stern. Finally Ingrams relented and with a sigh produced a bladed knife and proceeded to ease the cork bung from its housing. Advising the lad to sea-water wash the leather fish bucket, then to replace it conveniently under the gently oozing clear liquid sloshing and ferruling its way with the boat's movement. Sniffing deeply the night air Ingrams then placed his head deep into the bucket and snorted its bouquet. Holding a cautioning finger to his lip he whispered,

"We appear to be in luck young 'un for `''tis a scent o' French brandy wine."

Offering up the flexing bucket he gesticulated the lad should scoop liquid into a cupped hand yet should sup carefully, the reasoning behind his agreement for the lad to drink was that it would be a way of stemming the cold.

`Arghh." The lad threw the leather bucket at him. Ingrams" reflexes caught the vessel in mid flight, slopping liquid, however, did not stop and splashed his face. Obligated to lick the droplets as they went down his cheeks his grimace mirrored that of the lad.

"The liquid's turned into a damnable stinkibus." He slung the bucket down to the bilges after first sluicing it clean, then he banged the bung home with a firm thump from his clenched fist. "It happens that way sometimes, usually depending how long the casks been adrift under the seas surface." Shrugging his broad shoulders he added, "Some smugglers don't always locate their ship-dropped wares due to the sudden gales or tidal changes." He hoped this speech would allay his disappointment, in return he passed the remaining slice of homity pie the girl had afforded earlier. "Mayhap this will keep the cold from thy bones."

Tom miserably tucked into the dried out delicacy. "So what was in the barrel."

"White brandy from France laced with hidden caramel. Suppliers doth place a waxed tub of burnt sugar cane from the Indies, this gives the brandy its warming golden colour. Sometimes the rough seas break open this colouring tub and it forms a stinkibus taint to the liquor. ''tis meant to be added when the liquors run its smuggling course and delivered to inns like the Black Dog - dost thou see what I

121

mean."

"I would've seen." Tom grumbled lightly tucking gratefully into the last piece of homity pie. A smile lit his companion's face and he added the lad would have to put certain things down to life's experiences.

"Aye lad, at least though ye might just see the inside of a pirate ship. Be assured there bound to be a drop of the fiery liquid once thee and thy servant be safely aboard. That is if we don't be a getting ourselves a killed dead first." Ingrams settled down into the running boards, one hand holding onto the line affixed to a ship bound iron ring protruding from the aft. Deciding to tighten the painter, he reached up and made fast for the rest of the night.

"Clarissa." Tom murmured thoughtfully aloud, obviously he was still missing her.

"Aye lad ''tis up to the maid now. Best be settling thyself for a cool night ahead and try to get some rest." A perilous darkness descended on the bobbing cork in the inky-blackness all that could be heard was sea and ship noises.

●   * *
●

The rough cast-iron surface of the gun metal snatching at Clarissa's bared thighs, as she endeavoured to leapfrog along the length of the barrel, it grew wider to the breech stretching her thighs like the back of a broad horse. Finally to step gingerly down onto the wooden carriage and one of four pegged wheels, gratefully to touch the planked cambered deck from the swaying platform. Having carefully made out in the dimly lit area the ability to thus avoid ropes and other tackle securing the creaking cannon, she moved a heavy swaying hammock above her head to one side. She spied in the gloom of lit tallow stumps, row upon row of drawn-back cannons each side of the gun deck, dusty black, ominously half-illuminated by spluttering black lanterns.

"Oi. What are you doing here this night?"

A youthful voice complained from a position several feet above her head. Clarissa jumped out of her skin and spinning a circle to detect the direction of the voice, caught her breath as she found herself staring into a pair of dark eyes. The burning somewhat demanding look queried her being there that night. The blank facial expression of a young lad with a tousled head of black hair. A grubby looking youth, of approximately her own age looked down from a gently swinging hammock angry at being disturbed. Clarissa spoke before she was able to correct herself,

"Sorry, good sir, but if you please I be a stowaway." Her remark was on the advice of Ingrams. She waited to see if the excuse paid dividends. The boy relaxed, smirked, and appeared to relent.

"Sir? I b'aint no sir." Almost overbalancing, he rose to a part-sitting position to state proudly, "I be number one `powder monkey" on Teach's good ship `The Revenge".

"The good ship Revenge. That be strange for I was certain sure the name on thy vessel's bows did say Maracaibo."

"His Majesty's ship Revenge be here in these English waters unannounced." He retorted with more than a little contempt in his tone, swinging nimbly down from the precariously moving hammock, his raised arm prevented it swiping the girl's face as he did so. Affording her a puzzled stare and after a moment or two's silence he recalled his duty and asked authoritatively," Just what be ye a doing of here on board my ship. How can a young maiden spring from up out of one o' the seven seas - unless ye be a mermaid, of course."

The bedraggled look of her off-white calico nightwear, all sodden with sea-water and grime from clambering the caves and hostelry chimney now told a tale. The coarse calico linen clung to her fish shaped body like a dampened shroud, bare feet covered up by the lengthy hemline. Behind her back she wrung her hands in anticipation and fear of the unknown. Glancing over her shoulder back to the gun port, hoping for moral support from her companions. Then realising she was mortally alone in this sea venture, far flung from any safety of dry land. Braving it out she looked him square in the eye saying,

"Pray advise of thy name or title sir." Part-turning her head to avoid his darting gaze, also enabled her to seek an escape route should she need one.

"I aint got one - got a number though." The lad dressed in baggy knee-length breeches and loose fitting shirt gestured about him. "I'm number one." Then smiled at her confusion. "One to each gun d'ye see - a powder monkey."

"Son of a gun?" Clarissa said loud enough for the lad to hear.

"That's right." Nipper's slouched stance straightened brightly, his

123

tousled shock of sun-bleached hair and ever-moving dark eyes appeared to miss nothing as he spoke to her. Shuffling from one callused foot to the other, half-mast hung raggedy breeches and opened-to-the-waist shirt gave him the air of a youthfully nimble buccaneer. Not the stuffy uniformed King's Navy Marine, the girl was more used to seeing striding the narrow streets of Dartmouth.

"So ye know about ship children then, eh?" He sighed, folding his arms, endeavouring to look more important in front of this pretty young stranger.

The girl explained her reasoning behind knowledge of such nautical things.

"I overheard the term recently when my surgeon thought I was dying," She stated matter-of-factly, adding she'd been injured but was now on the mend.

It impressed the boy and he puffed out his pigeon chest, doing so whilst drawing her to sit alongside him on the gun carriage. They squatted summing up the way children do.

"What's a powder monkey."

"Thought you knew about ships,."

"I do not know about thy tasks aboard." She pursed her cupid lips. "I must say it sounds very important. Thou art very brave to hold such a commanding position." Softly the lies spilled yet the conviction was unquestionable.

Like minded, though the girl still felt she was losing her new found friend, the lying might placate the situation. He would be the only one to help her, yet she desperately needed to win him over first. Feeling sure the surly rogue Ingrams and the fawning Tom would be content to await her pleasure.

"The fighting men do so call me Nipper," he boasted proudly for he realised he had a name after all. Thoughtfully adding, "Then again they so do call every powder monkey as such because we do so `nip.'"

"Nip." Clarissa became curious.

"We powder monkeys nip flannel bags of black powder together for the firing of the big 32 lb-guns. Twelve stout seamen gun crew to each weapon on the gun deck on board 'cos it do so to fire such a large cannon." Nipper nodded towards the rotund barrel and showed prowess, "one of us lads to each gun crew means we prepare these black powder bags in advance, then stowed in the hanging magazine."

Pointing to the far end of the lower deck adding, "Takes one o' these charges rammed well home to the firing muzzle followed by wad, round shot then another wad all rammed in very tight, see. The gun captain pierces the bag with a pricker shoved down the vent hole, stuffing a hollow seagull's feather's quill containing black powder." Nipper took a deep breath concluding, "the cannon be then ready to fire.." Cocking his head knowingly to one side he grinned, "An alert gun crew can fire and re-load in under two solitary minute calibrations o' the ship's clock."

His companion was suitably impressed to say as much to the grinning lad. Then she gave a sudden start when a muffled noise interrupted their conversation. Nipper glanced over his shoulder to the shadowy lantern lit distant swinging of a hammock, and whereby a man's leg suddenly fell free and dangled outside.

"It's all right. Probably one o' the crew off-watch, mayhap still drunk on his ale or cider rations." A glance up and down the length of the narrowed deck showed the girl many such hammocks swung with the restless sway of the ship at anchor. "There be so many men in their beds - be they all drunk, too." Pointing down the lower deck illuminated by lights of many swinging lanterns.

"No, all beds be empty except for their belongings wrapped up and tied with a flaxen cord well apart from that one over there." Pointing to one solitary hammock nearby he then crossed himself with the sign of the cross many times rolling his eyes upwards, a gesture which failed to enlighten her and an explanation was left unsaid. Instead, Nipper mentioned something of equal import. "There be a meeting taking place on the quarter deck, our ship's captain be worried about crew getting mixed up with the skirmishing on the harbour side our crew be there on short shore leave, but our officers extend concern they'll not come back and we'll have to press a few back into service afore we sail home on the song o' the trades." Nipper became maudlin due to conveyed bewilderment. "Mayhap deserting to the Pretender's hurriedly assembled land army."

Becoming pensive he confided, "I've a task to do this night and that be to check on the maintop-gallants."

"Oh?" Clarissa failed to understand his nautical terms but took this to be sails.

"When topsails be lowered they be reefed in stays."

"What do they call the main sails?"

"If they be too deeply laden with stiffening breezes the call comes, "hands by the royal halyards, top-men aloft stand-by to clew up the royals and reef in those top-sails." Then the powder monkey became quiet for a moment, and suddenly he revealed the reasoning behind the meeting in the captain's stateroom quarters.

"A rowing skiff with a full compliment of eighteen sturdy yellow oars delivered two men to the ship earlier this night. Rumour has it one be the Duke o' Monmouth himself." Changing tack he inquired, "Wouldst thou like to see the stateroom and the finely dressed fellows of which I speak?"

Clarissa's confirming nod and inquiry of Black Ned prompted the lad to offer a proposition.

"We sail shortly after dawn if our crewmen return from shore at the sound of the midnight gun. If in agreement, I'll offer ye up to the captain. Mayhap ye'll sail with us back to the far off Indies." Haughtily the girl tossed her head in a very grown-up way, unseen before by the lad as more familiarly, the dusky maidens on the islands appearing much more forward in their approach to the seamen. Sulkily the girl batted her eyelashes, this inadvertent gesture too gave amusement to one unused to females. Clarissa confided her secret mission entrusting knowledge of two companions precariously situated nearby in the rowing boat. Briefly informing of the madman Jess Mandrake and the evil pursuance of her defenceless person. Also she told of the coach wreck and paper pardon for which her guardian had died. Concluding her lengthy monologue as a look of realisation crossed his face. Suddenly he gripped her shoulder crying out,

"Then we have the same mission. 'tis the very reason our ship be here waiting in English waters when we should be in Amsterdam looking for Morgan and his protectors."

"Hollands?" Clarissa queried linking two names familiar from the old inn.

"No Hollands be a drink o' gin. Old Harry's over there getting his picture fixed on canvas by a painter called Rembrandt. I heard tell twas for a step brother one Sir Thomas Morgan of Kinnersley Castle, Herefordshire." He puffed his jowls importantly, "Herefordshire be in another country called Wales." His phraseology was syrupy and confusing and it required careful interpretation.

"Painter." She smiled at the inference and lack of geographical knowledge.

"This fellow Rembrandt be a Dutch artist for fixing folk's likenesses to framed canvas," Nipper said sighing a little known confidence. "Morgan's nick-name be Harry though only to his friends."

"Not nipper, then," she blurted smiling mischievously. "'tis said he was a cabin boy, though now he be hoisted by his own petard."

They giggled waggishly and on cessation, found her hand gripped in that of the lad's who leant forward to confide in a much sombre note.

"If ye know where these papers are ye'd better say for it be good fortune and pure chance we be part o' the same mission this night." He squeezed the hand to lay emphasis on his words. "Because the sooner thou does the sooner we can rid ourselves o' these villainous waters and sail back to crystal oceans o' the Caribbean."

"Why are these papers important? So many innocents have died." She blurted.

Nipper pulled an apple from the folds of his clothing, bit generously into its flesh passing the remainder to the girl. Surprisingly fluent he went through the necessity of the missing yet coveted papers. How their captain was commissioned to convey the official documents to Morgan. Importance doubled as Charles was dead and his brother sat on England's throne.

"King James o' the Roman faith would give ol' Henry Morgan short shrift if he were found to be in England. Unlikely to feel affection for someone who behaved so blasphemously in the recent past, looting churches, using nuns as human shields whilst assaulting a fortress - monks and friars tortured. Though 'tis said he'd never knowingly pistolled a Catholic subject in his entire life. Yet Harry would." Indicating she should consume the apple as he continued. "Afore ye say I be a mixed in the ways of piracy on the high seas - mayhap I be mayhap I b'aint, just so happens we be escorting gold and silver bar bullion back from the Indies. Rumours abound the old king had an authenticated written agreement with Morgan. This ship be one of the converted treasure ferrying thus transporting Spanish booty from the Potosi gold and silver mines in far away Peru." He shrugged his thin shoulders,

"Perchance, fate took us by the hand whilst Morgan was ashore seeking the Amsterdam painter, Dutch authorities blockaded our ship preventing us leaving until the Protestants left for England. Eighty fighting men in two galleons armed to the teeth with mounts, cannon and ball left port only to be driven back in 24 hours by the great storm."

Clarissa nodded advising of her own experiences in the town of Lyme Regis. Pernickety advised as many as three thousand rushed to sign up to the pitch-fork army, joining the "cause" Pernickety saying as much to the girl. A hushed hour was spent deliberating their next move, finally the powder monkey confirmed he would help her and her companions in the rowing boat. Nipper took the girl's hand and led her across the cambered deck of blood and battle scrubbed planking. Together as one they began to climb a central companionway heading up to night air, then making their way toward the stateroom cabin in the ornate rear quarter. As they ran she still insisted he help her companions under the blue and gold painted gingerbread stern.

Chapter Nine   NOBLEMEN AND KNAVES

The sea the sea the rolling sea
'tis there to see like you and me
we're all at sea in little ships
what fragile ships relationships

Relationships mean you and me
me and you we're all at sea
the sea the sea the cruel sea
it comes between us you and me

It eats away relentlessly
unto ties that bind you to me
relationships mean you and me
me and you we're all at sea

The sea the sea the unforgiving sea
coming between us can't you see.
I can't forgive you, you can't me
then comes a rift in the family

Relationships mean you and me
you and me we're all at sea
like tears the sea the salty sea
erodes on touch you must agree

Working away remorselessly
keeping us apart for an eternity
relationships mean you and me
you and me we're all at sea

Poem: The Sea (after Rene Ashmore)

The black lacquered cabin door with its golden coloured brass
escutcheon plate surrounding a key hole afforded adequate viewing
for the kneeling girl as she crouched down on all fours. Clarissa had

found by alternating her spying betwixt an obstruction-free orifice, for there was no key inserted the other side, and that of a split-wood knot hole a little higher up at waist level afforded less chance of cramp. A banded lock confronting was without its heavy normal multi-faceted iron key which surely would have completely obscured her view of the men moving around inside the cabin. Pressing her face lightly once more against panelling and with bated breath, Clarissa listened intently to the muted conversation from behind the closed-off stateroom entry. A man's voice began his oratory.

"I am also assured by good authority the tale of Sir Henry Morgan, or his so called ill-usage of Spanish ladies at Panama is altogether a romance. For so careful was he that as soon as he had taken the town and quenched the fires he then caused most of the women of the city to be brought to one place and whereby he set the strictest guard over them. To prevent soldiers or others abusing them - gave orders prohibiting all men the offering of themselves leastways violent or injury of pain on sufferance of severe punishment. Under what loose Government his men are reputed to have lived. Affirming that few generals have kept their discipline more than he. Nor thought possible for him to have done all those great actions with men of so base and dissolute tempers as our Dutch historian friend paints them to be." Quoting from a voluminous book now slammed shut as the person reading hoped to apparently glean reaction to the quotable quotes within. His colleagues in the state room afforded his reading due-deference murmuring desuetude. A motley mixture of noblemen and knaves appeared to be holding an important meeting of minds, behind a locked door. Blue swirling smoke filled the air and underlined the fact the meeting must have taken place over a lengthy period of time. An overhung stateroom window was flung wide when awareness of the thickening atmosphere became apparent to the cabin's occupants. Unfortunately, this action gave rise to a fear that the cabin windows over-looked the jolly boat moored beneath them. This could prove a problem should anyone decide to hang out to breath in deeply the freshening night breezes.

Crouching down on all fours, her calico nightshirt gathered above her knees, even with concentration it was hard to discern how many men milled about occupying the spacious quarters - four probably five at most. Captain Dampier wandered into the restricting view now varying betwixt key and knothole alike as the girl bobbed up and down. Another attired in a claret coloured frock coat and blue powdered wig swaggered into view. This peacock addressed tersely by another as "my Lord Albemarle" along with another dressed of equal finery. Appearing now to be disagreeing with and heatedly maligning the quoted monologue and biographical details of one Captain Henry Morgan.

Although out of a direct line of sight, the girl felt it might be the one originally holding the book and from which he'd quoted so eloquently.

A braided and uniformed forearm came into her view through the knot hole, it reached to replenish a lead-crystal goblet of wine or possibly port on the captain's desk. A bell-shaped ship's decanter was used, re-stoppered and then placed briskly to one side. The dark serge uniform moved off, goblet in hand and the book tucked up under the armpit of the other arm, his slow pace across the decked planking paused within parameters of her limited sight. Luck portended she found herself able to glean the title by tipping her head to one side.

`Voyages and Adventures of Capt. Barth, Sharp and others in the South Seas"

Waiting and whistling low of her sucked-in breath, the kneeling girl realised she might be undone as a heart thumping minute passed, though finally it appeared no one had heard his misdemeanour. Nervously shifting her weight from one knee to the other made herself as comfortable as was possible in the circumstances. Her shoulder wound, adequately padded and bandaged now smarted with pain probably from the initial effort whilst clambering aboard ship. Momentary silence prevailed as extraneous noise was discussed though the cabin door remained firmly locked against all comers. Like minds seemed to conclude the disturbance had been conveyed from the open stateroom windows. A commanding voice spoke up and intervened the meeting was called back to the subject and the man in question. The conversation continued on the same tack as Dampier began to read once more having satiated his thirst, in so doing the prying young girl forgot her discomfort.

"You recall the expedition performed by Admiral Morgan against and the sacking of Panama, it was undertaken without commissioning from the then Governor of Jamaica, John, Earl of Carberry, Lord

Vaughan. It was upon account of new acts of hostility with fresh abuses that had been committed by the Spaniards against the king of England's subjects of Jamaica." Again he moved away to reach once more, presumably to whet his whistle from the goblet. Another moved into the restricted sight of the girl's watering eyeball, a rising draught from one of the opened windows made its presence felt through the oval-shaped knot hole. Through a misty haze she spied a man bristling with personal weaponry. A pistol thrust into a blue satin cummerbund embellished with a silver Damascus-twist binding ran its lengthy barrel. Finely embossed, a scabbard held a slim dirk and rapier style sword hung lower from crossed shoulder belts. Much earlier that evening Ingrams confided at length to them his meeting with the recently arrived Pretender. She and Tom voiced held affiliation with the news of a rebellious revival beginning in the West Country.

"It be truly exciting times." Tom had said with a juvenile fervour, "in which we so do live." Jittery as a titmouse at dawn, the girl set aside meandering thought and tried to converge her blurring vision on the cracked knothole.

An intervening voice commandeered her senses, she was afforded the apparition of a man she'd only dreamed of since his unexpected arrival on the pebbled shoaling beach close to the Cobb harbour wall.

"Enough. I have heard enough of this monologue of Morgan the terrible."

Monmouth looked tired and drawn. Realising things were not going as well with his blueprinted invasion. He had asked and was virtually promised help from privateers and pirates. Especially those buccaneers directly influenced by Henry Morgan and his `bilge rats" of Old Port Royal.

Monmouth's dour mood was clearly visible to the girl's naked eye. Silence and thoughtful pausing, perhaps choosing his next words or merely awaiting a reaction to his irritated statement of fact. D'Arcy Ingrams' words flooded back to the kneeling girl.

"Monmouth appeared to be personage of conserved bearing, yet soft of manner, a man no less, with fortitude and lustre such as befits a Prince - nay a king." Rowing across Lyme Bay Ingrams described his dark green velvet frock three-quarter-length coat, gathered at the waist. Trimmed with gold thread, crossed shoulder straps a bayonet thrust in one - long sword to the other. Also a blue Ribbon of State.

Red breeches, calf length brown leather boots broadly opened at the top and exactly as mentioned. Movement in the cabin concentrated her focus again, and suddenly the wine glass was whisked down as Monmouth tired of the orator with the book.

"Either Henry Morgan is with my venture or not. Time and tide wait for no man - especially one endeavouring to reclaim the throne for the people."

Monmouth hung his head as if undone, finding himself filled with a burning desire to abandon the meeting, leaning forward scooped up a feather bedecked Musketeer-style soft brimmed hat, then turned toward the cabin door.

"I find myself reluctant to tarry away precious time whilst the vilest of creatures sits upon my father's throne." Monmouth bowed courteously to the others making ready to take his leave. Still the girl found herself hanging on his every word and movement, remaining affixed to her spying through the aperture.

Despite Ingrams advising her that the Pretender mentioned a meeting with loyal Hollanders in the Amsterdam Free States, Henry Morgan knew Holland and thus acquainted kindly with the Dutch. Now though Morgan had disappeared to have his image placed on canvas for posterity. Saying as much to the others concluding with, "Gentlemen, I thank thee for thy hospitality, however time presses heavily on my person and there are many other reasons I stride England's green sward." He sighed heavily and flapped his hat at the side of his knee as he strode to pace catlike. "We thank thee humbly for thy shipments of arms, Ned, and for thy loyalty to England and her troubles and also the good offices of thy own Captain Dampier. Also the welcome treasure trove, or rather the generous portion allocated to the protestant crown and the English cause." Monmouth said, his voice crisp with sincerity.

Captain William Dampier, hydrographer and entrepreneurial buccaneer, shook hands with the Duke of Monmouth dipping a bowed head in salute, "Sire the gold Louis", German nobles, silver cob pieces of eight, were but the English crown's share of Spanish booty the late king Charles commissioned. I am merely completing my mission as a mark of respect to his memory. The King is dead - long live the King." A half hearted cheer was murmured about the interior of the cabin. Dampier released the grip, taking one pace backwards with a dapper bow.

The Duke of Monmouth was duly impressed at the courtesy of a true gentleman.

"Aye, captain, yet ye have a princely price on thy head and should steer speedily clear of these Dorsetshire ports." Monmouth suddenly realised his caution purported to both. He looked first to Black Ned and then back to Captain Dampier.

All three burst out laughing. Dampier confirming,

"Aye my Lord we all seem to wear that cap of fate."

Raucous was the merriment until it finally died and seemed to culminate with agreement from Monmouth who concluded,

"Late grows the hour, I should return to shore with pay for my forces and to begin my quarrelling war with my feckless uncle." Addressing another of the cabin's occupants out of sight to the kneeling girl. "I understood you too have a commissioned task for Henry Morgan." Bowing courteously Black Ned released Monmouth's grip and did swipe the nearby desk with a bared fist.

The action made Clarissa jump as she clapped a stifling hand over her own mouth to stop the gasp, beguiled by the rich tones of her step-father's booming voice. "Ol' Harry's in a deal o' trouble now this manuscript be published in the Dutch land o' Holland." Tapping the book with a vicious dagger, "telling o' his exploits and chronicling the like o' his compatriots like yours truly and his many swabs under direct control." Ned tilted his tricorn back from his brow and the spluttering candlemas of tallow lanterns caused the gold in his earring to glitter brightly. A flashing sprang from under a mass of hair coupled with a blackthorn growth of beard, red twists of coiled ribbon in his black beard gave a splash of colour as he strutted about cursing his luck for being away from his beloved South Seas. Black Ned twirled and tugged at a rogue curl with a thoughtful forefinger,

"Aye sire, ye must return forthwith yet not afore ye breaks bread and downs a bowl of rum with thy compatriots. 'tis way over the yardarm the red sun be down and placed to bed." Pouring liberal goblets of dark and golden liquid, slid drinking vessels across the desk one-by-one. Scooping the last bowl to his own lips he downed the draught in one single gulp.

"Harry Morgan be feared o' these shores as all we so might. Last visitation he were placed in the Tower o' London, so he was. Not an

134

experience to be repeated in a hurry I'll be bound, considering times in which we so do live." Blackbeard poured another measure of rum. "My crew and I be fair proud to serve under the auspices of Capn. Dampier here. We been paid handsome for getting the new understanding promised by the late king to his lieutenant governorship in Jamaica, 'tis said he don't want to die in the darkness o' disgrace. Any-road-up, Morgan won't trust this Duke o' York or treacherous offices alike." Ned faced head on the Duke of Monmouth. Out of character he tilted his head downwards in a most humbling salute. Unused to giving in to such self-effacing spontaneous gestures, it showed in the faltering of his next words.

"Henry Morgan wishes thy mission success milord. However conveys to thee a warning as follows, `my enemies be your enemies yet mine be a king's ransom away" Ned raised his eyes, "Why do I so feel that this smacks o' innuendo."

Monmouth smiled and touched his shoulder,

"Aye ye could be right about the possibility of innuendo. So how should thy servant translate this obscure verbal message from one so worldly as Morgan."

"One o' soul searching and watching out for thy back against closest friends."

Ned suggested raising his rum bowl in salute once more, then with gathering distrust in his tone suddenly rounded on another in the cabin. "Perhaps my Lord Albemarle can enlighten us." The sparsely fitted cabin fell silent with suspicion, falling on one who was in attendance by default - not by the more cordial of invitations.

"Already Sir Henry Morgan along with Captain Dampier have enjoyed all life's pleasures, from debaucheries to battle on the high seas." Albemarle nodded a hurrying courtesy for abruptness of his choice of words then continued,

"There are pre-supposedly copies of these aforementioned `letters of patent and marque.". Thus giving royal permit for the scouring of oceans for gold and silver by wreaking havoc on enemy shipping. James would appear to be making advances to France and Spain to put an end to the constant warring of our merchant vessels." The paraphrasing for privateers was left unchallenged.

"These rogue man o' wars found in the Indies. Jamaica, Tortuga, Hispaniola, Isle de la Vache and seaward entrances to the new Spanish

Americas." Clearing his throat slightly more nervously added, "Treasure-trove indeed, gentlemen, such glories ever behest by noblemen and knaves alike. Mayhap thou shalt hold in thy memory that the crown doth benefit to the tune of one sixth portion of any booty reclaimed. Yet according to rumour abounding the royal court - James is willing to forgo any such insurgencies into foreign policy and give up rights to the shuttling of anymore gold to these shores."

"What!" Ned Teach was sorely shocked at the disclosure. Then seeing the funny side he burst out laughing. "Then 'tis more for Morgan I say. And the devil take the hindmost for he'll not stop plundering the Spanish or the dastardly treacherous French.." Black Ned walked across the cabin to where the book lay opened up. Thumbing through to a page read out earlier quoted,

"Let the Great Morgan and Famed Buccaneer in his late enterprise make this appear - and who with but a handful of brave Englishmen frighted the whole of American Spain. And when he was upon the Indian Shore had he from England's King thus derived his awesome power. Charles II had been Crowned the Indies Emperor though the French king's boast of last year's campaign and what he's done to Old Spain - Great Morgan's fame shall last as long as there is beat of drum or any sound of War in the hearts of true hot-blooded English men."

Ned replaced the book having made his point then added informatively,

"In May 1685, last month, with honour saved and Charles our late King obviously bearing malice not toward him - Henry Morgan's spirits had lifted. So's not to die in the darkness o' disgrace." Referring ye to the court hearing whereby ol' Harry were so vindicated. Compensated with title and monetarily yet seeks, nay demands - promised pardon from several months ago in January this year."

Monmouth strode into her view, Clarissa heard him retort as if now totally exasperated by the whole affair. "In the year of our Lord Circa 1622, the Mayors of Lyme Regis and Weymouth reported these towns were despoiled and impoverished in attacks by Barbary corsairs. Turks no less from bases in the far off Muslim ports of Tunis, Tripoli, Sallee and Algiers, where the demand for English male and female slaves was immense." Moving to pace the floor he continued, "even reported sixty men, women and children were carried away from a Sunday's church congregation in Penzance, Cornwall." Clearing his throat added solemnly, "They goodly English folk were never seen or heard of again."

Albemarle interrupted his patience strained by one barbarian defending another of the same ilk.

"Your point sire - your point."

Monmouth placed an assuring hand on his shoulder.

"The point my dear Albemarle is buccaneering pirates and their reputation. A reputation that and which precedes them. Terrifying, legendary, abounding from the very earliest segment of our seventeenth century." Allowing his hand to slide free he continued,

"Indeed I tried to extol to my associate Ingrams just such a premise."

Albemarle, taken by surprise by a familiar name of his counterpart from the court of King James - recovered enough and in professional manner, calmed his voice before redress.

"Where exactly did you see this D'Arcy Ingrams fellow."

"In Lyme town, my lord Albemarle. It was the briefest of encounters. Nary a one I should care to repeat. The damnedest thing happened. T'were not for this Ingrams I should be skewered like a pig on a bed-spiked ambuscade."

Albemarle grunted under his breath whilst thinking aloud, "Then this D'Arcy Ingrams be close by?" Speaking loudly now as he further inquired, "where is this man who offered thee some speck o' salvation, sire."

"Alas dead, sir. He forewent his soul for thy servant. And very heavily it weighs upon my conscience these past few hours. His words will haunt me to the grave."

"What pray were the words so profoundly to thy mind, sire."

Albemarle needed to know if Ingrams was definitely laid to rest.

Additional from his patron Lord Duras, were thus to despatch his mission and the spy if he should deviate from the task in hand. Suspicions were he was a man for turning and not to be trusted, though this fact was realised too late.

"T'was a damnable four poster entrapment. T'were not for the man disturbing my repose, I, instead of he, should have tumbled to the depths of Hades." Monmouth shuddered saying,

"Spikes as long as a man's arm pierced and tumbled from the

137

canopy onto the mattress pinning him before the evil contraption spun on its axis. We found the caves underneath the old black dog hostelry in Silver Street. The local cellarman showed the place where his body should be hung. Yet my delay and the changing o' the tides already had whisked his soul out to seas deep coffers, never ever to be seen again." Throwing his arms high in an expression of sheer and futile hopelessness.

"The words, sire?" Albemarle asked. "The words which are memorable to ye."

"Luck wings the adventurer in his moment of despair." The cabin went quiet perhaps as a mark of respect for the dead adventurer.

Clarissa became uncontrollably excited knowing the circumstances which surrounded Ingrams predicament in the cave. A quiet man he had not extolled such derring-do detail afore his downfall. To him he was a hero. Her buckling knees were chilling from blood starvation, feeling them creak as she shifted about endeavouring to get comfortable. Wishing Nipper had already concluded his watch in the Crow's nest of the huge ship and would return to offer her the chance to relate their earlier adventure story. Missing his company, any company, for she was but a stowaway and would be treated as such if caught that dark night on board a pirate ship. Putting behind her thoughts of personal comfort, again she settled to her task of gleaning as much as she could through the peephole in the cabin door, also she hoped to hear more from her step-father, Black Ned. She had succeeded in finding him and was not about to give him up lightly again.

"It was and is Morgan's repute and that of his men I counted upon for to lead and inspire my polyglot of willing labourers and craftsmen alike."

Monmouth pushed to the back of his mind that which initially brought him to England, feeling by returning to London overland, he and he alone could persuade his Uncle James Duke of York to accept curbs on his Catholic powers. In fact to give guarantees of religious liberties perhaps to return to an army command for himself and a loyal friends - but it was not to be. Radical influential supporters claimed the crown of England itself, indeed instructed Monmouth to take and resume Protestant revival causation there. So here he was - swept along by the power of persuasion and here he would stay until the noble job was completed, finalised to the best of his ability. Captain Dampier moved into view of the knothole and placing a comforting hand on the shoulder of Monmouth, saying.

"This has been a meeting my lord Duke and other gentlemen - of great minds. Such diversity of intellect no pirate's chest o' booty or portmanteau filled with gold bars could persuade me to be absent from such a gathering." Turning to the desk he withdrew a black bottle sealed with a red-wax cap from a creaking drawer. Turning to the other end of the cork-screw, used it as a mallet, tapping brittle wax into a thousand splintering shards. Inserting the corkscrew he withdrew the cork with a loud `plop" and poured blood-coloured claret to a crystal goblet. Passing it up to the Duke he said softly,

"I salute ye sir and thy noble cause." Pouring another raised it in salute. Monmouth's introverted look gave Albemarle the chance to assess the situation without risk of immediate redress. Distraction was a strategy best known to all who soldier whatever side unto which their loyalty doth fall.

"Where pray are thy cavalry officers whilst you tarry on board."

Albemarle inquired innocently placing his treasonable allegiance on the line.

"My Lord Grey expounds with a small force against local militiamen in nearby Honiton. A taste for skirmish which will no doubt test the Royalist appetites for a fight - he leads a mounted foray with backing of soldiers afoot."

Monmouth became alerted to the fact he was being drawn further.

"Anton Buyse my Dutch gunner and his cannonade will direct ordnance with four huge guns my colours will be flown by the Blue, Red, Yellow, White and Green Regiments of foot. These totalling some three thousand men at this hour. yet we have much hope of more joining our cause en-route to Taunton. Though we have now at our command some 600 fine horse. Lord Grey of Wark, will no doubt have a tasty report for my eyes on my return and our meeting of minds."

Every eye in the cabin accept Monmouth's turned towards Albemarle for an explanation to the inquiry which was of no concern except to the Duke's army.

Suddenly it came after he sprang away from the group clutching a knife to the throat of Dampier, who in mid swallow, was taken completely by surprise.

"I be utterly at variance with thee - James, Duke of Monmouth. So I'm thinking it be best if I doth take my leave of ye forthwith.." A frock coat cuff ruff probably hid the knife that grew in Albemarle's hand. It graced the suppleness of the stretched throat of their Captain. A firm left fore-arm gripped his upper body. The `Coup de Main" took others in the modest stateroom cabin by complete surprise. Black Ned was first to recover his senses and wiping rum from his chin moved quickly to draw high his cutlass,

"Blast yer eyes ye fop and dandy! I never did place much store by them's as overdressed as a delicate sprat such as thee."

"Get back or I slit his throat." Albemarle warned backing away towards door.

Clarissa's scream was muffled yet not as much as she thought and this muted noise outside the cabin door afforded warning to the perspiring Albemarle.

Changing his mind and venue, he now headed for the opened stateroom window.

Silence befell the group as Monmouth touched Ned's shoulder, solemnly he shook his head at thought of any heroics until they assessed the situation.

Relaxing, Ned reluctantly backed off then glanced directly at the knot hole in the cabin door and wondered if he saw a blue eye staring back. Lowering the vicious looking cutlass, though whites of his knuckles showed clearly he was far from relaxed and still in killing mood. Monmouth broke silence with thoughts of distraction so's the situation might be neutralised, this was done by the mentioning out loud his musing thoughts.

"A kindly soothsayer recently warned of a traytor in the mist. I'm thinking his words were mayhap the misinterpretater and must have meant - midst."

Monmouth growled sliding his hand towards the cummerbund and his pistol butt.

"Thy soothsayer also warned ye of the `Rhine" yet thou doth reside a thousand leagues from Germany." Albemarle retaliated mockingly. Monmouth was astounded at what he felt was a private and confidential meeting betwixt a fortune teller and his client. News travels fast certainly and more so especially, bad news.

"A curse on thy treacherous friendship, sir, coupled with a plague on thy fortunes." Monmouth relaxed only when the oathing seemed to provoke the situation, also when too Dampier's eyes bulged due to pressure on his oesophagus from the quivering knife blade. Indomitable, the sailor became aghast at his predicament. Incredulously letting himself be so gullible. He, a pirate mariner and noted hydrographer, attributed to glorious ventures circumnavigating of the world almost thrice, chronicled dictionaries of the day listing his words such as, bread-fruits, avocados, pear, yam - even bringing to the world's notice the existence of the Pink Flamingo. Finally naming the worst storms ever spied at sea as `Typhoons".

Steely blue eyes flashed a warning to the others to keep their distance although his quick brain desperately sought his own solution. Was he to die ignominiously, not with a cutlass or brace of pistols blasting away at the sworn enemies of His Majesty the King. Albemarle, for his part, now reached behind and moved the window to extend fully open. His intentions very obvious - yet would he jump into the sea after he'd slit the throat of their captain or would he release his captive.

"Take care o' the scaffold; it be only a treacherous tongue away."

Ned's words were a veiled warning to the man deciding whether to plummet down the gun metal swells or not, throwing up his hand for silence, Monmouth gathered his thoughts. Black Ned would not be gagged and started chanting dire oaths and portents once more,

"Pirates, merchantmen and sea-generals on land always were twice as devious as Barbary corsairs."

Clarissa was fascinated by the subterfuge which had taken place. She clung to the doorknob and glued her eyeball to the split knothole with bated breath. Fear now forced her senses to succumb at last to removing the hidden dagger Ingrams had given her. Suddenly a hand clamped over her mouth and nose and she was lifted bodily into the air, a foul-tasting fishy cloth stuffed to her mouth and forced between her teeth to silence her welling screams. Her senses reeling, the last thing she remembered before passing out from lack of oxygen was the pinned-up sleeve of a frock coat. Only one person was known to her to be disabled so and that surely was "Jess the Pearly".

Chapter Ten   ROUGH DIAMOND

Rain washed clouds clear o' soil
Sun peeps out to dry and boil
"tis a goodly wash it'll surely be
billowing white for all to see
Four winds fluff them bright
putting grime and cares to flight
Poem: Clouds

* * *

"Man over board - man overboard!" came lusty distant cries urgently coloured with excitement topside. Reverberating down to the bowels of the ship, hearty screams and the accompanying rush of many feet, scrabbled back and forth on the deck planking.

These enhanced noises appeared to have brought the girl round from her dead faint. Clarissa blinked her eyes open to find herself bound head to foot with fuse cord, secured face-up sprawling the length of the broad-backed 32 pounder situated at the gun port and by which she'd entered the ship in the first instance. Presumably due to the huge piece of ordnance happening to be the furthest carriage mounted gun from the ship's lower deck companionway. The apple-core spied beneath was brown and dried with the passing of many hours whilst she crouched at the door, definitely the same jointly consumed earlier that night. Lying atop the cannon trussed like a chicken, the girl wriggled to loosen the lime-stinking cord bindings. Though the overall background smell below decks of the ship still rolling gently at anchor was one of stale spice, Ingrams commented earlier about her being a converted or taken East Indiaman, must have been correct after all.

Jess Mandrake had pursued her from the shore and now he leered down with a blood-shot eye as once again she lay firmly in his clutches. Annoyance crossed the solitary stare as he spake to her in hushed tones afraid of being overheard up on the top deck. Opened gun ports echoed sounds to anybody leaning o'er the larboard rail, gun-decks cleared of sleeping forms in slung hammocks, hearty jeering from above indicated midnight revelry of sorts - off-watch drinking and dice gambling.

"I observe thy senses return to thee little one." Jess waved the stiletto under her nose to lay emphasise that she lay quite defenceless. Clarissa shook a sleep-tousled head and blinked back misty tears. Looking away all she could observe was a dank darkness everywhere, most of the swinging lanterns had been extinguished as fire precautions aboard ship, regulations surrounding storage of black gun powder-kegs were strict, according to her friend the grandiloquent powder monkey, Nipper. Where was he in her hour of need. Recalling rotating watch cycles up the main masthead, betwixt boys and men during the full twenty-four hours aboard ship. Standing over the gothic apparition held a black countenance like the devil himself, over-sized dark tricorn and angled now looking for all the world like horns. Gun-carriage wheel grease, smeared over his face, it was an attempt to conceal his blanched features in the darkness, above all Jess appeared to be breathing fire. Chill sea air saturated the open gun ports and changed his quickening pants to that of a snorting mist. Recollections of the coach crash and struggling of downed horses that rain-lashed night appeared identical to the scene unfolding in front of the girl. Flared nostrils puffed inches long blasts of water vapour fell like invisible feathers onto her cheeks. Only by holding her own breath could she avoid the dreadful experience of breathing in the gaseous odours of garlic. The black patch in place, yet slanted above the man's hooked nose, the bony contours of his face part-concealed under a layer of dark salve yet still his deathly pallor showed. An epitome of evil the girl realising finally that he would be the last thing she would see on this earth. His foul smelling breath came closer and closer turning into hate-whispered threats as his face descended until nose to nose.

"Thou might have escaped my clutches down the chimney, and then the darkness of the caves thwarted me catching up with thee due to rising tides. By taking a differing route to the water front I spied ye rowing towards this pirate ship." Simpering triumphantly he expounded, "yet I still followed and caught up with ye my little vixen." Tapping a life-less sleeve with the blade laid emphasis to why she was to be duly sacrificed. "I knows what ye be a thinking about little one, how does old Jesse here row a jolly boat with one arm." More flickering annoyance sprang when he caught her smile.

Glancing away to hide the growing smile as her imagination ran riot, visions within saw a one-armed man circling in ever-widening arcs toward the horizon...

The knife blade caught her under the chin, lifting it slightly to catch the glint of the vengeful anger darting in his one good eye. Desperately tried to hide the smile only to be slapped with the hilt of the small knife originally handed to her by D'Arcy Ingrams. Jess became angry and told her that, "She'd best be quiet and show respect or he'd do for her there and then." The smile flickered once more waning only when she spied a satanic darkness in the depths of his hard look, irrevocable, the smile waned as she regained the seriousness of her isolated plight. Jess grunted satisfaction at the maid's new-found poise. "Thy name be not be "Peach"; thou be Ned Teach's brat and for which he should pay a goodly ransom." Grunting satisfaction at the widening of her eyes, advising her he intended to then kill two birds with one stone. "Thy escape from the inn surprises not thy servant sir, yet how didst thou follow out across the sea to find us aboard ship." Endeavouring to distract him was immediately trounced. "Hush up thy fork-tongued words, child, for whilst thy lips flatter me the poison of adders lurks under thy meanings." Jess tore free his red head band and rolled it to then thrust it deep into her open mouth. Straightening up he glanced about the shadowy darkness to observe the rows of slung hammocks that appeared to burst with personal effects. All except one - for this was stitched and securely bound with black fuse-cord. It was a shroud and ready for sea burial, its dead occupant oblivious to all the goings on about them. Grunting satisfaction, Jess decided inwardly that this was to be the way he would dispose of the maid Clarissa. It would take little effort to slash the stitching and insert her limp body. Noticing the girl beheld him with curiosity, sought to distract her.

"In the Cobb harbour I spied a small craft with a single oar fixed to the stern. I realised to manoeuvre the boat required a twisting-turning grip and I thus deployed out and seawards." Jess straightened to grin a real sense of achievement for a one-armed man.

Then he puffed himself up with misguided pride and grinned evilly advising her,

"Took me best part o' four hours o' the clock."

Clarissa's chin moved out of the way of his sharp cut-throat blade, blustering and gasping breath passed her lips this to the continued amusement of an infuriated Jess.

"Twas the purest knowledge which pleasured me thus and that I'd be soon placing thy scrawny carcass to a watery grave, to complete a sworn revenge that kept thy servant going against elements and chances of a flash storm rising in the bay."

Clarissa began to think quickly for every minute delaying him might allow her to cling to her life. Also the greater the chances of someone arriving to discover her plight. Recalling that Tom and Ingrams waited below in the jolly boat outside the gun portico, decided she would scream for help if she could spit out the roll of cloth. Her heart falling as she recalled Ingrams and Tom's intentions to moor and hide the tiny craft under the ship's stern. Jess knelt alongside and glared into her blue-grey eyes, the voice now became deathly soothing as he endeavoured to caress and toy with her senses.

"Dost thou know little one, officers once aboard be allocated a berth on the quarter-deck. Ship's carpenter then builds a wooden cot for his exact size. Officer lines and pads the cot with linen for comfort and is over-hung with a cloth canopy to keep peering eyes away." Jess gleaned casual interest as well as desperation in her expression before continuing, "Ordinary seaman, bless his wicked heart, has to make do with a hung sail-cloth bed. Bound hammocks contain all his worldly possessions. Hanging all around ye here on this lower deck like grubby washing in four winds." His voice lowered with emotion and this intonation instilled fear into the girl's fast-beating heart. So this was his intention.

He leaned menacingly forward licking his lips with a darting tongue and glaring with the one good though broken venules in his mono-visioned eye. "Should some terrible plague or accident befall our intrepid seaman once at sea." Jess squinted watching her expression change to one of horror as he began to relate the connection, Jess continued, "then corpse be sewn-up in his own bed to make a shroud. A cannon ball be placed at his feet to weight his corpse as thou needs cast-iron to send him hurtling towards the sea-bed." Unbeknown to the rambling highwayman, the girl had slipped her fuse-cord bonds deciding to choose that very last moment in one desperate attempt to escape.

Screaming heartily the girl tore her hands free and leapt to her feet making to run. Somehow anticipating this move, Jess dropped the dagger and scooped her once more up to bind her tightly under his armpit.

Nonchalantly he began carrying on with his monologue unabated by her dumb insolence.

""'tis said I be related to Catesby - Robert Catesby o' the gun powder plot back in the year 1605. He were a fine fellow who with Guido Fawkes and others did endeavour to blow up the House o' Parliament in London. Now I be about to do the same thing with Blackbeard's vessel the old *Revenge* so I be." With that he propelled the girl back down onto the wooden wheel of the gun carriage and drew his pistol, threatening her with ball and shot if she dared move again from that spot. Recovering he pushed the horse pistol back into his belt, then began systematically pouring black powder from the smaller half-kegs used for priming touch holes on the ranks of primed cannonade. Carefully winding his way between the rows of cannons, Jess snaked black gun powder from one opened keg to another at each gun station. Unseen Clarissa carefully awaiting a turned back reached down to retrieve the dagger and hid it away in her clothing safely. Completing his task he dropped the emptying keg alongside her then bent to look for the dagger. Turning once more on the girl when he failed to locate the missing weapon, perhaps discounting it as he gathered the cringing maid up into and under his armpit once more. Like a pet goose with its neck thrust forward he moved to the hammock ready for burial. Its off-white canvas shroud sealed and weighted like a cocoon suspended from the bulk-head beams hung heavy at the foot. Roughly by the highwayman held the squirming girl in his ever tightening grip, hand over her mouth as she now became frantic at his unbridled wickedness. For if he was to kill her then she would not allow him to prolong it the way he played cat- and-mouse. Tilting both their heads alongside the canvas coffin forced both their faces against the rough surface of the shroud.

"Difference being, my little one, is ye'll still be alive when ye hurtles to be eaten by the creatures o' the deep." Then sharply and without any warning the white shroud abruptly doubled then jack-knifed back into life. The twisting gyrating figure-of-eight movements up against the rope ties astonished Jess. Aghast, he dropped the girl his expression twisted in confused foreboding at the spectre in front of him. Especially after Clarissa's piercing screams penetrated every nook and cranny of the lower gun deck.

As Jess drew back in fright and shrunk down into the shadows of the gun-carriage, another noise from across the far side of the cambered deck greeted him. Prone in a head-up and terrified posture, the girl sprawled on the deck planking where she had been unceremoniously tipped by her abductor. She could do little but gaze hand-up-to-her-mouth at the rotation of the white shroud as it spun round and round in its hammock.

The jack-knifing began again between random circling. But had a corpse come back to life? Diamond beads of moist perspiration burst forth on the brow of the highwayman, as primeval survival instincts took control of his bodily functions creating havoc with his stomach. He wanted to be sick yet couldn't, he wanted to flee with haste yet his bowing legs failed him. Suddenly a lit lantern with its iron bands circling the flame, wobbled then smashed downwards to the deck and extinguishing itself. A moment later another light fluttered and died as if by magic.

In the half light across the far side of the shadow born deck a black silhouette of a male figure stood in the stairwell of the central companion-way, backlit by the upper gun deck and a red glowing embers alongside his eyes. The profile began to come into clear view, eyes glinted even at that distance, whiskers like a frightful meteor of black hair adorned the face. Fizzling tassels of black fuse cord protruded from underneath a jet black tricorn, wreaking odours of saltpetre and lime-water drifted across the dank air space. A red and yellow brilliance wreathed the apparition's head in a swirl of smoke. At some twenty feet distance away, the spectre began to glide forward towards them as if on oiled castors. A shadowy figure which held a cutlass erect over its head and noticeable coming closer by the minute to their side of the deck. Lanterns nearby caused the poised blade to glint revenge. It was Jess'' old adversary `Blackbeard the pirate'' and his worst wide-awake nightmare there confronting him once again; quickly drawing his horse-pistol, Jess placed it on full-cock. He held his fire and aim until the apparition was within range. Finally the girl slowly rose to her feet looking first to the spectre drifting across the deck towards them and then at the staring eye of Jess. Mayhap she was better off for leastways her tormentor was afeared for his life as well as she. Watching unravelling events she noted also that a third of the gun deck lay in darkness, all main lighting was on their side of the deck. This factor made it difficult for the highwayman to see clearly, rubbing his good eye to clear vision ready for an inevitable foray - placed the pistol to the cannon breech, drew a short epee from one of his thigh-length boots. He thrust it into the leather belt which also held his cutlass. No longer did he place faith in the lengthier rapier blades. Should he find it impossible to re-load in time his additional choice weaponry might be a life saver.

Taking up the pistol he whispered a warning to the girl,

"Move an inch and thou takes the first ball."

Muttering yet he dare not take his eye from the lengthening spectre as it loomed closer and closer to their side of the deck. By now the highwayman and the maid could hear equally the rasping breath of someone who had had too much to drink. Suddenly a loud clatter of a wood drinking bowl hitting the deck a few inches from where they stood - startled both man and maid alike. Jess spun on his heel first to the drinking vessel then regaining poise, looked towards darkness from whence it came. The neck nape hair under the bandanna and tricorn bristling like a dog ready for battle. Now conscious all the more of the perspiration traversing and tickling irritatedly as he strained his look and every facial muscle so's not to reveal inward fear. Clamped teeth, narrowed eye he waited for the attack beyond the darkness to begin. At long last out of the gloom and into view came a swinging lumbering figure wearing a red coat and black tricorn hat. Fuses fizzed and smouldering underneath its brim and this confirmed, as suspected, it was his old adversary from the port of Bristol -Ned Teach. Slowly his fore-finger tightened and the first then second impression was taken up on the trigger.

Jess levelled the pistol and aimed to shoot at the fiery head which came drunkenly closer - suddenly and without warning a huge hand, thumb forward, placed itself between flash pan and hammerlock mechanism preventing it from working. Spinning around, Jess looked from the useless weapon to the physique of a huge towering man alongside, then back to a distant thud which made him look toward what turned out to be a scarecrow swinging gently on a rope gun tackle. Its body an inverted muzzle rammer with guncotton mop-top, wooden ladle pole for the body, Ned's black tricorn atop - smartly adorned with a red tunic coat with four rows of shiny brass buttons. Looking for all the world like the pirate himself in the murky gloom of a lower deck. It even swayed toward them in a sauntering fashion of an old seadog due to the roll of the ship on its moorings. The realistic side-to-side sway was that which fooled him, but what was the noise the thud he'd heard.

"T'were a round shot angel hitting the deck which operated my ghost self, Jess." Blackbeard pointed to the crumpled bundle of clothing sprouting the 6 foot long wooden pole back bone. "Now Don't you think he be a handsome chap."

Both their clamped hands stretched out in front of them until Ned deliberately lowered the hold on the pistol. Then with a flick of his wrist, wrested and disarmed him in one deft movement. They faced each other and the grip to his right wrist remained firm and unwavering. But still affixed a powerful grip to his right wrist.

"There be a saying highwayman I be familiar with, `Pyrates take care o' the scaffold for it be only a treacherous tongue away" and thou hast a mighty treacherous tongue in thy head."

Jess wriggled and tried to free himself, a desperate ploy to distract his enemy. "Aye Ned Teach, yet merchantmen be nought but pirates on land - they be twice as devious as any sea heathen or black hearted Barbary corsair."

"Thee keep thy philosophising to thyself ye black hearted swab for I b'aint interested in silver-tongued words." Ned dragged the highwayman around by the scruff of his neck as he tramped about scuffing the trail of black powder into oblivion. Thwarting his plan to scuttle the thwarts of the huge ship. Jess Mandrake was dragged back on his knees to be slung roughly down onto the gun carriage, for it was the only gun station lit by swinging lanterns.

Still on her knees, Clarissa threw her arms around the thigh boot of her step-father calling him by his notorious title of Blackbeard. She clung there terrified that she might lose and not spy him again. Ned, not daring to take his burning glare away from Jess patted the tousled head of the girl and cooed her to be calm again. Brushing moisture away he looked deep into her tearful cherubic face.

"There, little one, there - and there's me thinking ye'd been done for in the old Ship Inn; ah, this woman called fate be a strange mistress and no mistake." Gently he pushed his adopted daughter toward the collapsed marionette wearing his clothing and made a request to distract and perk her spirits.

"Now be a goodly maid and fetch my hat and frock-coat. I so do feel naked without "em. Anyway them lit and fizzling fuses be still a bit lively and could reek a fair bit o' damage if left to their own devices." Giving her a gentle nudge he spoke as he watched her move to do his bidding. "My ship mates did thus Shanghai me back here to the old Revenge fearing commotion in the ale house would arouse interests o' the revenuers from a nearby cliff top." Black Ned watched her do as she was bade and was soon out of immediate earshot. Reaching to the highwayman he gripped his wrist with one hand and his black eye decal with the other saying,

"Thou be a thorn in my flesh Pearly and that b'aint nothing o' value under thy patch neither." Perusing what was under the eye patch closer then to withdraw satisfied he'd found no answer,

"Forsooth I always did think it were a ball o' polished ivory and now I be certain sure." Releasing the eye patch with a flicking action, Ned watched Jess recoil in pain and burning resentment for his old enemy. Taking exception to this he lifted him up by the throat, shaking his head so violently - his jaw and teeth rattled like pebbles in a wine glass. Laughing enjoyment at his victim's discomfiture, Ned recalled how earlier in the ale bar he'd observed the taunting then shooting of his young adopted daughter. Called over his shoulder for the girl to make haste and see the sport. The brief glance at the girl as she extinguished the still lit fuses by tipping them into a leather bucketful of brackish water. Unfortunately this was all the time needed for Jess to elbow ferociously at the offered back of the pirate's head. Taken fully by surprise, Ned fell to his knees crumpling the way the scarecrow had done moments earlier. This moment taken to unscramble the stars diving in front of his eyes, allowed Jess to make good his escape into the mainly furtive darkness of the lower deck. Scrabbling free he dived to cross the darkened camber of planking to leap up through the companionway like a demented rat running for his very life.

"Hell and damnation - `'tis ill luck abounds when a maid be aboard ship."

Out of temper he unkindly referred to the maid, Ned morosely rubbed the nape of his neck and quietly began uttering a string of fluent curses to be brought down upon the highwayman. The girl heard the noise and seeing what happened, returned over to his side with the red coat and the requested accoutrements. Raising the garment for acceptance by her step-father gathering her knife from inside a leg of her pantalette - made to spring for the stairs after the highwayman. Reaching out Ned stopped her in mid-flight swinging her completely off her feet to swing momentarily in the air alongside him.

"Here now, don't thee dare go after that scoundrel." He slipped the knife from her grip and grinned knowingly. "Ye be thy mother's daughter alright.

Now thee bide where ye be and answer some of my questions." Recovering from his ordeal, Ned gesticulated for the girl to sit. Then flung himself along the length of the cannon barrel and thrust his head through into the night air.

"Avast ye lubbers topside - can any hear my words."

A far away voice came filtering down through both the companionway and from the larboard rail on the main deck.

"Aye, aye, captain - what's yer pleasure, sir."

"A bilge rat be escaped up the central stairwell and should be reaching ye any moment. Kill the bastard dead for he be no good to man nor beast.."

"Where away." The unseen deck hand's voice replied against a background of lusty yells for the stowaway's blood.

"Mayhap the main companionway - Search the ship from stem to stern."

"Aye, aye captain."

Voices died as the scramble to be first in at the kill took place above them.

Chuckling Ned withdrew to return and flop alongside to a sitting position on the planking by the wooden wheels of the gun carriage.

"Tell me my daughter." Ned pronounced it `daugater". "Mayhap thou will care to give thy father a smidgen o' proof for his memory weakens with each passing year since my time in Dartmouth with ye - by what surname be ye known."

Advising that this was `Lovelace-Peach" caused a spreading of dark bristles on his black beard to a broad grin revealing white teeth. Clarissa grinned a personal triumph for this was the first time Ned had actually appeared to acknowledge there was a chance she was his off-spring. Swirling the red-frock coat up around his shoulders he placed the plumed hat nearby. Curling up alongside the girl softly and with a somewhat angelic smile he began to sing what appeared to be a nursery rhyme. Ned pushed her gently away saying,

"Don't ee give me no caterwauling in my ear girl, for my head be buzzing from that bilge rat old Pearly's moaning."

Clarissa recalled a rhyme her step-father sang lustily to her as a babe.

"Rain wash clouds clear o' soil
sun peeps out to dry and boil
goodly wash there'll surely be
billowing white for maids to see
Four winds fluff hanging bright
twill put all grime to flight"

Interrupting her he at last placed a fatherly arm around the girl's shoulder,

"If thou remembers how I used to sing my sea shanty, then thou must surely be my daughter - thy name be Teach not Lovelace-Peach."

They hugged from a sitting position and smiled into each other's eyes. The girl became serious and touched his arm for consolation of sorts.

"Why dids't leave us, father? Three short years and my mother left too."

"Aye, thy mother - there's a thought."

Ned became introverted to explain eventually,

"When I were a young man living in Bristol I decided to travel to the far off Cornish and Devonshire coasts to make my fortune.

"Twas there I met thy mother the fair faced Anne who just arrived in England with child. Thou were that babe and I be proud to have weaned ye off thy hell-cat of a mother." He grinned thoughtful contradiction. "The most fearsome angel I ever slapped a mooring on." Ned gave a leer pushing a tousled curl back from the girl's forehead, "But she were a comely wench. We decided we ought to splice the mainbrace and get married." Becoming melancholy he added softly,

"We decided it would be fitting for us to tie-the-knot in a little

152

church in Dartmouth. Me or her not wanting to be far from the sea and all.."

Clarissa felt him hesitate but was content whilst he chose the words which would let her down lightly.

"The king's navy ships moored and high in the water indicating they were light on supply. A dangerous sight for this means also they were so light o' crew one and the same time." Ned rubbed his chin thoughtfully for it was a long time ago. "We passed by the dockside whilst they provisioned with vittles for some far off parts. I nor thy mother, Anne had too many friends and mistakenly welcomed sailors hanging o'er the church wall taking an interest in proceedings." Shrugging broadly he added with a solemnity. "We had few guests and I took notice of a press gang taking an interest in our party leaving o' the little church, I hung back to pay clergy when I were grabbed. Spirited away by those devils in blue uniform and white trouser breeches. I were pressed into service for king and country." He grinned wickedly, "I made them pay more than the `king's shilling" for taking o' my hide out to sea - especially on my wedding night."

"Ye came home on shore-leave to see my mother."

This was the first time she'd realised the reason for the disappearance and remembering little yet recalled only seeing him occasionally. Clarissa had been placed to a private tutorial in a small convent, a guardian appointed and her every need in education and manners taken due care of - catered for by the timely arrival of sequester funds. These normally collected at a waterfront hostelry in Dartmouth by her mother. Anne Bonny retained her original married name and had not brought her up for many years, as she too went off back to sea to find Ned. Leaving the girl in the kindly employ of her guardian Miss Wilks. A kindly soul who would and did do anything for the child. It was the only real companion Clarissa had known during early childhood.

Ned's reaction was one of surprise. "Anne had a fire in her belly and I rightly considers 'twere put there by thy own little presence. She were a firebrand who consumed all and sundry. An all consuming presence gobbling up lesser mortals than thy servant or those of the same ilk." The profundity of his words made her look harder at the man she thought the world of and realised at the same instant he was no oil painting.

Edward Teach was a giant of a man blessed with a cauliflower ear and twisted nose. A shaggy faced pirate with large round gold earrings to both lobes, of towering physique and ringlets platted and twisted with red tassels in the coarse matted black beard from whence he took his reputation. Clarissa pummelled him in a fury, her tiny fists raining on his barrel chest like hail on an open deck.

"Why sayest thou unkind words about a woman who cannot defend herself." Clarissa rocked back on bared heels folding arms and looking a little less than cross. Glowering from under hooded brows, Ned rose and swept her up into his arms, holding her at eye level he began to walk back to the hanging shroud. Amused, by her spirit he though he spied a semblance of his wife in the girl.

"Thou be thy mother's daughter rightly enough."

Crossing from the gun port to where Jess forced Clarissa to look at the canvas coffin and this is where they paused, the girl stiffened with renewed anticipation of fear.

The bound shroud swung gently back and forth with movement of the ship at anchor, feeling a tightening of the grip on his hand he felt obliged to console her. "Within a year or two of thy fourth birthday thy mother Anne, in her infinite wisdom, followed ol' Ned out to sea for she were an experienced mariner and woman buccaneer of old." Breathing exasperation added,

"T'were either to locate and love once more thy true father Calico Jack Rackham or maybe - thy humble servant - I'd yet to decide which.. Any-road-up Anne found me in the Indies - Jamaicee," to be more precise. Because by then I'd tired o' the discipline of the king's navy sea-faring louts. Though not o' the sea itself, for she be a wonderful mistress at times but a lousy lover." Smiling at a known nautical banter which went completely over the maid's head. Ned shrugged and then decided to continue. "After a few years when I had gold and silver under my belt I returned to old Dartmouth to find thy mother had gone to sea to locate thy servant. In the meantime ye were placed with a kindly soul, Miss Wilks."

"Wilks," she corrected, "My governess Miss Martha Wilks sadly be dead, sir."

"Aye `'tis a restful state we all do so reach some day - some before their time and reaching their full span o' three score and ten."

"She were killed dead by that evil highwayman Jess Mandrake."

"Mandrake, eh. Allus were an evil tyke." Shaking off melancholia for the child's sake he murmured, "Poor Miss Wilks - she were a goodly sort and kindly soul and no mistake." Ned gave a comforting squeeze, "I had to say goodbye to thy little self forever for by repute I were a blackguard and no longer seen to be welcome in England due to my naval desertion."

"Where be my mother now." Clarissa inquired.

Pointing to the mummified corpse Ned lowered the child to her feet alongside him and said with feeling, "At sea women can bring men and vessels strife disillusion and jealousies." His eyes took on a quizzical look and he avoided the upturned face of the child. How on earth could he tell this maid her mother Anne Bonny was dead. How could he hurt her any more than he'd already done by denying her his presence over so many years. Although a wanted man, and who wasn't in this day and age, he should have made the effort in trying to see more of her in her tenderised years. Taking a deep breath he said,

"Thy mother Anne rests here little maid and has done so for the past day and a night, God bless her fighting spirit and soul." Despite holding her hand Clarissa whimpered trepidation, drawing back in fear from that which frightened her earlier confronted her again. Allowing the girl's shock and fear to subside Ned slipped a comforting arm around her slender shoulders. The tactile gesture had the desired effect and he felt her relax. Thoughtfully he stroked his bearded chin and in no uncertain terms said,

"There, there, little one, `'tis a fate we all draw one day though for some `'tis earlier than others." Ned watched the girl screw her eyes in fear as she shrivelled down to a willowy crouch, huddling hunched and tense as if waiting for something to happen. Suddenly it did. The canvas tomb jack-knifed again into life. Black Ned drew back in astonishment dragging the girl with him, he dived to draw a sheathed knife from his leather broad-belt. . . Clarissa screamed, unable to contain her outright terror any longer - she fled with flailing arms back to the comparative safety of the gun port. Trembling to crouch alongside the carriage, watching as her step-father approached wide-eyed and puzzled the briskly undulating hammock shroud. Shrugging he raised the knife to stab at the bound hammock.

"No. Don't thee kill her, sir - my mother be in there - she be alive."

Clarissa screamed and covered her mouth with her hands as the knife rose and fell to cut and slash at the waxed-twine stitching on the top of the canvas roll; Ned slashed and cut wantonly all the while growling for the blood of the powder monkey as he did so. . . The tousled head and grubby featured stable boy grinned a cheeky welcome as he suddenly appeared thrusting his head through the open gun port from the seaward side.

Calling softly he asked if it was safe to enter and join her. Clarissa turned and hastened him forward, yet with a cautioning finger held to her pursed pink cupid lips. Wet, shivering with sea spray and chill night vapours, Tom rode along the cannon's barrel horse-fashion up to its broad breech to eventually arrive right up alongside the girl.

"Shh!"

She waved him down alongside and grabbed his hand much to his delight, for Tom was more than a little sweet on the pretty maid. Nervously pointing to her step-father as he slashed at the gyrating shroud in the semi-darkness.

At the same instance the powder monkey, Nipper arrived in the companionway stairwell from a break in his night watch. He too dashed curiously over and threw himself alongside

"What happened. Why did'st scream so loud, Clara beau?"

Clarissa pointed to Ned at work with the knife, noticing Nipper had a sudden and fleeting look of fear as he watched his captain feverishly tackle the coarse stitching. "Mother of God." Nipper paled and making some excuse about leaving his knife up on deck rose and dashed past the pirate towards the stairwell. Ned looked round and spied what was happening - rounding on him, dropped the knife and tugged at a red ear of the powder monkey.

"Gotcha, ye bilge rat." Blackbeard shook Nipper painfully by his ear. "If I be a thinking what ye be thinking then 'tis the worst for ye. Ye bide awhile and see the outcome o' this exercise."

Ned murmured as the sailcloth bundle opened as the folds of slashed material fell to in a heap to the deck revealing.......

Chapter Eleven BEGGING YOUR PARDON

Some smile with lips
others smile with voice
some with good deeds
others without choice

Some with their actions
others with good heart
some don't know how
but eventually they start

Poem: Lost Smile

The moon became fainter and eventually hung low like a dimming lantern over the horizon. A silently heralded dawn was becoming radiant with turquoise hues and flecked with a gilding of burnished gold. Yet all the while the surrounding distant grey cloudscapes clung to the horizon like dirty linen, although they too were backlit and edged with silver gilt.

Mist-shrouded seas on an ever-moving surface hung with a transparent and ghostly veil. Above in a waning night sky, tiny Venus usually so bright began to fade into the charisma of a new summer's dawn.

Earlier at three bells the impotent pop of a swivel-gun alerted Ingrams from the restless creaking ship's quarter deck. Moments later from the thwarts he spied a ghostly flotilla of pirate vessels that scudded serenely past him in the middle distance. A raggedly fleet, yet each vessel of full-sail slunk silently past withholding illumination of their stern lanterns. Even from that distance Ingrams failed to detect movement in their rigging or on deck. Looking about and allowing his imagination to wander away from that uncomfortable place, there was good reason why he chose the stern for his repast. Knowing full well, bow figureheads, carved so lovingly by old salts ashore, were passed to naval ship yards for erection to the bows of man o' war galleons under construction. Ship-builders always installed a form of lavatory there. Circular holes carved in a plank either side of the bowsprit, chiselled masterpieces, invariably in the female form of mermaid or sea nymph were created for contemplation whilst all seamen were at their repast. Hence expressions such as "seeking the heads" and "place not thyself o'er the rail if winter skies predict a gale." Upper-deck gun crews idled near their night watch stations, originally they did spake in hushed whispers of a forthcoming sea journey. As night had lengthened their laughter mingled with pungent aromas of charcoal smouldering, further acrid smells of fish and foul cooking wafted down to his nostrils. Blue smoke swirled in a downdraught over the larboard rail to be dispersed by invisible sea zephyrs, cries from raucous dice or paste board primero, exhilarated their already heightened senses as presumably they used up earlier quotas of cider and ale allowance. Ingrams recalled sea journeys he'd endured whereby just 2 pints of water or thrice the amount of alcohol was there to be consumed daily. While stocks lasted of course. Illegally, the crewmen would retain substantial balances of their daily ration to be thus consumed above decks at night. Usually during ferociously fought gambling tournaments. Their up-front sea pay dwindling within days of an average three month voyage to some far off land. D'Arcy Ingrams became wary getting too close to the hull when they circumnavigated the ship on their initial arrival many hours before. Jolly boat not the slim sea skiff Ingrams was used to, manoeuvrable as driftwood. Or so he likened it to the lad. Using a rear rowlock he paddled the craft silently through the gathering swells to finally arrive and hove-to under the gingerbread stern. At midnight the poop swivel gun was fired instilling the wrath of God into their already taught nerves - a signal for all ashore to return forthwith. All those of the ship's crew that remained unconvinced of suggested dire moves into a land army of the rebelliously persuasive yet poorly armed soldiers in Lyme's hostelries. Gathering their wits they had slunk further underneath the ornate overhang of the stateroom and its overhead and suspiciously opened-up windows. Silence was the order of the night and remaining hours were spent uncomfortably lingering cold-cramped in the shallow gunwales. As night waned and dawn approached men returning from shore the far side of the ship, were immediately sent aloft to check on rigging. Their lanterns dotted and slowly moved about the rigging, in itself likened in the bright silvery moonlight to that of a spider's webbing. Later, cloud cover scudded over the full moon and their distant activities were seen only by the tiny pinpricks of lantern light. The wind was stronger at the stern. A deal of work remaining at a chosen mooring was entailed perpetually, that was until Ingrams located an iron ring with which to secure their boat's painter. Sea sloshed over the gunwales before the bow could be swung into the breeze and shoreward wave forming. The leather bucket utilised urgently to bale out bilges full of remaining stink of dead sprats and their leached oils in black brackish water.

Triumphant, though in moderate discomfort, Ingrams and the sea-initiated lad dragged on the remainder of clothing about their shoulders to settle down for the cool of night. Bolstered by moderate success in achieving the boarding of the girl, they hoped beyond hope for good news to come of her wanderings. Their mooring was fitful and uncomfortable, this due to the constant snatch of sea against line as they rode tender to the looming craft above.

Occasionally exchanging glances between cat-napping, Ingrams and the boy broke muted silence to offer speculation on their next move. Allowing his eye to wander along the lines of the ship rolling gently on the swell before him, Ingrams recalled warships could carry as many as one hundred guns. At first gun ports were constructed without any special design or set arrangement, the Dutch were first to arrange them in `checkerboard" fashion. Heaviest pieces of weaponry placed stably on the lowest of ship's decks. In battle the guns were always fired in volleys, primarily aimed at the rigging and masts of their enemy. This led to the development of the chain-shot cannonballs linked with chains or bars in pairs. They were called "angels". Thoughtfully he reminisced over his training, how a thirty-two pounder could impregnate and pierce with little resistance into two feet of English oak. Recalling how the bows of galleons were pointed like the galleys of old, although the stern towering above them was heavily ornamented with galleries, windows, carved panels and smaller painted figureheads or gilded insignias. In fact, every kind of mariner architectural decoration was there to behold, this vessel though held particular interest for him realising now that it was definitely not a converted East Indiaman, but a first class ship o' the line fighting vessel of the King's fleet.

* * *

Suddenly commotion above caused him to rouse himself from his rambling memories of his mind fitfully passing the long uncomfortable hours. South-Westerlies had died back and water temperature had risen again, this phenomenon portended of fog to come earlier and now this began descending rapidly in loose veils.

A sudden noise from up on the ship made him strain his eyes to see if he'd been spotted slinking underneath the over-hung stern quarter, then an upward glance made him go cold. There directly above him and at approximately twenty feet high two male figures struggled half-in and half-out of a stateroom open window. In misty moonlight back lit by the over-sized lantern in itself illuminated by six huge church candles, bathed what was clearly seen as two men battling in a yellowy glow. One, a more slender figure in a red tunic-coat lay hung at half mast out of the salon window. Rearwards he struggled with what appeared to be a man in dark blue serge cloth uniform - maybe the ship's captain. This might even be Dampier, the man he was supposed to meet and hand over the documents once smuggled aboard unseen by crew or Blackbeard himself.

Instinctively reaching inside his jacket lining felt for papers tucked safely away, the crinkly feel of parchment was impervious to sea water, knowing this gave him certain solace, what he did not know was the imperviousness of the oak-gall ink gracing its surface. Patting fondly secure in the knowledge that he'd almost completed his mission and afore-mentioned pouch of gold coins awaiting.

Remembering the life and death struggle above he made to slit the thin painter from the iron rung, enabling them to drift away from the direct line should one or both figures fall on the jolly boat. Quickly he tried to undo the whipping line holding the tender to the larger vessel but it was too late. Happening the way things did in these circumstances the slowest of motions unfolded in front of his eyes-D'Arcy Ingrams watched as glancing skywards, Dampier rounded on the figure in red, tearing the coat from his shoulders to elbow him from his precarious perch. Flailing the night skies with futility, like a cork bursting from a bottle, he soared towards them and the gunmetal surface of the sea. Gaining speed as he toppled downwards circular moving arms momentarily defying gravity by flapping he hurtled quickly towards the small rowing boat. Below the struggling man tried to get away from the inevitable - yet seconds later with arms and legs akimbo - the unwelcome intruder landed astride of the half-ankar cask with a tremendous bang.

Dazed and unable to comprehend good fortune by landing on something solid, the fallen intruder just sat there blinking at the confused D'Arcy Ingrams. Moments later, before either chose to speak and address the other, it was then an excruciating groin pain set in.

"Arggh."

Holding his private parts with both hands to groan inexorably. The small over-loaded craft did not sink immediately. Strangely considering its options. Then slowly, very slowly, and with additional top-heavy weights of an agonised rider and the still full half-ankar cask - the jolly boat complete with wide-eyed occupants rolled over and sank. Surfacing again, Ingrams screamed unrepeatable oaths at the man for not waiting until he'd untied the painter and moved the boat to a safer mooring. Who was this buffoon and what was his business on board The Revenge. Why did he choose to exit from the saloon stateroom window and not the traditional way down a companionway, rope ladder or gang plank like every other normal mortal soul aboard ship.

Activity on the deck above sprang from a need to lower the boats and find this blackguard, impotent gun shots to put the fear of God into anyone fleeing that night did the trick. Threats and abuse from Ingrams were duly ignored as they floundered opposite each other, the man trod water though began to slip beneath the choppy wave forms. Seemingly recovering a decorum as his discomfort waned, then took obtuse impertinence to thus introduce himself as Lord Albemarle. The courtesy seemingly taking priority and precedence over the fact that he now appeared to be drowning quite rapidly. Ingrams had vision of this buffoon saluting as he slid vertically underneath the sea.

Struggling in the choppy waters of Lyme bay, Ingrams angrily found himself also treading water to remain afloat in the heavy swell. Within moments of losing the boat he desperately tore at his jacket trying to free himself from its heavy clinging material. Remembering the precious documents in the calico blouson, grasped at the parchment then allowed his coat to drift beneath the gun-metal surface. With barely a cry for help, the fellow practised drowning by raising an anxious hand for possible assistance. Urgently now as

161

although devoid of his jacket, the white blouson shirt filled with salt water and dragged him lower and lower in the water. His terrified expression sea washed over by the swell as he rose and fell with its movement. Seemingly, he too placed great store by a similar sheaf of red-ribbon bound papers in his up-raised hand. Intent above all else on saving these documents. Waving them towards the figures hanging out of the stern window of the ship.

To D'Arcy Ingrams, a practised and strong swimmer, the document-goading to those aboard was like waving a red rag to a bull. Striking out towards the figure in the water, he was soon alongside and grabbing the papers from a wet grip - thrust them inside his own shirt. Then set about endeavouring to rescue the buffoon who sank him leaving both to flounder in the cold water. The drowning man's struggles subsided as Ingrams cupped a hand under his chin raising his bluing lips well above the surface, striking out for the direction of the half-submerged and bobbing barrel, he towed the limp figure behind him. Reaching the half-ankar cask now buoyantly riding higher due an influx of air.

Ingrams pushed him aboard likened to assisting someone in mounting a horse, winded yet grateful, he now found time to resume his former groaning. Endeavouring to join the man astride the cask, suddenly the rescuer felt the cold metal of a pistol muzzle pushed up hard against his right temple.

"Well my friendly rescuer and confidant what am I to do with ye until help arrives in the form of my sea-barge?" Albemarle's craggy features became recognisable to Ingrams in a growing half-light of dawn. Although it was prudent not to say or antagonise someone holding greater cards than he. The all-too- familiar rasping voice was coming from a drowned rat and not the lordly character he once knew at court. Lank curls of water-darkened hair bridged his nose and eyes, this originally concealed the dark identity.

Lord Albemarle was a confidant and close friend of the Earl of Feversham. He had probably been delegated to find Ingrams and retrieve the letters of marque documents. Yet he would not realise that he had recovered them and was actually carrying them with him that adventuresome night. The barrel and its writhing occupants began to drift away from the silhouette of the ship. Shouting aboard alerting the crew and snipers to take aim and "fire at will". Should the man-overboard scoundrel be sighted. D'Arcy Ingrams fast lost his bearings as mercifully a veiled sea mist began to swirl and gather about them in early dawn, they were now unseen by the heaving ship and crew at a tilting anchor. "I'll trouble ye for my papers inside thy vest, sir and quickly."

Albemarle removed the pistol from Ingrams' nostril and began prodding his ribcage encouragingly in the area of the obvious protuberance. Wet clothing, especially a calico blouson gave little protection to anyone endeavouring to conceal anything within. Let alone manifold quite bulky sheaves of parchment. In a quandary he reached inside his shirt and grabbed what he thought to be Albemarle's own snatched papers. Inadvertently he handed over his own secreted Letters of Marque intended for Morgan. Albemarle grabbed the wet bundle, without verifying validity - doubled them and thrust them back into the top of his waterlogged thigh length boots. Ingrams realised why he'd been drowning - fool hadn't kicked off his boots - God save us from fools.

Gloomily they watched each other from across differing ends of the barrel. Vaguely bemused, Ingrams watched as the man balancing in front stretched each leg up in-turn skywards and this action allowed water to drain from each boot. Securing the papers so's they wouldn't follow, then draining his mind calculating exactly how he would dispose of his enemy should the occasion present itself. Pursuit from the ship slackened and died. Flintlock pistol and musket fire waned, echoing into a far distance as the gap between them extended silently.

The lagoon which was Lyme Bay lay restless and fitful at their feet due to a change of tide pattern. Whirling zephyrs stirred up eddies on the swells of ever-moving crystal waters. A chill breeze, though barely noticeable, rose to roll and billow thickening fog over them. Albemarle's own flintlock pistol would not present a problem as black powder did not lend itself readily to an ingress of seawater, or any other kind of natural dampness for that matter. Yet what was the point in overpowering his new enemy, they would still be drifting together on a barrel in open sea. Too far from Lyme town or harbour to swim or even paddle the barrel if they had such an item as an oar or a plank to paddle with. "My rowing barge should be here shortly." Albemarle boasted taking his eyes reluctantly from the blank stare of the man opposite.

Summing each other up - each man decided they were both of the same age in their thirties, also of similar strength of character. Albemarle held Ingrams' gaze for a moment then looked back at the fast disappearing ship - for they were now heading out to sea and not drifting towards land as they'd hoped.

He also became concerned about their position yet seemingly making light of it perhaps by way of distraction leaned towards Ingrams and confided,

"Did you know there is a law punishable by imprisonment for a craft with more than six oars." Ingrams' laugh was spontaneous at the incredulity of the ridiculous man. So-much-so its infectiousness caused the confused and somewhat pompous lord Albemarle to join in, almost losing his perch on the cask at this impromptu birdsong of levity. Finally as their voices echoed in the dawn mist, Ingrams remarked casually,

"One doth suppose then my lord that there be no law against the type of craft without oars." More laughter came at unintended sarcasm. Yet tinged with reservation this time. "So how does my lord anticipate rescue from this our predicament. For one observes that we head out to sea at an alarming rate of nautical knots." Nodding toward the horizon added, "mayhap the tidal race will eventually drop us onto a beach - in France somewhere." Before Albemarle's reply came back, a distant slapping noise to port held both men's gaze.

Out of the swirling mist hovering a couple of feet above the sea surface was revealed eighteen yellow oars of a slender if lengthy rowing skiff. A long-boat no less, with orderly manned oars looming up out of filtering Venus and moon's light with no warning. Yet how on earth did they find them - drifting the way they were.

"I have failed to thank thee my dear fellow." Albemarle began realising he knew not the stranger's name who rescued him. Beckoning with the pistol to prompt such an offering of his identity.

"Paladin. Joshua Paladin and thy humble servant, sire," Ingrams lied. Albemarle grunted disbelief though nodded acknowledgement now becoming more interested in the approach of the life-saving boat and its silent crew.

"Well sir, uh, Mr. Paladin - ye saved my life and for which I be mortally obliged. Therefore I am obligated to afford ye the same service of basic humanity and thus ruling of the open seas."

He looked over his shoulder to the boat as it closed at an ever quickening pace, having spied Albemarle's wave of the horse pistol. Eventually drawing alongside the half-submerged barrel with two men aboard, the officer in charge gave the order to ship oars. Swaying upwards to a man, the crew rose to attention, their individual oars presented uniformly with the minimum of noise, then sat again with them criss-crossed over the sides. The eighteen- oared longboat had a rakish bow and overhung stern, swiftly designed for a goodly turn of speed. Naval personnel crewed the skiff, Ingrams concluded thoughtfully as he noted their quiet and totally disciplined efficiency. He also concluded with a sickening disdain that now he was out of the cooking skillet and into the fire. And what if someone should recognise him.

"Perhaps, captain," Albemarle began, "ye'd be a good enough fellow to assist my saviour and nautical colleague here, for we both be fair froze from dank breezes and chill of this night." Then Albemarle watched Ingrams' every move as he was brusquely and unceremoniously hauled from the bobbing cask and dragged amidships into the longboat. The wavering pistol followed his drowned-rat-appearance as he was thrust hand-over-hand by the crew deliberately towards the stern, once there he was forced to squat cross-legged in the gunwales. The lone castaway figure majestically tried to assert authority of the aristocracy whilst astride the barrel. Eventually assistance came with a deal of courtesy and reverence afforded an officer and a gentleman, aboard the almost wallowing long boat. The rowing skiff at once was allowed to drift clear of the sinking water-logged cask. As a parting shot, Albemarle stood and aimed his long-barrelled flintlock pistol at the butt keg that saved their lives. With barely an audible noise - the fizzing flash came as if the gun had been discharged in anger on half-cock. Briefly it illuminated the knowing smiles of the sombre rowing crew, though a respectful silence greeted the one lead ball shot as it rolled out of the end of the muzzle and fell with a gentle "plop" alongside the craft. The boarding officer-in-charge, doubled up and then shot a flamboyant hand to his mouth to cough a loud distraction to his men. Then straightened up to issue immediate orders to "lower oars" from their straddling rest position, and when ready - were to resume stroke on his singular command. In the blank wall of swirling fog and deathly silence they moved off under-sway once more. Slowly moving through the calm swells landward taking a bearing with Gold Cap hill on their starboard midships. Albemarle, out of embarrassment and with rising florid complexion, busily checking the bore and lock mechanism of the naval issue flintlock sidearm. Finally whispering an expletive - flung it in disgust down into the bilges, turning his back on the crew his self-conscious glower showing briefly to the part-smiling Ingrams squatting at head-height at the stern. He thought it prudent to hide head-down behind the lead rower. Seen over Albemarle's head, taking a short spell of time, the Geneva tub half-ankar cask disappeared beneath the waves.

Ingrams thought of the Chesil Banks sinking weights that must originally have been attached to the cask - used for collecting the hidden contraband offshore by the moonlight trade, only to be spirited away to places like the old Shambles by way of the tiny river Buddle inlet. Rowing at a fair pace, the heaving crew perfectly in tune with his counterpart, rowed their hearts-out to a stroke command from their captain.

"Pull - rest - pull - rest - pull - rest. . ." Into the swirling drifting sea mist and thickening fog they were soon lost to anything else at sea that day. Swiftly silent the boat cut through the green crystal clear waters of the bay, strangely asserted direction toward the harbour lights of Bridport.

* * *

Dawn 14th June 1685

Some unknown villainous scribe sent the heresy missive held by Albemarle, was now read aloud for the benefit and information of the captured King's man.

`The Duke of Monmouth purposeth to land and
set up his standard at the town of Lyme, a
small relatively quiet sea port of Dorset."
Dated 6th June 1685.

* * *

D'Arcy Ingrams thought this message must have travelled on one of the three ships anchored off-shore at Lyme's north shore pebbled beach. Two huge converted fishing vessels carried the bulk of the eighty soldiers, mounts, their ordnance and lighter equipment of musket and ball. The Dutch escort galleon, a swift vessel named *The Heldevenberg* cost the Pretender's wife who sold her jewellery to pay for the venture. A princely sum of £5.000 for services and navigation under guard to England. This ship too, now lay completely empty apart from a skeleton crew of aged seafarers.

"Well, my dear Paladin, having heard the missive from a fellow sea spy, ye knoweth why an officer and soldier of fortune, thy humble servant sir, fell from the gingerbread of a pirate galleon. Unfortunately shipwrecking thy good-self t'boot. Though thou sayest not why thy tiny jolly boat was so positioned under the stern of the ship Revenge."

"Maracaibo?"

"Nay sir, the ship be in disguise. It be actually Blackbeard's vessel."

"Aye The Revenge be Blackbeard's ship alright. Well good sir, I am certain sure that fate held its breath when ye fell from the heavens dictating I should moor there at the stern accordingly." A hardened look of growing distrust conveyed to Ingrams the truth be burdened with growing doubt.

"Fishing my lord Albemarle, lobster and crab pot baskets which were sunk earlier in the day. To be thus recovered later on the tethered floating corks with their accompanying sinker stones on fine jute. Though I did feel time and tide took me further from the harbour than was originally intended." Still no reaction from Albemarle, he elaborated in a final exasperating lie.

"I admit to becoming curious with a moored vessel tilting at anchor and flying no flag or navigational lights of convenience or not. Especially now in these restless times in which we live." Gesticulating for the orator to offer his hands palms up revealed a paleness without calluses, with a rueful smile, Albemarle took little offence at the deliberate lie. Instead said dourly,

"Quite my dear fellow, one supposes every fellow is entitled to a few dark secrets - I understand completely." Grinning knowingly his brightening expression cleared the air toward the man on horseback. Albemarle too, much safer on land than at sea, was astride a horse keeping pace with the King's man's mount as they cantered gently along the coastal road at talking pace. An hour earlier, having beached the longboat, the two officers found secreted horses awaiting their arrival on the beachhead. Plus an escort of some twenty or so cavalry out-riders to see them safely inland to Axminster.

As they journeyed almost to Lyme then to head at right angles inland, Ingrams heard one casual observer mention the Devon and Somerset Militia, he presumed Albemarle was officer-commanding and in charge. Also he must be the contact for the purveyor of the cryptic letter from The Dutch Free States.

Also he could now presume the slippery fellow had an offer to change sides to the rebel army. In his haste - and once he had the damning letter confirming the Duke of Monmouth's plans - decided to make good his escape from the lofty saloon stateroom window of the ship. Unfortunately to descend not into the sea but to land onto a small row boat. His nether regions compounded into oblivion by the barrel head. Continually musing just why this Albemarle's voice failed to ascend an octave or two.

"What I fail to understand is why ye were so situated in the first instance. Surely this be anticipation gone wild."

Ingrams quickly recalled verbally how he tried to row his craft from his descending line of flight. Insisting his crab fishing yarn, though in deeper waters was absolutely correct. It turned to be his undoing.

Albemarle, ever the gentleman with impeccable dress code and having donned red tricorn hat with a peacock feather, riding spurs, great coat, leather spat-breeches and an assortment of lethal side weapons, broke into a furious gallop for some unbeknown reason. Ingrams had but a moment to gather his thoughts and pace to draw alongside the man once more. Although he'd anticipated such questioning, his cold and starving wits had dulled and failed him. Riding alongside he looked across trying to discern the man's thinking yet avoided the twinkling darting gaze back. Finally Albemarle drew out a bundle of parchment from inside his tunic coat.

"D'Arcy Ingrams, King's man, was requested to and took it upon himself to deliver this official document headed "letters-of-marque" for Captain Henry Morgan, buccaneering assistant lieutenant to the governor of Port Royal in old Jamaica."

Ingrams' left hand dived into the calico blouson and tore out a similar sheaf of parchment without thinking, then he realised his reflex action might cost him his life. Shrugging his broad shoulders he reluctantly confessed,

"My dear Albemarle, thou doth indeed appear to have my classified documents by some sore mistake and quirk o' fate." He handed Albemarle's original papers over as they galloped alongside towards an ever brightening sky. Foolishly expecting to receive the other documents in return - though it appeared they were not to be forthcoming. Peripatetic - they rode on in moody silence.

Seeing the blank stare as his compatriot pocketed the documents he thought quickly, Albemarle reined in his mount as did Ingrams then his eyes challenged him and the commander said, "Why dost seek a title of knight errant, as this be the translation of thy coded nomme de plume. Thy dastardly nomme de guerre mayhap be a delusion of rising above thy station in life sir." His glancing gaze pierced Ingrams' soul as he waited for an answer.

Blurted out and sounding even less than credible it came as they rode side by side on the wayward coastal track.

"My liege. James II of England through his confidant bade me so to do."

Exhalation of breath, Albemarle's actions conveyed despair inexplicably, as he considered Ingrams' lies to muse aloud to his horse.

This conveyed that a more intelligent conversation could be had from the galloping animal. This ignorance gave the spy chance to glance at their general coast line direction. Finding themselves in a copse on the edge of woodland, others in the racing party having cantered on ahead. Yet would they return as soon as he and Albemarle were lagging behind and eventually to be sorely missed. It was too late. When Ingrams finally glanced back at his colleague, once again he pointed a loaded pistol, he assumed that this time it was with dry powder and ball.

Lord Albemarle indicated they should stop and rest the horses. When done the beasts whirled restlessly and snorted discontent by stomping their hooves.

"Please give credit to others not within thy King's circle who have privy to expanding historical facts also a knowledge of recent events." He sighed as he must have done many times before relating a tale he was about to repeat. Their horses spun restlessly, they too must have heard the tale before and would be gone from that place. "In 1683 two short years ago our liege Charles II was thought to be on the point of death. His bastard son Monmouth, became involved in a plot of assassination. His uncle, James, rightly sits enthroned as the King of England. The plot of assassination failed. Whilst several conspirators were dealt with on the "block" - Monmouth and several cronies fled. Monmouth was so exiled in the Dutch Free States. Then, almost on a point of reconciliation with his father, Charles died and Monmouth's uncle was crowned Imperial Catholic king of England."

"My lord," Ingrams began, irritated he should have common knowledge explained this way, but he was waved into silence and the monologue went on.

"James Duke of Monmouth is 36 years old. This passing of the years one would assume to be round and about the age of us both, my dear Ingrams." Grunting satisfaction when he received a curt nod from his compatriot. Their mounts decided to graze head down having long since lost interest in the conversation. Lending an almost idyllic pastoral moment to their differences, the sun now broke through the darkness with rays of orange brilliance. Soon illuminating the promise of a fine new day. Misty veils were swiftly rising soon everything would be all one could ask for weather in England in the month of June.

It was the sight of the waving gun which brought Ingrams back to the reality of the moment and the dire situation in which he now found himself.

"Therefore Monmouth was persuaded by his uncle William of Holland and others in the exiled English aristocracy to lead an invasion party. Thus to land nearby in the port and harbour town of Lyme. There he planned to go about a summoning-up of a rag-tag army from Protestant supporters here in the West.

"Ye do naught but fail to astound me sir." Ingrams spat softly. "The very fact ye are so well informed. What mayhap dost ye think ye'll do to one who serves the English crown so readily as one such as I."

"Methinks it would serve all concerned if ye were to meet with a riding accident." he waved the gun indicating Ingrams should get closer to the cliff edge. "Just so's we might all rest easy in our cots this night." Albemarle raised the horse pistol and took careful aim at his adversary's chest. The anticipated report from the weapon was to be the last thing he and my Lord Albemarle would hear, or so he thought. When the curl of hovering blue smoke subsided and the echo of gun fire waned, Ingrams widened his fear-screwed gaze to see Albemarle wincing with dire pain. Gripping sorely the bloody torn hole in the padded shoulder of his uniform. Pistol still falling, bouncing off the saddle horn to a grassy mound at his startled horse's feet, his mount throwing back its head at the released charge, yet had astonishingly remained quite calm in the circumstances.

The man moving slowly forward on horseback was instantly recognisable as Lord Grey, the Duke of Monmouth's second-in-command and 1st cavalry officer. He held a smoking flintlock in his grip. Having led a skirmish against the nearby Devon and Somerset Militia, based at Bridport, had been sorely routed leaving six dead. Their horses bolted with the noise of battle, leaving a contingency force of foot to "mop-up" - he'd led the retreat to Lyme and reported previously unknown strength of their enemy at the town. There they had sighted up the coast road and followed Lord Albemarle and his mounted men for some three miles at a safe distance. When the cavalry outriders had gone on ahead of them, they'd decided to move in on Albemarle. Yet it was then they found him holding the deadly weapon on D'Arcy Ingrams, this tale informed the King's man just how they happened to be in the right place at the right time. Unto which he conveyed his grateful appreciation.

After formal introductions took place, Lord Grey's consternation over the circumstances in which he found Ingrams were put into words. Voiced after watching the tending of his wound and fastening of Albemarle back onto his saddle.

"Sir. Though I believe ye to be on the side of justice, unfortunately I overheard thy tale related to my lord Albemarle, therefore I believe ye possibly to be a spy for the Rump Parliament - indeed a King's man for the present Catholic King, James II." Lord Grey nodded for his mounted contingent of men to watch over Ingrams whilst others continued affording a courtesy wound pad for the doubled-up and now very disgruntled Lord Albemarle. Assisting in the field dressing placement, a less than considerate D'Arcy Ingrams at the same instant removed the blood-stained documents from inside the injured man's vest, this done without his enemy even realising it. Partly due to pain partly to deftness and sleight of a thief's hand. Albemarle was allowed to ride away with the group of rebel army riders virtually unbound, for in column, they assumed him to be of no real threat now badly injured and in obvious pain. When the party moved off on advice from Ingrams, advising of the party of 20 outriders Grey decided to double-back and track round them.

Lord Grey's skirmishing party and its prisoner were barely two miles down the track towards the town of Lyme when Lord Albemarle had made good his escape into dense woodland. Whether by design or default, D'Arcy Ingrams smiled and, without being noticed, gently touched the thickened bundle of documents under his armpit tucked into his vest. This was indeed a bonus.

On removing them from the bloodied captive he'd noticed documents which should have been handed over to Captain Dampier of the good ship Revenge. They were a permit to seek treasure trove subsidised by London merchant bankers and the aristocracy, the words stating one sixth going to the Crown. Ingrams looked admiringly at the great waxed red seal affixed to the papers of Parliament noting it was a motte not unfamiliar to him. He too held just such high office warranted by official documentation - *agent provocateur*.

Chapter Twelve ALL WHISPERS BE LIES

One love to give
one life to live
one smile to smile
braving a last mile

One kiss to kiss
one love to miss
one tear to cry
one fearful sigh

A salty tear to weep
a gentle touch to keep
the kindly hands caress
though now hold even less

Poem: Thy Love

* * *

10.00 am 14th June

D'Arcy Ingrams was dragged down from the snorting Arab stallion by the cavalry officers, hurriedly bundled out of the public eye and into a sunlit hall way of the three-storeyed house in George Square in the centre of Lyme Regis.

"New Monmouth House" was the hastily painted new address scribbled in tar on a temporary hand-painted sign depicting the sanctuary and headquarters. Thrust roughly into a shadowy north-facing front room. Now feeling far from happy he struggled back up to his feet and cautiously he looked about him. Imposing the building in the quiet square was of one of the more select parts of town, guarded well outside. He could only presume the Pretender must be in temporary residence there. Looking about he assessed the opulence of silver salvers and candlesticks gracing dark wood sideboards and a centralised and lengthy oval table. Several chairs strategically placed as if a meeting had been hastily convened then abandoned. Momentarily alone with his thoughts, distant voices permeated the walls, Ingrams noting finally with a grim satisfaction that the sitting room door opened. At last he would find reason for his incarceration. A man dressed in sombre battle clothing was immediately recognisable, yet with an unusually gaunt stare. Entering to address him personably by his little used title, well one of them anyway. Seeing him, the man with a military bearing immediately brightened and his face cleared of care.

"D'Arcy Ingrams, my dear sir - fortuitously it would appear ye doth busily employ the most excellent of guardian angels." James, Duke of Monmouth smiled a genuine welcome on seeing the King's man again, and shook his hand strongly. "We are most glad to spy ye safe and well I hope." A nod and returning smile from Ingrams silently answered the hearty inquiry. Monmouth's smiling blue eyes and genuine lusty greeting conveyed delight as they concluded the violent shaking of hands. Moving apart Ingrams could now assume things did not fare well with regard to training of locally recruited regiments. Monmouth waved his guest toward a chair beckoning for him to seat himself opposite, the scattering of chairs still afforded him thoughts of a discussed stratagem of forthcoming skirmishing, either interrupted or broken up in total disarray. Only then did he notice further such signs, part-empty drinking vessels pushed to one side, wooden cups of coloured liquid placed to one side on a side table. Failing to sit down immediately, Monmouth strolled thoughtfully over to the tall window as if choosing his next words carefully. Side-on even his silhouette looked fitful and troubled, the sea spy put this down to being drawn by responsibility of a forthcoming life-and-death venture. Yet to his credit, the figure remained stalwartly upright, a far away look in his eyes was only to be expected. It took a brave man to invade England with such poor resources and manpower, as he moved back across and into focus he withdrew a chair from under the drop to take his place at table.

"I trust I find thee in robust health, sir." Ingrams offered the pleasantry to break a growing atmosphere. They sat closely opposite, a closed jug containing a cordial of summer fruit juices was slid brimming full across the surface towards him.

Monmouth watched him fill a heavy crystal goblet before deeming it necessary to reply. "We are well sir - yet pressing matters which lay before one are momentous, nay bordering on the calamitous." He sighed and looked into Ingrams' very soul as he suffixed,

"Thy servant would seek advice from his peers and due blood ties I consider thee as such."

Ingrams buried his nose into the goblet, protocol abounded he would think long and hard before being drawn into a conversation over politics of the country.

Recalling their fractious meeting and confrontation, original eye contact in the bedchamber, noted a glint of fervour, an inspired anticipation for his forthcoming endeavours. Yet observing the man opposite readily he spied that spark of fervour and raw enthusiasm had definitely waned.

James, Duke of Monmouth spoke distracting the spy from the dour profundity of his own muses. Inquiring of the spy's subsequent adventures after an obvious escape from the revolving mattress device in the George Inn.

What followed was an in-depth account of Ingrams' rescue and precarious journey out to the pirate vessel - including an impetuous exit from aboard ship which had sunk his jolly boat. The latter unbelievable segment bringing much levity to the earlier somewhat formal proceedings of their reunion.

The documents were mentioned for obvious reasons. Apart from the fact they were issued many months earlier by his late father, Monmouth showed little curiosity in their existence. Business past is business concluded they concerned themselves with business in hand.

"I owe thee my life therefore and despite sensible advising of my commanding cavalry officer, Lord Grey - I am obligated to afford thee thy freedom. This then concludes any further indebtedness should we meet on the battlefield." Monmouth rose and strode head-down along the length of the narrow room. It was the actions of a man reassessing his thoughts and past deeds. Perhaps justifying a need to confide and deceive all in the same instant. Pausing he turned to address Ingrams with a strange sincerity.

"To effectively escape death twice in the past forty-eight hours seems a tad lucky, sir. Would'st confirm to thy servant that thou art a lucky man." A friendly smile impetuously flickered then waned. Perhaps finding himself in the embarrassing position owing a mere

175

commoner his existence that day. Perhaps because the conversation was ebbing. At the same time he wondered if his gratuitous good fortune was something to be nurtured and propagated to be used to advantage. Or merely born under a lucky star to be one of nature's favourites.

"Man makes his own luck, I feel, though it is when the `devil" steps in that man's troubles can thus begin all over again."

"Aye, sir and we all have dark devils within the far recesses of our soul." Monmouth agreed, looking pensive, reiterated thoughts carefully before confiding an incident which caused recent changes of plans and his possible fortune.

"Since, fortuitously for thy servant, we last met up, Thomas Dare my pay-master was shot dead by one Andrew Fletcher. He was the competent commander of my 2nd Cavalry Brigade. In disgrace he has been returned aboard the Dutch frigate "Heldevenberg" this is why the substitute Lord Grey, rode with a skirmishing party to nearby Bridport. Not my natural choice of overall cavalry commander, yet I have little choice due to a diabolical outcome of personal quarrelling amongst my officers."

"Aye my Lord, amongst other pirate sloops the Heldevenberg sailed past me presumably for the Dutch Free States this past night. I noted such movement on the horizon before the flying man hit my rowing boat." Ingrams reiterated the initial introduction to Albemarle and his inadvertent rescue. "Led by Lord Grey and Colonel Venner, I was met by the retiring skirmishing column some two miles east of Lyme. Happening upon my person as I was about to be despatched to kingdom-come, Lord Albemarle holding a pistol to my forehead undoubtedly using it upon me had not thy cavalry captain wounded him in his shoulder."

"Yet ye were classed as too dangerous once Albemarle made good his escape. However, Lord Grey advised me ye boasted of thy escapade in the flood caves. Also calamity surrounding Albemarle's plummet onto thy moored craft." Monmouth allowed himself a broad grin, "Canst confirm he actually landed astride a large brandy barrel located then in thy tender." He found this most amusing.

"A half-ankar cask my lord Duke; 'twas full of a stinkibus liquid purporting to be French yet long since past its best taste and flavour." Monmouth noted Ingrams' curt nod and wicked grin taking pleasure as he added,

"Then he'll not play the "father" for awhile - I be a thinking."

Avoiding retaliation, Ingrams remained concerned over his own personal predicament.

"Albemarle confided an alias or mayhap thy code name to my commander." The Duke went on looking darkly hard before saying, "'Paladin - knight errant and so be this correct, sir."

D'Arcy Ingrams considered his response yet failed to confirm the name afforded him by the Rump Parliament. Generously the questioning was not pursued and thankfully it changed tack, Monmouth shrugged, "My Lord Grey reported incorrectly encountering Albemarle's militia company as did he embellish skirmish and confrontation with the Devon and Somerset's foot soldier brigade at Bridport."

"Dost mean my Lord Grey be an embroiderer of the truth, my Lord Duke." Ingrams smiled, knowing full well what was to come. Monmouth nodded confirming the cavalry was led by Grey, yet attacked from a flank, was fought off by the Dorset Militia. His soldiers of foot caught up and saved a complete rout.

"My heart lays heavy with history-making much against my better judgement. I fear the time be not ripe, less fortuitously since the Inter Regnum twixt Commonwealth and re-instigation of monarchy, originally in the guise of my blood-kin father, Charles Stuart."

Ingrams knew precisely what the Duke meant hastening to change the subject.

"Thou knowest of the whereabouts of Blackbeard's step-daughter, Clarissa and her stable lad friend from the spies in the town?" Ingrams queried.

"Aye, word reached me days ago Ned Teach's ward lay recovering from a murder attempt - the lad's name escapes me though."

"Tom. In service originally to known infamous Lyme hostelries as The Olde Shippe Inne up the coast a spell and The Black Dog in nearby silver street. Unwittingly thy servant forced the boy to transfer allegiance to the sea who can be a cruel mistress. Bravely, when the highwayman broke into the girl's sick-bed attic, Tom helped her to escape death. En route to the sea by way of an underground smuggler's cave, he and the girl rescued thy servant hanging inverted in the bell mouth. This chaste girl be the only living witness twixt Jess the Pearly and the hangman's gibbet." His breath rattled in his chest nervously recalling the close call in the cavern. "I found it necessary to pursue the children for information pertaining to this wanted felon, combined with more pressing ventures of thy father's "whispered pardon" for the pirate king. Thoughts of my freedom might cloud over in thy head - this be not my aim and I beg of thee to reconsider should this be the case."

Monmouth extended himself with further obvious knowledge of the day.

"Letters-of-patent carrying the great seal be but a passe-to-porte by Parliament to authorise and enable the bearer to enjoy privilege or to do some act. So be ye on some mission to thwart thy servant in his new endeavours, sir."

"Perish such devious thoughts, my lord. Yet if I tell thee my endeavours be separate to thy cause and in no way be treasonable towards thy presence in Lyme." Rising he afforded his benefactor a brief but humbling bow - he was no fool and certainly did not want to dally with this man's senses, especially if he were to eventually be his king. "Thy father, a month before his death, afforded a state pardon to the perpetrator of his great treasure ships. Old Spain might be placated if these vessels, whilst traversing the oceans with gold and silver mined from Peru and Potosi in the Americas, and by his own Barbary pirates did fail at last to shuttle the same betwixt England and the Indies. This larger-than-life villain be a legend in his own lifetime who seeks no more than to die with clear conscience forgiven by his native land. He is the Lieutenant Governor of Jamaica and Tortuga, Captain Henry Morgan the Terrible."

"I know naught of the letters of marque or patent. Though thy youthful helpers be safe aboard the good ship *Maracaibo.*

"The Revenge."

"Aye *The Revenge."*

Monmouth discounted past business directly concerning his dead father and his black-hearted friend's wishes. Returning by distraction to Ingrams' original concern - that of the children's whereabouts. "Yes Ingrams, thy wards be safe and well. I be obligated to allow ye thy freedom so mayhap it be best if ye travel once more in the moored ship's direction." Monmouth added softly, "this business of intrigue and spying - be it well paid if thou succeedeth? I of all people can guess the price of failure if thou doesn't." Then stopped him from answering by a raised hand. "Mayhap it be thine own business and I shall no longer inquire of ye where thy political loyalties lie. 'tis best I know not for it mayhap cloud my judgement by releasing thee." Monmouth withdrew his close-up perusing of his face.

"Thy little wards be safe in the care of the privateer Teach on the afore-mentioned vessel. Apparently there was a last ditch attempt on their lives from this dastardly Pearly fellow who boarded ship and tried to abduct the maid. Thwarted thankfully by the girl's step-father. The tale relayed to thy servant by good captain Dampier.."

Ingrams appeared most concerned with the children's welfare and inquired with bated breath, "Ah, I'm glad his guns were spiked and presumably the perpetrator was the known rogue we had the misfortune to mention earlier this night."

"No, this blackguardly rapscallion were known as Jess the Pearly."

Watching Ingrams smile to confirm the villain to be one and the same.

"I see - well apparently he abducted the maid aboard and was about to despatch her when the Barbary corsair apparently rescued her. 'tis a smite interesting that this privateer should turn out to be the missing step-father."

"And what of the highwayman aboard. Was he despatched in the furore."

"Disappeared without trace despite a bow to stern search by a full crew."

Ingrams angered and Monmouth noticing this inquired why so.

"The scoundrel has stolen a twinned document from thy late father."

"Ah, the King be dead - long live the King," Monmouth mused irreverently.

The bad taste was not for Ingrams to moralise on maybe the devious musing referred unto the wicked uncle James - though in a metaphorical context.

The Duke recalled the earlier statement about the missing document.

"The Whispered Pardon." He finally acknowledged nodding thoughtfully, concluding, "Twas thought to be a nonsense and its presence reached me in the Hague. My advisors thought it best to

179

inform me though placed no real value to such whimsical nonsense from my father's pen. Although in hindsight it just might have put pressure on the pirates to throw in their lot with my cause."

"Aye, my lord and what a formidable force they would have made sailing up the Thames to strike at the very heart of the Rump Parliament."

"Aye, we be all experts in hindsight."

The Duke turned away and paced the room spinning on the heel of his boot on reaching the tall window. Confronting Ingrams from afar he directed his forefinger at the bulge in his shirt to inquire.

"And what of the bloodied documents inside thy vest sir."

Looking down the spy noticed a blanched crimson stain from Albemarle's wound had changed his sea-discoloured calico blouson into a brown patch, clearly showing an outline. Reaching inside and gripping jointly the two dampened sheaves of parchment. Sighing loudly, as if undone, placed them carefully side-by-side on the table's surface. Temptingly positioned for the other man to reach over and examine them. The Duke moved closer to the table and slowly reached out saying, "Do I so dangerously tamper with history, Mr. Ingrams?"

Direct questioning ignored, his companion merely raised the goblet and sipped his cordial before responding. "Presumably thou dost not refer to these documents I consider to be of some import." Shaking his head and refraining from gathering them yet, Monmouth continued to peruse them only from a distance confirming eloquently if not adamantly, "This sir, is yesterday's history today, circumspect and deliberated upon over turbulent years of English politics. I, on the other hand, hope to be tomorrow's history, so do I deserve tomorrow's history today as I now reject yesterday's history."

It was all getting too complicated for the simple mind and straightforward thinking of a spy in the pay of the Rump Parliament. Though it seemed apt to offer some sort of retaliation to the colourful if somewhat confusing oratory.

"An old legend purports there is only today, tomorrow never comes and that yesterday be gone forever. Mayhap it be best if thou dost concern thyself only with tomorrow's fate my liege." Ingrams purposely allowed himself the slip of social etiquette. Impertinent of him to suggest anything to his betters, yet it had the desired effect -

180

the documents slid back across the table unopened. Ingrams left them there. He felt the gesture would show that he too was in no hurry to tamper with history - yesterday's or that very day.

"Events weigh heavily on thy servant, D'Arcy Ingrams, sir. My cavalry officer, himself a competent officer with military experience, chose to shoot dead my pay-master. A silly quarrel over a black stallion. It was not for the likes of these men to decide their own and thy servant's fate. Individually they knew their rightful place in these turbulent times and latent history making. They decided a personal quarrel would thus change the outcome of my war, yet I shall foray forth to do what man should do when requested of him."

A sporadic conversation over the next twenty minutes passed relatively slowly as the two bared their souls to the other man. Somehow Monmouth knew that fate had intervened and this solitary incident could change the outcome.

That morning was to be the last time D'Arcy Ingrams, King's man and spy and the Pretender to the English throne, James, Duke of Monmouth were to meet.

Somehow they knew this and each respected their individual pathways would not cross on the same side again. Parliament had already risen and offered full support to James II, King of England, offering up also by placing their great seal behind the armies of the realm and for just defence of the Crown. Rising to approach and grip the other's hand in friendship, the bond created by the giving back of the other's life was poignant yet fragile.

Ingrams would have died for Monmouth in the bed chamber of the old inn, albeit in the heat of the moment, yet this honouring of an unwritten pledge of loyalty placed him in his debt. It paid off because now Ingrams' life was equally handed back to him on a silver platter, and with the Pretender's blessing. A companionable arm thrown around his shoulder, Ingrams was guided out of their private conference down the corridor to the door from whence he came, then at the opened doorway a black silk, silver braided tricorn hat with a sweeping turquoise ostrich feather was handed over to him. Informing of its provenance that it had belonged to his father, Charles II, recognisable whilst worn by Monmouth, and so its relative return to obscurity would be best for both parties. Donned with pride, the door held poignantly back for Ingrams to access the busying little street in

Lyme town, and although a meandering side street yet it accessed the main thoroughfare by way of a narrow route.

A curt nod from Monmouth was the final gesture as they stood expressionless eye-to-eye for one brief moment in the doorway. Unconsciously sweeping the hat from his head, D'Arcy Ingrams bowed low and deeply, he afforded to James, Duke of Monmouth the highest of honours humbling himself for one last time.

Then looked about him for a gap in the passing, milling, yeoman farmers as they stumbled along laughingly under an assortment of crude weaponry on their shoulders. Heartily hailing a last goodbye from the bottom of the steps outside the entrance, D'Arcy Ingrams turned away pulling the hat down over his eyes. Yanking the coat collar up even on that warm day gave a modicum of concealment, then slipped away with silent thanks for his freedom, melting into the crowds and sunshine of that June day took only a minute or so. Even though it was an hour before Ingrams realised he'd left Albemarle's duplicated papers lying on the rich patina of the dining table at the mysterious house in George Street.

Chapter Thirteen MORS VINCET

Thy prisoner Clarissa am I
captured from thy first sigh
and from thy first smile
never more free to while

Bonded together by unseen chain
weighted by need to be with ye again
thy prisoner be ever doomed
though so willingly groomed

Trapped behind bars of love
softly held like a dove
thy eyes thy kisses thy touch
light thy face to mean so much

In calico pantalettes or lace
twinkling blue eyes fair of face
a love as gentle as thy breath
never dreaming o' escape "till death

Poem: Prisoner

"Dalliance and frivolity be the downfall o' many a young suitor."

Pernickety grumbled gently struggling to invert cut-down bottles into still wet brown mortar under the rook eaves of the Black Dog Inn. It was the secret sign of the night traders, indicating a safe-house to passing flaskers and regular crocodiles of passing smugglers.

"Churches and clergy have grown fat on proceeds of smuggling," Pernickety had said, "'bout time we put a stop to their high goings-on, mayhap earn ourselves a bit o' kill-devil t'boot." Her statement initially had referred to her missing stable-boy Tom, and how so willingly he'd run off with the maid to trace her missing father. No loyalty from servants she'd complained.

"So what's the old parson done to upset ye now?" Jake inquired mockingly.

"Let's say he estreated in default o' payment for liquor." Pernickety wittered heaving and squinting at the flash of sun on green bottle bases.

"Don't think ye should use the word "kill-devil" in the same sentence as the church or the clergy, could be incitement to portend o' bad luck."

"Rumbullion be rumbullion our Jake, and the devil take the hindmost I say."

"Aye mayhap ye be right, Pernick." Jake capitulated to her womanly wiles.

Distracted as he stared to the top of the lofty ladder at the welcome arrival of the summer swallows, they dipped and dived high above on insects drawn up by rising heat of morning. Indigo blue sky and warmth of summer sunshine in England was all a man could ask for. Despite on an empty belly with no chance of satisfying vittles "till this busy-body completed her clandestine task. Business was profoundly brisk and need for more fruitful supplies of illicit beverages was sorely required. Town full of red-leg strangers, the Black Dog's fit to burst every night, yet kindly so, Jake still found time to wonder what happened to the maid and their cheeky stable lad. Abducted no doubt, mayhap put to the sword by one of these dastardly murtherers in their town. His thoughts raced over events of the past few days, he now found himself longing for a smidgen of peace and quiet of past summers in a quieter port. Witnessing as they did, the uprising of Oliver Cromwell and the Roundheads, Lyme Regis then had been under siege for many weeks. Now, it seemed all sorts of angry skirmishing was beginning all over again and for what purpose this time. Who cared for the throne and the politics o' the day - they still had to find heavy taxes.

A plaintive seabird's cry as it swooped low over the roof seemed to agree, and have an accord with his musing as he stared up at her teetering atop of the makeshift step ladder. Perspiration bounced from her brow to her forearms, or was she just glowing for this was a term she always used. Women glowed, men perspired and horses did sweat. His thoughts came back to another grand over-used saying of hers that men required six hours o' sleep, women seven, only fools did thus require eight. Shouting louder, assuming the man had failed to appreciate her concern - now repeated the earlier statement.

"I said our Jake, that dalliance and frivolity be the downfall o' many a young suitor." It warranted an answer and she half-turned atop her perch and was now looking down at his puzzled face at the base of the ladder.

"Young Tom ye mean." He toyed with her emotions.

"Why now. Just who d'ye think I was a meaning of."

"Dunno, could be the Duke." Jake offered playfully bored.

She fixed him with a beady eye, "Well now - supposing ye could be right."

She turned back to the finality and success of her task, pressing the ends firmly into the pliable mixture. Then with a brief warning of her intentions, made to descend the rickety structure to a safer altitude. Quickly she went back down the ladder to stand alongside Jake and confirm the sign was discreet yet effective for business.

"According to the local chatter the Pretender's mistress pawned her beautiful family jewels to help pay for his visitation to these here parts." She folded her arms authoritatively as if coming by the knowledge increased her status as a female. Jake nodded grimly and glanced around him then leaned towards her added,

"Aye, only after the good Duke pawned his own family jewels and finery."

Jake tucked his thumbs into his waistcoat and puffing himself up importantly, he added with equal knowledge of such idle-talk, "T'were to pay for weaponry, musket and ball, heavy cannon, militia horse and.." Stopping mid-sentence when, head-down, a stranger approached from behind to stand silently close by.

Jake and the woman failed to recognise the destitute impoverished look of the hunched man with sea salt-stained clothing, strangely adorned with a fashionable black silk hat with an unusual ostrich feather. The manifestation one of a down-at-heel aristocrat, his one redeeming feature that of an expensive fedora hat and flouncy feather. Pulled well down over his eyes he moved right up to them before stating rudely,

"Thy ale be likened to brackish water o' little taste and substance."

Felicity Pernickety was astounded. Mouth-open, speechless that any man could speak to her so. Glaring first to Jake who seemed to find his remarks amusing, then back at this abhorrent stranger. Snorting indignantly she carefully rolled up her right sleeve ready to pummel him into the dust.

She exercised her right to summary execution for such stated treason

in front of a witness with regard to the quality of her foaming ale, the man added a suffix only this time a lilt of laughter could be detected.

"Of course, I myself be partial to a smidgen of home-baked homity pie and the tangy taste o' quince marmalade." D'Arcy Ingrams tipped back his hat from a broad grin and mischievous dancing of his twinkling blue eyes. After laughing sheer relief at unnecessary avoidance of confrontation, Pernickety could do nought but slap the impudent villain lightly across the face, then slipping a powerful arm around his broad shoulders, invited him quickly through the door to safe cool shadows of the old ale room of the Inn.

• * *
•

It was not long before a wooden trencher of piping hot food and a vessel full of ale lay before the man devoid of black hat which at first masked his appearance. Squatting as he was at a window bench table, Ingrams apparently had not forgotten his manners by so placing the grand adornment over one knee. Tucking ravenously into his meal of her aforementioned homity pie and steaming potatoes from Ireland floating in a thick greasy gravy.

"Careful your feathers don't interfere wi' thy vittles." The woman playfully sniggered flicking a forefinger at the hat. "You know - I be unable to recall

if I liked ye or not, especially now I know thee to be one of those London fops." Giggling helplessly she was relieved that soon she would receive news of her ward and little Tom the stable boy. Yet not afore he'd slake a raging thirst and fill himself with good food. Smilingly Ingrams threw down his pewter spoon and rubbed her chin.

"Ye must have done ma'am, for thou hast fed and watered me thus proud."

Ingrams grinned up at her whilst spooning the slurry of pastry, cheese and baked vegetables into his mouth. "Thy homity pie and thy pottage doth go afore ye in repute - I'll wager a goodly sum."

"Silver tongued knave." Pernickety mumbled as she rose and made

186

to leave
her seat opposite. Standing she rounded on Ingrams saying,

"It was the good doctor which did tell the reasoning by which ye turned up soon after happening on his shop that way."

Pernickety threw down the gauntlet of challenge. She now wondered how Ingrams would thus deal with it. She added in the same breath,

"Gentlemen o' the night was thy cover for more dastardly doings - tub man's batman no. Smuggler, no. King's man, yes - I'm a thinking."

D'Arcy Ingrams moodily began eating again, at least he would satiate his hunger afore she bundled him out into the street again - for this was the direction things were building. The woman recalled the incident whilst they carried the injured maid to the harbour of Lyme looking for a ship's surgeon. How they happened upon the doctor's residence, yet soon confronted by the King's man's interfering. Completing his first meal for a deal of time by mopping liquid to a goodly chunk of her coarse brown bread, glowered respite from the domineering statements. Sliding the empty wooden platter away he challenged her fecklessness with his eyes.

"Where be the good doctor in these difficult days."

"Where every Englishman and decent law abiding citizen be these days."

She snapped back recovering from the piercing glare.

"Certainly not here in this hostelry." Jake added and shot a smile at Ingrams. "And surely not in old Lyme, either." Ingrams continued the jape and they burst into light-hearted laughter, supping his ale, he felt he ought not have jested with the woman, especially about the way she kept her liquor for it was superb, golden clear, an after-taste which smacked o' malt and fine spices from the far East. His imagination wandered to quieter times and cool winter evenings in London taverns, where her kept ale would be well received and even probably lend itself to a good mulling from a red hot fire iron.

"My apologies ma'am for the earlier jesting and remarks about thy ale, for it be insurmountable by unique taste, colour and fine qualities." Capitulating, Ingrams shrugged an apology to make up for his gushing.

Nodding her concurrence, slowly the woman preened herself like a jay bird - running long fingers through her hair, finally tossing her head to pout like a sixteen year-old. Perceptibly quick to relent, half-suspecting he was making merry with her senses any-road-up. Poking him playfully she said,

"Thy apology be acceptable to thy servant. And to answer thy question "bout the good doctor." Suddenly she was startled by the entrance way opening and glancing round did spy two furtive looking men. Strangers to her eyes -though many were those dark days of insurrection and rebellion. Entering they sat down nearby the ale counter and looked pointedly at her for service.

Pernickety could think of nought more but additional funding for her overflowing coffers. Her maxim to make hay whilst the sun shone in its heaven, hurriedly rose to her feet by way of servile reaction, then leant over and whispered hurriedly to Ingrams,

"Temple was in the ale house yesterday, he mentioned there was to be a testing of ball and powder in the next town o' Bridport. He were on-call to deal with wounding o' any o' these skirmishing foot soldiers and cavalry men."

Making her way toward the newcomers she turned briefly to tap a forefinger alongside her right nostril. The wink he also spied conveyed silently that wagging tongues in front of strangers was not to be recommended in those uncertain times. Several minutes later the woman re-joined Jake and Ingrams involved in deep discussion about the caves known to be beneath the cellars of the ancient inn. It was the timely rescue effected by the maid and Tom that Jake was impressed with. And to think the precious bundle he'd carried so far at death's door weeks earlier, had repaid tenfold this action by saving someone else's life.

"How be the babes." Jake had wondered aloud his back to the newcomers and far enough away not to be overheard.

"Safe aboard ship, or so I be reliably informed." Ingrams remarked casually, though it was not enough information for the volatile Pernickety as she made her presence felt.

She leaned forward to whisper, "How safe - be safe."

Ingrams looked over the woman's shoulder to the strangers who seemed preoccupied with the leisurely consumption of their served vittles and tankards of foaming ale, glancing back at her with a knowing if sycophantic nod, he said, "The source shall we say be impeccable and not to be questioned."

"Ah, ye mean the Du....."

A powerful finger shot forward and pressed her lips preventing the rest coming out, Ingrams' response was anticipated by the lighting-up of her face as she realised of whom he spake. Hushed voices from the other side of the room had stopped as well, Pernickety became aware of this and began gossiping about the fine sailing weather for the ships in the harbour. The murmur of distant chatter started up again and they soon reverted to their subject once she stated rather loudly,

"Sly devils them flaskers - tried to dump "slack-casks" on me they did." Puffing herself up she thumped the table-top pretending to make no never mind of the stranger's and their constant whispering. "Her wound." Pernickety mumbled, her back to the men to prevent lip reading.

"My little Venus's chest wound - how be it."

"It fares well. The boy Tom has looked after her and seems more than a smite sweet on her tiny personage." Ingrams grinned broadly, it was the way adults did whilst discussing the pubescence of the young who suddenly awoke to life and its fruits. One stranger rose and walked towards them sparking a change in conversation. Dwindling now to ramble once more about all and sundry about them in those unsettling days and nights. This change of tack warned the woman, whose back was still turned, that someone approached. Ingrams stated loudly,

"Twas then we caught a Danish slaver off the coast o' Sierra Leone."

Jake brightly took up the fictional yarn continuing with, "On the way back to port ye must have encountered white water on the Portland Race and Plymouth Roads for there was bad weather abroad at the time."

"Aye, that we did."

Reaching the huddled group the man menaced over them with a biting question. "Which one of ye be known as Squire Ingrams?"

All three looked up at the hovering middle-aged man with iron greying hair and appeared only part-dressed in a seafarer's clothing. Blue breeches, sail-cloth shirt, turned down knee-boots. Black coarse woollen half coat, narrow lapels and brass buttons emblazoned. A white spotted red neckerchief protruded from under his black silk tricorn. Jauntily placed, the hat held his dark matted hair in place along with a silk neckerchief which clung to his throat. This was withdrawn as he spoke and it wiped a perspiring face. Patiently he awaited an answer from the sitting group. D'Arcy Ingrams' bravado took an initiative by speaking first and sparing the other's embarrassment by the necessity of revelation. Rising to his feet from between the high-back settle and table he said now realising the man was in some of the highwayman's clothing.

"Who so might be inquiring after him,." Hand slipping underneath his frock coat to where a knife lay thrust deep into his waistband.

"Didn't give a name. Only paid for a message to be delivered and that was that the man known as Ingrams was to meet with him later this night at the Black Dog Inn." Hesitating when realising nobody had really helped him in his inquiries. Relenting somewhat due to the defiant and stony silence he added,

"He'd a document for this Ingrams and spoke of some importance attached."

"Where was your contact when he requested this meeting."

Ingrams asked knowing he'd get little or no information unless he revealed a sprat to catch a mackerel, adding quickly, "Mayhap ye can describe this man so's if we run into this Ingrams we might pass on a somewhat fuller and detailed bulletin."

Looking disappointed at not identifying who he'd come about, the lone seaman shrugged his shoulders and said,

"Mischievous looking sort o' character. I rowed him back from my lobster pots in the bay - hailed me from aboard a ship moored off-shore." He sniffed recollection adding, "Bony nose, thin features, pallor like death itself - topped off with a black eye patch over one eye." The man took a grubby brown leather pouch from his pocket, tossing it up and down in his open hand. This action rattled coinage within - with a roguish grin he turned away saying,

"Well I've done what I was bade to do and been paid handsome. Whether I've delivered the message to the right person or not - 'tis good ale money."

He winked down at D'Arcy Ingrams rather pointedly, then turned towards his colleague who rose to meet him at the door and they made ready to leave.

The other fellow carried a bundle of clothing which fell apart as he stood awaiting the return of his colleague. Jess's wine-coloured frock coat and thigh length boots tumbled to the floor and was hurriedly gathered again.

Checking to spy everything of value had been secured once more and now standing in the doorway, the first seaman glanced back to call cheerily,

"Tell this man to meet the black-hearted rogue here at nine o' the hour this night. That is - if he wishes to see the aforementioned documents again."

As his companion with the clothes bundle made his way into the street closing the huge door behind him he left his comrade to add, "Mayhap he's another interested party to dally with." With a friendly knowing wave he placed a hand on the latch, "Mayhap it will whet this Ingrams' appetite if he knows there be a swapping o' the documents should he be so interested. A gold coin balance to grease the transaction be all that's necessary."

Pausing to let his words to sink in, then turned away and was gone to the brilliant sunshine outside. Creaking shut on its hinges the door now appeared to seal-in a poignant atmosphere, it was several moments before anyone spoke.

Pernickety took a deep breath and sighing heavily, finally spoke. "Be these documents the ones the good doctor informed of?" She nodded anticipating agreement from Ingrams and smiled when it came. "And ye be a King's man inspired to estreat these dark orders from the crown." She was nodding in unison again only this time the gesticulation was checked.

"Thou needs to know little more for thy health's sake now be a goodly woman and fetch more ale for Jake and myself." Watching her leave and silver coins changed hands underneath the table once an agreement was made in her absence of a near future task for the big man. Jake nodded silent acceptance of the deal and made to follow the strangers, the latch falling gently on his fleeting departure. When Pernickety returned to the settle with a jug of ale she immediately noticed the absence of her manservant. Falling on Ingrams to scold him vehemently, "Blast yer eyes, Ingrams ye shouldn't involve innocents in thy skulduggery." Leaning forward and placing the brimming ale jug down she growled, "How much coinage did ye give my tired-witted beast o' burden."

191

"Nary a bent farthing." Ingrams lied nodding to the back house. "He be merely taking nature's necessary relief at thy heads woman."

Holding her head at a questioning angle and staring hard with one eye she glowered until he relented and said softly, "Three pieces of eight - pure silver cut from a bar cob coin from the Potosi mine in New Spain. More Danegeld than thy poor wretch hath seen in many a long year, I'll warrant." Ingrams knew he was stating the obvious for the woman burst into tears, snuffling she spoke through a grubby nose rag.

"That loveable giant doth mean all the world to me. Excepting me, nobody can control his desires and excesses, give the lout too many coins o' the realm and he'll get deadly and stupid drunk - as sure as eggs be eggs."

Ingrams rose and placed a comforting arm around her shoulders as he spoke softly, "Then I have inadvertently wronged ye ma'am. Though my intentions were intended to be honourable, I certainly meant thy man servant no lasting harm." Giving her an encouraging shoulder hug he added solemnly. "I have a task to do which rests heavily on my heart, for thy maid Clarissa saved my life and I wrongly involved her in my dastardly task to deliver some papers of import. It pleases me that she be safe and away from the evil doings o' the highwayman, Jess Mandrake."

"Amen to that." Pernickety snorted into her kerchief.

"Thine own goodly nature and service in helping to save her life has probably brought ye a lasting life-long friendship with the maid. She so spoke kindly of thy loving tenderness toward her." His syrupy words were to gloss over his wrong doing with her manservant, yet it was important to his mission she did not intervene in any way later that night.

"How can a lump o' lard like me be wrathful to thee and thy business and

for helping her locate her father, Ned. Clarissa Lovelace Peach is a loveable little girl who was dragged back from entering death's door itself."

"Teach ma'am. Peach were afforded her by her piratical parents. The slight change in her surname was to prevent the authorities associating her with Ned Teach and Anne Bonny's wrong doings past and present tense."

"Ned Teach - o' course. Now thy servant sees."

Felicity Pernickety looked kindly up into his blue eyes and ceased her snuffling, then she stated rather matter-of-factly as she reached for and briefly touched his hand.

"Even if she did steal my stable lad from me and all his services - honest little tyke that he was." Snuffling once more she felt her tears well as she complained, ". Now my Jake be gone forever as well."

"Not forever - an hour o' the clock only. Ye mark my word."

Ingrams smiled without the woman noticing, for it mattered not about her own feelings, greater political events were at stake here and he was content in the knowledge she might allow him into the back house. Hopefully safe in the place known to inn keepers as the squier - where casual visitors, apart from customers purchasing illicit liquor, would-be smugglers delivering the wares or parsons and tavern keepers purchasing them. All would arrive at dead o' night and only with the woman's permission aforehand. Making for an upstairs bedchamber on further advice from the woman and only after a cautionary word about the two strangers, Ingrams hoped for some well earned sleep. Relaxation until evening and the pre-planned meeting with the highwayman - forewarned, so say, by the friendly seafarers. Reaching the bottom tread of the stairwell and was called upon to wait awhile, Pernickety caught him up and thrust a large white highly glazed porcelain chamber pot into his hand. Holding it high up by its handle, then looking first to the empty pot then at the curious twinkle in the woman's eye, complained that it appeared to be completely devoid of ale. A slap on the back to send him on his way causing him to trip the treads.

"I think ye hath had enough ale for one session."

Thanking her for her sarcastic concern, he turned away and holding the pot in front of him, slowly made his way upstairs.

Pernickety smiled to herself over the past hour or two's events and recalled his saucy dalliance with her on their meeting again.

"I too be partial to a smidgen o' quince marmalade." Gripping her portly middle with both hands she laughed until she shook vigorously. "And don't we know it, my girl, and don't we just know it."

Chapter Fourteen   THE HANGING MAN

Thy candle be my mantle it illuminates the night
opulent translucence will burn with silent light
shaft of waxy substance as tender as thy skin
hallowing flame always will warm the heart within

The candle dance is gracious to visions in my heart
conjoining gaze doth prophesy therefore love will start
spiritual smoke will rise thus the flames expire
like man nothing lasts forever soon its light will tire

Wispy smoke dashes atop burning flaxen ember
previous night like previous life will anyone remember
spiralling smoke be like casting o'er a veil
spirit soul floats upwards unto where we know so well

So as the spent candle our duty to life is through
rising grey mist of time thus drawn from you
swirl the helix upwards to where you can be mine
affectionately meet in harmony of a hallowed place divine

Poem: Candle Dance

Sunday 14th June

The long room of the Black Dog Inn fell to a whispering silence. A yellowing candle stump sitting on the ale counter flickered violently in the draught and went out. Others in the hostelry took over the task of illuminating the ale house as the jollity and countenance of the drinking den in Silver Street died away and finally ceased.

The inn's occupants knew the front door had opened for fresh smells of brackish seaweed-laden breezes permeated the stuffy atmosphere, suddenly the inert swirling clouds of blued wood smoke rushed to escape. Originally the men huddled pleasurably over their dice and primero games, now though they turned their curious heads to spy just who was framed in the doorway. Sharply the ambience was broken as the battered front door, blackened and sprung with age, slammed back onto its hinges with an horrendous "crack". This blatant and unnecessary action flaked white distemper from the wall, causing it to flutter like snow onto the flags. A pair of sea boots stepped amongst the scattering, distantly aloft of his shoulders the muted roar of a turning tide suddenly filtered inside. Sinewy alert for quickened movement and with the cat-like stealth the man entered the low portals. His presence instantly cast a shadow of apprehension on the proceedings, a silhouette recognised by the notoriety of his black eye-patch. Slowly and furtively Jess Mandrake stepped forward into the ale room full of muttering. Shabbily adorned in tired nautical clothing, discoloured hop-sack breeches supported by broad brass-buckled belt, dark-blue half-length coat concealed a yellow woollen smock and a white shirt with its collars flicked out. Barely recognisable in sea-going attire, no longer the look of a lone horseman and known road-robber on borrowed time from the gibbet. Satisfied the personage he sought was not residing at the long room counter or ensconced at table, appearing to relax, dragged off his hat. No longer anticipating trouble from the inn's occupants, yet the tremulous forefinger of his solitary fighting hand stroked the quillion cross of his naval long sword. Still sheathed, though loosely hung for prompt action. Carefully he scanned the scattered cliques of gamblers and card players in a shadow-hung chamber sparsely illuminated by one candle and a roaring log fire; England known to be chill after sunset on long summer evenings.

Miss Pernickety hurried from a side room waving an iron skillet screeching as she emerged for him to, "Shut the front door or put thyself back on the street." Then paralysed with fear as she realised who it was in an instant - decided to brave it out. Shaking the heavy skillet she afforded him a defiant toss of her red hair.

Jess had already felt the power of her right arm and sullenly grunted acknowledgement, slowly he moved clear of the door. Once inside he leaned back and reached over his shoulder - flipping the latch into place. Slamming the door he complied with her irritated demand, pausing to adjust his eye patch flung himself into the nearest bench settle table by the bowed window.

Pernickety, realising the lengthening room shadows were unacceptable to her older groups of card playing gamblers due their tiring eyesight, busied her-self now by putting a lighted spill to many scattered lanterns. They swung from age-and-smoke-darkened oak beams checkering a sagging ceiling, encouraged into movement by the draught from an opened doorway. The church candle's faltering flame became upright to resume its full brightness, with an acrid stinking of tallow fat its high flame eclipsing the dark figure in the corner. A flurrying shower of sparks suddenly combusted upward as a heavy log settled into nights of deep white wood ash. Roaring flames stretched lazily at the broad chimney set well back into the inglenook. The flaring gave a momentary burst of additional light and revealed a hovering presence of another figure squatting in a shadowy corner.

A scrawny spiky-haired street-urchin cowered then glanced up from a trencher of hot food provided earlier by the ever-benevolent Pernickety. It was her way of gently pressing a new stable-lad into service, but only after conditioning him to regular meals and a straw bed for cool nights. His squinting gaze darted, reflecting the ever moving firelight, the ebony eyes seemed to flash fear alerting others in the room to be wary of him. Rags covered his bare essentials, well just about enough to remain humanly decent. Patches of exposed flesh were grubby and in dire need of thorough cleansing. Painfully gaunt, darkened rings surrounding the piercing stare deep set into a facial pallor appearing one stage away from death. The ten year old overcame a natural reaction to take flight, gradually his head lowered and slowly the lad concentrated once again on the only square meal he'd consumed for many days.

Jess the Pearly discounted the lad as being no threat to him and leaning forward thumped a table with his fist calling for service, at the same instant voiced his thoughts loudly,

"D'Arcy Ingrams where be thee - damn and blast yer eyes."

Felicity Pernickety scurried to fill a clay jar with foaming ale and grabbed a tankard holding both with a single grip, gripped in the other hand was her skillet for continued protection. Crossing back to place them both before the slumped figure. The insisted precaution bringing separate vessels, was a common practice, mainly due to the covert practice of a King's shilling placed into the base of an ale mug. Easily downed unless the more stately ale houses could afford glass bottomed tankards, an expensive exercise, especially when the pewter tankards could easily be switched during a distracting conversation anyway. Once the ale was quaffed, the victim was taken to have accepted the first pay of the crown and thus forced unwittingly and recruited into the King's Navy. Passing press gangs toured nightly the ale and beer houses and would spy a chalked signal on their portals - placed by their spies who so did the dirty deed. Encouraged inside by the mark the officer would inform the victim of his plight, men would then drag the unsuspecting fellow out into the street never to be seen by his family again. Biding her time whilst ale was poured from clay pot to pewter tankard, and only then did Pernickety receive a cartwheel penny and silver farthing for services rendered unto the testily volatile highwayman. Jess the Pearly reached out and gripped her forearm, he leaned forward and muttered softly,

"I've a score to settle with thee and thy damnable pot. If memory serves - I've only just recovered from thy blow to my cranium." Thrusting her backwards to pour himself ale he advised, "Now get thee back to thy serving woman, I'll be settling my other account with ye later."

It was dark outside the inn and a rising wind sighed through an overhead cracked pane of glass. Spider web perforations allowed street noises and revelry from regular evening gatherings, apparently rejoicing in news which arrived from the latest fights and flights of Monmouth's rebel armies.

Watching her leave the room Jess turned on other men crouched over ale pots and their playing cards, desperately trying to ignore disturbance to their evening. Scared faces glanced away to avoid further confrontation of eye contact with the known villain.

"Ye best be minding thy own businesses - I'm thinking, good sirs."

One group played the popular card game primero whilst others scattered in shadowy corners tossed pairs of dice, gambling low denomination silver coins for amusement and pleasure. By turning their backs on his presence they hoped this might exclude them from further trouble brewing-up later in the evening. The inn's occupants were all of advancing years yet this did not stop them muttering confided discourtesy on the stranger's lack of etiquette and social qualities. It appeared only the willowy youth lay oblivious to the road robber's presence that night. After initial shock of seeing him enter the hostelry, the lad now slept noisily by the fire side. Otherwise engaged, the usual bout of rowdy fun seeking soldiers failed to turn up for a second evening now. All regiments having departed Lyme for the latest localised battle or skirmishing. Monmouth's motley army was hammered into as good a shape as any despite being ill-equipped. Wagging tongues and keen gossiping advised locals differing colours denoted regiments apart. Pernickety had received inadvertently enough such informative gossip over the past week to become a fully fledged spy. Musing inwardly the well known fact that anything can be preserved in alcohol except secrets, especially when half the part-time soldiers frequented her hostelry from time to time.

Jess rose from the window seat and crossing the floor to throw himself bad tempered into a fireside wooden settle. High-backed he felt the seat would afford good support for his disablement. Close to the lad now, Jess relaxed, placing his hat on the seat preventing anyone, unless invited from placing themselves down alongside. The one-armed, one-eyed man felt under threat of surprise must think ahead and cover his blind, vulnerable side. He looked at the front door with his naked eye then to a brass carriage clock on the nearby mantelpiece, trying desperately to recall where he'd seen the timepiece afore. Miserably he noted the clock and he held something in common - only having one arm. The hour hand and calibrated dividing numerals gave semblance of passing minutes. One eye restrictively affording perspective to distant objects, Jess rose to glean exact time by ascertaining it was now five minutes to nine of the hour, deciding a King's man might arrive shortly. That was, if he wanted to negotiate the whereabouts of the missing documents as desperately as he'd been led to believe by his emissaries.

The lad in the fireplace belched, his shrunken gullet rebelling at the comparative strangeness of a well-cooked generous portion of piping hot food. Waking at the experience, yet without trace of embarrassment for his ill -manners, wiped a sleeve over his brow to rid himself of perspiration created by the heat. Another phenomenon he was unused to at that time of the evening, the warmth from a glowing fireside. Disdainfully Jess looked down upon him perhaps seeing his own misspent youth, how he went from the gutter and begging to petty thieving of wealthy women or merchant purses in crowds amused by street traders or minstrels. Then to fall further and further down the ladder of debauchery to robbery with violence, finally ending up in London's Newgate Prison or "bedlam" as the inmates termed it. Escaping by desperately disguising himself as a turnkey. Fleeing and flouting law and order ever since. The musing of his fortuitous luck remaining unfettered by the law brought on an evil grin, sadly misinterpreted by the lad to be a friendly smile. A curled-lip leer quickly turned into a rising glower and put him straight in no uncertain terms, running the haunting turnpike, even stealing traveller tolls from turnpike-men themselves, yet now, he thought, if he played his hand carefully he might make more money this night than he'd seen in a lifetime.

Looking down at his dark blue serge cloth coat, Jess thought over his trip back to land from the anchor-tilting moored ship in Lyme Bay. How the sailor who agreed to row him ashore, his own craft retrieved by an irascible fisherman, this blackguard of a seaman demanding his fine velvet three quarter length coat, black silk tricorn edged with silver braid, brass buckled shoes and a final insult - disrobing from his finely stitched hose and breeches. However the rapscallion did offer up the naval broad sword of some grandeur and his own sea-washed warm clothing that chill evening afore. He should have killed him with his own sword. Too late for self-recriminating doubts now. Withdrawing a scuffed leather pouch of silver coins he pushed a groat under the nose of the mesmerised and rudely staring youth,

"Here, take thyself off and fetch an ale flagon for thy benefactor along with." He dead-lamped the young boy with his one good eye, "A small cordial for thine own thirst - but be quick about it!" Grabbing the bony arm of the youth as he rose to go, "And I'll be a having of the change in pennies o' the realm from the scurvy crone in the kitchens." Grumbling continually of the reckoning he had to settle with the woman, he watched the lad leave then to stare at the flames licking over a huge log. Losing himself within the atmosphere of warmth, the flames creating pictures of happier days when he was a whole fellow and much desired by women. How he'd romanced the young damsels when younger, and had he not sunk so much ale and trounced them so willingly he might have provided for a more comfortable dotage. The willing street urchin returned with a brimming clay jar only to trip and promptly slosh half the contents over Jess's foot. Leaping to his feet the highwayman kicked the air and cuffed the lad resoundingly, this vehemence caused yet more ale from the clay jar to be lost. Handing over the half-empty vessel and a smite o' change, totally disheartened the youth slunk back to his perch amongst the greying ashes. Sullenly to sip his cordial which fared better in the fracas. None of his volume was lost. Jess noticed this fact and snatching the drink away from the lad, poured some of the sweet summer berry cordial into his own ale - smirking as he returned what was left of the lad's beverage.

Grateful for anything in his life at that moment in time, the boy fell on the slops so as not to lose any more to the cruel actions of the highwayman.

Though now his own pewter tankard brimmed with flat liquid, and one deep sip told Jess he'd made a bad mistake, with a growl of distaste, he rose and spat indignantly onto the kindling of the fire. Flames hissed then roared to protect themselves against this dire effort to douse them. Ash erupted spouting white flurry over the lower part of his boot and this added to his fury. Furious at his own undoing the concoction in his hand was now totally unpalatable, Jess shook his fist at the youth. Again the leering faces glanced their way and then turned away from the leaping antics by the fireside. Angering due to being the focal point of attention once more, Jess demanded to know just what they were staring at; when no reaction was forth-coming he challenged each in turn, striding the length of the ale room stalking like a hunter stalks his prey. Eventually rounding on one such man hunched over and playing a card game of primero. Dressed all in black, of scruffy and unkempt appearance, yet at the same time strangely youthful underneath it all. This bundle of tied rags whose skin did not portray that of a beggar or a thief, continued to ignore his challenge and merely flick his paste boards onto the table surface. Slowly after a second confrontation did the man reach out and take up his wooden bowl of dark rum. Holding it to his lips and supping loudly he turned to hold the highwayman's mono-gaze himself part-concealed by the drinking vessel. Jess felt challenged by the dumb insolence and affronted, eventually he repeated his earlier question, "Well what be ye looking at."

The man kept his gaze firmly on the highwayman's blazing defiant good eye.

"Why don't ye answer me?" Reaching forward Jess hysterically pounded the table with his bony clenched fist, this action caused the man's drink to spill slightly and dribbles of golden liquid leached from the corners of his mouth. Suddenly rising to a height of over six feet, and placing the spent rum bowl to one side - head-bowed the dark clothed stranger dragged off his tricorn along with its flouncing ostrich feathers. At last this act of a modicum of humility told Jess the man was about to humble himself in front of his betters.

Holding the black accessory in front of his chest, the man's hand slid up inside the crown and withdrew a small wheel-lock pistol, exposing it he reached and placed it at the highwayman's temple on full-cock with a loud "double-click."

Jess the Pearly finally realised he was looking into the twinkling blue eyes of the one he'd come to meet and bargain with - D'Arcy Ingrams. Concealing the weapon back under the headband and from others in the room with a swaying movement of the tricorn silently advised the stunned highwayman to sit opposite him. The gun and hat was lowered into Ingrams" lap then the other hand scoop-gathered paste boards and began to deal a two-handed card session. His original gambling opponent, a man of enormous proportions, rose automatically from his seat and with a knowing wink, slid away to another table.

A buzz of excitement went around the room like wild fire. Ingrams, on hearing this disturbance rose briefly and glowered about him putting a stop to the raised voices. Revenuers and law and order spies were never far away. As he sat down he noted a more normal level of conversation was resumed.

The game of Primero began and was reluctantly taken up by the astonished Jess.

"Ye be a hard man to find "Pearly." Ingrams began, as he watched him take up the cards with difficulty - dancing fingers shook violently and failed to grip the thinning paste boards.

"There's many a man that has said that afore he died violently." Jess said with little conviction knowing his vitals faced the broad-gauged small-calibre pistol underneath the table. D'Arcy Ingrams looked past the threatening gaze deep down into Jess's very soul, he leaned forward saying quietly,

"If ye be trying to make yours truly nervous, mayhap it be best if I remind thee that this gun bodes well with a hair trigger." Withdrawing from a face-to-face confrontation he sat upright, noting with cruel satisfaction that Jess began to perspire profusely. Jittery expressions crossed his brow and the bony nose acting like a barrel-tap as tiny droplets of fear-induced sweat ran from the end to his clothing. Any thought of retaliatory action would be put off awhile, Ingrams decided as he once again scooped up the cards and dealt a second hand. Deliberately leaving the naval sword on him for if Jess was intending to retaliate, it would be this weapon and not one secreted about his person. The rather obvious way his captive closed his legs defensively on command now brought a smile to Ingrams' face. Lowering his eyes to hide this inadvertent reaction was what the highwayman was waiting for. It took a fleeting a moment for Jess to fling the distraction of playing cards at his face and to seize chance at escape by pushing the table on top of him. Springing lively at the same instant up to his feet and poking the gun to one side, withdrew the sword - he sent the pistol flying. Jess leaped about jabbing lively at Ingrams as he now rolled about sprawling on the stone floor, rolling and twisting away from the wild frenzied attack. Avoiding the offensive thrusting of the prodding weapon, he revolved into a puddle of spilt beverages from whence the table overturned, fervently dodging the "sword- dance" realising he'd also underestimated his partially disabled enemy. Knowing too it would only be a matter of time before anticipation let him down and he would be skewered by the long sword like a stuck pig. Suddenly as if by some mystic levitation - Jess was dancing above and in front of him. Lifted bodily from his sword-thrusting intimidation to a futile kicking of his legs, now danced like a demented jester in mid-air. Hairy arms clung to his midriff swinging him to and fro - then closed tighter and began squeezing the very life out of him in a tremendous bear hug. The sword fell to the flags with a loud clatter, this noise prompting the gyrating Ingrams to leap up to his feet, kicking the weapon to one side he thanked the good offices of the massive stranger- the hunter was now the hunted.

"''tis in thy debt once more and a very grateful one too."

Ingrams spoke sincerely to the man of gargantuan proportions holding Jess likened to a limp rag doll, lowering him to his feet, the giant turned and walked back to the table from whence he'd came. A brief nod was all the acknowledgement Ingrams beheld as he retrieved his fallen pistol. Once again he covered his enemy with powder and ball from the cocked weapon.

"Blast yer eyes." Jess said, smarting with pain and rubbing himself round his waist checking to see if any ribs were broken. D'Arcy

Ingrams leaned towards him whilst he was about his business, reaching inside the man's vest withdrew a document containing the Parliamentary seal. Placing it on the now uprighted table, he waved him to sit once more.

"Thou be a dangerous fellow, Pearly." Reaching over he tore the black eye patch from the highwayman's face exposing the pure white ball which kept open the socket. "Mayhap it be best if I doth hold something thou treasures and thus to put thee under threat o' ransom." Tapping Jess' temple sharply with the pistol, a left hand shot out to catch the white ball as he removed the false eye. Holding it high in front enabled him to keep spy on the highwayman, whilst glancing at the object in the palm of his hand.

"Thy pride and joy, eh Jess Mandrake. Why 'tis naught but a rounded piece o' ivory from the East." Jess looked extremely uncomfortable. Ingrams had to decide whether to put this down to nervousness at downfall or worry about what he thought was an object of real value. Deciding to find out - why not. A moment earlier this heathen would have stuck him with the sword and walked off with his purse, only luck and interference of the kindly giant saved him to fight on another day. The woman approached from the back room now the commotion was over, she was not stupid and survived many such skirmishing due to such lordly diplomacy.

"Ah for sure ''tis Miss Pernickety herself - how fare ye ma'am. I'll be having a puncheon of good port wine broached and enjoyed by all of my goodly friends here this night. Bring thy servant here some French red wine also some genuine Crowlink for my lofty colleague and stoutly handsome friend there."

Touching her arm before she hurried off added sombrely,

"A last resort would be Porter, but if this be so smash the red wax and tug the cork ready for our delectations," Ingrams watched her smile at the thought of goodly business that night.

"Or a keg cup o' Hollands, wi' the sweet smell o' juniper beads — that's if ye've no Crowlink for my colleague Jake, over there in the snug."

"Schnapps? Well apart from surviving an altercation why else would ye be a celebrating this night."

Pernickety grunted wiping her hands in her apron then picked up another bench seat overturned in the fracas. Ingrams part-turned away from Jess adding, "The Crowlink is for my friend." He nodded to the big man who turned his back on her and resumed card playing with others having moved the far side of the room to the window seat.

Pernickety looked about her, eventually spotting who he meant and walking over bent forward to take a closer look in the half-darkness, "Jake! Be that ye in a powdered wig?" She gave a spurt of speed and flew to cuff him alongside his ear. Rebounding from the sharp blow, Jake rose to tower over her out of harm's way - knowing she could no longer intimidate him when at full height. "What in God's name be ye doing dressed up like a fop and dandy, wearing a silver grey wig and all." Pernickety folded her arms to stare up at him, also she knew this stance always meant business to the humbling man.

"Twas done for the best Pernick - poverty abounds in my brain and I felt I needed a change." He reached out and tapped her shoulder, "Mayhap ye'll be a doing what the man requested, eh." Affording her a knowing wink. She huffed and turned to look again at the stranger in black with the wheel- lock pistol. "Yet again, D'Arcy Ingrams ye be causation o' my troubles or tribulations."

Snorting disgust, she turned on her heel and made for the scullery and the securely locked liquor store. Jake grumbled loud enough for Ingrams to hear him. "Ol' Pernick be like a Carrack flapping up the English channel from Germany or a Caravel travelling east o' Spain." Then he smiled adding curtly,

"Don't let her tantrums bother ye until she lets fly with a broadside."

He sat down to resume his card playing though rubbed a sore cheek.

D'Arcy Ingrams chuckled at the man's definition of the dowager that was his temperamental employer, then turned his full attention to the seething highwayman opposite him. "Sit thyself down quietly highwayman, best relax "till thy drink comes for I feel the good Lord must have had a touch o' the "squitters" when laying thy bones." Conceitedly smiling at the wit of his own words, then carefully watched the man do as he was bade. A momentary silence befell him as he begrudgingly replaced the eye patch to cover the empty socket and straightening his tricorn - Jess slumped into the seat opposite.

Pernickety returned with a glass of Schnapps on a round pewter tray for her manservant and placed it down in front of him. Crossing back to Ingrams she glowered and then positioned a dark bottle of red wine and two rough-cast glass goblets to the tabletop. Ignoring the dead-lamping she'd tried to effect, Ingrams waved the pistol and with his free hand filled to push a brimming vessel toward him.

"Thy drink villain - we have business to discuss this night. I'm thinking it best be done in a smidgen o' comfort." Ingrams watched him instinctively push the goblet away with a terse shake of his head while staring at Pernickety.

"I'll not be scuttled by thy poisonous potions. If ye intend to do for me then it'll have to be by your own devices. Any-road-up I'll not trust the inn-keeper or her manservant from this moment onwards."

Pernickety could not contain herself any longer in his presence, placing the drinks tray to one side then shrugging a premature apology to the seated Ingrams, rolled up her right sleeve, recoiling back then forwards with a resounding wallop - knocked the highwayman from his chair with a ferocious punch.

"There you are you blackguard. I've wanted to do that ever since ye blasted my little Venus child. That little maid never did anyone any harm yet because she was in the wrong place at the right time ye tried to kill her dead."

Brawling fists thrust to her hips, she glared angrily down at the highwayman sprawling on the flagstones.

"Ye be fair lucky I don't do for you right here and now. Poison indeed."

Turning away, a florid colour rising to both cheeks and to much applause and laughter from the other men in the room, she spun on her heel to make off towards the kitchen and a good cry. Mortally fearful for her little maid's welfare and continued absence for twenty-four hours now.

D'Arcy Ingrams burst out laughing and called to Jake the far side of the room, "Thy initial rout and defeat o' this man is thanks to ye my friend. My indebtedness will increase thy bursary accordingly."

Jake nodded silently toasting his colleague, hurriedly casting a paste-board to the table surface for he had a winning hand and lacked extra need to talk. Jess rolled onto his good arm and crawled to his feet then back to the perch opposite a grinning King's man. Ignoring the flow of blood, he grabbed the document from his vest and waved it about him saying,

"I'll be relieving ye of this it has to be with its rightful owner afore the morrow's dawn tide." Ingrams stuffed it into his vest grimacing as he pulled the neckerchief's content from his side pocket, the white globe nestled in the palm of Ingrams' hand as he looked hard at Jess, "Ye agreed with thy servant that this be but a piece o' carved ivory." The man opposite nodded yet his pursed lips held a deal of mystery. Ingrams took it up with forefinger and thumb holding it over the wine goblet. Casually he dropped it into the liquid and it disappeared with a loud *plop*. Jess did not move. A puzzled look grew on his face; why had this man done such a thing, what could it possibly prove - suddenly the expression in his eyes fell from contempt to puzzlement as the surface of the brimming goblet erupted. It began effervescing and foaming violently. Realisation came to Jess's good eye as he saw the priceless bauble set aside for old age, rapidly begin to disappear in front of him - so it was a pearl - a gigantic South Seas pale blue-white pearl and absolutely priceless. . . The action of the red wine proved this fact. Anticipating the move to recover the fast reducing effervescing white ball, as the frantic man dived his fingers into the goblet, Ingrams slammed the flat of his own hand over the vessel trapping scrawny fingers forcing whimpers of anguish. Turmoil in the goblet ceased after a few more moments, and releasing his hand allowed both men to look at the clearing contents in the goblet. Barely altering its red glowing tint or even adding anything to its volume, yet now he took it up and held a worthless potion instead of the priceless object. D'Arcy Ingrams grinned rising to his feet to thrust the wheel-lock pistol into Jess's gaping mouth, pushing its way betwixt his foul halitosis-laden breath and the blackening bad teeth.

"Drink it, Jess, for ''tis an aphrodisiac and'll do ye the power of good. 'Twill put back fire in thy loins and a lusty desire in thy wicked heart."

Ingrams began tapping the side of the trigger guard lightly with his impatient forefinger. Jess remembered mention of the "hair-trigger" so swiftly moving his head to extract the pistol from between his lips, he took hold of the goblet and raised it mockingly to Ingrams. Slowly, very slowly he raised the vessel to his lips. Ignoring the sea of staring faces watching his every move, he threw back his head and sunk the contents, at the same instant howling like a wolf as liquid leached from both corners of his cruel mouth.

"Arghh!" he cried melodramatically whilst screwing up his good eye he drank deeply, lowering the goblet he continued with the caterwauling of despair. Part in sheer horror at having to consume his "eye" also the trauma of losing his life's security and insurance for old age. Even if it had been stolen from a London merchant in yet another post chaise hold-up. Lowering the empty goblet to the table, Jess's squint turned to a bulging glare of hatred for the man opposite him. Ingrams would not leave the room alive if he had the chance this tormentor would pay dearly for the indignities of that night. D'Arcy Ingrams called for Pernickety and she arrived clutching a rag to clear the spilt liquid from the table top. Snuffling and groaning unto him about not being able to see and enjoy the company of the little maid Clarissa. Grasping her arm to shake more important events into her concentration, he whispered to her ear about safe haven for the incarceration of the villainous highwayman. As he advised her earlier that he would himself be gone from that place and into the night. Finalising business at hand he could be away and back to London from Lyme town and all its brewing troubles of a civil war.

She nodded agreement indicating he should bring the prisoner and for both to follow her towards the stairwell door. Once there she carefully lit a candle and placed it into a holder then turned back to him to advise,

"Best place him in the lockable storeroom under the stairwell. No wait. ''tis now full o' spare tables and benches." She failed to mention it was because of the escapade earlier whereby Jess went out of this room up the chimney - although it was not a total lie about the hostelry's spare furniture.

"Best if ye take him to the attic where the maid recovered her health. Oh, and mind the floorboards. They be a smite unsafe so ye tread carefully or thou'll end up in the store anyways." Passing the candle holder for their illumination, opened up the stairwell door and stood to one side with a knowingly wicked wink of her eye. It did her heart good to see Jess Mandrake finally getting his rightful come-uppance.

Bundling the highwayman to his feet then across to the low doorway then to traverse the narrow staircase. Forcing him in front he held the pistol to his buttocks prodding encouragement. Saying he would blast away his vitals should he so much as stumble. Due to difficulty encountered by the one-armed man climbing the stair treads with the banister the wrong side, they reached the attic after several minutes of slow climbing. Once there a large wrought iron key protruding from the door lock and this was removed by Ingrams.

Ducking their heads underneath the beamed eaves, both prisoner and gaoler entered and looked about themselves.

Thrusting the highwayman across the boards to the singularly small window allowing moonlight to filter in. Ingrams reached for and lit another candle stuck into a discoloured wine bottle. Spluttering reluctantly into life it gave a modicum of illumination, yet this remained isolated to an area over the fireplace. The fire breast looked as if it had received a deal of attention as it appeared freshly mortared and pointed. Only then did Ingrams realise that this was the one mentioned by Tom and the girl.

Now they had extra light, he closed the door and leaned back against it deciding how to secure the highwayman. Placing the pistol off-cock he thrust it into his belt whilst looking for a place to secure his scallywag, whose own eyes roamed over to the familiar fireplace. His heart openly fell when he saw it had been boarded and bricked up again. Though affording a second glance he noted it hadn't been done very well - a make-shift job which might be useful.

He looked to the tiny window remembering earlier he'd no chance of escape that way, angrily recalling the mob below who jeered his soot-blackened head wedged in the frame. Another score to settle with the maid and the boy.

The stairs creaked outside, Ingrams spun and gripped the pistol again, part-turning he aimed the gun away from the highwayman towards the door.

As if a prayer had been answered the door flew back and cast Ingrams into Jess's open arm grabbed Ingrams from behind, grappling further by wrapping a leg around him in a wrestling grip. At the same time seizing the pistol butt with the King's man still holding on - the gun pointing every which way in their wavering double-grip.

Jake was the lumbering intruder and stood aghast in the doorway clutching a coil of ship's rope and the recovered naval sword. Having anticipated the need for ship's chandlery, yet all he could now do was watch as the wheel-lock pistol vacillated in front of his eyes. Both men continued their struggle for control of the weapon his revolving gaze remained fixed quite hypnotically.

Watching and waiting his chance Jake dived forward and made a grab for the weapon from the wrestling grips - not realising it had already been placed on full-cock only becoming apparent when it abruptly erupted with a loud "Bang". The pistol inadvertently fired point-blank into the huge man's chest, crumpling to his knees, head-bowed, body finally tilting forward in the juxtaposition of a broken marionette. Jess was first to recover his senses after the explosion, and although enveloped in a cloud of blue gunsmoke, having the most to lose dived forward and grabbed at the fallen sword to round on Ingrams who was left clutching an empty, worthless still smoking muzzle-loading wheellock.

Prodding the chest of his tormentor with the sword until his arms raised akimbo sideways. Ingrams did not feel the point piercing his chest for he could only stare at the downed giant, his gaze filled with remorse and self-recrimination at his own stupidity. Jess grinned triumphantly and watched with sadistic delight as a thin but copious flow of his red blood trickled down the navy blue serge coat - hardly noticeable in the light starved attic. Ingrams suddenly became aware of the pin-prick puncture and clutched at his chest in sharpening pain. Blood trickling out from between his fingers immobilising any immediate thoughts of retaliation.

Turning his attention to the attic door, reached behind him and closed it against more interfering visitors. He did this with difficulty sword in hand.

Searching the King's man was easier once the highwayman swapped the sword for a hidden dirk dagger. Going through his side pockets of the man now holding a neckerchief to the wound, he located the iron turn key and carefully revolved it in the lock. Leaving it half-turned against a duplicate perhaps thrust from the otherside, someone downstairs might just have heard the shot. Growling his words at the wounded man he said menacingly,

"Thou hast taken my pension which was my life savings, I would have done anything to keep it safe." He poked threateningly with the dirk, "apart from a priceless value t'were the finest thing a man could treasure next to that of his own sight, for 'twas a bluish grey lustrous iridescent pearl" that was how the merchant advised me afore I put him to the skewer. Sounded fine and noble, and I recalled his words whilst removing the bauble from his dead corpse."

D'Arcy Ingrams was barely listening to the wicked story telling as he failed to believe his foul luck his taking gaze off this rogue for a second time. He should have learned his lesson from earlier, now the woman Pernickety's manservant lay dead at his feet, this through his own act of sheer carelessness. Thoughts whirled his brain preventing him taking-in what was going on, though when he did, he realised the coil of rope from Jake's body had been threaded through a "deadman's eye" metal loop in a ceiling beam.

Jess was now dragging a three-legged foot stool across the rotten floor-boards. The highwayman now nodded for him to mount the stool and stand beneath the dangling rope.

"Thy boots King's man. Peel off thy stocking hose as well. Place thy bared feet onto the stool for 'tis of import ye should feel everything."

Jess the Pearly watched as he did as he was bade, then to stand upright on the unsteady piece of old and rickety furniture.

Retrieving the long sword Jess placed the sword, hilt-down, the point up to the man's crotch. Propping the foil guard onto the seat of the footstool.

This action definitely dissuaded quick movement on pain of severance of his very vital organs. The dirk jabbed threateningly in his back to remind him, on pain of death, not to make a false move.

"Well don't ye just stand there - weave thyself a hangman's noose, make it strong enough to take thy neck and thy bodyweight."

Stooping he placed the still lit candleholder beneath the stool then looked up he confirmed the noose was made correctly. Rising with difficulty he said,

"Place it around thy neck and take up the slack."

Jess regained his sword having watched the man do as he was told, then made the rope fast at the other end to the brass door knob. Once secured, the coarse jute rope was twanged by the evil humour of the highwayman, then he crossed back towards Ingrams. Undoing the suspended man's coat he pulled each arm out of their sleeves in turn. Placing them by his side to then release the buckle of his belt - securing his arms straight and tight. Laboriously buttoning up the frock coat again with his manipulative bony fingers, Jess afforded himself the luxury of a boastful sneer on turning the tables on his tormentor. "Thy luck do seem to be escaping thee today, Squire Ingrams, but fear thee naught for soon, very soon thy troubles will be over."

Nodding down to the footstool he grinned openly at Ingrams" predicament. D'Arcy Ingrams was unable to follow the highwayman's gesticulations as he dare not move for fear of slipping to oblivion. Against all odds he stood on tip-toe barely daring to breath let alone glance downwards, grunting disgust and moving his head irritatedly about sideways to loosen the noose. What he Jess, did not know was that he'd spied a loose board close to the stool before the restricting head-up position. If only he could entice the highwayman closer towards the weakened point he just might......?

"Well, King's man - not so clever now, eh."

Jess came closer to gloat and as he stared slightly upwards to the grim features of the balancing man, jaw set and bracing to what was inevitable, suddenly he remembered the recovered documents inside his blouson.

"At least I still hold thy parchments of some import."

A futile and stupid remark it may be for the man was a natural thief and murderer, he was able to remove them from his lifeless body at a later time.

"Time enough for bothering when ye've left us."

The heat from the candle at last began to do its job, fumes from charring wood filled the restricting air space in the small attic. In a short space of time the wooden under-surface of the stool would be unbearable to stand on. Inadvertently, the balancing man would dance and kick the piece of furniture from beneath to do the dance of death at the end of the rope. The balancing man would inevitably become - the hanging man.

D'Arcy Ingrams had to think fast, controlling the tremble infiltrating his voice box he tried to inform Jess as casually as he could, "Blood doth render a legal document useless. And it would thy sword has pierced a lung and I be bleeding like a stuck pig."

Jess thought the man now teetering on the stool might have a point and so he came towards him having placed the sword up under his armpit. Stretching out, yet still supporting the long sword the one-armed highwayman reached inside the blood stained calico shirt for the bundle of papers. As soon as he raised his arm further, Ingrams

211

drawing away slightly to encourage this, the inevitable happened. The sword slipped and fell blade uppermost, Ingrams catching the quillion cross-guard hilt with his knees as it tumbled past him, the gyrating effort almost causing him to unbalance completely.

Again the sneer crossed his lips as he tore the documents from the hanging man's blouson, stepping back to glean a better picture of someone teetering on the brink of his own extinction.

"What good d'ye think that'll do ye." Jess moved from one foot to the other laughing and cackling uncontrollably so. "I may have but one good arm but ye have none now I have bound thee and trussed thee up like the carcass of a chicken ready for the bake oven." Stepping sideways to observe better then to guffaw loudly at a man clinging to the upturned sword with his knees, likening it to that of a drowning victim grasping at a passing straw. Oblivious and unaware of the shift of his bodyweight on loosened rotten and weakened boards, sensationally reacting to 12-stone bodyweight with a resounding "crash!"

Tilting upwards allowed the highwayman's right leg to penetrate right through the rotten floor boards and into the wooden slats of the ceiling of the store room below. Jammed fast in splintered wood, Jess stupidly called out in futile fright for the teetering man on the footstool to assist. D'Arcy Ingrams having more pressing things on his mind, realised he too was about to hang himself by over-balancing in all the commotion of entrapment. Feverishly he resumed his personal struggle to release himself from his predicament, watching out of the corner of his eye - for the head-up position afforded little else. Fired by the will to live he tried to manipulate the heavy sword to a better position, thus to make use of its precarious presence now rather close to his vitals. Further noise came from beneath them as both he and Jess struggled to free themselves. Luckily Jess was far enough away not to grab at the wobbling foot stool and use it to prise himself clear, for all adjacent boards about him had begun to split and crumble with his weight. The tighter his leg sunk through the floor, now right up to his thigh, the more the wattle and daub ceiling batons acted like an all-enveloping mantrap. Ingrams regained his delicate balancing act to compare stuck-up spikes of splintered wood around Jess's groin to that of the appetite of Esox Lucius -the voracious fresh water shark preying on dying compatriots seemed rather appropriate. Fleetingly the comparison did little for his burning toes as he stood on one foot to the other to cool before standing down once more. The highwayman's gyrations proved useless, his left leg doubled underneath and becoming more cramped by the minute, his right dangling free somewhere through the storeroom ceiling. An iron nail had pierced his thigh and blood stained his breeches around the groin area on the right side. The more Jess tried to struggle free the more he slid through the rotten mixture of floorboards. The balancing man tried not to hear the wailing pleas of anguish of the trapped man, instead concentrated on shaving upwards the sharpened point of the sword. Offering it up against the embalming frock coat and its buttons, shorn cotton thread slowly yet surely relinquishing each button in turn. After an eternity of struggling with the precariously balanced weapon its keen edge finally allowed his top coat to drift open. Ingrams could now concentrate on attacking the strength of his leather belt. Avoiding its tough immovable brass buckle, set about the toughened leather itself, for this would take longer also the quickening motion and dance-of-death was beginning. Increasingly the heat raised the temperature of the squab and he sprang lightly from one set of toes to the other, nimbly so - trying not to upset the foot stool's fine balance on the sprung boards. Knees together the sword still propped and gripped as the acrid smell and fine spiralling of black smoke rose from under the smouldering piece of furniture, permeating every facet of the tiny room. The stool seat surface was hotter now and beginning to be a desperate race against time and his tenacious endurance.

* * *

•

Mandrake the highwayman threw back his head and screamed the most harrowing human scream Ingrams had ever heard, equalling the bitterest height of any sea battle aboard the cruellest of ships. Almost unbalancing as the attention was diverted to his part-severed and securing leather belt and delicately tensioning from the hangman's noose. A tipped balance was swiftly juggled to retain momentum, only then did he find himself able to listen to the agonising gurgle of an injured man uttering oaths and curses to a world which had betrayed him. Ingrams then thought he heard why Jess was in further predicament as he sank forever lower through the splitting floor

213

boards - muted growling of some devil dog chewed and attacking his exposed leg in the storeroom below. Jess ceased incessant screaming long enough to plead wretched questioning to the dangling Ingrams,

"How can the animal reach me whilst up on the anteroom ceiling." Terrifyingly the gnawing and snarling noises began again, the balancing man put his struggles out of his own mind whilst ceaselessly carving away with the upturned sword. His numbing knees precariously letting him down as many minutes had passed while he tenaciously carved away at the belt. Then with a final desperate expansion of lungs and bunched arm muscles - his arms were finally freed. Just as he grabbed at the rope noose tightening around his throat, one of the foot stool legs snapped off and tipped him away. This action flung the sword down - out of reach to either victim. The hanging man swung free back and forth several inches above the floor, tension taken up again as the slack was taken up in the coarse jute line. A creak of straining rope against the dead man's ring in the beam and brass door knob, creaked jointly with this pendulum of dry weight. Ingrams had one last desperate idea and with trapped fingers tucked into noose to save himself choking swung himself deliberately towards the highwayman's head and shoulders still protruding. Jess was still being attacked relentlessly by some unseen beast, his shoulders and one arm flailed the air above him and he wailed agonisingly. The hanging man's legs searched and found his victim. A hunched form and yet a human island refuge. Straightening his arched back - in a flash Ingrams managed to release the ever tightening rope from his throat, cruelly and deliberately to step down from the man's shoulder to yet more screams as crushing extra weight thrust his victim further through the hole and into the devil dog's jaws. Rubbing his neck from the purple scar of a rope burn, though eventually he gathered strength and fortitude to kneel alongside the man in agony. Yet he did nothing for a moment or two.

"Tables and chairs, Jess, 'tis a storeroom 'neath thee and that be how the devil dog be attacking thy left leg."

Attempting to dead-lift him from his armpits only to confess the man was stuck-fast, his action seemed to deter the animal from his attack and the growling underneath both men ceased as quickly as it began.

"Get me out - get me out!" Jess screamed his one darting eye pleading for mercy up and at his victim, finally with a throaty sigh he slipped into a deep unconsciousness - his blanched expression told of some unseen horror beneath him. D'Arcy Ingrams endeavoured to drag him free of the hell-hole yet as the attack was resumed from below - a howling and snarling ended up in a weird tug-of-war between man and beast of a raggedly human being, raging defiance and the pandemonium of the man's screams for the beast to let go and the alternating howling of a wolf at bay as the attack continued unabated. The hound of hell was indisputably gnawing away at bone and sinew, instantly and as quickly as the horrific noises began everything became deathly silent. The beast having gone back to whence it came. Blood clots and splashes hid what was yet to come as he pulled him clear of the splintered boards, offering an unavoidable shudder at what came out, all that remained below the highwayman's right knee was a musculature tangle of dangling white flesh and chewed bone. His right foot had disappeared. A furtive glance down through the torn hole in the ceiling confirmed this fact, Ingrams turned his attention to what was left of the highwayman's leg, mangled and lacerated the right leg was beyond recognition, torn into strips of chewed bone and flesh. It was his turn to feel physically sick, turning his head to vomit freely as his stomach churned nauseous movement. Wiping his face with the back of his hand he glanced downwards to sum up the broken man slumped on the floor - he who apparently killed innocents for their valuables was totally free of pain lying unconscious on the floor. God repays! D'Arcy Ingrams thought darkly whilst searching for the bloodstained documents, then suddenly his thoughts were interrupted by a noisy pounding on the attic door. A pitying glance offered to the man at his feet, Ingrams rose from one knee and turning the key in the lock having stepped over Jake's prone form to do so. Miss Pernickety's portly frame filled the doorway, she stood there arms folded demanding to know,

"What in the hell was going on in the room." then she saw Jake's crumpled form face down at her feet, a broad pool of blood seeped away from his chest wound. Breath sucked in as she tried to gasp his name in a growing show of horror, then throwing herself on top the woman wept openly. Sobbing all the while between tears of remorse for the treatment she'd afforded her manservant. Then rose to tear dementedly at her flame red hair in dire consternation, only then did she spy the horrific spectre of the road robber's mutilated and shortened half leg. She swooned dead away her head revolved backwards and then forwards from one awful spectre to the other. Her manservant dead, the evil highwayman's stump profusely oozed blood and gore over bare boards of the attic. D'Arcy Ingrams turned away to complete his business with a grunt of disgust, for the woman cared not of his own dilemma, retrieving the documents he recalled the young girl's words -

"Why have so many innocents died for these papers?"

Secreting the parchment package to a bloodied vest he returned to check on the condition of the manservant, suspecting a faint pulse was put down to his distracted heightened imagination. Propping her up she seemed to recover her senses within a minute or two, now recovered though she continued to shake her head in disbelief, then bundling the King's man out of the attic to the top of the stairs indicating he should go below to the empty drinking den. Assuring of her intentions to follow after checking on the injuries of the dying thief. And to pay last respects to Jake at the same instance for there was little else she felt she could do for him. Wiping her eyes with her sleeve, accompanied the unsteady perpetrator of this death and destruction to the head of the staircase, turned to look hard into a moistening face,

"Brave man thy Jake. 'twere he that saved my life. Aye, that he did." Touching her shoulder gently did little but make her shudder contemptuously. Ignoring the flicker of annoyance turn to outright anger in her blue eyes he murmured,

"Of little comfort to you at this moment I shall leave a gold coin for a proper incarceration and burial in the local graveyard." Instead of grateful compassion anticipated she screamed mercilessly, "Ye bane worth it, King's man, saving thy hide b'aint worth the candle." Thumping him roundly on the chest forced blood to spurt through spread fingers which nullified the injury.

"Death and destruction do follow ye, King's man everywhere."

Fresh darkening of the calico blouson turned red. Oozing blood indicated he too was injured. Wincing and doubling up Ingrams slipped his hand across a darkening stain spreading out from the wound. Pernickety touched it and her eyes silently apologised, nodding her head and with pursed cupid lips for him to leave, she stood back to watch him stumble down the narrow treads. Then with a sniff, turned on her heels and went back into the room and closed the door as if it was a shrine. A make-shift tourniquet would have to be made for Jess. Looking about decided on a piece of wood originally the broken leg of the foot stool, then came linen from one of many under-petticoats. This done dragged his scrawny unconscious form into a corner and propped him up to save further leaching of his life's blood. A knees up into an inverted sitting position. A tourniquet of twisted cloth above the knee stopped the blood flow immediately. Though she realised she would have to return regularly to release pressure until a doctor could be reached. He then would decide on whether to effect proper amputation or a cauterising of the gaping leg injury. This done, she fell to her knees over the prostrate form of her manservant Jake and said a brief prayer. - there wasn't any way she might place the huge man in a semblance of dignity due to his bulk. His corpse would have to wait the strength of many men the next day when the hostelry was full at midday. Perhaps kindly souls would bear him downstairs to the storeroom where a makeshift coffin could be built for the dead giant. From the doorway she afforded a last longing gaze to the fallen man. Maybe thinking of what might have been. Only then did short stout legs send her like a spinning jenny down to confront the King's man for answers to the destruction of manservant and highwayman alike. D'Arcy Ingrams was half sitting, half-slumped totally exhausted on a ladder-back chair the experience in the attic left him dazed and with a far off look in his grey blue eyes. Protocol abounded as he awaited the woman's pleasure before requesting from her good auspices a stiff bowl of rum. Tearing at his salt and blood stained calico shirt - the woman revealed the fine stab puncture in his upper chest. Clean, yet having entered several inches into flesh and bone, bathing and dressing. Again her knee came up and another layer of cotton calico petticoat was shredded to make-do-and-mend as a wound pad. This done she disappeared only to return after a moment with a wooden bowl of hot water, proceeding to bathe and tend his chest wound. The sea spy winced and grumbled with the stinging interference, whispering between clenched teeth and pain pangs of the black devil-dog's attack which tore off a human leg. Demanding to know why she kept such a ferocious beast in her store room. Horror-struck, Pernickety remembered the legend of the ghostly spectre purporting to haunt the old inn - the notorious black devil dog. An apparition known until recent events only by legend of many years past, quickly adding that she hadn't placed much store by the tale, assuming there was but a mere grain of truth in the rumour. Remembering the legendary defence mentioned to the girl she added,

"Ye should have tossed the beast a silver coin or a share of thy vittles." Adding then Jess would've been safe from its fearful reputation, the woman offered a genuine fear by rolling her eyes, crossing herself not once but several times then turning back to tend his wound added sincerely,

"Spying the beast in person portends o' death for it manifests itself into the shape o' Beelzebub himself according to local folklore."

Abruptly a cacophony of stumbling and cursing made them look to the stairwell as something was endeavouring to come down the constricted stair treads with great difficulty. A man's voice muttered oaths as he approached the ale room.

Pernickety and Ingrams stared at each other then decided it could only be the struggling of the fatally injured highwayman. The fluent cursing giving an inkling that it could only be he. Glancing about the empty tavern for a weapon, the naval sword having remained on the floor of the attic, along with the spent empty wheel-lock pistol. There was nothing, a distinct clattering and ping of metal accompanied slow progress downwards, suggested the sword accompanied whosoever lumbered towards them. Ingrams' own secreted weapons had been removed by Monmouth's troops on his initial capture and abduction to the house in George street. Pushing the woman to one side, he grabbed a pewter flagon half-filled with stale flat ale - then he dived behind the stairwell door gesturing for her to take her leave by the main door. Rushing to do so, Pernickety then seemed to change her mind and then hurried about the long room extinguishing candle lit lanterns - puffing at each in turn. Soon they were in comparative darkness awaiting their advancing adversary soon to burst from the stairwell. In terror as the noise came closer, Pernickety began to shake with fear, urgently she whispered as she stood to one side of the staircase. Ingrams failed to appreciate what she rambled on about, instead turned his attention to the stairs holding high the tankard ready to strike. Yellow pools of flickering light wavered down towards the open door well, whoever it was must have picked up the candleholder to illuminate their way. Miss Pernickety, her eyes flashing a warning to Ingrams as they stood opposite and behind the stairwell door stared wide-eyed at each other.

"God's tooth woman, leave me room to swing the tankard!"

His grumbling sparked further the potential terror of what was coming toward them and containing her fear no longer - Pernickety dived over to his side of the doorway. In an instant and cowered behind with both her arms encircling his waist in terror, the King's man, more restricted than ever, elbowed her backwards. Suddenly the looming shadow arrived on the last tread and fell forward into the room with great difficulty - Ingrams leapt into action and tossed ale into the figure's face momentarily blinding and enraging the huge man.

"Blast yer eyes D'Arcy Ingrams." The towering figure teetered and rounded on them as he clutched at his chest wound, "through thee I be half-killed if that wasn't enough thou be trying to drown me in stale drinking ale, t'boot."

The voice belonged to Pernickety's manservant Jake. Clutching a gaping firearm wound in his chest and bleeding profusely, he stumbled down the rest of the stairway to fall into their arms. It was a near mortal wound which required immediate attention, the profuse blood letting brought about by his laborious movements from the attic down to the drinking den of the ale house.

"This was on the floor beside the foot stool, methinks ye could've started a building fire."

Ingrams took the holder and flickering stub of tallow looking in mouth-opened-amazement at the reincarnation of the giant he originally assumed to be dead -so there must have been a pulse after all. Assuming also the big man in his haste to return downstairs could not have seen Jess in the shadows once the candle was removed for he would surely have put paid to him there and then. Pernickety thought otherwise about his reincarnation and said so vehemently,

"You buffoon, our Jake." Pernickety screeched, "pretending t'be dead when thee aint." Rushing forward she grabbed at his hand, Jake recoiling in horror wrongly assuming she was about her usual attack position and threw his head back out of reach. Instead she guided him gently then lowered him into a nearby wooden settle saying, "Dr. Temple, the apothecary be in town until tomorrow's skirmishing, word abounds he be joining the rebels. I'll make haste and get ye medicinal help as soon I be sure of his whereabouts, in the meantime I best be making ye more comfortable." She rushed off for some water leaving Ingrams to lean over the giant and smilingly offer his thoughts.

"I be relieved ye be safe and alright after all big man." D'Arcy Ingrams reached for his pouch and poured a cascade of silver coins down into his opened-up palm. "Thy bursary sir; thou doth deserve every penny." He watched as the man nodded gratitude then he looked heavenwards. Ingrams heard him say, "Thy servant sorely believes he has some praying to catch up on." He grabbed at his broad shoulders in friendship, then making sure he was not going to slide off the bench into unconsciousness he grabbed up the sword and candle-holder diving up the stairs warily to the attic again.

Once there his eyes met with a renewed scene of the total devastation of the attic. Yet strangely the highwayman had disappeared completely. He left behind him a trail of darkening blood which led from the window corner to the fireplace. His topcoat was flung to one side as the narrow hole through which he'd made his escape was too small to take but the slenderest form. The foot stool still smouldered and this was extinguished with a slosh from the water jug nearby - Ingrams wondered why he'd omitted to do so afore. From the corner the coil of rope had gone, no longer swung the hangman's noose from the makeshift gibbet on the ceiling beam. presuming this assisted the injured man's escape down the chimney rungs. Taking up the discarded coat Ingrams placed the candle holder to one side as he rummaged in the pockets for anything and everything. Eventually silver coins spilled from a purse along with a map. In shadowy half-darkness the other candle in the bottle probably illuminating the highwayman's way out. Surprisingly, D'Arcy Ingrams found other parchment documents secreted in the lining of the coat - three in all were hidden there. A momentary silence befell him whilst he racked his brain how they could turn up on the highwayman. Then he concluded that Jess saw him leave the house in George street and then entered to find the documents on the dining table, well at least his mission could now be completed without further ado, for the highwayman was history. Horrendous injuries such as he sustained that night would indeed put him out of the running as far he was concerned. All D'Arcy Ingrams had to do was to return to the ship in the bay and hand over the documents bound for Henry Morgan to Blackbeard the pirate.

Retracing his steps downstairs found the surgeon Temple present and bending over the agonised form of the manservant Jake. A small calibre ball had been removed and he was now stemming the copious flow of the man's blood. Miss Pernickety was apparently in the scullery boiling water and searching for fresh wound linens.

"How are ye doctor." Ingrams sang out approaching him from the stairwell.

Turning slowly to see who addressed him at that God forsaken hour, Dr. Temple momentarily paused from closing off the chest wound.

"Why if it isn't the 'sea-spy'." Looking first to the front door then to the scullery said turning back to his task, "best not be found by the rabble gathering outside the tavern at this unearthly hour Mr. Ingrams, for if they caught a King's man here tonight I'm afraid ye'd not be long for this world."

"Will the big fellow be alright, Doctor Temple?" Ingrams asked politely whilst ignoring the warning pertaining to his very survival.

"Aye sir - he'll survive. Plenty of flesh to stop a ball o' that size and dimensions, although a larger musket load may have put paid to his shenanigans."

Jake looked up from his wound and grinned at Ingrams as he winced in pain managed to blurt out between tight clenched teeth,

"It took more than a lady's purse gun to send me on my way, eh."

"Aye Jake - thou be a tough piece o' meat and no mistake." Ingrams offered whilst listening intently as he looked over towards the inglenook fireplace and wondered if Jess would suddenly appear covered in black from the hearth. A fresh pile of loose soot covered the previous night's embers yet there was no sign of the one-legged highwayman. He could only assume that he must have struggled up to the rooftops and over the slates to safety of sorts. The downward hung rope in the chimney a blind to put off potential followers. Watching with satisfaction he observed the good doctor finish his flesh probing and then with a grunt of satisfaction, a piece of clean linen prodded into the wound, a splash of high-proof rum spirit cleansed and completed the task.

Withdrawing with a satisfactory grunt, Temple made for the scullery to cleanse his instruments, making ready for the fray that was to come later at dawn.

Jake looked down at yet more silver coins now being pressed into his hand saying, "But ye paid me earlier this night, Ingrams."

"Aye that I did, Jake, but these coins be from the dead highwayman's purse. I thought ye might approve of his paying for thy treatment considering he caused thy discomfort."

"That I surely do - be the bounder dead then."

"Aye - or if not then he may well be for the poor wretch had his leg so chewed by a hell-hound he'll need a wooden peg to get walking again."

Then watched the man nod agreement as he pocketed fresh pieces of eight and four to his own purse afore the woman Pernickety returned from the scullery.

"Thou art a brave and true friend," Ingrams offered sincerely, then added he knew from the maid the way out from the Black Dog Inn's cellars. Deciding after the timely warning from Temple this would be the best exit that night. His respects paid to both men and the kindly auspices of the woman, he moved to the other side of the room skulking momentarily in black shadows before offering a brief wave of his hand. D'Arcy Ingrams - King's man, slid from the gloom of the inn unseen into the scullery below, once there he looked for the cellar door, and before diving through toward the waterfront - grabbed a roasted chicken from the bake oven spit. Tearing at its flesh he stuffed pieces it into his mouth and pockets as he made for the cellar door. Shooting the iron bolt back he suddenly felt the room go quite cold. Glancing somewhat nervously over his shoulder he spied a large black dog watching his every move. It crouched down in a darkened corner and appeared ready to spring. Remembering Pernickety's words he slowly reached into his purse and with-drawing a handful of silver farthings, tossed them towards the shadowy black beast - accompanied by a drum-stick of warm greasy chicken.

Disappearing immediately, the shadowy apparition seemed attracted to the wavering lantern light of the huge kitchens. Shrugging off the image of the hell-hound he dived into the dark moist dankness of the cellar caves, hoping to find the right one which led them originally to the harbour edge. Beginning to break into a run Ingrams turned to look back when he thought he heard a noise behind as if someone was following. Glancing over his shoulder he saw the enormous black beast again, this time staring at him from the entrance to the passageway.

The doorway having been left open for brief illumination into the hewn-stone corridor leading to the bell mouth cave. On seeing him turn, the animal sat domestically down on its haunches and held him with its fixed stare. It appeared to have a piece of boot leather in its mouth. Shuddering before turning to go, D'Arcy Ingrams found the strangest thing that struck him was the gaze of the now docile beast, for in silhouette the burning eyes glowed a definitive marigold yellow.

Chapter Fifteen

Crystal sea with a crystal dream
marbled turquoise breaker's cream
rushing hither snow-capped foam
purging tides there will roam
shelving cove and tidal race
dashing pebbles on changing face

Gold cap adorns all Lyme bay
witness the start of the eleventh day
the undercliff of Monmouth beach
a raging crown came within reach
Rapscallion Royal be on the Cobb
strutting there to begin the job

Thieves vagabonds and ne'er do well
murthering freebooters and scoundrel
then come ye hence think not to pause
your presence required 'tis for the cause
Seadog, Cavalry, Militia too.
Pike and Scythemen for Regiment Blue

Four days delayed training Regiment Blue
this gave the King's men and Militia too
much time to gather at Bridport true
skirmishing followed whereby cavalry flew
Monmouth's infantry saved the day
confronted with prisoners the cowardly Grey

Then sped to Taunton Monmouth King
`Jacobus Rex' the maids did sing
on again to Bridgwater Towne
desperate pursuit of England's Crowne
banners unfurled their colours did sleep
promises of loyalty ever thus to keep

Ever onward unto Bristol the Citye
halted its progress more's the pitye
Keynsham its bridge all found smashed
swing towards Bath their presence abashed
fading thoughts of London to march
war-whetted appetites thus did parch

Doubling back to Mallett Shepton
conscious Feversham's armies crept on
Cathedral Wells then back to Bridgwater
tired bedraggled lost taste for slaughter
Perusing Royalists from St Mary's church
Monmouth's idea sprang from his perch

A night attack with the help of a guide
mayhap turn the tables to rebels side
with thousands of men totalling four
set out via Chedzoy to reach dark Sedgemoor
soothsayer warning nought but a dream
`twixt darkness and shine beware the Rhine"

Silent the army over moor did creep
Protestant cause desperate honour to keep
traitorous shot rang out a warning
the battle began and raged till morning
all was lost as the first ray of dawn
found Monmouth, Grey, Anton Buyse all gone.

Until later near Ringwood found in a ditch
in shepherd's clothing heavy of stitch
by Militia men ever hard to please
found starving pockets a mere handful of peas
escorted to London thrust before James
Monmouth prostrate refutes all claim

A Whispered Pardon yet none to hear
at last cost King Monmouth dear
joined on the scaffold by bungling Jack Ketch
five blows of the axe failed to detach
discarding his blade for fear of his life
the Sheriff of London did pass him a knife

Then back to the Tower albeit late
transported by Thames through traytor's gate
spurned by a country having given his love
a winged soul takes flight of a dove
gone now the cause and all seems peculiar
buried at peace St Peter's ad Vincula
Mors Vincet - Death Wins.

Poem: The Whispered Pardon   Miles Hawke

* * *

   24 hours earlier lower gun deck - The Revenge

Bolting veins of jagged lightning tore the night skies asunder. The forked barbs darted and flashed to illuminate the lower deck down through the opened up gun ports of *The Revenge*, Blackbeard's sardonic title for his heaving craft still careering back and forth at anchor. The ship's surreptitious identity painted-out to illuminate the more tranquil name of *The Maracaibo* continued to grace her broad-beamed gingerbread stern. Lightning swiftly followed catching companionably up with a deafening "crack" from accompanying disgruntled sister - thunder.

   Summer storm squalls eventually began to abate. They subsided almost as quickly as they had begun, although now a refreshing dash of heavy rain drummed audibly on the hull. Hopefully heralding a final diminishing to the inclement weather that night. Terrified at being left to face up to this ordeal, a torpor clouded the maid's senses after the distracting sounds of thunder likened to earlier rebel gunfire on the main-land. Standing, feet apart for balance, the tall privateer hacked and chopped at the tight stitching on the bound hammock.

226

Continuing to gyrate and twist some six feet up off the cambered deck planking. There appeared to be no audacious plan to placate the muted pleading voice from within. Though the pirate interjected periodically with some murmur of appeasement, mayhap to assure the person within he was doing his mortal best to offer up deliverance. Two mucky-faced children knelt huddled together like blackbirds on a vine, Clarissa resisting Tom's tug at her sleeve and with hushed tones begged him to be quiet.

"Whist Tom, my step-father be opening a tomb."

Nipper, terrified at the fearful dilemma unfolding stood alongside Blackbeard, reaching to remove a flag from a sail locker to prevent shivering, probably attributed to outright fear anyway. Black and white the material was tightly drawn about and it was recognised immediately as the Jolly Roger pirate motte. This one portrayed a whole skeleton, eerily the skeleton had horns, and sported a drinking goblet in one hand a cutlass stabbing symbolic enemy heart in the other. Hysterically the continued slashing took place at the sailcloth mummification. The hammock swung violently loose suspended between two overhead deck beams within the confines of a gun crew's quarters. As it undulated back and forth, the children on the gun carriage trembling arms reached over to cuddle up to the other. Never before had they witnessed such goings-on. The shroud ceased vibrating as the slashed folds of coarse tattered sailcloth fell away and down to land beneath on the deck planking. The dimly lit section revealed the quivering form of an irate and furious woman. A shocked pallor distorted with quivering despair and fury rolled into one as the pirate's spouse lay there on her back. Clarissa could not contain herself and ran screaming forward to hug her father's waist, hanging and clinging in a terrified stupor. Tom climbed the cannon breech and slid backwards further down the barrel until his feet protruded out through the port into the fresh sea air, lying there as if riding a phantom iron horse. Puffing unable to catch his breath, having heard tell of tomb robbers and the horrendous things befalling such men. Nipper froze with fear then gathering his wits made to run past the awesome sight of the body and make for the stairwell. Grabbed once more by the irate Blackbeard. Collared by a red ear he was drawn up on tip-toe to look into the beady eyes of the angry Ned Teach. Clarissa clung to his waist whilst he ranted at the terrified powder monkey and cabin boy.

"This be your doings, ye little bilge rat."

Ned shook Nipper like a rag doll then twisted his head towards the prostrate form only now beginning to move about in the hammock again.

"I'm blind, I'm blind!" A shrill voice from above cried in anguish. Black Ned let go of Nipper the powder monkey and reached over to peel tiny coins from the woman's eyes. Her eyes blinked and focused on the man towering above.

Ned furthered his temper at the boy only this time held the low denomination coins in front of the young lad's darting gaze.

"What's this, ye lubber."

"Farthings, sir - silver farthings." Nipper knew what was coming and screwed up his facial muscles against the battering that was to come, and opening his eyes he still hung loosely from a red ear. Pre-empting incorrectly but then relaxed his grimace too soon, Ned waited for this moment and cuffed him roundly knocking him violently down to the deck. Slowly he rose to his feet, head-bowed listening while chastisement abated and reasoning took over.

"Now thou knows it has to be pennies on the eyes o' the dead, for no folk be worthy o' silver coinage if they be going down deep to the sea bed."

Blinking her eyes, the woman opened them completely and on seeing his piratical face threw back her head and wailed out the scream of a banshee. Ned took hold of her wringing hands and tried to placate her by cooing gentle soothing words,

"There my proud beauty thou be safe for 'tis young Nipper o'er there that ye should rightly blame. T'were he that advised o' thy death and I were too busy with affairs o' State to check on thee and thy condition." Blackbeard reached behind him and withdrew the quivering little girl, sliding his arm around Clarissa, thrust her forward into the woman's view over the edge of the hammock as it swung lightly with the rising swell.

"Anne Teach - this be thy daughter and hath thy pride of face I'm thinking." He grinned proudly and reached to ruffle the young maid's hair fondly.

"What d'ye mean - I bane worth no silver coins."

Anne Bonny glowered angrily glancing first to Ned then ignoring

228

the maid to Nipper. He, fascinated slowly approached with his fist thrust deep into his mouth in sheer horror, seeing what he thought was a body coming back to life.

Realising she had been freed from bondage, yet the woman in the shroud still feeling breathless and wretched, sat bolt upright in the hammock - almost losing the precarious balance afforded to such an unstable sleeping post.

Ned slunk behind the girl knowing full well the temper befitting to any knave who so roamed seven seas - and she was a ruthless pirate t'boot. Powerless to resist her blow as the woman's fist shot forward and struck him in the eye. Nipper guffawed at his recurring expletives and then froze as he realised he too was still in reach. Rounding on him in frustration, Ned gave vent to the smarting pain over his eye, walloping the lad once more let go of the hammock causing the recoiling woman to be catapulted downwards to the deck.

Indignantly without ceremony, she rose shakily to stand looking up at the huge Black Ned, who, embarrassed beyond all reason cuffed the powder monkey once more as the lad rose to take his punishment. Ned held his blackening eye making plain to the boy by stating angrily.

"I warned you about stitching the nostrils." He screamed through his opened fingers holding the injury.

"How dost thou think the saying came to be "a stitch in time saves nine" because that be the minimum water depth a body be sunk - 9 fathoms." Rubbing the eye prevented further attacks as he kept his guard up.

"A corpse in a cloth shroud would scream blue murder if ye stitched it and it weren't dead – that's why the last stitch goes through the nose." A wail of anguish came from the petite Anne Bonny as she stood alongside the almost casual chastising of the cowering lad. Tom joined them as the spectre was awakened and staring hard at the black bearded man wailing relentlessly. Ned continued waving her to be silent with a nonchalant movement of his hand as he sought to explain further. "For t'would sparked a bit o' life d'ye see. And if it hadn't a sea water depth of at least `nine-fathoms" be required as that be the minimum depth for burial at sea." Ned drove home the point ignoring the gathering fury in his wife's eyes. Recovering her composure after the ordeal, Anne was wearing a crumpled yellowing calico night garment similar to that of the nearby maid. Staggering to regain lost sea-legs, Anne Bonny waveringly made headway to the side of the ship and the open gun port. Once there, knelt and breathed in sea fresh air. Bending slightly further she could spy the distant lights of the shoreline town of Lyme Regis. Rising from all fours, Anne supported herself on the breech of the cannon and turned to demand further explanations.

"Anyway why didst thee not bury me whilst we be anchored here in the bay."

Ned placed his hands on his hips and throwing back his head guffawed loudly,

"My dearest beauty, this close to the land o' Dorset ye would have gone in and out with the tide at a fair rate o' knots. And my lads could've waved at you twice a day."

Composure fully restored, Ned anticipated the next move from his estranged spouse, mockingly he bowed to avoid the hurled object scooped up and flung toward him. This mutinous act made all the more treacherous as he found the missile bursting into splinters of wood about the beam above was his favourite drinking bowl. Furious he drew himself to his full height and fair bellowed across the under deck to the pathetic figure leaning against the cannon,

"Anne o' the Indies, ye hell-cat it be best now if I leave ye to introduce thyself to thy own daughter. Our daughter Clarissa. Afore ye be up to anymore mischief this night."

"Aye mischief ye can't control." Anne paused and recalling the word asked "Daughter?"

Staggering forward she began to look harder at the maid, standing to one side holding his arms akimbo Blackbeard proudly announced,

"This be thy maid Clarissa, she be all growed up now. If ye hadn't followed me to sea thou would have seen her developing yourself." Tucking his thumbs under the lapels of his frock coat, Ned Teach puffed himself up proudly. Nodding first to his wife then to the widening eyes of the young girl alongside. Vulnerability showed, fury left her and she looked a shell of her former self. Frailty and remaining strength left and her small frame gasped breathless for air as if having some sort of panic attack. The others ran to her side, moments later when Anne caught her breath and composure, Clarissa was the first to speak after plucking up the courage. "If you please, ma'am, why did ye leave me to run off to sea all those years ago - was it to find my step-father or this other pirate Calico Jack."

Anne looked fondly at the young girl and reached out and touched her with unsteady fingers, though ignoring her question she stated softly,

"Oh them's manners, my little girl's all growed up now and with manners that befits the aristocracy." Possessing little care for the woman's condition Clarissa slapped her face with a swipe of her flattened and open hand, repeating the question gained a shocked look and modicum of respect. Pleadingly and out of frustration the woman looked to her erring Black Ned for advice or assistance. This came in the form of statement, looking first to the confused expression on his wife's face and determination in the maid's sparkling blue eyes. "Aye, lass - she be your daughter alright."

●   * * *
●

Black Ned left the maid with her mother to sort their differences and was hopeful an amicable tryst would result after the soul searching abated. Mayhap after a formal signing of necessary `pirates articles" for the maid Clarissa and her keen friend young Tom the stable lad, they would become members of the crew and therefore could not legally testify to any wrongdoing they might harbour a grudge over. Tom would be trained in ship's duties as a cabin boy or powder monkey to a gun team.

The maid would not be sent home to Dartmouth because there was no one to care for the child now the diligent Martha Wilks was dead, she might just as well remain reunited with her true mother anyway. Clarissa would be trained in all nautical endeavours, starting with running bare foot up the shrouds to the "yards," reefing of sails would be too much for her to handle at her age and physique - though eventually she might be strong enough. Probably to take her respite in an officer's quarter deck cabin rather than deck down or swing a hammock aloft with the rest of the gun crew.

Black Ned Teach decided to leave them to get to know each other and made his way up on deck via the central companionway. Unfinished business dictated he should locate the missing prowler if only to make him suffer before he dies. Up he strolled on the poop deck, for t'were against all ship o' the line rules to smoke a pipe below decks without a cap on it, this in itself caused for a ruining of the cool smoke in a lengthy churchwarden clay pipe.

* * *

A leaden dawn offered grey light of morning. Slowly it was stealing over the sea's choppy surface barely visible through swirling sea mists. And maybe this promised summer warmth and a fair wind later on in the full light of daytime. These factors would be essential if they were to catch the turning rip tide to set full sail for their journey to the Dutch Free States later that morning. Scanning gunmetal waters to the direction of Lyme and its weakening harbour lights, Ned looked for the small boat arriving out of the mists at the parent vessel.

Stuffing the soured clay with rough tobacco shag, then fingering his favourite style pipe bowl, a wheatsheaf moulding, stuffing it deep he thrust it between tobacco-yellowed front teeth. Producing a silver tinderbox the pirate struck a shower of sparks onto the mixture of dried black combustible leaf. Once lit, he puffed merrily away until the blue smoke haloed and wafted around his head in the stillness of dawn mists. Sniffing the wave of smoke he found himself listening to what he thought was the solitary and distant sound of an oar moving water. Strangely this should have been a pair of oars and yet he could have swore he heard only one as he enjoyed his solitary smoke. There was no continuance of echo or sound of oars that creaked and strained against a carvel planked hull as it plied itself against the salt water swell. Now dawn's early light was making its presence felt he also knew his crew would return from their merrymaking of yet another anniversaire, spent birthday revelries which cost dear in temper and dour spirits. With bad heads and sour disposition the crew would go reluctantly about their chandlery duties until dispelling all memories of quaffed ale lost in fitful sleep. The rumbullion-soaked salts would appear in the long boat through the sea mist to arrive alongside the thwarts, then piped aboard with pomp as any Navy marine in full uniform would expect when back from authorised shore leave. For it was the way of the sea and protocol abounded, albeit tongue in cheek for a privateer employed under letters-of-marque and ready to set sail for the Spanish gold galleons of the far off Indies. If fortune

232

proliferated and favoured the brave, the pirate vessel would catch the noon tide and leave that God-forsaken place with or without the pardon documents. To return via the Dutch Free States and freedom of sorts, leastways more freedom than England held that moment in civil war preparation. Black Ned Teach took a long draw of tobacco smoke and breathing it out through his nostrils watching it move to waft toward the distant high peak of the majestic Gold Cap.

Early grey light was striking the headland and illuminating the Dorset downs eerily, its undercliff tumbled down towards to the gentle wash of lapping sea on barely visible beach head. Finishing his pipeful of baccy he tapped the clay out to the heel of his boot and said, growling aloud to no one bar himself.

"Where be thee, D'Arcy Ingrams, ye black-hearted swab, for old Harry Morgan will see thy torso hanging from the mainbrace if thou lets him down o'er this damnable paper-pardon! Aye to be sure - that he will..."

* * *

An hour passed and the only visitors on board was the ramshackle crew arriving back from shore leave and the past night's merrymaking. Three part-submerged jolly boats almost swamped in the restless tides of the open seas beyond the safety of the harbour. Long boats were stowed and the rubber-men crew washed slumber and excesses of the night from their eyes.

Once sober then to climb up into the yards to check halyards, sheets and braces, all fore, mizzen and top-gallants including main Royals, ready to slip away on the first ebb of tide. The excess of shouted orders topside was enough to blot out the arrival of Blackbeard's expected visitor, despite taking to his leather-bound spy glass. . . The mist was patchy due to the rising temperature of an orange sun, and it was in one of these swirling fog patches that D'Arcy Ingrams slipped unseen back onboard the good ship, Maracaibo from a small tender. Neither man realising that the evil Jess Mandrake slipped by both villains a mere cable's length in the sea fog quietly operating a one-oared ship's tender.

Ingrams had tied the boat aft to the same iron ring up under the overhang of the gilded stern quarter, then swiftly scaled a rope up onboard ship left earlier by the treacherous lord Albemarle. Albemarle having missed the intended escape route by a few inches in his haste to escape from the stateroom cabin, only to plunge unabated onto the head of the sea spy.

"Turn thy head in this direction and I shall be forced to despatch ye with a black powder ball forthwith. Think on my words and do not raise thy voice, a nodding o' thy tricorn will suffice as ye search seaward wi" thy spy glass."

"D'Arcy Ingrams no doubt - well I be expecting ye sir, if only to thank ye for assisting my daughter, Clarissa, to find her errant step-father. Aye that I do without reservation." Blackbeard kept the telescopic glass to his eye.

"She and young Tom be goodly kinder, I shall fair miss their pubescent banter and I be envious of thy ward and her young suitor's future aboard thy ship for furthering the ventures when back in the Indies."

"Harry Morgan be expecting something o' great import from thy clutches."

"Aye, Ned - Morgan won't be disappointed with what I've brought - but "tis only a part o' the pardon document which accompanies me this dawn. That bounder Mandrake lifted the cover page and section with the great seal of Parliament."

"No matter, Ingrams, "tis the main pardon we and old Harry be after."

"I be concerned that this renders the document worthless as the great seal be the final say-so and legal approval on such a royal pardon from the late Charles II."

"Be ye English Protestant, Ingrams?"

"I be anything ye want me to be, Ned Teach."

"Aye, ye be a King's man, alright. Only a sea spy would change the colour o' his cloth to suit his surroundings. I saw a lizard in an exotic clime which could do the same - be ye a lizard or a snake in the grass, D'Arcy Ingrams?"

"I be anything ye want me to be for neither of us be what we outwardly appear to be this day, Ned Teach or should I say-Blackbeard the pirate."

"Aye - ye be right Ingrams. Or should I say, D'Arcy Chavasse Penhalligon?"

"Then Henry Morgan's done his background into my birth well and passed on to thee genuine information instead o' half-truths. Did he also inform thee that I be o' the French Huguenots and at any moment we do so expect to be driven out of France to England by the Sun King Louis X1V?"

"Aye, Ingrams - but didst know Morgan be sat in the Hague with William considering placing his weight behind the Pretender's rebellion in nearby Lyme town?" Black Ned lowered his spy-glass grumbling his arms leached of blood and caused him great cramp. He did as he was bade and kept his gaze seaward.

"That I did not, Ned - so Morgan would take on the King's Navy, eh. Well give my good wishes for the venture and convey a message to his ears when thou hast a chance to leave this God-forsaken Dorset coast."

"The message, sir for I would be gone from this place."

"Tell Henry Morgan it is not always best to strike whilst the iron's hot."

"Ol' Harry be not akin to riddles - best explain further so's I can avoid his wrath and collect my 2,000 silver pieces o' eight."

"Advise him King William o' the Hague himself informed king James II of the forthcoming rebellion, even offering to assist quell the same by landing troops and horses a smite after the Pretender did a few days past."

"Noblemen and knaves - bounders the lot o' them!"

"Aye, Ned, blackguards and scoundrels which I do so deal with every waking hour o' the day so think on thy lot and enjoy thy freedom whilst thou can."

Black Ned Teach reached slowly into his three-quarter-length coat pocket and withdrew a velvet purse which rattled with coins. Tossing it rearwards he said quietly,

"Make sure the family o' the late Miss Wilks gets this bounty for "tis all I can do to appease myself for the mortal soul who placed herself in such great danger in delivering this to Ol' Harry Morgan."

"The woman has no kin, Ned - I checked in Dartmouth when offering to recover this pardon document for the crown."

"Thou be a counterfeit two-sided coin alright, Ingrams. Well then give it to the woman who cared for my maid Clarissa - mayhap split its contents wi' her and the goodly surgeon who removed the bullet-ball splinter. For "tis 50 gold Louis and will keep them both in reasonable luxury for the rest o' their days."

"Dr. Temple, the ship's surgeon, has left for the rebellion against the crown, and I doubts we'll see him again. The woman Pernickety who rescued the maid and found the surgeon will be mortal grateful for the money. If I ask her to keep a portion o' the bursary to one side should the doctor return; I'm sure she is trustworthy enough so to do."

"Where is the maid, Clarissa Lovelace Peach for I do owe her my life."

"Teach - Peach be a protection. She be below decks wi' her mother, Anne."

"I was informed a while ago that Anne o' the Indies had died."

"Aye, I tried to bury her at sea only she weren't having any o' it!"

"Some women are hard to kill, Ned - take thy Clarissa for instance."

"Then we'll seal our bargain this day wi' a pinch o' snuff, Ned. If I can trust thee to keep thy head turned and not identify yours truly, that is?"

"Aye that ye can, D'Arcy Ingrams King's man and sea spy - then ye'd best be off before my men wonder why I be rooted to this spot and not screaming orders at them." D'Arcy Ingrams slid out of the deck cabin shadow and approaching the ship's rail reached over the right shoulder of the pirate. The opened snuff box allowed Ned to slip a finger and thumb into the tobacco dust and remove a handsome pinch. Pausing only when he recognised the chaise silver, gold inlaid diamond encrusted box richly appointed with king Charles II's portrait as soon as the lid flipped shut.

"That be Ol' Harry Morgan's silver snuff box, t'were given to him by the late king himself -God bless him - why he were wondering what happened to that these months past?"

"Aye, seems that way, Ned. I recovered this item from a post chaise wreck dropped by the highwayman, Jess Mandrake who so caused it. Although there was more to him then than the last time I clapped eyes on the dastardly fellow."

"So he caused the death o' my step-daughter's guardian, Wilks."

"Aye and many innocents that travelled with her, Ned.. 'tis always so when history is furthered without shame or favour to neither cause. It be always the innocents that so suffer and always will be throughout time immemorial."

"Best be gone, King's man - I shall convey thy thoughts to Harry Morgan." Teach sighed and flapped a hand near his side to lay emphasis to his words.

"Thy documents be on the cabin roof under a lead sinker weight - have the courtesy to wait a moment or two before leaving the ship's rail to effect disappearance. I am thy servant, sir."

"Aye, Ingrams and I yours - begone sire."

"I have one detail to check in the papers before I leave thee sir, be good enough to await my say so before turning thy head. Have I thy word on this?"

"Aye, that ye have, D'Arcy Ingrams - but make haste. I tire o' this game."

It was ten minutes before Ned Teach realised the sound of paper parchment being flicked was done by the rising breeze. Turning to walk towards the bundle of papers, he spied they had been so arranged by the lead weight as to be irritated by the sea wind rattling through its loose-leaf pages.

The broad red ribbon slid back a deal to allow this phenomenon and give the sea spy a chance to slip quietly away and escape unnoticed.

"I can see why thou hast lived so long in thy devious trade, King's man."

Ned Teach chuckled as he scooped up the papers and arranged them with the ribbon once more.

"Aye that I can indeed you slithery serpent." Ned Teach stroked the red tassels in his black curly beard and thought over their conversation and how he must advise Morgan to reconsider his help in the forthcoming West Country rebellion, and with that placed to the back of his mind he strolled up to for'ard quarter to yell orders for the ship's departure.

* * *

August 1685

Later that summer a lone hunched figure dressed in heavy-stitch dark navy-blue serge clothing was seen grumbling to himself and gazing seaward from the end of Lyme's Cobb to a distant point beyond the horizon. The man stood with difficulty against a stiffening sea breeze on the 16-foot high sea defence wall, he braced himself with his hand-made crutch whilst balancing on one leg.

Lyme Regis Cobb is a 680 foot long moon-shaped structure of driven oak tree-trunk stakes, cobbled together with huge chunks of solid quarried rock, making the town one of the primary ports outside Bristol. In all winds and weathers the solitary journey was quite an ordeal for a man with one arm, one eye and one good leg, for it was easy to lose balance against the elements on the canted angle of the lengthy sea wall. Especially when senses and physical abilities be impaired. Jess Mandrake thought bitterly about his plight as he laboriously made his way down the carved rock steps known as "Granny's teeth" - spying daily for a ship which might never arrive. Yet his pilgrimage at dusk and dawn every day was a mystery to the industrious fishermen of Lyme Regis as they began or finished their working day on the eventide.

Jess the Pearly spoke to no one, always refusing point-blank to answer curious questioning or indeed enter into any casual conversation about the elements or why he was on his lonesome quest that day. He was a man alone. Dressed all in black standing there on the harbour side's highest edge, peering out as if some kind of ritual, a homage to the sea and all its changing moods. Sometimes blankly he would stare into a rising sea mist, or glowering with one angry eye the other covered with a black patch, to give uncontrollable spasms of suppressed anger. Jess Mandrake stood with some difficulty on the uneven surface of the huge carved stones of the Cobb, his stump affixed to a roughly hewn shaft strapped to what was left of his lower leg. The thinning crutch made out of a tree sapling tucked neatly yet firmly underneath the armpit of the coarse weave of his thick coat.

Occasionally the curiously eccentric figure was heard to mumble to himself, and only once was it audible enough for any translation by passing seafarers who in turn repeated it in the local hostelry of the Silver Street Black Dog Inn hostelry. The seaman held the local's attention when he related the phrase which seemed to fascinate and transfix their imaginations as he said,

"Where be D'Arcy Ingrams, blast yer eyes!"

In late summer after a fine day and evening at sundown, there standing unsteadily watching and keeping his daily vigil amongst a spiral of rising white sea birds, the cripple Jess Mandrake turned to leave his vantage-point at the end of the harbour wall.

Earlier and having made his way laboriously on his hand-fashioned crutch, with iron will, he hobbled back from the far end of the Cobb. Hunched over and cruelly embittered with fate, the figure with the makeshift gnarled crutch was attracted to a flash of late evening sunlight glinting off what might have been something silver. A snuff-box mayhap? The distraction had come from a nearby alleyway at the edge of the town, although perhaps it was nothing. Then again he thought he heard a distinctive double sniff as a line of tobacco-powdered snuff was taken up from the back of a hand into grateful nostrils.

It was much later in the evening whilst quietly and deep in thought quaffing a quart of ale in the *Black Dog Inn* that he cursed his slow wittedness and foul luck. For only then did he recall one man sought so zealously in the recent past had such a reflecting dazzling chaise-silver snuffbox. The King's man and sea spy known to him as - D'Arcy Ingrams!

THE END

GLOSSARY

1. Letters of Marque or A Commission to a private person.
2. Letters of Patent A document under the Great Seal authorising a person to do some act or enjoy some right.

3. Coup de Main	Double cross
4. Black powder	Gun powder
5. Blouson	Calico shirt
7. Gingerbread design	Ornately carved stern of a ship
8. Door stoop	Door step
15. Homity Pie	Leek, potato, cheese, crusty top.
20. Half-ankar cask	Barrel 4½ Imperial gallons
24. Rumbullion	Dark Rum
26. Kill-devil	Rum & Brandy mixture
27. Murtherers	Murderers
29. Pretender	Duke of Monmouth
31. Smidgen	Small amount
34. Rapscallion	A good-for-nothing
35. Slack casks	Underweight barrels
38. Flaskers	Smugglers
39. Pottage	Peason or bean stew or soup
40. Mulling	Red-hot fire iron plunged into wine or ale to make it warm
45. One-handed clocks	Watchmaker John Bennett invented the hairspring in 1686 allowing minute hands on clocks and pocket watches
47. Crowlink	Schnapps
48. Deadlamped	Closing one eye, head to one-side glowering threateningly with other eye
50. Hollands	Dutch Gin
51. Porter	Dark brown beer made from charred or chemically coloured malt
52. Portoise	Gunwale of a ship
53. Caravel	Swift Spanish/Portuguese Merchant vessel
54. Carrack	Large Merchant galleon
55. Clarissa Lovelace	Lovelace - accomplished libertine
56. Angels	Bar or chained together cannon balls used for bringing down ship's rigging/masts.